My
Mother's
Choice

D1440770

BOOKS BY ALI MERCER

Lost Daughter
His Secret Family

My Mother's Choice

Ali Mercer

bookouture

Published by Bookouture in 2020

An imprint of Storyfire Ltd.
Carmelite House
50 Victoria Embankment
London EC4Y 0DZ

www.bookouture.com

Copyright © Ali Mercer, 2020

Ali Mercer has asserted her right to be identified
as the author of this work.

All rights reserved.
No part of this publication may be reproduced, stored in any
retrieval system, or transmitted, in any form or by any means,
electronic, mechanical, photocopying, recording or otherwise,
without the prior written permission of the publishers.

ISBN: 978-1-83888-692-9
eBook ISBN: 978-1-83888-691-2

This book is a work of fiction. Names, characters, businesses,
organizations, places and events other than those clearly in the
public domain, are either the product of the author's imagination
or are used fictitiously. Any resemblance to actual persons, living
or dead, events or locales is entirely coincidental.

For David

Prologue

Laura's Diary

Since leaving him I've found myself doing all kinds of other things I wouldn't normally do. Coming here, for a start. I didn't even think twice about the drive – all those hours on the M4 with Dani in the back, the rain sheeting down when we got to the West Country, the tangle of lanes and bad signposts at the end.

But we made it. And Dani was so good. It was almost as if she knew how badly I needed her to be calm and patient. It was like having a mini adult with me, who had decided to be kind and supportive and help me to follow through on what I'd started. It was not at all like having a real adult with me – at least, not if that adult had been my husband.

If Jon had been with me – under other circumstances, at a more ordinary time – he'd have been impatient with my driving, and I would have had to turn a blind eye to his.

But Dani said, *Don't worry, Mummy*, when I took yet another wrong turn, when it was long after dark and she should have been bathed and in bed. *We'll get there.*

And then we did, and I drew up outside the dark little cottage and the key was under the pot of lavender in the front garden, just as I'd been told it would be. When I went in and flicked the switch the lights came on and I saw the cottage for what it was: a small, plain, sparsely furnished lifesaver. A place where Dani and I could live simply from day to day, lying low, eating and sleeping and making trips to the beach. A chance for me to rest and recover, and regain my strength to face what would come next.

We slept well in our unfamiliar beds – we were too worn out by the long drive for either of us to have trouble sleeping – and this morning we walked down the lane to the corner shop to buy eggs and tea and juice and milk for breakfast. I'd come away in such a rush, I'd only packed enough snacks to see us through the journey.

I'd forgotten to pack sunhats, too. Luckily they had a rack of them in the shop. I chose a straw Stetson, and Dani picked out a bright yellow cloth hat.

'There'll be no losing you in that,' I said to her, though the truth is there's no losing Dani anywhere; her bright red curls make her stand out in any crowd.

They sold stationery next to the till. I picked up a packet of felt tips and some paper for Dani to draw on. Then, on impulse, I added a couple of ballpoint pens and a pad of lined A4 paper, with a spiral-bound spine so it opened up like a book.

I said to the lady behind the till, 'You're quiet this morning.'

'Oh, it comes and goes,' she said, ringing up my purchases. She had a Scottish accent. I suppose Cornwall is full of people who have come from somewhere else, drawn by the warmer weather and the sea and the desire to get away.

'We're at Curlew Cottage, at the top of the lane,' I told her. 'Are you Mandy?'

'Yes, that's me, the one who put the key out for you last night. It was an impulse thing, then, you coming here? They said it was a last-minute booking.'

'Yes, it was. Thanks for your help.'

Did I look like a runaway? She looked us over and took in my rings, the solitaire diamond and the gold band, which I've carried on wearing because in spite of everything, I'm a long way from being ready to give them up. Her own wedding ring was stuck on her chubby finger as if it hadn't come off for years.

It was obvious she wanted to ask more, but she restrained herself and just said, 'Well, looks like you've got good weather. Might as well make the most of it.'

'We will,' I said.

Dani wanted us to wear our hats straight away, so Mandy snipped the tags out for us and we walked back up the lane to the cottage with them on. It felt almost as if we were on holiday. Or it might have done if I knew where home is going to be when we leave.

And now here I am, sitting at the garden table in the sunshine with one of my new pens in my hand and the A4 notebook open in front of me, and Dani next to me, drawing.

I thought I could make to-do lists, map out my next move. I could note down what I want, figure out all the problems I'll have to solve to get there.

But instead the pen and paper just make me want to write… write for its own sake, to make a record, though I have no idea who for. Like sticking a flag in the ground to say *I was here*.

If only I could swim back through time to the beginning, when nothing had gone wrong, when none of the mistakes had been made. But there is no going back. There is only the present, and my whole future rests on what I choose to do next. Dani's, too. Because Dani *is* my future. But she is also his, and that's what makes it so hard to know what to do for the best. It's not just about *feelings* – betrayal and love and guilt. It's about blood and earth, the ties that bind us to people and places we only think we can leave behind.

Everything that happens here seems important and unreal at the same time, weighted with possible consequences even if it's nothing out of the ordinary in itself. Like a dream that seems to be trying to tell you something, maybe even to warn you, but you have no way of knowing what it means.

I have a decision to make, and I am putting it off. I don't want to face it. Not yet.

In the meantime, I have to protect Dani. She needs to know that none of this is her fault.

And most of all, I have to make sure she never finds out what he has done.

Chapter One

Dani

Ten years later

On the morning of my fourteenth birthday Aunt Carrie looked knackered, which was nothing new. Birthdays weren't all that easy for me either, but I figured the best way to deal with it was not to think about it too much, whereas Aunt Carrie was the brooding sort. She thought about all of it a lot – much more than was good for her – and it kept her awake at night. You only had to look at her face to know: pale, beaky, with deep little lines round the mouth and eyes and the expression of someone who suffered from a near-permanent headache.

Still, at least she'd remembered. There was a card and a parcel waiting for me on the dining-room table when I came down for breakfast. I assumed Dad had forgotten – not for the first time.

'Happy birthday,' Aunt Carrie said, and carried on eating her toast.

'Yeah, well, it's not really that different to any other day, is it? I mean, I've still got school and stuff.'

Aunt Carrie looked wounded. I ignored her and put down my bowl of cornflakes and set about opening my present. I already knew she hadn't got me any of the things I wanted. OK, maybe a PlayStation was a big ask, but a phone that wasn't two years old would have done nicely, or the new Sims game. But no, it was obvious from the shape of the package that she'd got me books, something called *I Capture the Castle* with a girl in a drippy white dress holding some flowers on the cover, and *Rebecca*, which had spooky-looking writing and an old house.

'I hope you'll enjoy them,' Aunt Carrie said. She was always on at me to read.

'Yeah, I'm sure I will.'

I pretended to take in the blurbs on the back, then put the books down. I knew I'd probably never get round to tackling them. There were quite a few books about the place, but the only ones I ever looked at were the romantic ones Aunt Carrie kept in her bedroom, which I sometimes peeked at for a laugh when she was out. None of the men I'd ever met were at all like the heroes Aunt Carrie liked, putting themselves in harm's way to save helpless girls, or turning from mean to soppy because of a single kiss.

I knew it made her sad that I preferred playing on the computer to reading. But then, lots of things made Aunt Carrie sad. I didn't hug her or anything – we didn't go in for a whole lot of that. In fact, we spent most of our time together in the house as physically far apart as possible, whether we were watching telly or eating or doing weekend chores. I wasn't mad keen on having my personal space invaded – not by anybody, including Aunt Carrie. It didn't help that my hair was so curly, which meant people often wanted to touch it, but I'd developed a pretty good glare that meant they usually got the message and backed off fast.

'I've put some money in your savings account,' she said. She was always on at me to save, too.

'Thanks.'

I opened my birthday card. It had a picture of an elegant, long-haired lady lying in a hammock, writing in a notebook. If that was her idea of who I was going to turn into when I grew up, I figured she had another think coming.

'Thanks,' I said again, and set about eating my cornflakes. Aunt Carrie didn't say anything, just nodded and tightened her lips. She carried on sitting there at the round dining table, looking out through the French windows that she was always so careful to lock in case of burglars, staring at the birds splashing and playing in the birdbath.

Poor old Aunt Carrie. You had to feel sorry for her, in a way – or at least I might have done if I hadn't found her so annoying. She never could have expected to find herself lumbered with bringing up her little sister's kid more or less single-handed. But as it turned out, she was stuck with a cuckoo in the nest – a curly-haired, freckly, stroppy cuckoo, who had refused ballet lessons and wasn't always polite to grown-ups and got into trouble at school. And didn't read. Worse still, the nest was empty apart from us. I was a cuckoo without any siblings, and she was a mama bird without a partner. It was a recipe for resentment on both sides.

I had a pretty shrewd idea what was on her mind, and I had at least as much right as her to sit round feeling sad about it. But actually, I just wanted to get away from her. So I finished as fast as I could and said, 'Right-o, I'd better get going.'

She didn't actually answer, but let out a gurgling kind of noise that probably meant she was crying, or trying not to. I decided the best thing was to ignore her and went to wash up my bowl. There were times when chores were actually quite useful.

If there was anything I'd learned in my fourteen years on the planet, that was it – to keep my feelings to myself and out of sight, like the dirty laundry we put in a wicker basket with a lid, and that Aunt Carrie sorted through and turned into neatly folded and ironed things that she reproached me for not putting away properly.

The other thing that was helpful was to discourage anybody and everybody from asking questions. People who knew a little bit about me were sometimes curious. They wanted to know what was it like having a dead mum, did I remember her, did I look like her, did I remind my dad of her and was that why he didn't want to see me very much and so on and so forth. They wanted to know how sorry they ought to feel for me.

But my answer – the only one I was prepared to give them – was that they shouldn't feel sorry for me at all. I didn't want hugs and pats and sympathy, and if anybody tried all that with me, I was more likely to want to punch them on the nose than anything else. And that went for Aunt Carrie, too.

I wasn't in the greatest of moods when I rocked up at school, and the day didn't improve.

Nobody really knew it was my birthday, so there wasn't a lot of fuss. I should have been relieved, but I just found myself getting more and more fed up. By the time I got to French, which was the first lesson after lunch, people were pretty much avoiding me. They didn't know me that well, but on the whole, they knew me well enough to keep their distance when I got angry.

French was boring at the best of times, but was almost unbearable on a warm afternoon. Mr Matthews, our teacher, seemed to feel the same way. He set us some work to do and got on with his marking, and his head bowed so low over his desk at the front that once or twice I thought he'd actually managed to doze off.

The task he'd set us was to write a paragraph describing our families. We were allowed to make stuff up for this kind of task: it didn't have to be strictly accurate. Maybe Mr Matthews appreciated that some of us didn't go on holiday or do anything much at the weekend or feel like describing where we lived. Or maybe he felt that if there was any chance of being entertained by our efforts, he should take it.

But I didn't feel much like being entertaining. Instead I decided to write something that might wake Mr Matthews up.

J'habite avec ma tante. Mon père habite dans le meme ville. Je le vois quelquefois.

I live with my aunt. My dad lives in the same town. I see him sometimes.

J'ai une photo de ma mère dans ma salle de chambre. Elle etait très belle. Je suis dans le photo aussi. J'avais quatre ans. Aujourd'hui j'ai quatorze ans. Mon père a oublié mon anniversaire.

On ne parle pas de ma mère.

I have a photo of my mum in my bedroom. She was very pretty. I'm in the photo too. I was four. Today I'm fourteen. My dad forgot my birthday.

We don't talk about my mum.

There! Hopefully that would give Mr Matthews something to pay attention to. I'd pressed so hard as I was writing that I'd poked little holes in the paper. I had no idea if the French was right or wrong, and I didn't care.

The next lesson was science. I sat next to Josie Pye, who was skinny and little and always got picked on. She was there before me – she was that kind of kid, always on time, always trying her hardest, never realising that didn't really get you anywhere. As I settled down next to her and got my pencil case out of my bag she muttered something I didn't hear, then slid a card in a bright pink envelope across the desk.

She'd gone bright red. I said, 'Is that for me?'

'Yeah. It is your birthday, right? Happy birthday.'

There was a packet of sweets stuck to the envelope. I took them off and tore it open. Inside was a card with a Cocker Spaniel on the front. The dog had big dopey love-me eyes, a bit like Josie – the kind of look that brings out either the soft side in people or the nasty side, depending.

'Sorry it's a bit cheesy,' Josie said. 'It was either that or one with teddy bears and flowers on it.'

'It was nice of you. Thanks. I like dogs, but my aunt won't let me have one,' I said.

Gemma Case, who was sitting in front of us and who was one of the people who especially liked to make Josie's life a misery, turned round and stared at us. I glared at Gemma and she turned away.

Mr Hodge, the science teacher, started droning on about what happens when an unstoppable force meets an immovable object. I opened the sweets Josie had given me and offered Josie one.

She hesitated – she wasn't one for breaking rules and eating sweets in class was one of many things we weren't supposed to do. But she took one, and I took one too and pocketed the rest. We sat there discreetly sucking our sweets and the teacher didn't notice, and I thought that perhaps school wasn't quite so bad after all.

When I got home there was another, much bigger surprise waiting for me.

I spotted it as soon as I came out of the alleyway that led from the bridge over the stream to our road. It was leaning against the front of the house with a big pink totally over-the-top bow tied round the crossbar and a helmet dangling from the handlebars by its straps.

It was a bike. A beautiful gleaming silver bike. I knew at once who'd left it there. There was only one person in the world who would get me something like that and then not stick around to see my reaction to it.

He'd at least taken the precaution of locking it – though knowing Dad, he would have been confident of his ability to get it back if anybody had nicked it. He seemed to have pretty good connections with Kettlebridge's small semi-criminal underworld. Once, when Aunt Carrie's elderly neighbour had her new terracotta window-boxes nicked, Dad had intervened and the stolen goods had been returned within twenty-four hours, left on the neighbour's lawn with an extra potted geranium by way of apology. Aunt Carrie hadn't even seemed to find this particularly remarkable. 'Your dad has his ways,' was all she had said.

The bike had a substantial D-lock securing the front wheel to the frame. No sign of any key. I imagined Dad standing here, snapping the lock into place, stepping back to admire his handiwork and imagine my reaction, then driving off. Or maybe he'd asked someone else to leave it here. That was the thing with Dad – I never knew. He was a mystery.

Anyway, I'd have to get hold of the key to the D-lock or I wouldn't be going anywhere. Maybe he'd left it with Aunt Carrie at her office in the town centre, to dole out after a short lecture about road safety when she got back from work.

I unlocked the front door to find a big white envelope on the doormat. My name was written on the front in Dad's spiky, almost illegible handwriting: *Dani*. I tore it open and a key fell out. I scooped it up and held it. Freedom! Freedom, direct from him to me.

The card said HAPPY BIRTHDAY on the front, with balloons. It took me a while to decipher what he'd written inside.

Bob from the bike shop reckons this'll be the right size for you. Take it to him to check and he'll make sure it's OK. Ride safely, and don't go anywhere you're not supposed to.

He'd signed it, *Dad x*. The kiss looked both hesitant and deliberate, like something he'd thought about.

I dumped my schoolbag and went back out. Everything fit: the key in the lock, the helmet on my head. I tore off the pink ribbon and left it lying there. It looked like the aftermath of a party. But as far as I was concerned the party was only just beginning. I straddled the bike and found – not to my surprise – that it was exactly the right size for me. That was the power of Dad; people tried to do things right for him, to please him. Apart from me. I didn't see why I should, and anyway, what could be worse than to make an effort and still be mostly ignored?

But I owed him a big thank you for this. Still, I couldn't quite bring myself to feel grateful. Couldn't he at least have put the card through the door this morning?

I took off down the road. It had been a while since I'd ridden a bike – I'd outgrown my old one a couple of years before – and I'd forgotten what it felt like, the sense of speed, the lightness of it. Of not being in contact with the earth. Like swimming if water was air. Or flying.

Maybe he really did love me, after all.

But in that case, why did he make it so hard for me to love him back?

Chapter Two

It all started with a broken rule. I'm not one for blindly following orders, but I will say this. If you ever decide to do the one thing you've been explicitly instructed never to do, you should be prepared for consequences.

Once I had my bike, I wanted to make the most of it. As far as I was concerned Dad had given me the keys to my freedom – the chance to get away from home, Aunt Carrie, Kettlebridge, anyone I knew and all the old familiar roads. Aunt Carrie didn't see it like that, though, predictably, and it wasn't long after my birthday that she decided to lay down the law.

She tackled me after dinner, which was the usual time for her to give me a talking-to about anything that was bothering her – I spent most of the rest of my time in my bedroom, and she knew I hated her coming in when I was up there. She was washing up and I was drying, and I could tell that something was wrong. She looked hot and flustered, more so than she should have been, given that the heat had gone out of the day. Then, all of a sudden, she came out with it.

'I hope you're being careful when you go out on your bike.'

Was she about to try and put some kind of limit on how far out of Kettlebridge I was allowed to go? 'Sure I am. I always wear my helmet. You don't have to worry. The bike shop checked everything, so it's as it should be. And I promise you I'll always make sure I'm back in time for dinner.' I had a sudden burst of inspiration: 'It's good exercise, isn't it? Better than sitting home playing on the computer.'

Aunt Carrie looked up towards the ceiling, frowning slightly as if checking for cobwebs. I held my breath. Then she fixed her gaze on me. Aunt Carrie had green eyes; Mum's had been brown, like mine. In the photo of Mum that I had on my bedroom windowsill Mum's eyes looked warm and loving. They were the eyes of someone you wouldn't mind hugging you. Aunt Carrie looked like someone who probably wouldn't want to hug you even if you let them.

'This is all very well right now, but when the nights start drawing in I want you back before dark.'

'Sure.'

Well, that was no big deal. Autumn was ages away, anyway.

'There is one other thing. I know your father would say this as well.'

How bad could it be?

'No swimming.'

I stared at her.

'No river swimming, I mean,' she said. 'You can go to the pool anytime you want.' She looked as stern as if we were talking about drugs, or thieving, or sex, or the kinds of things that mothers of teenagers were supposed to worry about. But she wasn't my mother. And she was talking about something it had literally never even occurred to me to try.

'OK, fine, but why are you making such a big deal about this all of a sudden?'

She put her hands back into the washing-up bowl. 'Because it's dangerous. River water is dirty water. You get a mouthful of that, heaven only knows what kind of shape you'll be in.'

'I'm not planning on swallowing any river water, Aunt Carrie.'

She gave me the disdainful look that meant I was being facetious when she was trying to talk about something important. 'Kids are always getting into trouble in open water. You get a heatwave, like now, they suddenly think it would be a great idea to cool off wherever they like, and next thing you know they're getting tangled up in the reeds and not making it back up to the surface. There's a reason why we have swimming pools, you know. Besides, you shouldn't swim anywhere unsupervised.'

I could feel my face beginning to crack into a grin the way it always did when she was stern with me. I couldn't help it. Being told off by anybody made me want to laugh. It was a reflex reaction that inevitably made people even more annoyed with me than they already were.

'But I don't even like swimming.'

Swimming lessons at school had not been much fun – too cold, too much hanging around. The only redeeming thing had been that I could actually swim, so was spared the humiliation of being in the bottom group.

My dad had taught me, back when I was little. It was one of my earliest memories, maybe the earliest of all – being suspended in blue water, very deep, and him just a few inches away, within reaching distance, having let me go. What I remembered was the feeling of panic – of my body moving almost involuntarily, like someone scrabbling at a cliff edge before falling – and then realising that I wasn't going to sink. That the blue water was holding me up. Dad was still there, just a few inches away, and what he had wanted me to learn was that I didn't need him.

I knew now that the water hadn't even been that deep. That had been at the leisure centre in Barrowton, a few miles south of Kettlebridge, and he'd taken me there because at the time Kettlebridge didn't have an indoor pool of its own. Looking back, I was impressed that he'd bothered. I'd already been living with Aunt Carrie then. He hadn't been around for all that much of my childhood, but at least he'd taught me something.

'I just want you to promise me that you won't do it,' Aunt Carrie said. 'How would I explain it to your dad if anything happened to you?'

'He probably wouldn't care.'

'Don't be such a brat. Do I need to ask him to talk to you about this?'

I looked away, shrugged. Suddenly I felt like crying. All this fuss over something I didn't even want to do and had no intention of doing.

'OK,' I said. 'I promise I won't swim in the river.'

'Good girl,' Aunt Carrie said approvingly. 'As long as we've got that clear.'

I made my escape to my bedroom as soon as I'd dried the last dish. Back to the world of my computer game, where all the families and their lives and their houses were under my control, and there was nobody at all who could tell me what to do. At least Aunt Carrie had given up on attempting to ration my screen time; I think it actually suited her to have me quietly occupied, so she could have the telly and the living room to herself.

If it hadn't been so hot, I might have found it easier to keep my promise. But as it was…

One day, after school, I found a spot that was a little like a beach: a small sandy patch by the edge of the Thames in a village called Little Tipthorpe, a few miles downstream from Kettlebridge. The river was wide and slow there, and the bank sloped gently down to meet it. There were some people swimming a little way downstream. I stayed at a safe distance and watched them, bobbing around in the water and laughing, and I remembered what Aunt Carrie had said about dirty water and people getting tangled up in the reeds, and tried to tell myself that they were making a stupid mistake.

The water wasn't that tempting, after all. It wasn't as if it was blue and sparkling. It was the colour of diluted mud. It was just that the day was so sweltering, and the breeze coming off the river offered a little of the same kind of relief that you might get from being by the sea.

The next afternoon was even hotter, and when I got to the same spot by the river I had it to myself. I sat on the sandy bank and took off my socks and shoes and edged forward so I could dip my toes in the water. That couldn't do any harm, surely.

Cold! But it was good. Such a relief!

I put both feet in. I could still see them through the water: perhaps it wasn't quite so dirty after all. I watched the movement of the surface, the current rippling and threading across it. It was like watching the flames of a bonfire – it was always changing, and yet it still kept going. Except a fire would burn itself out, eventually, and the river just kept on flowing. It was lower today than it sometimes was because we had gone so long without rain; all the grass was parched, and the worms and snails were in hiding. But it would take a lot more than a heatwave to dry up the Thames.

I didn't even consciously decide to go in. One minute I was sitting there on the river's edge and I was still a good girl, abiding by the rule Aunt Carrie had made. And the next I was taking my T-shirt off over my head.

When it was really hot we were allowed to wear our PE kit to lessons, and I had on black cycling shorts and a black sports bra, which could have passed for a bikini. But anyway, there was no one around to see. I let my feet down into the water and touched earth, soft and boggy. Then I stood and it took my weight. A few more tentative steps and I was in – in up to my neck. I swam a couple of strokes and then I was in the middle of the river.

It felt so good – so right! This was how a swan would see it: the banks with all their raggedy grass and pink flowers at eye level, high as hills, and the blue canopy of the sky stretching overhead. And the water was so soft and smooth. Like silk. Dirty silk. No, like familiar old clothes you put on for comfort. How could anybody deny themselves this? It was so free. Like flying might be. But why would you want to fly, when you could float instead?

A dragonfly looped by, its body as bright blue as a jewel. I circled round and headed back towards the bank. A quick dip, that was all. Nobody would ever know.

I clambered out onto the patch of sand without difficulty and sat there for a while longer, watching the river go by. I was dry within minutes. I smelt of the river, though – of mud and rain.

And I didn't look too clean. That was all right, though. I'd be able to shower before Aunt Carrie got home. She thought I was always showering and took much too long over it. It wouldn't be anything out of the ordinary for her to come back and find that I'd already washed and changed.

It was all going so well… until it wasn't.

I didn't even realise Aunt Carrie was already home until I was halfway up the stairs to the bathroom. Then I heard my name and turned to see her standing in the hall at the bottom of the stairs, looking up at me as if she already knew I'd done something wrong.

'Dani? Couldn't you hear me? I called you.'

Would she be able to tell? I could still make out the whiff of the river on me, and Aunt Carrie had a particularly acute sense of smell. She was always opening windows and changing air fresheners and sprinkling scented oil on bowls of potpourri.

Also, my stupid hair would give me away. I hadn't checked what it looked like, but it always went extra curly after getting wet.

I said, 'What's up?'

My heart was hammering. I liked to think that Aunt Carrie couldn't get to me, that it was a matter of indifference to me whether she was angry or not. But right then and there I discovered I'd been kidding myself; I did care, and I really didn't want to have to face her if she found out that I'd been swimming in the open after she'd explicitly told me not to.

Maybe she even had a point. Maybe it had been a stupid, reckless thing to do, rather than a cool adventure that was just too tempting to resist.

'I'm not well,' she said. 'I have the beginnings of a migraine. That's why I came home early. I think I'm going to have to lie down. How was your day?'

'Not bad. Hot,' I said. 'I'm just going up for a shower, actually.'

I turned my back on her and made to start back up the stairs. The next minute she said, 'Dani?' in the sergeant-major voice she used when I'd done something specially wrong, and I knew the game was up.

'Yes?'

I sounded too innocent by half, but once you've committed to behaving as if you're above suspicion, it's hard to stop – even when you know you've been rumbled.

'Get back down here,' Aunt Carrie said, and it was clear that at least one of us was about to go in for some straight-talking.

I went down the stairs to face her and caught sight of my reflection in the hall mirror. My hair looked pretty wild. It had been relatively subdued during the hot dry days, but now it had sprung back into action like a drought-hit plant that finally gets a good long drink of water.

Aunt Carrie wrinkled her nose. 'You smell like you've been rolling round in a bog.'

I shrugged, tried a smile. I couldn't help but look sheepish, and I knew I looked it, too.

'You've gone and done exactly what I told you not to do,' Aunt Carrie said. 'You have, haven't you? I asked you not to do one thing. Just one thing. How could you deliberately disregard me?'

I gave the tiniest shrug. 'It didn't do any harm,' I said. 'It was just a tiny dip. To cool down. I was only in the water for a few minutes. Other people do it all the time.'

'You have no idea what harm it could do.'

'Look, OK, I know I shouldn't have done it after you asked me not to…'

'Not asked. Told. I told you not to.'

'It was just a one-off thing, OK? I can see it really bothers you and I promise I won't do it again.'

She folded her arms. She was looking at me as if she absolutely hated me. I'd never seen her like that before – staring at me as if I was an actual enemy, rather than a kid she'd ended up being saddled with and had brought up out of a sense of duty. She opened her mouth and then closed it again. Her lips tightened in a little grimace of disgust.

'I'm not going to do this any more,' she said. '*He* can deal with you.'

'Look, I'm really sorry, OK? I know it was stupid to do what I did.'

She shook her head. Suddenly she looked more sad than angry.

'I'm going to call your father,' she said. 'He has to be the one to talk to you about this.'

'But Aunt Carrie... is that really necessary? I won't even go out on the bike after school any more if you don't want me to. I'll come straight home and do my homework.'

'I need to tell him.' She picked up the phone, which lived on a little table next to the hall mirror.

'Please don't.'

She looked at me with her eyebrows raised. It was the kind of look she might have given to someone who was trying to sell her something, before making it clear that she wasn't buying.

She said, 'You'd better get in the shower and clean yourself up.'

Then she went into the living room with the phone and I heard her saying, 'Jon? It's Carrie. We have a situation here.' She closed the door and I couldn't hear any more.

We have a situation here.

Why was she reacting in such a wildly over-the-top way?

She'd said she had a migraine coming on. Probably she wasn't feeling too great.

Dad wouldn't take all this as seriously as Aunt Carrie had... would he?

I trudged up the stairs to the shower. If only I hadn't gone into the water... If only Aunt Carrie hadn't come home early... but what was the point of regret? I'd screwed up, and now I was going to have to face the consequences.

Better the devil you know. Aunt Carrie could be difficult, but I'd lived with her long enough to be mostly immune to her. Dad was the devil I didn't know at all.

Aunt Carrie knocked at my bedroom door while I was getting dressed after the shower. I was sitting on the bed, putting my socks on. Left to myself I'd have gone barefoot as much of the time as possible, but Aunt Carrie had a horror of bare feet. Bare anything, in fact. I said, 'Come in' as politely as I could manage, and she came in and stood with her arms folded and looked down at me.

'He's on his way,' she said.

'Now?'

'Oh, he can be fast when he wants to be.'

This was as close as I'd ever heard her come to saying something critical of him. She put her hands to her temples and rubbed them. Then she let out a sigh.

'Is he angry with me?'

'More concerned, I think. Understandably so. I'm going to go and lie down.'

She withdrew, leaving the door open. Annoying – as if I didn't have any right to shut her out.

I closed it and picked up the photo of my mum that lived on my windowsill. It was covered in a thin film of dust, like everything else in my room – it was down to me to keep it clean, but usually I left it until Aunt Carrie made me do it. I loved that photo, though. It was the one thing of mine I would have saved if the house burned down, and I felt bad for neglecting it. How was it possible to neglect something you loved? Was that how Dad felt about me?

The photo showed a pretty woman in a brown dress, looking back over her shoulder at the camera and laughing. She was holding the hand of a little girl in a pink coat, and the colour of the coat matched the pink of the ribbon in the girl's red hair and the pink of the blossoming cherry trees that lined the path where they were walking. You couldn't see the little girl's face: she was focused on the path ahead, and wherever they were going next. By way of contrast, the woman didn't appear to be in any hurry.

I had been four years old, and my dad had taken that photo somewhere in London the spring before Mum died. I found a tissue and wiped the glass to clean it, then tapped it gently with my forefinger.

'If only you could talk,' I said out loud.

Then I put the photo back in its place on the windowsill and turned away to switch on my laptop.

About half an hour later the doorbell rang and there was Dad, a tall, shadowy figure with reddish hair, distorted by the wavy lines in the glass.

Dad was one of those people who have a presence. On the rare occasions when he came to Aunt Carrie's house, he changed it: made it seem smaller somehow, less of a fortress – less Aunt Carrie's kingdom and more like an ordinary house, two bedrooms plus box room plus garage and two little squares of garden, front and back. What was it that made him stand out the way he did? I'd seen it time and time again – waitresses, DIY store attendants, teachers at my school the few times he'd ventured anywhere near the place. They fell over themselves to try and please him, even if he was a stranger to them. If they did know him, or knew of him, they tried even harder.

Everybody wanted to impress Dad... except me. Lately, I'd gone out of my way to do the opposite.

But as I opened the front door to him I couldn't help but wonder if I'd overdone it.

Chapter Three

Dad said, 'You ready, then?'

'What for?'

He narrowed his eyes at me as if I might be an idiot, but he was going to give me the benefit of the doubt and not tell me so.

'Your aunt wants me to talk to you. So we'll talk. I have to sort out a couple of things at work, so I'm going to leave you at White Cottage for a bit. Then I'll take you down the road for dinner. OK?'

'OK.'

'You'd better say goodbye then. I'll be waiting.'

'Sure,' I said, but he'd already gone.

Aunt Carrie was lying in her bedroom in the dark, with the curtains drawn. I peered in at her from the doorway.

'I'm going out with Dad,' I said.

She propped herself up on one elbow. I could tell from the way she moved that it hurt.

'I've always done my best by you, Dani. There were things I wanted to say to you. But he didn't want me to, so I didn't.'

My heart was beginning to beat faster. I said, 'What do you mean? What didn't he want you to tell me?'

'You'll find out soon enough,' she said, and rested her head on the pillow again.

I backed out, closed the door and went out as quietly as I could. It felt as if the house might explode around me.

Dad was outside in the pick-up truck that he sometimes used for stuff to do with the garden centre. Getting into the cab next to him didn't seem like much of an escape.

We set off in silence. He didn't put any music on, which was a sure sign that he was building up to saying something. Usually he liked to listen to jazz as he drove. That was his favourite – old, bluesy songs about rivers and work and bad women and doing wrong, and then regretting it.

He didn't speak till we were on the main road, heading towards the outskirts of town. Then he said, 'I was worried when I got the call, you know. I thought something had happened to you.'

That wasn't too bad a start. At least he didn't sound angry. To my surprise, he sounded genuinely concerned, and I felt my powers of resistance beginning to ebb away.

When Aunt Carrie was telling me off I'd felt indignant and self-righteous, as if she was being completely unreasonable. That had been much easier to cope with than Dad speaking to me so gently, which I wasn't at all used to. The time we spent together was usually awkward, but in a different way – a special kind of awkwardness that came out of us not really knowing what to say to each other, even though we were father and daughter.

But really, what was the big deal?

I began to feel guilty. Another unfamiliar experience, because why should I, where he was concerned?

'I'm fine,' I said, a little sulkily.

'So I see. Your aunt, though… not so much.'

'That's not my fault. She was feeling ill anyway. That's why she came home early.'

Dad turned slightly and shot me one of his looks – a quick, piercing glance that seemed to say there wasn't much point in pretending to be different or better than I was, since he would see right through me anyway. It made me feel even worse. Like he'd just accused me outright of not caring about other people, and of just doing what I wanted to do without stopping to think twice about whether it would upset them.

He said, 'It's her fault for having caught you, is it?' His voice was still gentle.

I didn't answer. I was feeling angry again. It struck me that all of this – collecting me, preparing to give me some kind of talking-to – was about Dad keeping Aunt Carrie happy. He had to do it, whether he wanted to or not. All she'd had to do was summon him to talk to me, and he'd come running.

We drove out of town in silence, crossed the river and passed through woods and fields. This was the exact same way the way I'd come earlier today, cycling towards my disgrace, not that I'd known it at the time. But instead of carrying on towards the river we took the left turning just before the sign for Rosewell's Garden Centre – easy to miss if you didn't know it was there, but then, there was no reason for anyone to go that way unless they lived there or had business there. And then we pulled up outside the house.

It wasn't far out of town, but it might as well have been in the back of beyond, especially when the garden centre was closed and there was nobody around. It was everything Aunt Carrie's house wasn't: old, isolated, and right out in the countryside, with farmland all around. It could be cosy in winter, especially if you stayed close to the fire – but it was the kind of cosy that comes from knowing you're surrounded by the dark. And it was cool in summer, the kind of cool that goes with thick stone walls and no neighbours.

We went into the house; the wind chimes in the lobby rang to announce our arrival. Dad left me with the TV on and permission to raid the fridge and went off to the garden centre. I watched *Friends* and wondered if I should just apologise, if that would make all of this easier – even if I hadn't really done anything wrong. Other than disobeying Aunt Carrie's instruction and breaking my promise.

But if the instruction was unreasonable, I didn't see why I should have to follow it.

Then I remembered what Aunt Carrie had said. *There were things I wanted to say to you. But he didn't want me to, so I didn't.* I began to feel sick with apprehension.

Maybe there were things I was better off not knowing. Maybe Dad was about to tell me something I really wouldn't want to hear.

Dad was gone for about an hour and when he came back he showered, changed and drove me to the pub down the road in the big old saloon car that he'd had for as long as I could remember.

'Have whatever you like,' he said as we scanned our menus.

I folded mine and put it down. I didn't feel at all hungry. I was too anxious. This clearly wasn't just a straightforward telling-off. Usually, when we went out, there was an unspoken understanding that I shouldn't choose the most expensive things on the menu. But now he was treating me. As if he was about to tell me something really awful and felt bad about it and wanted to make up for it.

I said, 'I'll have the same as you.'

'Nothing like knowing your own mind.'

'I do know my own mind,' I said. 'That's why we're here.'

'Hmm. About that.'

He regarded me thoughtfully. He looked almost as if he might be about to crack into a smile – as if he didn't really think I was such a dreadful person after all. Then he said, 'I do understand why you did it, you know.'

'You do?'

This was getting weirder and weirder. The whole thing was so strange, it was actually uncomfortable looking at him across the little table. It was like staring at an optical illusion.

'Sure,' he said. 'You were hot and you wanted to cool off, and you did it because Carrie told you not to. I get that. It can be pretty irresistible to break the rules, especially if you don't know why they're there.'

Was this a trap? I said, 'I wasn't in the water for very long. But anyway, it was a mistake and I won't do it again. I'm sorry, OK? Now can we stop talking about it?'

'I wish we could,' he said evenly. 'But we can't.'

We stared at each other. I got the impression he was steeling himself. For a moment I seemed to see right through him and I knew how uncomfortable he was, and how much this was hurting him. And then something shifted and it was just Dad, Dad who I hardly ever saw and who couldn't possibly care about me all that much. But here he was, trying to do parenting, and about to attempt an excruciating heart-to-heart because Aunt Carrie had nagged him into it.

He said, 'How much do you remember about how you lost your mum?'

My heart started beating even faster. I pictured the woman in the brown dress in the photo on my bedroom windowsill, smiling at the camera, holding my four-year-old hand. A woman who was spoken of so rarely, she'd become like a secret I kept to myself.

I said, 'Not much.'

'But you remember something.'

'I remember a long drive, with you in the driving seat. And her not being there next to you.' I still dreamed about that, sometimes. It had been Aunt Carrie sitting next to him instead. 'I remember being in Aunt Carrie's kitchen.' I hesitated. 'I asked her if she was going to be my mummy now, and she said no, she'd never be my mummy and my mummy would always be my mummy.'

He flinched at that, but didn't say anything. I said, 'Are you sure you want to talk about this?'

'I don't,' he said.

'I know,' I said. 'Aunt Carrie never talks about her either. Nobody does. It's almost as if she never existed.'

'It's not like that for me,' Dad said.

In the photograph there was cherry blossom. She'd been happy. That much I knew for sure. That much was obvious. She'd had no idea she wouldn't live to see another spring.

'I think about her a lot,' I said.

'I do too,' he said.

There was a silence between us, as if we'd both made a confession. It was on the tip of my tongue to say that sometimes I felt as if she was thinking about me, too. Not watching over me – it wasn't as if she was a presence I could sense, or at least, not as if she was anywhere nearby. But it was as if she was reaching out. Trying to send me a message that couldn't get through.

I didn't say so, though. It would have sounded like a fantasy. Like something I'd made up for comfort. Not that it felt like that. It wasn't exactly comforting to imagine that your dead mother longed to be able to talk to you and couldn't.

The waiter came to take our order, and after he'd gone I leaned forward and said, 'I think I must have blanked out some of what happened. I don't remember the funeral.'

'That's because you didn't go,' he said. 'Do you remember what happened on the beach?'

As he said this, I thought that perhaps I did remember. Or at least, I could remember the beach. Unless I was just imagining that too? Had I seen a photo? There wasn't much detail. Just the line of the shore, long and curving, and the sand and the sea and a blue sky overhead with a few clouds in it. No people, as far as I could remember. As good as empty.

'I think maybe I can picture the beach, and the sea,' I said. 'Where was it?'

'Cornwall,' he said. 'North coast. Near a village called Port Mallion. That sea was the Atlantic.' Then he sighed. 'She drowned,' he said.

I stared at him, took in the whites of his eyes and the bristles in his beard that were a different colour to the rest of his hair, more sandy and less coppery.

'I thought she had a heart attack.'

'No. Not a heart attack. A brain attack. A massive stroke. But that was later, in hospital. When I got her out of the water she was still alive.'

'You mean you saved her.'

'I tried to save her.'

'You got her out of the sea. That's saving her.'

'I wasn't fast enough. It was too late.'

His expression was almost pleading. What did he want me to say? *You tried your hardest. You couldn't have done any more.* But why should I? How did I know, anyway? I would only be saying it because I thought it was what he wanted to hear.

For the first time, I found myself looking at him in a different way, as if he was nothing to do with me. As if I was a detective, or a judge, weighing what little evidence there was in the balance: *could* he have tried harder? Done better? *Should* he have been able to save her? What he was telling me was that he had tried and failed. And I had never, ever thought of my dad as a failure.

Did he cry about her, ever? It was awful to think of him crying. Howling and shouting and throwing things and breaking things, maybe. But sitting with tears dripping down his face?

He was my cowboy dad who rode into my life in his pick-up truck and then disappeared again. That was the nature of heroes, to come and go. He could abandon me and still be a hero. But weeping, sobbing – that was not how a hero behaved. A hero was all about action. Protection and vengeance. And yet he hadn't been able to protect her, and how could you take your revenge on the sea?

Suddenly I realised I really didn't want to think about it. About the water closing over her head, getting into her lungs. About what it would be like, not to be able to breathe. To realise you were dying. They said that when you drowned, your whole life flashed before your eyes. Had she relived everything in the time it took for him to reach her and pull her out?

'She didn't want to be buried,' he said. 'She wanted to be cremated, and for her ashes to be scattered on the Wildcroft Hills. That's as good a place to feel close to her as any.'

The Wildcroft Hills were a local landmark and beauty spot, about seven miles from Kettlebridge. Everybody who lived nearby knew them: they stuck up out of the surrounding flat river valley like a sign you were nearly home. You could see them from the train to London, and from the roads all around – if you headed east from where we lived, sooner or later they'd pop up, two smooth round mounds topped with clusters of trees. Up until then I'd taken about as much interest in them as I took in the towers of the nearby power station, or the blight affecting the oak trees that you passed on the road south out of town.

He said, 'For me she's all around here. In Kettlebridge, and at White Cottage. Even in this pub. But the bit of her that's still alive is in you.'

'But I'm nothing like her. As far as I can tell. I mean, I definitely don't look like her.'

'That isn't true. OK, so you have the Rosewell red hair. But your eyes are very like hers. She was stubborn, too. Just like you. Once she'd decided something, that was it. She was slow to make up her mind, though – you're more impulsive, more like me. You do something and think about it later. She liked to weigh things up.'

I looked up at him again and suddenly I was conscious once more of what he was feeling, and it was hell. It was like a burning pit all around my heart.

'You loved her, then,' I said, and it was only when I said it that I realised this was what I'd really wanted to know. It hadn't exactly been obvious, after all, given that he never spoke about her. It just felt all wrong… not just like grief, but like something else, too. It felt like shame.

'Of course I loved her,' he said, almost angrily, and that was when I knew that I couldn't ask him any more and didn't want to, because if I did the moment we were in – a moment that was almost tender, an attempt to talk about something we never, ever talked about – might turn into something else.

The tie between us was so fragile, I didn't want to risk it. It was one thing him being at arm's length, the way he usually was. But what if something volcanic happened, and I couldn't even have that? I'd already lost Mum. I knew I couldn't bear to lose Dad too.

I said, 'I remember you teaching me how to swim.'

His face cleared. 'Yeah, well, someone had to,' he said gruffly. 'Your aunt wasn't going to. She hates swimming. And the school was worse than useless. They weren't going to do anything for ages. And we do live in a place with open water. You need to know how to look after yourself if something happens and you fall in. Which is not the same' – and at this point he looked at me sternly – 'as going out looking for trouble just for the hell of it.'

'OK, message received. Over and out,' I said, and was relieved that the conversation was back to being something more normal. Perhaps this bit of it was the kind of talk that pretty much every kid had with their dad at one time or another.

'The thing is, you have not to fight it,' Dad went on. 'When people fall in the instinct is to panic, but that just makes it worse. Water is weird stuff. It's not like anything else in the world. If you let it, it'll support you.'

'Like floating,' I suggested.

'Exactly,' he agreed. Then he said, 'Look, Dani, maybe you could do me a favour and cut your aunt some slack. She does care about you, you know. And this should go without saying, but she was devastated by what happened to your mum. We all were.'

I shrugged. Then I instantly felt bad. 'OK,' I said. 'I'll try not to be such a pain.'

'Just think next time, OK?' he said, and shook his head. 'Sometimes you really do remind me of me.'

I had no idea how to react to that. How could I – a fourteen-year-old girl – possibly be like him in any way? Then the waiter arrived with our mains and we tucked in, and he asked me about school, which was obviously the kind of thing he felt he ought to talk to me about, and I complained that it was boring and he told me to try and make the best of it and it seemed as if everything was back to normal, if things can ever be normal with a father you don't really know.

So that was it – the end of the big confession, where he told me what had happened to my mum and how he hadn't managed to save her. I knew neither of us wanted to talk about all that any more, or even think about it. It was like a dead weight of sadness that would pull you down if you let it, far from the ordinary world of being told to do your homework over a side order of chips, right down to the depths.

After I'd finished my pudding he paid up and took me back to Aunt Carrie's. He seemed to be ready for the evening to be over, and I was too. I felt all at sea, as if everything I'd been used to – even my own self – had just changed, even though it didn't look any different.

Maybe this was what life was like for him all the time: this sense of something missing, of everything being adrift. Maybe that was why he was always restless, never far from moving on to the next thing. He just didn't want to stop, because then he might have to start remembering. But he probably found she slipped into his thoughts at odd times, whether he wanted her to or not – just as she did with me. The only difference was that I had so much less to go on.

All this time, I'd assumed it was just me who thought about her – that woman with the brown eyes and the smile, looking back over her shoulder as she walked beneath the cherry trees. But I couldn't have been more wrong. At that table in the restaurant, he'd seemed tormented by his memories of her.

There was a light on in the sitting room when we pulled up outside the house; Aunt Carrie must have recovered enough to come downstairs. Usually when he dropped me back he didn't come in. It was a ritual: he stayed in the car, I'd go to the door and just before I went in, I'd turn and wave, and after the door was closed I'd hear him driving away. Waiting outside like that was one of the things he did that let me know he was looking out for me. That even if I didn't live with him, even though he hadn't brought me up, even though most of the time it felt as if I barely knew him… he still cared.

I hesitated before getting out of the car. Was everything really just going to carry on as normal? The strangeness of the day was like a weight on my tongue. The heat, the water, Aunt Carrie's fury. Was it fury, or fear? What was she so afraid of? I knew there was more to ask, more to know – the same sick, creeping feeling you get in a scary film, when there are more threats out there in the dark, when being home doesn't mean being safe.

Aunt Carrie opened the front door before I could rummage for my key. She looked very pale. I turned to Dad and waved – I couldn't make out his expression, he was just a dark shape in the car. And then I closed the door on him and was alone with Aunt Carrie again.

After spending time with Dad she seemed smaller, less of an authority figure. A sallow woman, anxious and washed-out. The hallway was painted a watery pale green, and the dim light had a bluish tinge that made her look even more sickly. It was a bit like being stuck in a fish tank.

She folded her arms and said, 'Did he talk to you?'

'He told me my mother drowned, if that's what you mean.'

'It's good that he told you.' Her eyes were fixed on my face, studying it as if it might reveal the precise details of what he had said. As if she didn't trust him. Then she said, 'Then you'll understand why I reacted the way I did.'

'I don't think you were freaked out because I might have put myself in danger,' I said. 'I think you were freaked out because I didn't know how she died, and that he tried to save her and couldn't.'

Aunt Carrie drew breath, exhaled.

'He did his best,' she said.

Suddenly I felt completely deflated, as if there was nothing left to resist any more. What was there to fight, anyway? There was nothing more to know or say, and nothing to be done but to carry on.

I said, 'Is it OK if I go to bed now? I'm pretty tired.'

'Of course,' Aunt Carrie said. 'Good idea. After all, you've got school tomorrow. A normal day.'

I went upstairs to my room and picked up the photo of Mum from the windowsill and sat down on the bed to study it.

She looked so alive. So happy, and so free. So much more so than Aunt Carrie in the hall just now, or Dad across the table in the restaurant. All of us seemed to be trapped – trapped by missing her, by having lost her. By the huge hole she'd left in our lives when she disappeared.

That night I dreamed about her, more vividly than I had ever done before.

I dreamed I was walking along that path past the cherry trees with her. I wasn't a little kid any more but she was still the age she'd been in the photo. That's what happens to the dead. They get stuck in time, like insects in amber, while everybody else keeps on moving.

I wasn't holding her hand, and she didn't say anything. There was nobody else there, nobody watching. Directly ahead of us, washing across the end of the path, was the sea.

'I don't think we're going to be able to go home,' I said, but there was no answer.

Then I saw her face, very real, very close to mine. She wanted to speak to me, but she couldn't, and I called out to her and I realised she knew I was calling even if she couldn't hear me, and I saw how much it grieved her that she was powerless to respond.

I jerked awake and took deep, gulping breaths, and the air was such a sweet luxury and I was so grateful for it, so glad to be still alive, and then I sobbed because she had been there in the dream, and now she had gone again.

That was when I understood the point of ghost stories. The dead always want to tell us something, maybe something we would much prefer not to know. But they can't. They can't speak. It's only in a ghost story that we can find out what they're trying to say.

Chapter Four

My memories of Mum added up to hardly anything. It was just glimpses, like lost bits of a jigsaw puzzle that turned up years later when all the other pieces and the box had already gone in a clear-out. I remembered her absence more than her being there. What I couldn't remember was anybody actually sitting me down and explaining what was going on when she disappeared.

This was what I remembered.

Getting into the back seat of Dad's car and seeing Aunt Carrie in the passenger seat instead of Mum. A long drive. Aunt Carrie's kitchen, which had tall, dark cupboards and smelt faintly of boiled vegetables. A stale, shut-in smell. Aunt Carrie's telly screen flickering before a cartoon came on. My relief that her telly worked. Telly was so comforting. So familiar. The same programmes, whichever house you watched them from.

Asking Aunt Carrie if she was going to be my mummy now. No, she told me. Your mummy will always be your mummy. After that I didn't ask any more questions. I had already figured out what they weren't telling me, which was that Mum wasn't coming back, and Dad was never going to take me away with him.

I don't know how long it took me to work it out. A while, maybe. Then I knew. I didn't say anything, though. Maybe I realised there wasn't anything anyone could do about it – it wasn't like a bruise or a graze, something that was easy to kiss better. It was too big for that. It was a shock that turned into fact; it just *was*, like a bomb crater in the middle of the road.

Life had changed. We weren't going back to London. Dad brought over my clothes and toys, and after a while he moved back to Kettlebridge, to an old cottage just outside town, but I stayed at Aunt Carrie's. I was sad, but I didn't cry about it into my pillow – it wasn't that kind of sadness. It was a heavy sadness that pressed on my heart like something that could stop me breathing.

And then one day it was sunny and I walked along the road by myself from the shops back to Aunt Carrie's house with one foot in the road and one foot on the pavement, and nobody saw me and nobody told me off, and no cars came and killed me and I was happy. Because there I was, and the sun was shining and I was alive.

That feeling stayed with me. *I'm here. I'm still here, even if she isn't.* It made me reckless. Other kids learned not to dare me, because I'd do whatever they'd suggested before they had time to regret it. The sadness stayed with me, too. It wasn't constant; it came and went like the weather, and I wasn't always conscious of it. I became familiar with it. I acclimatised. I learned that the sadness sometimes rose up and was almost overwhelming, then subsided into something that was in the background: the difference between being at sea in a storm and hearing the waves from a distance.

There were so many occasions that forced me to miss her. At sports days and parents' evenings, I was the kid whose aunt came along instead of her mum or dad – and that was only if Aunt Carrie could get the time off her job at the council. It was the same when I got into trouble, and Aunt Carrie was summoned into school to hear about whatever it was I'd done. I was Aunt Carrie's cross to bear, that was for sure. The way she looked sometimes told me what a burden I was. And I was sorry about it, but it didn't seem to stop me doing things I shouldn't.

I heard about those mums who knew they were dying in advance and wrote their kids letters to open on special occasions, one for every birthday until they were eighteen. I didn't know whether to envy those kids or pity them. Wouldn't you be desperate to read the next letter – wouldn't you want to race through all of them? And each time you'd have to wait for a whole year, and it would seem like forever.

And then it would come to the same thing in the end.

Absence.

When someone's missing who ought to be there, it makes everything strange and out of kilter. My childhood was weird. All of it. It was as if I had grown up in a ceasefire, and if I started to try to find out what all the fighting had been about, I'd risk triggering the return of all-out war.

When I got older I figured that I was better off living with Aunt Carrie than I would have been with Dad. Maybe I reminded him too much of my mum, and that was why he couldn't cope with having me around – even though, as far as I could see, I didn't look especially like her. Or maybe he just wasn't up for being a full-on, full-time dad, or didn't think he'd be any good at it. But anyway, if he wasn't that bothered about me I wasn't that bothered about him. I decided to try not to take it personally. After all, he was virtually a recluse; he ran his garden centre and then he hung out at White Cottage on his own, and that was it. It wasn't like he had anything much to do with his other daughter, my very boring grown-up half-sister Michelle, or Jade, his witchy first wife. Dad was as close to me and Aunt Carrie as he was to anybody, which wasn't saying much.

And then, finally, after that hot summer's day when I swam in the river even though I'd promised not to, he told me what had happened to my mum.

It didn't help. It still felt as if most of the jigsaw was missing. Worse still, I felt angry with myself for not having asked more questions when I had the chance, and for not daring to open up the subject again.

And then I came across Josie Pye crying by the bridge after school, and I flipped. I couldn't bear to see it. And that was how I ended up finding the one thing in the house that Aunt Carrie really wouldn't have wanted me to uncover.

How does it happen that somebody becomes a target, and everybody knows and nobody does anything about it? Why Josie? Why does it happen to anybody? It was like a kind of bad luck that attached itself to her, that she couldn't shake off. She wasn't the only kid in school who was little and skinny and nervous, though it didn't help that she had the wrong kind of jeans, the wrong T-shirt, the wrong trainers. Cherry Marsden and Gemma Case, who were her main tormentors, didn't hesitate to point any of this out.

In theory, we all knew about bullying – how bad it was, and how important it was to speak up when it happened. We'd talked about it in citizenship class, and we'd been allowed to wear non-school uniform on the Friday of Anti-Bullying Week, as a sort of treat that was also meant to encourage us to remember what we'd learned. But none of that helped Josie.

She suffered in silence, but everyone knew when she was suffering. She had a very expressive face, and you just had to look at her to know what she was feeling. That was probably part of it. Cherry and Gemma were bored and mean, which was what made them dangerous; they were looking for entertainment. They had got into the habit of picking on her, and they were like addicts. They didn't know when to stop.

When I spotted Josie standing by herself on the bridge over the stream and crying, I knew it had to be something to do with Gemma and Cherry, though they were nowhere to be seen. There were a few other people around, but not many; I was a bit later walking home than usual, as I'd queued up for the ice-cream van after school. Nobody was paying Josie any attention. I finished my ice cream and went over to join her on the bridge.

'You OK?'

She shook her head slightly and carried on staring down at the water. I looked down too, and then I saw what she was upset about. Her schoolbag was down there, right in the middle of the stream.

'Did Gemma and Cherry…?'

She didn't answer. I said, 'What those two want is a good kicking,' and stooped down to get my socks and trainers off. The next minute I was splashing through the stream. It had been hot and dry for so long, it was much shallower than usual – there was no way anyone could think it was dangerous, and anyway, Aunt Carrie hadn't said anything about paddling, only swimming. Besides, she never need know.

I got hold of the bag and waded out, and gave it back to Josie. 'There you go. Hopefully it'll dry out all right. Might smell a bit funny though.'

She looked at me so gratefully I wanted to tell her to stop it – this was me, after all, no one special. 'Thank you,' she said.

'No big deal.'

Then she started snivelling again. 'They told me nobody likes me.'

'Well, they're wrong,' I said. 'Don't let them get to you.'

Should I have put my arm around her? I had no idea. If I was her, I wouldn't have wanted anyone touching me. I'd probably have decked them one.

'But they're right,' Josie said. 'Nobody *does* like me. I don't have any friends.'

'*I* like you.' There was a small silence, broken only by Josie's sniffles. I thought maybe she didn't believe me. 'I like you a lot better than I like Gemma and Cherry, anyway.'

'Yeah, well, I guess that's something,' Josie said in the funny voice that means someone is about to burst into full-on floods of tears and is trying not to. 'Anyway, I guess I'd better be getting home. Mum'll be wondering where I am.' And then she bolted.

I stayed and watched the stream for a while. It looked so harmless. There was just about enough water to wet your feet, nothing more.

You wouldn't have thought that it could turn into something that could kill someone. But eventually it would flow into the Thames, and then into the sea. And all along the coast people would go and look at it and say how beautiful it was. Even at that beach in Cornwall where my mother had died.

Then I put my socks and trainers back on and went into the alleyway that was a shortcut to Aunt Carrie's house.

The alleyway had a high brick wall on one side, separating it from people's gardens, and a wire fence on the other, marking the boundary of the woodland around the stream. I smelt cigarette smoke, and then I turned a corner and saw Gemma and Cherry.

Gemma dropped the cigarette butt and put it out with her heel and Cherry said something and they both laughed. They were looking at something on the ground. Not the cigarette butt. A snail, slowly making its way across the path towards the woods. Cherry said something to Gemma and Gemma lifted up her foot and stamped on it.

I charged at them and yelled, 'What did you go and do that for? It wasn't doing you any harm!'

They both stared at me in astonishment. The snail was on the ground between us, a splash of slime and grey sludge and broken shell. I had my fists up and my blood was raging. I was ready to hit either of them, or both. I might not have been able to stop. I'd never been quite that angry before.

Gemma's mouth hung open. She stepped back and glanced at Cherry for guidance.

'I never thought she'd actually do it,' Cherry said appeasingly.

Gemma scowled. 'What's the big deal? It's just a snail. My dad smashes them up all the time. He has a special post he uses to do it.'

'Yeah, well, both of you had better watch out,' I said. 'Because if either of you upset Josie ever again, you're going to be the ones getting smashed up.'

'You can't go round threatening people like that,' Cherry said. 'I'll tell Miss Baldon and you'll get suspended.'

'You won't tell anyone. Because if you do, I'm going to flatten you the way Gemma flattened that snail.'

Gemma and Cherry exchanged glances. I glared at both of them with all the venom I was capable of and said, very slowly so as to leave no room for doubt, 'You leave her alone. Because otherwise I'm coming for both of you and I'm going to make you sorry.'

They were both wavering. As usual, Cherry was the one who decided what to do next. 'Come on, Gee, let's go back to mine,' she said. 'This is stupid.' The two of them scuttled off, and I had the alleyway to myself.

I stepped round the remains of the dead snail and let myself into the house. Upstairs in my bedroom, I stared at the picture of me with my mum until it seemed to be of two people I didn't know and had nothing to do with. And then I thought of Josie, crying by the stream. My mum looked like she would have known how to comfort someone. So why didn't I?

A few days after that, I made a big step – for me. I asked Josie if she'd like to come to my house after school.

It was a big step for Aunt Carrie, too; she wasn't keen on having other people in the house, and we never had visitors. But I asked her for permission and she said yes. I was making an effort to be good, after the business of swimming in the river and her getting Dad to talk to me. And I suppose she was trying to be generous.

Then I betrayed her trust completely, though it didn't feel like a betrayal at the time.

Josie and I had the house to ourselves; Aunt Carrie was still at work. We ate some wafer biscuits and drank lemonade, and then we went up to my room and Josie noticed the picture on my windowsill and I said, 'That's my mum. That's the only picture I have.'

'That's the *only* picture?'

'Yeah, that's it.'

I felt slightly sick. Because once Josie had questioned it... it seemed ridiculous. How could it possibly be the only one?

'My aunt's kind of a neat freak,' I said, and my voice sounded wobbly. 'You've seen what this house is like. I don't think there's anything else. She's not the kind of person who has stuff cluttering up the place.'

'It's not clutter. It's your mum. Have you ever asked her?'

I shook my head. 'It's not the kind of thing we talk about,' I said. 'She's not very easy to talk to about anything. Especially Mum.'

Then I explained about me going swimming and how angry Aunt Carrie had been, and what Dad had told me. It was difficult at first – I'd never confided anything like that before. But it got easier. Josie listened with a shrewd look on her face, like a detective, and didn't say anything. If she'd been shocked or offered sympathy, it would have stopped me in my tracks.

When I'd finished Josie said she was sorry about what had happened to my mum. 'But I still think it's weird there aren't more pictures of her,' she went on. 'There must be some somewhere. Where does your aunt keep things in storage? What about the Christmas decorations? Where do they go?'

And that was how I ended up going in the loft, with Josie standing on the landing underneath the hatch and holding the stepladder, and peering nervously up at me and the darkness in the roof of the house. If Josie hadn't encouraged me, if she hadn't helped me, I might never have done it. And I never would have discovered what there was to be found.

Normally I went up in the loft with Aunt Carrie twice a year, once at the beginning of December to bring the Christmas tree and the decorations down, and once in early January to put it all back. When I was younger it had been my job to hold the ladder steady while Aunt Carrie hauled herself up into the space; later, when I got taller than her, she'd asked me to be the one who went up there. The stepladder wasn't quite tall enough, even though I'd grown, and there was always a scary moment when my toes swung in the air and I levered myself up into the hatch.

Once I'd made it, having managed not to fall down the yawning void of the stairwell, there was something else to be scared about. There weren't proper floorboards up there, so if I failed to rest my weight on the ceiling joists I'd crash through the plaster into the bedrooms.

I climbed up the stepladder – 'Hold it firmly, Josie! Don't let it wobble!' – and reached up to turn on the light. It was a single bulb, not enough to dispel the gloom entirely but enough to see your way around by. Then I put my arms either side of the hatch and pushed myself up and there I was – in the forgotten space of the house, the dark triangle where Aunt Carrie stored the few things that she needed to keep but wanted out of the way, out of sight and out of mind.

Bits of sunlight glimmered around the edges of the roof tiles; that was something I'd never noticed when I went up there in the depths of winter. It was hot, too – usually it was freezing. There was the box with the Christmas tree in it, the same tree we'd had every year for as long as I could remember, and the box for decorations. Next to it, as usual, was a big old rucksack – when had Aunt Carrie ever gone away for long enough to need one as big as that? It must date from the time before she'd had to look after me. Back when she'd had a boyfriend, a phase of her life I was very dimly aware of but that had been over before my memories began.

I clambered round, taking care to step only on the beams, and inspected the rucksack more closely. It was stuffed full of something. I unzipped it and opened it up.

Josie called up, 'Have you found something?'

'A load of old clothes,' I said.

Could they have been my mum's? It was hard to connect them with the woman in the brown dress in the picture on my bedroom windowsill. These weren't the clothes of a woman who wore dresses. Or who had a child.

Black jeans, black tops. A dark red velvet jacket that smelt of rain and joss sticks. A plum-coloured waistcoat that looked like it might have once belonged to a dapper old man. A pair of black Doctor Marten boots in a plastic bag, with traces of mud still clinging to the soles.

Right down at the bottom, there was a shoebox with an assortment of bits and pieces inside – a wrist bracelet from a festival, a Zippo lighter that didn't work, a cassette tape with song titles written out by hand and a tarnished silver ring adorned with a skull.

I was definitely getting an Aunt Carrie vibe off this stuff – though who knew? Perhaps it had been my mum's. After all, she'd had a life before she'd had me... more of a life than she'd had afterwards.

I put everything back. And then I saw it, on the other side of the loft, beyond the water tank that wasn't needed since Aunt Carrie'd had the combi boiler put in, but which had never been removed.

An old trunk. The kind of thing people took on sea voyages in films made in the golden age of Hollywood. It looked as if it had been there forever, had maybe even been left there by a previous owner of the house. In the usual way of things, with Aunt Carrie on the landing down below urging me to hurry up, I might never have noticed it. It certainly would never have occurred to me to check it out.

I called out to Josie, 'I'm going across the loft,' and began to make my way along the beams towards where the trunk was resting.

'Be careful,' Josie called up.

Past the water tank. The point of no return. I was so far gone now, I might as well carry on.

There was an old wasps' nest hanging just above the trunk: a pale, papery, distended globe, like an old light with its power gone. It must have been a blissful place for them, given that the loft went undisturbed from one year to the next. A haven.

And then I was undoing the catches on the trunk and pulling up the lid and resting it against the beams of the roof.

It was almost empty. All there was inside was a dark green paper bag with something in it and an old A4 notebook with a doodle on the front cover of a couple dancing.

A weird shiver ran from the top of my head down my spine. I reached for the paper bag and took it out of the trunk. It was brittle to the touch and light, and it rustled. The things inside were wrapped in tissue paper. I took them out and unwrapped them. They were Christmas tree decorations – four of them. Posh, old-fashioned ones. A golden pear, a glittery bow, a star made of pearl beads and a small pair of silver bells, attached by a silver cord.

Josie called up, 'Have you found anything?'

'I'll be down in a minute,' I said.

I wrapped up the decorations and put them back, and then I took out the A4 notebook and opened it.

The handwriting was a bit slapdash, as if it had been put down quickly and without worrying about whether someone else could read it. It was in ink, not biro, and not all the words sat on the lines, and the dots of the 'i's were floating off above their letters and the 't's were barely crossed. Still, it looked pretty. It looked like music, which was something I didn't know how to read at all – all those squiggles rising and falling that, if you knew how, you could translate into the 'Moonlight Sonata' or whatever.

And then I read the beginning of the first page.

Since leaving him I've found myself doing all kinds of other things I wouldn't normally do. Coming here, for a start. I didn't even think twice about the drive – all those hours on the M4 with Dani in the back, the rain sheeting down when we got to the West Country, the tangle of lanes and bad signposts at the end.

But we made it. And Dani was so good. It was almost as if she knew how badly I needed her to be calm and patient.

I closed the notebook and shut my eyes. My mum had written that. About me. I'd been there with her. And I'd been good! Really good! Nobody thought I was calm and patient. Literally nobody. But I'd been patient for her.

I was never a weeper, but my eyes prickled and I felt as if my heart was swelling up in my chest. I breathed in deep and took in the smell of the attic: wooden beams, heated-up roof tiles, insulation, dust and hot, still air. It smelt like a barn with no animals in it.

Then I opened my eyes and flipped down the lid of the trunk and tucked the notebook under one arm. I made my way back across the beams, faster than I'd crossed them in the first place but not too fast.

'I'm coming down,' I called out. 'Can you take this?'

I reached down through the hatch and passed the notebook down to Josie, who had come up the stepladder to take it. Then she backed down and I wedged myself into position and let myself drop down until my feet landed squarely on the top of the stepladder.

Just before I pulled the cover across, I remembered to flick off the light. I came down into the hallway to see Josie looking up at me as if I was an astronaut who'd come back from the moon, holding out the notebook as if she wasn't sure it was safe to touch it.

Chapter Five

It always seemed to be raining at the recreation ground by the bridge. Or at least, that was how I remembered it from when I was little. This is how it used to go: I'd whine and moan and make a nuisance of myself, and Aunt Carrie would finally summon up the energy to take me round there, by which time the sunshine that had made me want to go there in the first place would have disappeared. And then it would start to pour, and Aunt Carrie would sigh and say we had to turn round and go right back again.

But it wasn't raining as I walked there with Josie. Maybe we'd broken the curse of the rec. The A4 notebook was in my schoolbag, and I couldn't help but be conscious of it every step of the way.

It was like carrying round something from an alien planet. The kind of thing a kid in a film would pick up and think was interesting or harmless, and then it would turn out to be a homing device that, once accidentally activated, summoned invading forces from across the universe to attack the Earth. And yet it wasn't heavy. It was lighter than all the books and rubbish I usually had in my bag, so light that if I hadn't been aware all the time of what it was and what it might have inside it, I might even have forgotten it was there.

Josie and I didn't say anything on the way. That was something I was beginning to appreciate more and more about Josie: she knew when to shut up. When I'd said I wanted to get out of my aunt's house, she had seemed to understand, or at least she hadn't questioned why. She'd suggested leaving a note, though – I'd been all set just to get out of there. Instead I'd stopped long enough to scribble down something about going out for a bit and then walking with Josie back to her house. Fair play to Josie, the note had probably been a good move: it wasn't all that long till Aunt Carrie would be back from work, and the last thing I needed was her on the warpath.

The little shelter that was part of the play equipment was free. Usually there were a couple of older teenagers in there, smoking and putting off the little kids from going near it. But that day it was all ours. We sat down on the bench under the cover and Josie said, 'Well, aren't you going to have a look?'

'No. No way. I can't sit here reading it with you looking over my shoulder.'

'I wouldn't try and read it.'

'Yes, you would. What else are you going to do, just sit there like a lemon?'

'I don't mind. I've got my book.'

'Your *book*. You could seriously sit there reading your book while I've got my dead mother's secret diary on my lap?'

'Is it definitely hers?'

'Who else's would it be? It talks about me. Right there on the first page, she's going on about driving down to Cornwall with me. And anyway, it's obviously not Aunt Carrie's. Different writing. Aunt Carrie's writing is a mess, like she really doesn't want anybody else to be able to read it. Which is kind of weird, for such a neat freak. This is like… I don't know… A bit rushed, but it's *pretty* writing. Pretty and brainy. Not like mine.' I hesitated. 'I mean, I suppose I can't say for sure. I've never seen my mum's handwriting before. Not that I can remember. But who else's diary would Aunt Carrie be hiding in the attic?'

I was thinking of the photo on my bedroom windowsill, my mother smiling in the brown dress, holding my hand with no idea of what was about to happen to her. The thought that I had found something with her handwriting in it did my head in. It wasn't so much the idea of what the handwriting might say – I hadn't even begun to think about that yet – as the idea that she'd *touched* it. The diary was something she'd thought about, spent time over, kept going back to. People talked about committing things to memory. She'd committed something to paper. It came to me that I was terrified of finding out what.

I'd imagined it being like a homing device for an army of aliens. But it was more like a portal. A portal straight across time and space into her mind, into whatever she'd been going through when she wrote it.

I said, 'Maybe it's a really bad idea for me to read it. I don't know, it could be kind of personal.'

'That's true. I wouldn't like it if someone read my diary,' Josie said.

'You keep a diary?' I couldn't imagine that she had anything much to write in it.

'I do,' Josie said stiffly. 'It's just a way of remembering what I did. I mean, it's nice to look back at the old ones and see how much I've changed and how childish I was then.'

'Yeah, well, if that's your idea of fun then, you know, go for it.'

'Honestly, it's good, you should try it.'

'Yeah, *so* not my thing.'

'I guess it was your mum's thing,' Josie observed.

We both paused to think about that for a moment, sitting there in the shade and looking across the sunlit playing field in front of us. There was a woman walking her dog on the far side of the field, alongside the trees in front of the fence; on our right, a couple of mums were chatting while their kids played on the climbing frame. I couldn't quite make out what they were saying, or what the kids were saying, but it was nice to listen to – the sound of ordinary happiness, people going about their lives.

That was what we'd lost, me and Mum. All the days when we could have come to places like this, days that wouldn't have been memorable or remarkable in themselves but that would have added up to something: a feeling of being safe. Of being lucky. Of being loved, I suppose. I'd never really thought about whether Aunt Carrie loved me. She probably did, but it wasn't too obvious.

'I don't get it,' Josie observed. 'The way you went up into that loft and climbed around up there – you didn't even hesitate. But now you've got this thing and you don't even seem like you want to open it.'

'Maybe it would be disrespectful. Maybe it's hidden away for a reason,' I countered. 'There might be things in there she wouldn't have wanted me to know.'

'There might be things in there your *aunt* wouldn't want you to know,' Josie said, then gave me a sly sideways look as if she knew full well that would make me want to read it.

'You said you wouldn't want anyone reading your diary. How do you think you'd feel if your future daughter did?'

'I don't think it would really be that interesting, to be honest. So I guess it would be kind of embarrassing. But, you know… I don't think I'd really mind. I mean, it's nice to think she might care enough to bother.'

'Well, that's one way of looking at it.'

'OK, I know it's meant to be rude to read other people's diaries. But I'm not sure that applies under the circumstances. You know, I think it's different when… when someone's not around.'

'I guess it is,' I said.

I reached for my schoolbag, which was sitting on the bench next to me. Normally I would probably just have dumped it on the ground. Then my mind played a strange little trick on me. For an instant, I pictured *her* – my mum, the smiling woman in the brown dress from the photo on my windowsill – right there beside me, about to start telling me something. Except she wasn't smiling. She looked devastated. Desperate.

And then she was gone again, and it was just me and Josie Pye in the rec, me with an old A4 notebook on my lap.

I looked again at the doodle on the cover. So she'd been a doodler, just like me. The connection only went so far, though. I drew fat little comedy monsters when lessons got boring, or caricatures of my teachers. I would never draw a couple dancing, not in a million years.

The woman in the doodle was wearing some kind of ball-gown with a big swishy skirt. Again, not my cup of tea, but it was obvious that Mum had enjoyed drawing it.

She had been a romantic. Romantic, and into clothes. Who else would draw something like that? Whereas I'd always been put off by anything too soppy. The princesses I liked didn't dance with princes, they fought with swords. Or whatever came to hand. And there weren't that many of that kind of princess. It seemed like they were fighting a losing battle.

I flipped over the cover. What was that story we'd done a project about back in primary school? Pandora's box. Girl gets given a box and is told not to open it. Girl opens it because duh, of course she does, human nature. And out pops all the misery of the world. But the last thing that comes out is the thing that will make it possible for people to bear everything else: it's hope.

Each of us had made a box as part of the project. Mine hadn't closed properly at all. You'd have had a job keeping anything at all in there, whether it was curses or blessings.

As I looked down at what Mum had written, I didn't feel hopeful. I was scared. It was an unfamiliar feeling and I didn't like it one bit. I'd never really bothered with fear. Other girls were vain about being pretty, or popular, or having nice new trainers. I was vain about being brave.

When it came down to reading what my dead mother had written, I wasn't brave at all.

Since leaving him I've found myself doing all kinds of other things I wouldn't normally do.

'She wrote it after she left my dad,' I said to Josie. 'I'm in it, but it's going to be full of stuff I don't remember. It's too weird.'

Josie was looking at me with a strange light in her eyes.

'Dani,' she said, 'your aunt is your mum's sister, right? Older sister? Younger sister?'

'Oh, older. I think so, anyway. Though I reckon Aunt Carrie was born ancient, so it probably would have seemed that way even if she wasn't.'

'Well, did they get on? Were they close? Does she ever talk about her?'

'Nobody talks about my mum. Absolutely nobody. I have no idea what she was like. Did people like her? Did they love her? I don't know. Apart from that photo I showed you, she's just a blank. It's like they erased her.'

'Then how can you *not* read the diary?' Josie said. 'You owe it to her. To colour her back in.'

'Because I know how it turned out,' I said. 'I know what happened to her. And when she was writing this, she had absolutely no idea what was coming.'

'You don't know how the diary ends,' Josie pointed out.

'I suppose that's true,' I said.

I closed it, and turned it over and opened the back cover.

'You can't do that,' Josie said. 'That's cheating.'

'I'm only going to peek,' I told her.

I flipped through the blank pages at the back. There were lots of them. Would she have carried on writing, if she'd lived? Or would she not have felt she needed to?

And then I came to the last page she had written on, and the final paragraph.

In a minute Dani would remember that she was supposed to be hungry and come in asking where her lunch was. She needed everything to be as normal as possible, the same as usual in spite of the heat; she needed to be able to carry on believing that what adults did made sense. I hoped she wouldn't notice

*the mark on my face, that it would have faded enough by then
to be inconspicuous. A mother who'd just been hit was the last
thing she needed to see.*

I closed the notebook again.

'Josie,' I said. 'I think there's a possibility my dad might not be
a very good man.'

Chapter Six

I wasn't really all that keen on seeing other girls with their mums. Unless they hated them. In which case, fine. But if they were being nice to each other… ugh.

Then I would feel hollow, like there was nothing to me, like I could just blow away in the wind and nobody would notice. And feeling that way made me angry and being angry usually ended up getting me into trouble. So I wasn't crazy about Josie's suggestion that we should go back to her house for a bit. But it was beginning to rain, just as it always did at the rec… and it wasn't as if we'd have to spend any time with her mum, anyway. We could just hide away in her bedroom, and I could read my mum's diary in peace.

'We could say we're doing homework,' Josie suggested. 'I won't bother you. I might actually *do* some homework.'

'We haven't got any, have we?'

'Yes we have. French. History. But you've got plenty of time to catch up. It's not due yet.' I noted that she didn't suggest that I could copy hers. 'I have a reading chair in my room. You can sit there. And I'll sit at my desk. Mum said she was going to make biscuits today, so we can have some before we go up.'

Home-made biscuits. Reading chair. *Definitely* someone else's life.

'Yeah, it sounds pretty good, to be fair. OK, I'll come.'

I put the notebook back into my bag.

The last line I'd read came back to me. *A mother who'd just been hit was the last thing she needed to see.*

Well… maybe Josie was right, and I shouldn't jump to conclusions, not before I'd read the whole thing. I should probably give

Dad the benefit of the doubt… But I'd been doing that for years and years.

The lost feeling I'd always had – the sense of being out of my depth and not wanting to rock the boat – was turning into something else. Suspicion. And along with that, there was anger. Which I was well used to: it was how the world usually made me feel. But I wasn't used to being this angry with *him*. Usually I was just resigned.

Maybe this was how people began to feel before they went and did drastic, terrible things, things no normal, sane person would do.

But if I was going to have it out with him, or go crazy, or both at the same time… I had to be sure.

First of all, I had to read the diary. That was the key to it. Then I wouldn't have to wonder any more. I'd know.

Josie's house turned out to be my idea of heaven.

It wasn't that different to Aunt Carrie's house, on the face of it. It was a pretty normal kind of house, with a lawn in front and a car parked on the drive and neighbours all around. But inside, it was different. It smelt sweet and fresh, like pine cleaning products crossed with baking, and was as bright and cheery as a house in a TV advert.

To top it all off, there was Josie's mother in the kitchen: a woman in a yellow shirt and jeans stooping over a worktop to ice a batch of biscuits, helped by a girl with fair hair and glasses who was presumably Josie's kid sister.

'Mum, this is Dani,' Josie said.

Mrs Pye looked up and smiled, apparently completely unfazed by having a kid she'd never met before rock up uninvited. She seemed nice. Really nice. I felt a sudden ache somewhere near my heart, like a cross between hunger pangs and a stitch.

'Hi, Dani. I'm Lucy,' she said.

I made an awkward sort of grunting noise in acknowledgement. I wasn't often tongue-tied, but then, usually I didn't care what people thought of me. And I didn't want to make a bad impression on Mrs Pye – I couldn't bring myself to think of her as Lucy, even if she had just given me permission.

Mrs Pye had the kind of smile that makes you feel like smiling back, even if you didn't feel at all like smiling to start with, and short blonde hair that made her look like a motherly pixie. If Josie turned out like her mum, sooner or later her ugly duckling days would be over and she'd turn into a fully-fledged swan.

'That's my sister Annie. Annie, this is my friend Dani from school,' Josie said.

Annie looked at me blankly. Shy, like Josie: little and skinny, too. She had on the green-and-white gingham dress that was the summer uniform of the primary school round the corner – the one I'd gone to – and it made me sad to think that once she was surrounded by kids who were bigger and older, she might end up being bullied the way Josie was. I grinned at her, and she managed a small smile in return.

Josie went over to inspect the biscuits. 'Can we have some?'

'They're for the bake sale,' Mrs Pye said. 'But there are cupcakes in the usual place. Help yourself.'

Josie scurried round, assembling things and placing them on the island in the middle of the kitchen: plates, lemonade, glasses and a round flowery tin that turned out to be where the cupcakes lived. I felt like Edmund in *The Lion, the Witch and the Wardrobe* confronted with his first taste of Turkish Delight. One of my primary school teachers had read that book to us at the end of the day to bore us into good behaviour just before home time. I hadn't liked it all that much, but I kind of liked Edmund. When it came to stories, I usually liked the person you weren't supposed to like.

Mrs Pye said, 'I've heard a lot about you, Dani.'

'Really?'

I didn't like this at all. Probably Josie would have told her I didn't have a mum – it was the most obvious thing to tell anyone about me. Mrs Pye was bound to feel sorry for me. She looked like the kind of person who went round feeling sorry for people.

'Nothing bad,' Mrs Pye said hurriedly. 'Only good things. I hear you stood up to some girls who were being nasty to someone else.'

Josie shot me a pleading look. So she didn't want her mum to know that she was the one Cherry and Gemma had been picking on. If Mrs Pye knew about the way Gemma and Cherry treated Josie, she most likely would have been straight up the school complaining. And then probably things would have got a whole lot worse, and Josie would have ended up having to leave.

Maybe, at the end of the day, it wasn't all that much help having a mum like Mrs Pye. Though it might be a comfort, at least when compared to having a guardian like Aunt Carrie. Once or twice, when I was younger, I'd tried telling Aunt Carrie stuff about school. She'd bent over backwards to be all reasonable and try not to take sides, like the other person had a perfectly reasonable point of view. It had driven me nuts.

'I don't like people who think they can bully other people and get away with it,' I said. 'But I guess that's the thing about bullies. Nobody much likes them, so the only way they can get people to take any notice is by frightening them. And then people are too frightened of them to tell them where to get off.'

Mrs Pye looked slightly alarmed. Maybe she was thinking that I knew about bullies from my dad. And given the way the diary ended – that line about Mum being hit – maybe I did.

'Do you think there's an issue with bullying at school?' Mrs Pye asked me. 'I got the impression from Josie that what happened was more of a falling-out than anything more sinister.'

'I wasn't really thinking of school. Or home. It was just a general point. That's the impression I get.'

Mrs Pye's face cleared. 'Oh, well, in that case you may very well be right.'

'Mum, can we finish doing the biscuits?' Josie's kid sister pleaded.

'We should go do our homework,' Josie said to me with a meaningful glance at my bag, which I'd put on the stool next to me.

'Sure.'

I stood up and shouldered my bag. Josie started to clear away the things we'd left on the table, but Mrs Pye said, 'Don't worry about that, I'll do it in a minute. Dani, will you be staying for dinner?'

How nice was that? No wonder Josie sometimes looked as if she was astonished by the real world outside her front door. Especially when people were mean to her.

'Thanks, but I don't think so,' I said.

It seemed like the safest thing to say. I wasn't sure I'd be staying anywhere. The notebook in my bag seemed like something that might have the power to explode everything, and take me somewhere else completely.

A mother who'd just been hit was the last thing she needed to see.

Perhaps Mum hadn't wanted anybody to know she was being bullied either. Especially not me. The four-year-old I'd been back then. Who was probably pretty clueless, as four-year-olds tend to be.

But little kids make fast learners, especially as they get older. They notice things like bruises and raised voices, and sudden silences. Sometimes they know better than to ask too many questions. Other times, they stumble across the answers they didn't know they needed.

What exactly had my mum been running away from? What if it had been my dad, and she'd decided she had to go before I saw something I shouldn't? What if he had caught up with her before she could escape for good and take me with her?

It would make sense of everything if my dad was a villain. It would even made sense of why I always had a sneaking sympathy for the baddie. Because kids do love their dads, don't they? Whoever they are. Whatever they've done. Even if the dads don't really deserve it.

I picked up my bag and followed Josie upstairs. My heart was pounding. So much for not being scared of anything. I was scared like crazy, and not just of what I might find out. I was even more scared of what I would have to do afterwards.

What I had got my hands on was evidence, and it didn't make a blind bit of difference that it was old. It was down to me to speak out for my mum if I had to, because who else was going to do it? Not Dad, that was for sure. And not Aunt Carrie either. She must have read whatever was in the notebook. She was the one who'd hidden it, after all. And she'd never said a thing.

I'd always thought they kept quiet about Mum because they were sad. But what if it was because they were guilty?

Josie's bedroom was very nice – clean and warm and bright, with a bouncy carpet – but very far from cool. She still had stuffed animals on the bed and framed Flower Fairy prints on the walls. Predictably, she had a desk and chair in there, by the bed – she was exactly the kind of kid who would have a desk and chair in her bedroom. There was an armchair, too, in a corner, with a floor lamp beside it.

'Your bedroom is massive,' I said. 'If I had a room like this I'd never come downstairs.' Though I only ever came down for meals anyway.

'It's not *that* big,' Josie said, a bit defensively, but I could tell she was relieved. She must have been nervous that I'd tease her about the cuddly toys.

She went over to the armchair and turned on the floor lamp. 'There. This is my reading chair. All yours.'

The armchair was comfy all right, but I felt like someone was going to come along any minute and tell me to get off it. I tucked my feet up underneath me – I'd already taken my shoes off. It was the kind of house where nobody treads dirt in.

'I can't believe you have a special chair for reading,' I said.

'I asked for it,' Josie said. 'I chose it. It was a joint Christmas and birthday present.'

'Guess you must really like books.'

'Of course I do. Don't you?'

'Well, let's just say I would probably have chosen a different present.'

Josie sat down at her desk and got her planner out of her book bag and opened up her laptop. 'I'm going to do my homework now. Just tell me if you want anything.'

And then she put headphones on and turned her back to me.

It was very quiet. If I really concentrated, I could just about make out the radio chattering away downstairs in the kitchen. But otherwise there were no distractions. No distractions and no excuses.

This was it, then. It was time. Time for me to get as close as I would ever be to my mother.

I was going to *invade* her. I was going to read something she would never have meant for me to read.

I unzipped my bag and took the notebook out and opened it.

But Dani said, Don't worry, Mummy, *when I took yet another wrong turning at journey's end, when it was long after dark and she should have been bathed and in bed.* We'll get there.

And we *had* got there. Problem was, she had never made it back. It was time to go and find her.

As I began to read the room around me fell away: the chintzy wallpaper, the big window with its view of garden trees and blue sky, Josie tapping away at her keyboard. I wasn't there. I wasn't me. I was her, a woman with a little girl in a cottage by the sea. A runaway.

But what was I running away from?

Chapter Seven

Laura's Diary

It's our second night in Cornwall, and Dani is sound asleep.

I peeked in on her just now and she looks so sweet and peaceful, the picture of childhood innocence and bliss, tucked up in the blue flowered sheets that came with the cottage – clean but faded, and smelling of lavender – and cuddling Bear, the red of her hair still bright even in the gloom.

Right from the start, one of the things that touched me most about motherhood was seeing her sleeping. After all, who else can you watch when they're asleep, apart from lovers and children? The married are less likely to find each other fascinating – however little they know of what goes on in each other's heads when they're awake.

I love watching over Dani, always have done, ever since her very first sleep in my arms. Her smooth, fine skin, the eyelids – delicate as veined parchment – the miniature features that are hers, but also remind me of a jumble of other people. Jon's red hair. My mother's heart-shaped face. And, when she opens them, brown eyes like mine.

When I told her we were going away, she said, *Is Daddy coming?* And I said, *No, he's too busy with work. It'll be fun, just you and me, won't it?* I was half afraid that she was going to persist, the way she so often does: *I want Daddy to come! I want Daddy to come!* But luckily she didn't.

To tell the truth, there's always been another reason to cherish the time when Dani's asleep: she can be quite a handful. Other little girls always seem so docile, so pretty, with their little pink dresses and their shiny shoes and their fairy wands. Dani has never been up for any of that. Other things she doesn't like include queueing, taking turns, sitting still for any length of time. She's calmed down a bit now, but when she was a toddler I couldn't let her out of my sight for a minute. If she saw an open door – or found one she could open – she'd be off, toddling merrily down the street as if on a mission to expose herself to danger. It was like being a bodyguard to an occasionally adorable celebrity with a very short attention span and a wildly unpredictable temper.

Jon dotes on her. Always has. She can wrap him round her little finger. Just one of those special, cherubic smiles is all it takes, and I believe he'd do anything for her.

How am I going to explain to her why I need to leave him behind?

When it comes down to it, will he fight me for her?

The real shock of all of this is how little I knew him. But how can you know someone, anyway, at the start? You take a lover on trust. You do that because that's what you're designed to do – that's what your body is telling you to do, and that's what the whole world is telling you to do, or so it seems.

And then – if you're me, at any rate – you wake up and find you have a child and a ring on your finger and a husband who might as well be your most conniving enemy rather than your dearest friend. Who might not have done things so very differently if he'd been hell-bent on destroying you right from the moment you met.

And yet it was so sweet, once upon a time.

Can I bring myself to remember it? Can I bear to?

If I don't remember, I cannot tell this story honestly. But is it possible to tell it honestly, however hard I try, however much I force myself to look back? I don't know. Does it matter? Who am I telling it for?

For myself, I suppose. To try to find a way back. Because I am lost. I am here in this cottage by the sea with my daughter, and yet

I might just as well be in the midst of the deepest, darkest wood, with no map and no sense of direction and no idea how to get out.

After all the lies, it seems important to try to find the truth.

It has to at least be possible to try.

Was I a fool to fall in love? I suppose I was. It's easy to be wise with hindsight. Jon dazzled me. I thought he was wonderful. And the way we met was part of that. From the start I saw him as a prize I had no chance of winning, and didn't deserve anyway – and had no right to so much as daydream about, because back then he belonged to someone else.

I first set eyes on him in the last century, when I was sixteen years old, and I met him because I was incapable of saying no to my mother.

I was new in town, an innocent who always had her nose in her book, who had read plenty about romance but had never come close to experiencing it. We had moved to Kettlebridge because Mum had finally agreed to marry Phil, her nice but boring boyfriend, and that was where he had a nice but boring house. My sister Carrie had already left home for university and was only back for the holidays. But I had two more years of school to go, and Mum decided, in her wisdom, that it would help me to settle in if I did the very last thing I felt like doing, and got involving in performing in a play.

The phrase 'get out of your comfort zone' was used, and 'being part of the community'. I think she honestly believed it would build my confidence and do me good. And so it was that I joined the Kettlebridge Amateur Dramatic Society and was cast in a small part in their production of *Macbeth*. And that was how I met Jon's wife.

I was in awe of Jade right from the start. Her Lady Macbeth was spectacular: the intensity, the glamour, the murderous rage – it was almost effortless, as if she was barely acting. But she wasn't friendly or approachable, and she didn't bother with small talk. She was the sort of person you observe sneakily, from a safe distance, while hoping she won't notice what you're up to and object.

She was twenty-three then, seven years older than I was, light years ahead in terms of life experience and – this was what really struck me about her – she was sexy, the kind of sexy that would make someone think twice about catcalling because she also seemed as if she wouldn't hold back on picking a fight with anybody who annoyed her. She looked like a sultry Sicilian widow, all dark eyes and glossy hair and philosophical gloom, and she had a languid, unhurried way of moving, as if she lived in her own special climate where there was always a heatwave, even if, in Kettlebridge, it was cool and grey.

Jade insisted on finding her own costume for the play. It was a long, form-fitting dress in close-fitting jersey, the colour of ivy. It could have had a touch of the Disney villainess about it but, on Jade, was a reminder that not everybody looks terrible in poison green. My own costume, by way of contrast, was a reminder that not everyone is pretty in pink. It looked like a bridesmaid's dress, which was probably what it was. It had a full skirt and a sash and flouncy sleeves and frills, and was just slightly too low cut for comfort. I couldn't help but wonder if the original wearer had hated it as much as I did.

I didn't complain, though. After all, the character I was playing, Lady Macduff, was only on stage for about five minutes before running off to get murdered. All I had to do was look sweet and innocent and remember a couple of lines. No one would pay me attention until they heard me scream.

But on the day of the first performance Jade's green dress was still hanging on the rail a quarter of an hour before curtain-up. And that was when Mr Reed, the portly town librarian who was directing the play, told me I'd have to take her part.

There were two dressing rooms backstage at the Old Hall Theatre, one small and dark, the other relatively light and spacious. The women had been given the bigger of the two – the women and I: I was the youngest cast member, and I still thought of myself as a girl and not a woman. I assumed we'd been given the better dressing room because of Jade, not because of our gender. She probably wouldn't even have had to drop hints about it.

The rest of us – me and the three witches – were all ready, and trying, in our different ways, to keep our nerves at bay. I was reading through my scene, Lesley Johns was flicking past pictures of famous people in a magazine, Mary Tilsley was eating chocolate and Eloise Cummings, who worked as a beauty therapist, was touching up her witchy make-up, even though every wrinkle was already perfect.

Then Mr Reed rapped heavily on the door and called out, 'Ladies? Are you decent?' and it was obvious from his voice that he was more nervous than any of us.

'You can come in,' Lesley called out, and he bustled in and stopped short in front of the green frock on the rail.

'No sign of her, then,' he said.

'Not yet,' Lesley said. 'But I'm sure she'll make it. We all know how much she wants to do it. She won't let us down.'

He turned his face and hands to the ceiling as if pleading with unseen forces for mercy; he didn't look panicky so much as doomed. 'She's not answering her phone,' he said. 'Something must have happened.'

Mary Tilsley surreptitiously dropped her chocolate bar wrapper in her handbag. We weren't supposed to eat or drink in costume, a rule that Mr Reed had been very insistent about but was now too preoccupied to remember.

She said, 'What about her husband?'

Mr Reed looked horrified. 'Oh, no, I couldn't possibly. Even if I did have his number.'

Lesley licked the tips of her fingers and turned the page of her magazine. She said, 'They're probably fighting. Or making up. With couples like Jade and Jon, it's always one or the other.'

Eloise put down the powder brush, adjusted her witch's cloak, examined her reflection in the mirror and let out a small sigh.

'It could be the baby,' she said.

At first I didn't understand what she meant. Was Jade pregnant? If so, it wasn't at all obvious. Then Mary said, 'She's not a baby any more. She must be two or three by now.'

'Still very little to be left with a babysitter while her mum swans round going to drama rehearsals,' Lesley said disapprovingly.

'Yes, well, Jade was never going to be one for sitting round in playgroups singing "The Wheels on the Bus", was she?' Eloise said.

'I'm sure she's done her fair share of that. As we all do,' Mary said.

'She's been spotted in town buying vodka,' Lesley said. 'Not the sign of a happy mummy. And my nephew said he heard them bickering like anything in the hardware store.'

'The vodka could have been for someone else, and all couples bicker in the hardware store,' Mary pointed out.

'It's the curse of the Scottish play,' Mr Reed said. He settled heavily in the empty chair next to me, the one where Jade usually sat, and folded his arms and shook his head. 'Mrs Reed told me not to do it.'

Then Eloise turned towards me and said, '*You* could do it.'

Four pairs of eyes were instantly fixed on me. Mary said, 'That's it. *You* could be Lady Macbeth.'

I felt myself turning an ugly shade or red. 'I couldn't,' I said.

Mr Reed leaped up out of his chair. 'Of course! Why didn't I think of that? You're always reading it. I bet you know all of the lines.'

'Now that's a brilliant idea. The show must go on, Laura,' Lesley said. She inspected her wrinkled reflection in the mirror. 'I haven't gone through all this just to have it cancelled at the last minute.'

'But I don't know it. Not well enough to perform it,' I said.

'Then carry the script with you. Don't worry, nobody will mind. They'll know you're just standing in. They're not going to be expecting very much,' Mary said kindly.

'Why do I have to do it? Anybody else could read the lines.'

'You're the only one who could get into the costume,' Mary pointed out.

'That won't fit me,' I said, staring at the poison-green frock hanging on the rail like a piece of incriminating evidence. Jade was much more voluptuous than I was, and I didn't fancy the idea of trooping across the stage looking like a toxic deflated balloon.

'Well, it might be a bit big, but at least you'll be able to zip it up,' Mary said.

'You could always stuff your bra with a couple of old socks,' Lesley said helpfully.

'Can't I just wear what I've got on now?' The flouncy pink dress suddenly seemed like the safest and most reassuring outfit in the world.

'You can't be Lady Macbeth in that,' Mr Reed said decisively. 'You'll have to change. No need to panic, you're not on for the first couple of scenes. Mrs Reed can be Lady Macduff.'

I could see that Mrs Reed would probably fit into the pink dress, and would be willing to, for the sake of the play. She was tall and brisk and bony, with the figure of a woman who likes to keep busy. And as for me – my sister Carrie's nickname for me was Pinhead, because that was what she said my head looked like on my narrow body. She was curvy herself, but always wore tops and jumpers so outsized she could have been any shape underneath and nobody would have been any the wiser.

Eloise looked at me accusingly. It wasn't as if they were all encouraging me to step up to the role – more as if they were annoyed with me for not jumping at the chance.

She said, 'So are you going to or what?'

I hesitated. I'd spent so much time in rehearsal, watching Jade, wondering how anybody could be so confident…

Then I got to my feet.

'I don't need a script,' I said. 'I can do it.'

Mr Reed exhaled and clapped his hands. 'Good girl. We'll all just have to do our best.' He checked his watch. 'No time to waste. Witches, you'll need to take your positions in five minutes.' And with that he hurried out.

I reached round to my back to tug down the zip of the pink dress. Mary said, 'Laura, love, do you need a hand?'

'I think I'm all right,' I said, but she ignored me and came round to unzip me. I stepped out of the pink dress and Mary took it from me and passed me the green one. I was conscious of them all politely trying not to look at me in my plain white underwear as I dropped it over my head.

It fit. That was the first surprise. Mary did it up, and I smoothed it down. It was like being encased in supple green armour, and it smelt of Jade.

But when I turned to face the mirror, I saw that I didn't look like her. Not remotely. I looked like a bolder, harder, more ruthless version of myself.

'Well, that's not so bad, is it?' Mary said.

'Pretty good, I'd say,' Lesley commented. 'Makes you realise what a snug fit it was on Jade.'

'I didn't know she had a child,' I said, smoothing down the fabric of the dress over my tummy.

'I think you should try on the rest of your costume, Laura,' Eloise said.

She went over to the prop table, where Lady Macbeth's crown was laid out ready. It was a small silver tiara, set with seed pearls, that Jade had worn on her wedding day.

'I'm not sure I should,' I said. 'It is Jade's, after all.'

'You'll have to wear it,' Mary said. 'Otherwise people won't understand what's going on when Lady Macbeth becomes a queen. You can't be a queen without a crown.'

'Don't worry about Jade,' Eloise said. 'She isn't here, is she? Besides, don't you want to see what it looks like?'

And I did. Mary was standing behind me in her witchy make-up and holding out the tiara as if acting in a coronation, and Eloise and Lesley were egging me on, and I wanted very much to see what I would look like if the long green dress was topped by a crown.

Mary moved forward and laid the tiara gently on my hair, and I made no attempt to stop her.

All three of them gasped and then sighed.

'You look beautiful,' Lesley said.

'Very elegant. Like a proper queen,' Eloise observed.

Mary folded her arms. 'Stunning,' she said. 'You're going to break a few hearts, that's for sure.'

Then there was a rush of air into the room as the door behind us was flung open wide and Jade stormed in.

'What do you think you're doing?' she yelled. 'Get out of my dress!'

Mary, who'd been standing so close to me, instantly backed off, and Jade came right up to me and snatched the tiara off my head.

'Don't you ever dare touch my stuff again,' she said.

'I won't,' I said. 'I didn't mean to. We thought you weren't coming.'

'Once I've decided I'm going to do something, believe me, I'm going to do it.' She put the tiara down on the dressing-table, then faced me again. 'Turn round.'

I did as she said, and she pulled down the zip at the back of the green dress and I took it off and passed it to her. I tried to stand as tall as I could, to look her in the eye. Suddenly it seemed vitally important to salvage something from this, but I wasn't quite sure what.

'I'm glad you made it,' I said. 'I wouldn't have been a very good stand-in.'

Jade shook her head. 'It's always the quiet ones,' she said. Then she looked round at Lesley and Mary and Eloise. 'What's up with you three witches? Cat got your tongues? You'd better get yourselves backstage. You're going to be on in a minute.'

It seemed no time at all before I was back in the pink dress and Jade was in the green, and we were alone together in the dressing room. She put her feet up on the dressing-table and got on with the big sexy blockbuster she was reading, the kind of book my mum wouldn't approve of. I went back to reading my copy of the script. I knew I should have been relieved. But I just felt humiliated, and, worse, ashamed – because after all, who was I to think I could play a leading role?

When I finally made it out onto the stage for the five underwhelming minutes of my one and only scene, there was no missing the handsome red-haired man sitting right in the middle of the auditorium, a few rows further forward than Mum and Phil and Carrie. He was head and shoulders above everyone else, and he was watching with an amused, ironic expression, as if challenging us all to impress him. He didn't seem to be particularly impressed by me, but then, just as I'd expected, neither was anybody else.

There I was, on stage, supposedly not far from the centre of attention, but a long way from the centre of his. And there he was, in the audience, ignoring me. He was so distractingly charismatic that I nearly forgot my lines, and was relieved when my part was done.

That was how I first set eyes on Jon. If anyone had told me back then what would happen between me and him later on, I would hardly have believed it.

If they'd told me just the beginning, I would have been thrilled. If they'd told me more, I'd have been stuck with the exact same dilemma that I have now: not knowing whether to run for my life or accept my fate.

Back in the dressing room I listened to Eloise and Mary and Lesley talking about him. Jade was on stage, doing her sleepwalking scene, and they always chatted more freely when she wasn't there. That was how I found out his name and who he was married to.

'I don't usually fancy men with red hair,' Eloise said. 'But I could make an exception for him.'

'Don't let Jade hear you say that,' Mary said.

'As if I would,' Eloise said. 'Mind you, she deserves to lose him, the way she's carried on.'

'Why anyone would want to play the field when they've got a man like Jon Rosewell is beyond me,' Mary said, and sighed.

So Jade was cheating on Jon? That seemed extraordinary. I found myself in complete agreement with Mary. How could anyone have so much and then throw it away?

They didn't dare show their disapproval to her, though. After we'd taken our final bows she produced a bottle of champagne, and they all said they'd have some and cackled as she tipped it into the plastic cups that someone had rustled up.

She was literally flushed with success; I'd never seen her look so happy. I made my excuses and went out. As the door shut behind me I heard laughter, and had the uncomfortable sense of being the butt of the joke.

The only way out was through the auditorium. The theatre was in an old building, a relic of the ruined abbey that had once dominated Kettlebridge; a keen civic society had put in a stage and curtains and steeply raked seating, but the walls were still made of rough bare stone and ancient dust shimmered in the light that seeped through the cracks.

It was all empty and quiet now; the audience had already gone out. As I made my way towards the exit at the back the place suddenly seemed immensely spooky. Ominous. As if I might suddenly find myself shut in, and unable to escape.

If I really were to vanish then and there, to disappear completely… what kind of impression would I have made on the world? Barely enough to leave a trace.

I pushed open the double doors at the back of the auditorium. In the courtyard below, people who had been to see the play were milling round nursing drinks from the table Mrs Reed had set up. Jon was there, his red hair glinting in the sunshine, swigging beer from a bottle. He looked potentially dangerous, like a tetchy bull in a field. Mum and Phil and Carrie were standing in a little cluster to one side, and I went down the steps to join them.

Phil was checking his watch, and Carrie was bound to be itching to get away so she could have a cigarette – Mum and Phil didn't know she smoked, and I'd been sworn to secrecy. But Mum was looking round for people to meet. As I approached Jon drifted into her orbit, and she saw her chance and accosted him.

'You must be Jon Rosewell. I don't think we've met – I hope you don't mind if I introduce myself. I'm Betty Rivers. This is Carrie, my older daughter. She just applied for a job in your garden centre. Which is just lovely, by the way, one of my favourite places in Kettlebridge. And this is Laura, my youngest, who was in the play.'

Jon took the hand she'd offered him and shook it. Then he shook Phil's, and the two men eyed each other up as it they belonged to different species and weren't quite sure what the other was good for. I didn't think Carrie was going to make a very good impression either. She was all in black despite the heat, and she was wearing black shades and matte red lipstick and scowling. Her hair was naturally light brown but she'd dyed it darker – closer to the colour of mine – and the contrast with her pale skin made her look unhealthy. She didn't come across as someone you'd much want to employ.

But then Jon turned towards her with something not too far removed from a smile, as if he didn't find the way she looked off-putting in the least.

Then there was a small collective intake of breath from all around us as Jade emerged from the theatre, out of the green dress now and wearing a strappy black top and shorts. She was smiling triumphantly as she came down the steps, as if she really was a queen about to greet her loyal subjects.

'Nice to meet you,' Jon said to us all, and went over to join her.

They embraced, and he congratulated her. Phil said, 'Perhaps it's time we weren't here…?'

As we made our way out Carrie said, 'I really don't want to work in the garden centre,' a bit too loudly to be discreet.

'You might not get the option,' Mum muttered. Then she said to me, 'Well, there you are, you did it. That wasn't so bad, was it?'

I decided not to tell them that I'd nearly ended up in a starring role. The thought of Jade snatching the tiara off my head was too awful to revisit. Instead I said, 'It was OK, but I really don't think acting's my thing. After this play finishes, is it OK with you if I don't do any more?'

That caught Mum by surprise. I never usually rejected anything she wanted me to do; she got so much resistance from Carrie it seemed unfair for me to do the same.

'I don't think either of you girls appreciate anything I try to do for you,' she sniffed, and put her head down and walked very fast to the car with Phil trotting along behind her, hurrying to catch up.

'Well, the worm has turned,' Carrie said, raising her eyebrows. I didn't reply. I felt faintly irritated with her – even more than usual. It was something to do with the way Jon had looked at her. Not as if she was stroppy and surly and the last person you'd want serving you in a garden centre, but as if she was someone it would be good to pass the time of day with – someone interesting, someone worth talking to.

And he hadn't even noticed me.

It wasn't surprising, really. I understood it. Carrie wasn't glamorous like Jade, but I could see that in a way, there was something attractive about her rebelliousness and sulkiness. I was used to her dominating things at home, but it would've been a nice change if, just for once, when it came to the outside world, I could have held my own.

*

Mum did let me drop out of the drama club, and at the end of the summer I started at my new school and began studying for my A levels and making plans for my future, and it never occurred to me that Jon would be in it.

I made some friends at school but they were slightly awkward girls, a bit like me, who didn't entirely fit in and who didn't have relationships, or sex. The division between us and the kind of girls who *did* have relationships seemed stark. They shaped their eyebrows and had contraception and broken hearts; we listened to music and wondered what it would be like to feel the things that people sang about. They were living their lives, lives that involved love and hope and betrayal. But life was something I was still building up to. I was scared of it, if I'm honest. And now I think I had good reason to be.

Chapter Eight

Laura's Diary

This morning I woke very early and lay in bed for a while listening to the distant whisper of the sea. It's so different to the background sounds of our flat in London – the traffic, the police sirens, the upstairs neighbour's washing machine. Here we're surrounded by light and ocean. I can see why people used to be sent to the sea for medicinal cures, and why they still come here when they grow old. And there's nothing like water that stretches to the horizon and beyond to help you with a sense of perspective.

But is perspective really what I am looking for? Do I wish to be able to look at what he did and shrink it to a tiny point surrounded by distance, and say, *Well, it cannot hurt me now?* Or is it courage I'm looking for – the courage to leave him and stay away, to refuse to listen to his pleading and persuasion and promises to change, to start over?

It would all be so very much easier if I didn't love him still. But even here, though I am grateful to wake so very far from home, I miss him. I miss him when I wake up and he's not in the bed beside me. I miss him in the car, at the breakfast table, at the beach. I miss him when Dani does or says something new and he's not there for me to exchange glances with, the glances that say, *Look what we made. Isn't she a miracle?*

Maybe all this will fade, in time. But it hasn't yet. I came here to escape from him and he's still here. And part of me doesn't ever want him to fade, to shrink and become distant until he's just a memory of how I used to live years ago, when I was still married, in a time and place that even then, it will still be impossible to forget.

*

I'm at the kitchen table now with my cup of tea and my boiled egg, wondering how much longer Dani will sleep in. I don't want to wake her, though. She must need it; it must be doing her good.

I don't want her to know what her father did. Not for years, and maybe not ever. I don't want it to become a tale she tells other people about herself, about her family, late at night when she's drunk and sad, or when she's confiding in a new lover. I don't want her to be someone who has those kind of stories to tell.

Would she forgive him? The idea of her knowing fills me with shame. But how could she understand what I'm doing now unless she knew?

You never know, with children. They'll accept what they're presented with when they have no choice, just like any of the rest of us. But they can be harsh. I know that, having been harsh myself. I couldn't understand how my mum could settle for boring, bloodless Phil after my dad. It's taken me till now to realise that one person's boring and bloodless might be somebody else's gentle and reliable, and that those are not qualities to be sniffed at.

Why didn't I see it coming? Why didn't I get away before it was too late? I could have had a whole different life – one of those lives that women can have if they're both lucky and wise, with no betrayal, no rage, no discoveries that turn everything you thought you knew inside out.

They say you can't choose who you love. I'm not so sure about that. I didn't choose Jon, exactly, but also, there came a time when I chose not to resist.

*

The autumn after I first met Jon, Carrie got a steady boyfriend. She was in the last year of her degree then, and let us know that she was going out with another student, a boy called Stick – at least, that was what she called him, and I never heard her refer to him by any other name.

Stick was long-haired and grubby-looking and smelt of something I later discovered was weed. Still, he was willing to be brought home at Christmas to meet us, which seemed to mark a new stage in the development of her relationships – although Mum and Phil were at a loss as to what to say to him, especially once he'd introduced himself as an anarchist.

I didn't see all that much of Carrie. In the holidays, she was either working at the garden centre, sleeping in, or at festivals with Stick. I could understand why she didn't want to hang out in the house much; Mum kept having home improvements done to remodel Phil's house in line with her tastes, which kept her happy but was noisy and intrusive. Phil spent a lot of time hiding out in his study, and I hid away in my room as much as possible and lost myself in reading books.

After Carrie graduated she worked full-time at the garden centre for a while and applied for lots of jobs, without success. Mum gave up asking her how it was going. Then she got a job in a local pub that served food, which she said was better because of the tips and because she didn't have to get up so early. Once in a while Mum wondered aloud whether Carrie would ever sort herself out with a proper job – but only when Carrie was safely out of earshot. Somehow, even though Carrie was still living at home, it felt as if she'd already left; she was usually either in her room or not there.

And then, a year and a half after *Macbeth*, Jade decided to throw a New Year's Eve party at White Cottage, the house Jon had inherited from his father and that his father had won in a game of cards. That was one version of the story; the other was that it had been security for a bad debt, and Jon's father had lost no time in laying claim to it and kicking out the original owners. At any rate, it was where Jon had grown up, though his childhood was one of many things about himself that he was never keen to talk about. Carrie was invited, along with everybody else she knew from the garden centre. And to my amazement, she asked me if I'd like to go with her.

Of course I said yes. Part of me had been hoping for a gesture like that – for the sister I remembered from long ago, from before our dad had died, to come back. Besides, we were getting older. I was in my last year at school. She'd graduated and had got a job, even if she hadn't left home yet. She was an adult, and I almost was: if we weren't going to find our way to a friendship now, then when would we?

Stick wasn't around at the time – that was the other reason why she asked me. He'd inherited some money and had decided to spend it on a winter trip to Thailand; since Carrie was broke, he had gone away on his own.

'He wants to live,' Carrie said, 'rather than spend it on a deposit for a house or something like that,' making the last point with a little grimace of disgust.

I privately thought that life in a home of my own would actually be just as special as life on a beach overseas, but didn't say anything. Both Carrie and I knew that life could carry on like a calm stream or a country road, stretching ahead out of sight, and then suddenly be interrupted; we had learned that when our dad died. That had made Carrie reckless and angry but the effect on me had been the opposite. I was cautious. Careful. If I'm really honest, I was frightened.

But in the end, perhaps I just wasn't careful enough.

The party was fancy dress – not my cup of tea at all. Even less my cup of tea than an ordinary party would have been. When Carrie told me that, my heart sank and she looked at me across the dining table and laughed.

'Oh come on, it won't be that bad. The theme is 1950s. I expect there'll be a load of Pink Ladies there. All you need to do is get a big skirt and tuck your T-shirt in and put your hair in a ponytail, and you'll be fine.'

'Are you going as a Pink Lady?'

'Of course not. I'm going to go as Olivia Newton-John at the end, in skin-tight black and heels.'

Mum's eyebrows shot up, and Phil looked uneasy. I said, 'Do you think Stick would have dressed up?'

I half expected Carrie to bite my head off, but she didn't.

'Oh Laura, stop feeling sorry for me,' she said. 'I'm fine with him going off without me. Honestly. That's how it is in long-term relationships. You have to give each other space. You have to let the other person do what they need to do.' Then, before it could all get too cosy: 'So when are you going to get yourself a boyfriend, then?'

'Carrie, please,' Mum said. 'Laura has other priorities.'

Carrie pulled a face. 'No she doesn't. She just doesn't know how to *live*.'

I said I didn't want a boyfriend, and Carrie told me I'd end up dying alone and being eaten by my cat, and our relationship was back on its usual antagonistic track. But I was happy anyway, because at least she'd asked me to go to the party with her.

Right from the beginning, the night of the party felt like magic.

It started with a taxi ride, a necessary extravagance because Carrie and all her friends were planning to drink and I couldn't drive. The bridge that led out of Kettlebridge was all lit up with Christmas lights still as well as the old Victorian lampposts; the river was black as ink and looked as thick as treacle, stretching away into the deep darkness of woods and fields to either side. And then we passed along a short stretch where leafless trees crowded the roadside, and the headlights picked out the depth of the shadows just beyond the verge. I never even saw the turning. One minute we were hurtling along the road, and the next minute we had turned off onto a narrow lane dotted with a few parked cars and then the taxi pulled up in front of the house.

That was the first time I saw White Cottage. It wasn't exceptional; there are houses like it all over the country, squarish buildings in whitewashed stone that perhaps originally only had one room downstairs and another overhead, with bathrooms and other rooms added on by later inhabitants. It was built on an incline with a hill at its back, and had long, narrow sash windows that looked south over fields that stretched towards the Thames and beyond. Nobody knew exactly how old it was. Now there was a motorway half an hour away and a fast rail link to London at the same distance, and White Cottage had become valuable, but that wasn't where its real value lay. There was just something about it, and I thought so as soon as I saw it.

That night it was buzzing; there were lights on at every window and fairy lights wound round the gateposts and the rail that ran along the raised patio in front of the house. The whole place gave off a vibe of enchanted energy, as if it was drawing people towards it much as the Pied Piper had fetched children towards his cave.

I could hear music coming from inside – decades-old rock 'n' roll, upbeat and summery. Through the glass pane of the front door I saw a crowd of people in a big rustic kitchen, with corn dollies dangling from the beams and a red-flagged floor and an old-fashioned range set in a recess, and a row of copper-bottomed pots hanging from hooks in front of it. It was the cosiest, most hospitable kitchen I had ever seen, and everyone in it was chatting like long-lost friends, as if this was the best party they'd ever been to.

Carrie knocked and gestured, and someone in a polka-dot dress with a bottle of beer in her hand broke off her conversation and came to the door to let us in. The air smelt of Christmas: citrus and cloves and brandy, sweet and spicy and warm.

'Happy New Year,' said the girl in the polka-dot dress. 'Welcome to another time.'

Someone else served us both a ladleful of mulled wine from the pot on top of the range, and we went through to the big living room, where all the furniture had been pushed up against the walls to make space for dancing. A few people were already twirling and turning in the middle of the room, their faces as shining and hopeful as children putting on a show. There was no sign of Jade and Jon's daughter, but there was a big photo of Jade holding her on one of the shelves in the alcove next to the fireplace, a professional portrait photographer's best effort. Jade was smiling winningly for the camera, dressed in a top that was just tight enough to look sexy rather than maternal, while the little girl – about four years old by now – looked bemused, as if baffled to find herself being embraced at such length.

Straight away Carrie spotted someone from the garden centre – someone who'd come dressed as James Dean in a check shirt and jeans, with a gelled-up quiff. He looked pretty good, if a little too conscious of his own hotness.

'I'm going out for a smoke. Do you want to come?' he said to Carrie, ignoring me completely.

'Sure,' Carrie said. 'You'll be all right, won't you, Laura? I'm sure there must be someone here you know.'

'But Carrie… what about Stick?'

Carrie rolled her eyes. 'You are so prissy, do you know that? Just saying no to everything doesn't make you good.'

'It's this way,' James Dean said, jerking his head in the direction of the white-painted staircase that led up out of the room. 'You have to go upstairs to get out. It's because the place is built into a hill.'

The two of them went off together, and I spotted the three witches from *Macbeth* perched on a sofa in the corner and went over to greet them.

They'd all come as Marilyn Monroe, though Lesley had already taken off her platinum blonde wig. She was sitting in the middle, dressed in a white halter-neck sundress, while Eloise, to her left, was in a gold lamé costume that looked as if it had come from a hire shop, and Mary, who had a plateful of party food on her lap, was resplendent in fuchsia pink, accessorised with a necklace of chunky paste diamonds.

As I approached Lesley raised her cup of mulled wine and said, 'Well, look at you. Laura Rivers, all grown up. Aren't you pretty as a picture? You look like a princess.'

Mary dusted sausage roll crumbs off her upper lip. 'So where's your boyfriend?'

'Oh, I don't have one.'

'Well, that makes no sense at all,' Eloise said.

'I guess I just haven't met anyone I like,' I said.

'Oh, well, there's your mistake right there,' Eloise said. 'You absolutely don't have to like them. Not unless you're planning to marry them, in which case it's a bonus. You just have to *want* them.'

'Personally, I'm just glad to be past all that how's-your-father,' Mary observed. 'Takes up so much time and energy, when you could just be sitting quietly in front of the telly.'

'Don't say that to Laura, she's got all that yet to come,' Eloise said. 'She probably still believes in love.'

'And so she should, at her age,' Lesley said.

'I don't, actually, particularly,' I said.

'Oh, you will,' Lesley told me. 'Don't you listen to these two jaded old cynics. Romantic love is a powerful thing. Just about the only thing that can be even more powerful than the love of a parent for a child. Family is in the blood. But two people have to fall in love to give it a heartbeat.'

As she finished speaking there was a sudden hush and stillness, even though the music was still playing. It was 'My Baby Still Cares For Me', jaunty and upbeat as if everything in life could be easy if only you let it be. But the dancers had stopped dancing and it wasn't Lesley who had distracted them and interrupted every conversation in the room. It was Jade.

She came slowly and heavily downstairs, her expression as sombre as if she was on her way to attend a funeral. She was dressed for the party, though; she'd curled her hair and painted her face like an old movie star's and was wearing an ice-blue satin dress with a skirt that swished with each step she took. She made no attempt to greet or acknowledge anybody, but crossed the room with her head held high, as if to prove that she could be a lady as much as anyone. When she came to the sideboard next to the kitchen door, she paused to open a drawer and took out a set of keys, which she dropped into the ice-blue handbag she was carrying. Then she walked out.

As if a spell had been broken, people began to move and talk again. Mary started eating pretzels and Eloise said, 'Do you think we should leave?'

'Why would we do that? Party's only just started,' Lesley said, wafting her hand to fan herself. 'She'll be back. She probably just did it to prove a point. That's what some people are like, hooked on drama.'

I said, 'I hope she's all right.'

'Oh, sure she is,' Mary said. 'Don't you worry about her. She's probably gone off to see one of her boyfriends. If anything she's been having a bit too much of a good time lately.'

'It's not right, not when she has a child,' Lesley said.

'Making best possible use of the babysitter,' Mary observed.

'I suppose I'd better go and find my sister,' I said. 'She's missed all the drama.'

'She's older than you, isn't she?' Lesley said. 'Shouldn't she be checking up on you, rather than the other way round? Usually it's the older sister who's the responsible one.'

I smiled at her. I thought, but did not say, *Yes, but usually the older sister didn't come down one morning and find her dad dead of a heart attack on the floor.*

Carrie had stopped me from seeing Dad. She'd made me stay in my bedroom while Mum rang 999 and waited for the emergency services to arrive. By the time I came out his body had been covered up with a duvet, as if he was sleeping.

I'll always be grateful to Carrie for that. It still amazes me that as a child – just eleven years old – she had the presence of mind to protect me. However much we bickered later, and however much she seemed to dislike and resent me, her first instinct had been to take care of me.

'All families are different,' I said, and withdrew and went up the stairs.

The doors along the upstairs landing were mostly shut, but one was ajar. The door to the garden was on the left ahead of me; I could see the dark of the night sky through its glass. But as I walked towards it I heard something that made me stop in my tracks.

It was a soft moaning sound. It was the kind of noise a woman in an old film might have made when she was in labour – if she was being brave and ladylike trying not to yell the place down. It was the sound of someone who was in pain, and it was coming from beyond the door that was only just open.

Then I heard someone swearing. Turning the air blue.

Definitely *not* a lady.

I knocked on the door that was ajar. Nobody answered. I pushed it open wide and went in.

I was in a bedroom. Jon and Jade's bedroom. There was no farmhouse cottage vibe here. It was all glamorous red and charcoal grey and mahogany and black; it could have been the lair of a seductress or a Casanova, but you wouldn't have expected it to be shared by a married couple who had a baby.

Jon was standing by the mantelpiece, cupping his right hand with his left. He said, 'Is she still here?'

'You mean Jade? She left.'

He groaned. 'She said she would. I didn't think she'd actually do it. She's left me with a handful of broken knuckles and a bunch of guests I didn't want. How's the party? You can't be enjoying it that much, or you wouldn't have come nosing round here. Or do you always wander into people's bedrooms when you're in a strange house?'

There was an indentation in the wall next to the mantelpiece, the size and shape of a fist. That was how angry he'd been – he'd hit the wall hard enough to mark it.

I said, 'I heard you moaning from the hall. And swearing. I was concerned. If you've broken something you should go to A&E. There might even be someone downstairs who could drive you.'

'You're sensible, aren't you? Sensible *and* nice,' he said. 'I'm surprised you even want to talk to me.' He inclined his head towards the dent in the wall. 'It's a stupid thing to have done. Not sensible at all, and definitely not nice. You must think I'm a fool. A fool with bad impulse control. The worst kind.'

'If you don't want to go to A&E right now, at least let me get you some ice for it. You must have a pack of frozen peas in the freezer downstairs. I could bring them up.'

'What, to spare my blushes? I wouldn't count on us having anything in this house. Keeping a well-stocked freezer isn't my wife's forte. Nor mine.'

'I could check.'

He smiled. He was beginning to look a little less pale. 'Well, aren't you the little Florence Nightingale, carting peas through the party to help heal the host whose wife has just walked out on him.'

'Has she?'

'Has she what?'

'Walked out on you.'

Something in his expression shifted. He stepped forward and sat down on the bed, still cradling his hurt hand. His shoulders slumped. He looked up at me almost pleadingly, as if I could help him.

'I'm going to lose my baby,' he said.

I moved closer to him, sat on the bed next to him. There were still several inches between us. A safe distance. A safe, respectable distance.

'Maybe you and Jade can still sort things out,' I said.

'I didn't mean Jade,' he said. 'I meant Michelle. My daughter. My little girl. Jade will want custody.' He sighed. 'She's a good mum. Devoted. I've always said that. People don't give her credit for it.'

There was a sudden cold draught across our backs as the door behind us was flung open wide. Carrie said, 'Laura, what on earth are you doing?'

Jon straightened up. He turned, and looked from me to her. He said, 'How do you two know each other?'

'We're sisters,' I said. 'I was Lady Macduff when Jade was in *Macbeth*. Do you remember?'

He frowned as if he didn't quite believe me. Not the first time I'd had that reaction. Then it came back to him: 'You were in pink. You looked embarrassed.' He turned back to Carrie as if he was still puzzled – as if there was something he was missing here, something she might be able to explain.

Carrie folded her arms and leaned against the door jamb. I had never thought of her as a judgemental person – the opposite, if anything – but the hard look in her eyes suddenly reminded me very much of Mum.

Jon flexed his right hand, as if testing it. He didn't wince or make a sound.

'I don't know about you two, but I could use a drink,' he said, and got up and went out.

'What were you thinking?' Carrie hissed as we followed him downstairs. 'He's married.'

'Barely. Jade just stormed out of the party. Anyway, we were just talking.'

'Nobody just *talks*. That's not what men are *for*.'

'So what were you doing with the James Dean lookalike, then?'

'Speaking of which…' Carrie said, spotting him on the far side of the room. 'Remember, I'm just trying to look out for you. Find someone your own age to flirt with.'

Then she stalked off to join him, leaving me both indignant and a little bit ashamed. After all, I hadn't done anything! What right did she have to accuse me, and to be so suspicious?

And yet… if the opportunity had presented itself… could I really be sure that I would have done the right thing, and turned it down?

I turned to see Lesley, Eloise and Mary still perched on the sofa, taking it all in. They were watching me with identical expressions of slightly patronising sympathy, as if they'd known all along that my sister didn't need my help and I was the one who wanted to be looked after.

It pains me to admit that I was lonely before I had Jon. But I was, and I had been ever since I lost my dad.

The thing about being lonely is that it's what carries on after you've got used to being sad. Lonely is when you have got used to being on the outside and looking in, and you don't even mind it any more. You're safe on the outside, and at least you can see what's going on.

But once in a while you get drawn into the action. And then you stop being lonely, and maybe you even forget you were ever sad. And there you are, right in the middle of your own life, and somebody else is there with you and you're happy.

By and by, you stop seeing. You stop looking. And in the end, you forget there could be anything to look out for.

Chapter Nine
Laura's Diary

Today Dani and I went to the special beach. It was mentioned in one of the tourist information leaflets left on the telephone table in the living room, along with the takeaway menus and the instructions on how to use the immersion heater: St Angel's Cove, a six-mile round walk along the cliff path from Port Mallion or an easy drive. 'No facilities, but quiet and scenic,' the leaflet said. It sounded perfect. Not that I've got anything against Port Mallion beach, which is quite near the cottage, but I wanted to go somewhere that Dani and I could have to ourselves.

We set off as soon as Dani was up and dressed and had finished her breakfast. 'Is this right, Mummy? Are we lost? It doesn't look like there's any beach,' Dani kept saying on the way. 'Are you sure we're nearly there?'

Then we rounded a bend and it was there in front of us – the cliff-top and the bay, and the sea stretching to the blue horizon.

There were no other cars in the patch of gravel set aside for parking on the headland. We made our way down the steps set into the cliff to the beach, and it was completely deserted – like an island we'd discovered. It was so sheltered, it seemed to have its own climate – softer and milder than out on the cliff-top, where it was sweltering today.

We took off our sandals and the sand was as soft as carpet under our feet. The sun shone and the water sparkled and everything was golden and blue, like an old religious painting, like stained glass that has been freshly cleaned. We both paddled and I thought how wonderful it would be to swim, to plunge into the water and be cut off completely from the heaviness of life on land, from our ordinary landlubber clumsiness. To be light and free. But I didn't dare because I didn't want Dani to follow me, and I didn't quite trust her to stay in the shallows, even if she promised she would.

There are some places where you feel time falling away from you, as if all the bad things that have happened don't matter any more. As if you've left everything you wanted to forget behind. Dani was happy too, enchanted and enchanting: completely absorbed in the task at hand as she set about making sandcastles, her red curls escaping from underneath her yellow sunhat.

Being there with her, watching her so happy and busy – it was bliss. She's so perfectly plump, with that smooth baby-like skin that smells as sweet as biscuits and milk at bedtime and makes me want to hold her tight and breathe her in and keep her close forever. Not that she likes it when I linger too much over embracing her. She doesn't like me being soppy, doesn't see the point of it: she's not a sentimental child. And I love that about her, too.

We ate sandwiches and played ball and wrote in the sand, and the tide gradually receded, exposing wet sand and bits of rubbery seaweed. Finally, when Dani was beginning to stumble with tiredness, I said it was time to go home. She didn't protest – another sign that the place had worked some kind of magic on her. Once she was in the car she nodded off almost instantly and stayed asleep all the way home.

She's sitting at the table outside with me now, drawing. She has drawn the cottage, the shop, and our special beach. Each time she draws the background first, and then carefully adds two stick people, one for her and one for me. And I can't help but suspect this is her way of asking a question she can't bring herself to ask, because young as she is, she knows it will upset me: *When is Daddy going to come?*

Or maybe it's herself she is protecting. I don't think she would want to hear any of the answers I might give her. And if she moved on to *why isn't he coming?* I would have no option but to lie.

If I had never found out, if we had all just carried on as we were, this loss of innocence wouldn't have happened. She would have been able to include both me and Jon in her pictures without thinking about it. She could have relied on us being the bit of the background that didn't change.

But we are where we are. I've lost my innocence too. And among all the questions I keep asking myself is this: *Would it really have been better to know from the start?*

After the New Year's Eve party at White Cottage, the next time I met Jon was in London, five and a half years later.

Since I'd been living in the city I'd got used to the way it cramped the view of the sky, so that on grey days you almost forgot to look up. But that day the sky was full of drama and light and shade, high clouds against a serene expanse of blue, and I couldn't help but notice it as I made my way across Trafalgar Square. I almost missed him.

It was the flash of red hair that caught my eye, visible beneath the brim of his straw Panama hat. But it took me a moment to place him, as it does when you see someone you know in a setting where you don't expect to come across them. He had his back to me and was holding up a camera – an old-fashioned, chunky thing – and peering through it to take a picture of one of the fountains. He lowered the camera and turned towards me with the abstract gaze of someone who's looking out for their next shot. Then his expression changed and I approached him and he said, 'Laura Rivers. What on earth are you doing here?'

'I might say the same to you,' I said, close enough now for us to have to decide whether to shake hands, lean in for a kiss or keep our distance.

And then we were moving closer and our cheeks were almost close enough to touch. Not too close – a polite air kiss, the sort of greeting a youthful aunt might give you, if you had one. He smelt of lemon-scented aftershave and sun-warmed skin. He smelt... I don't know how to describe it other than to say he smelt just right.

He withdrew and put the camera away in the messenger bag he was carrying with the strap slung across his chest. His shirt was a couple of buttons open at the neck and short-sleeved, and his forearms were lightly tanned and the hairs on them were golden rather than red.

I said, 'Nice camera. Are you into photography?'

He shrugged. 'I like taking pictures. I'm not sure I'm any good at it.'

'Have you ever been to the National Portrait Gallery? I've just been there. There are lots of great photos.'

'No, I've never been. I guess I should go sometime. Funny how you can live in London and not get around to these things.'

And then there was a pause – not an awkward one, but the kind that is an opportunity to either say something or leave it unsaid. That was when I noticed his eyes, which were a light, clear blue, shaded by the brim of his hat.

'Jade and I broke up,' he said. 'I don't know if you heard.'

'Oh. I'm sorry to hear that. No, I didn't know.'

'Well, why should you? I guess you've moved on, left Kettlebridge. Do you live here now?'

'Yes, in South London, near where I work. I'm a primary school teacher. How about you?'

'Yeah, I've got a flat in the South-West London suburbs, so it's easy to get back to White Cottage. Depending on the traffic, of course. It's close to Jade and Michelle, but not too close.'

He said Jade's name without any emotional heat, as if she was a fact of life to be negotiated, like a mountain or the weather. But still... Jade.

I thought of the conversation I'd had with him in the master bedroom at White Cottage after he'd punched the wall, and how Carrie had accused me of flirting. And maybe she had been right.

I said, 'Do you miss Kettlebridge?'

He shrugged. 'The house has tenants in it. I go back because of the garden centre there. I'm just about to open another one near where I live here, so, you know. Busy. You just missed Jade and Michelle, actually. I took Michelle to see a film at Leicester Square, and then Jade came here to collect her and take her off somewhere else.'

Just as well I hadn't bumped into him five minutes earlier. I was pretty sure Jade wouldn't have wanted to talk to me, and would have made it obvious that she thought I should move along as soon as possible. And maybe she would have been right. Because what was I doing lingering?

I told him I was going to get on the Tube and make my way home, and he said he should be heading back too, and I asked if Embankment station worked for him and he hesitated and said, 'Yes, could do. I think so. Why not?'

As we left Trafalgar Square there was another silence between us. He was walking at a slight distance from me, as if it had occurred to him that getting too close might not be a good idea, and his face had the wary look that people have when they're not sure whether you're about to try to scam them or just ask for directions. It was as if we had been treading water and had both decided to allow the current to carry us downstream, but neither of us was quite sure where we might end up.

It would have been hard to keep talking, though. The Strand was too busy for that, clogged with traffic and passers-by. We crossed over and turned off onto the narrow street that leads down to the river Thames and Embankment station. And then there was a sudden movement in front of us, and Jon bounded forward as someone I hadn't even noticed – who'd been walking along in front of us – crumpled and fell to the ground.

It turned out to be an old lady – short, grey-haired, and both confused and embarrassed by her fall. Jon helped her up and waved aside her determination to send us on our way. She could stand, but it was obvious that it was going to be a struggle for her to walk. He suggested that she should get her ankle checked out; she said she was fine, thank you very much. He offered to hail a cab for her, and after briefly mulling it over she said, with dignity, that she thought that might not be a bad idea.

The three of us made our way back to the Strand, and the next black cab to come our way stopped for us and Jon helped the old lady get inside. After a brief exchange with the old lady and the driver, he passed the driver some cash, stood back and slammed the door, and we stood side by side and waved at her as the taxi pulled into the traffic and drove away.

I said, 'That was nice of you.'

'Anybody would have done the same.'

And that was when I really fell for him. That was all it took, finally: the revelation that Jon Rosewell, who could punch a hole in a wall and had a fierce and glamorous ex-wife, was also capable of being kind to old ladies and thinking nothing of it. Suddenly I was falling or perhaps I was flying, and he was looking at me as if I might be a spy about to set a trap for him, or perhaps someone who was about to save him and there was no way of knowing which.

I said, 'If you're not busy… would you maybe like to go and get a drink somewhere? Just a quick one. If you have time. I still don't know all that many people in London, to be honest. It's nice to see a familiar face.'

All around us people were strolling towards good times; London was in a holiday mood, had taken on some of the sun-soaked idleness of a seaside resort. He hesitated and I could see that he wanted to say yes, and was surprised by wanting to say yes, and that saying yes was not easy for him. Then he looked away from me, down the street towards the river.

'OK,' he said, and shrugged.

And so we crossed over Hungerford Bridge and found a place to have a drink on the South Bank, where we could sit overlooking the river. It was still warm, but there was a fresh breeze that seemed to come from the sea miles away downstream, where the Thames flowed into its estuary. We talked about London – I decided to steer clear of the subject of Kettlebridge, didn't want to remind him of White Cottage and the end of his marriage, or remind him of my sixteen-year-old self, because that might have made him think again of Jade who had been the star of the show when I was not much more than a walk-on.

Then, somehow, we ended up talking about gardening, not a subject I knew anything about though it was clearly comfortable territory for him.

He visibly relaxed as he told me some of his favourite plants for a garden: herbs, like rosemary and lavender and mint; climbers like jasmine and clematis; and fruit trees – 'You can't beat a peach tree espaliered against a west-facing wall, the old-fashioned way.' Just the words made it seem as if we were somewhere else entirely, surrounded by greenery that was hazy in the fading heat and scented like a feast.

The first couple of drinks led to another round, and then we agreed to move on. We strolled further along the South Bank, and neither of us said anything about how we ought to be heading home. Instead I said I was starving and then we walked past a pizza place and Jon hesitated only briefly before suggesting we go in.

I didn't hesitate at all before agreeing.

It wasn't like any date I'd ever been on. Perhaps that was why I didn't think of it as a date. I wasn't worrying about whether he liked me or I liked him, or whether my hair had gone weird or my eyeliner was smudged, or about whether I was going to make a fool of myself eating and how we'd split the bill and whether or not we should see each other again. It was just me and him in no hurry, spending accidental time together on a summer afternoon that had somehow turned into evening.

People say 'we clicked', and I guess that's what they mean – it's the point when a bumpy ride becomes smooth, when something that has been fraught with difficulty is suddenly so easy it's a mystery as to why it was so tricky before.

Times like that are meant to sustain you later on – to give you something to look back at and say, 'Just then – when it was just us and we were new to each other – we were perfect.' But they're dangerous, too, even though they don't feel it, even though they seem like the best thing that could ever happen to you. They're dangerous because they're so precious, and they seem as if they should last forever – and afterwards you don't want to let them go, and are willing to do things you ought not to do to get them back.

When we had finished we split the bill, and when we came out he thanked me rather formally for a lovely evening and said we had better go and find a Tube stop, and I couldn't think of an excuse to disagree.

By this time the daylight had faded and the river was darker than the sky, murky and treacly and throwing out scattered reflections of brightness. We walked along to Blackfriars Bridge and the dome of St Paul's came into view, pale as a moon against the washed-out blue of the sky. We paused to admire it and then he said, 'Come on, let's get you to the station. You shouldn't be on the train too late, with a bunch of drunks and louts and who knows what.'

'I can look after myself,' I said as we set off again.

'The best way to look after yourself is not to need to,' he said.

The road on the far side of the bridge was lined with big, glass-fronted office blocks, apart from an ancient-looking pub that must have been on that spot long before office blocks were even invented.

'We could go for another drink,' I suggested. I was tipsy enough to be bold; I felt invincible, which is not the same thing as being brave. All I knew for sure was that I didn't want to let him go. Not yet. I knew we weren't done yet.

But he sighed and said, 'I should be getting home. You should, too. Before we both end up doing something we'd regret.'

'Who says we'd regret it?'

'Laura, please… Don't think I'm not tempted. But we can't do this. We really can't. We've had a good time, and now we have to say goodbye.'

We had come to a standstill on the pavement. To passers-by, we might have looked like a couple having an argument. I said, 'Why are you doing this?'

He stood looking down at me. I put my hand on his sleeve. It was the first time I'd made contact with him. Whatever was between us seemed to be wrapping itself around the pair of us like an invisible coil, pulling us together as it tightened.

'Don't pretend you don't feel it,' I said. 'I know you do. Don't you want to find out?'

He was studying my face. His expression was serious and also slightly helpless.

He said, 'Find out what?'

I slipped my backpack off my shoulders and rested it at my feet. His hands came to rest either side of my waist. He looked confused, as if he'd just been hypnotised into doing something against his will, or had exposed himself to an attack and was surprised to find himself unharmed.

He said, 'I'm a bad bet for you, Laura. You don't know very much about me. And what you do know should be enough to put you off.'

I put my finger to his lips. I said, 'Forget about all that. I don't care. We're here, aren't we? What matters is now.'

Something changed in his eyes and I knew I'd won. He seemed to lift me up, though I was still standing on my own two feet, and we kissed, hesitantly at first, then not.

I had never kissed like that before. He tasted like hunger and I knew beyond a shadow of doubt that I was what he needed. We fit together like two dancers who have already rehearsed all their moves and have finally found the right stage on which to perform them. I was thinking of nothing but the kiss when a piece of knowledge dropped into my head, clear but ghostly as an echo or something remembered, even more shocking than the kiss: *I'm going to marry him.*

We broke off, paused, looked at each other.

He said, 'This isn't a good idea.' But he didn't move away.

There were still passers-by all around us, moving towards the station or back the way we had come, across the river. Well, people could kiss, couldn't they? What business was it of anybody else's? I was doing my best to blot them out again when someone approached us – someone male and slightly built. He darted forward, almost close enough to touch, stooped and then shot off into the distance, and it was only once he was out of sight that I realised my backpack had been stolen.

There was no point even attempting to chase him. He had completely disappeared, and had taken my cashcard, keys and phone with him.

Jon lent me his phone to call the bank and cancel my card, and then he said, 'What are you going to do about getting back home? I mean, I can cover your fare... but are you going to be able to get in?'

'I rent a bedsit. I don't have any flatmates, and I can't get hold of the landlord out of hours. I could call a locksmith, I guess.'

He studied me for a moment. He looked calculating, as if he was working out whether I was a risk worth taking. Then he said, 'There wasn't anything in your bag with your address on it, was there?'

I shook my head. 'That's good. One less thing to worry about,' he said. 'Look, if you like, come back to mine. I have a very comfortable sofa. Though I suppose I should be the one sleeping on it. You can phone the police and file a report at your leisure, get a good night's sleep, and sort out getting back into your bedsit in the morning.'

Of course I said yes, and in the end we went down to the Underground together.

Sitting side by side with him on worn seats in the hot, strip-lit carriage, I had the strangest sense of being very still, as if we weren't moving at all, as if it was only an illusion that we were rattling along with everybody else. As if we'd been frozen in time.

I already knew that I'd remember that night, and that it was the beginning of something. And even though I had no way of knowing what lay ahead, I knew it was special and rare to be filled with so much hope about being with someone else, and about what might happen between us.

Chapter Ten

Laura's Diary

This evening the phone rang. A horrible, shrilling sound, like something out of a nightmare. By the time I picked up the line had gone dead, and the number came up as unobtainable.

Dani said, 'Who was that, Mummy?'

'Nobody,' I said and pulled the phone cord out of the socket.

'What if it was Daddy?'

'It can't have been Daddy.'

'Why not?'

Because he doesn't know we're here. Unless someone has told him. But she wouldn't do that – would she?

'Because Daddy's very busy looking after all the plants in the garden centre. That sounded like a very good game you were playing – what was happening?'

She didn't look completely convinced, but gamely explained about the argument her toy animals had been having, which involved the husky and the sheep fighting with the eagle. She didn't ask any more about the phone call and I hoped she'd forgotten about it, though I certainly hadn't.

Now she's in bed and I'm awake and alone, and the cottage – which has been such a haven – seems shadowy and sinister.

Too isolated. If someone came here to butcher the pair of us, who would hear us if I called for help? Maybe it wasn't smart to disconnect the phone. But there's no way I'm going to plug it back in again. The whole point of being here was to be left alone, after all. To have time and space to make a decision.

Who am I going to become as the years go by? Can I bear to live not only with betrayal but with its small-scale day-to-day aftermath: disappointment, bitterness, disgust? Could I get used to it?

My heart is pounding still, and I don't think I'm going to sleep.

Is he home alone tonight, hundreds of miles away at White Cottage? Is he drinking by himself, pacing the floor? What is he planning?

I should have known that you can't escape a marriage by running away. I have forgotten how to do without him. And I've forgotten how to be alone.

Of course he's going to come for me.

I am afraid now. I am afraid of seeing him. I don't really know why. He has never hurt me, not physically anyway. Still, he has a temper, and the thought of being cornered by him fills me with dread. I'm afraid not so much of what he'll do as what he'll say, and of what will be left of me when we part again.

And yet it was so sweet, in the beginning. Is it always like that? Is every love affair that goes wrong a tragedy in which high hopes give way to disaster and only the audience emerges unscathed at the end, glad to go back to their own lives and thanking their lucky stars they weren't any closer to the swordfights?

I still remember our first argument. It was one morning not long after we'd started seeing each other, and we were eating scrambled eggs in his flat. I put my cutlery down on my plate and stretched and thanked him, and then I said, 'I don't know what they're going to make of this back in Kettlebridge.'

He put his cutlery down too and stared at me. His eyes were suddenly cold. He didn't look like a lover; he looked like an examiner who had hoped for better.

'Why would they make anything of it back in Kettlebridge? Do they need to know?'

'I didn't really mean Kettlebridge. I guess I was really thinking about my mum. But anyway, I'm sure she'd be fine about it. I mean, it's not as if you're still married…'

'I am, technically, actually. On paper.'

'Oh.'

I stared down at my plate. Why hadn't he told me before? Then I looked up at him. He was watching me with a mixture of sympathy and detachment, as if he knew I was going to be upset but also thought that there were much bigger things for me to be upset about.

'We just need to get the decree absolute, and then it'll finally be over,' he said. 'It's a technicality.'

'So technically, I've been sleeping with a married man.'

He pulled a face that was half a grimace, half a smile. 'I suppose you could put it that way.'

'I wish you'd told me earlier. I'm not the kind of person who does that kind of thing. And if I'm going to become the kind of person who does that kind of thing, I want to know about it.'

'You didn't ask.'

'I didn't know I needed to.'

'I'm sorry,' he said.

And he really did seem to be sorry. He looked like a puppy who has no idea whether it's going to be kicked. I couldn't help but relent.

'I guess it's OK. I never really tell my mum anything anyway. Or my sister. But will you tell me when it's all properly finalised?'

'I will,' he promised, and I felt a huge rush of relief. After all, it wasn't that big a deal. It was a much bigger deal that he had a daughter. Michelle was nine by then, old enough to have a mind of her own, and I was already nervous about maybe meeting her one day.

Looking back, I can see that he and I were both on our best behaviour in those early days. I was in love for the first time, and I approached our relationship like a lawyer building a case for the defence. Only the evidence that suited me was allowed to be part of it. And the evidence was that he was in love too, and perhaps it wasn't for the first time but – I was almost sure of this – it was different to before.

We didn't speculate about the future, not then – or at least, we never touched on whether we might be together in it. It was as if we were both terrified of tempting fate. We carried on as if we didn't expect to last, as if we both believed that circumstances could change any minute and tear us apart. We were as light-hearted as if it was a duty, and in bed we clung to each other as if there might never be another chance. The city went on around us, tolerant in its indifference, full of strangers who were busy with their own lives and barely noticed us.

My working weeks passed by in sepia – it was as if I wasn't really there, not fully, not all the time. Days in the classroom were peppered with flashbacks and daydreams. As the minute hand of the wall clock ticked towards home time, or as I read to the children who were gathered on the carpet for register, I would find myself thinking of him.

I didn't confide in anybody. I had few friends and kept them at arm's length – I'd always been like that. There were just two people in the world who knew me well enough to coax or bully the truth out of me: Mum and Carrie. And it was very unlikely that Carrie would, since by then I barely saw her from one Christmas to the next.

She and Stick had moved to Leeds, where she was working for a travel agency and he was doing something in computing. I assumed she was happy. They went on lots of holidays to exotic, far-flung locations, and happiness for Carrie seemed to mean being on the move. Presumably being with Stick suited her, even if I didn't really get what she saw in him. He'd been around long enough, after all.

I didn't see Mum all that much either, but by early October it was several months since I'd visited, and I took the train back home for Sunday lunch.

The taxi I took from the nearest station took the road that went past White Cottage. *White Cottage!* I was at that stage in love where you want to be able to see the world as your lover sees it, remember their memories and share their dreams. So to be driven along the road that had been his way home for so many years, and to pass the turning to the house where he'd grown up, was like being let into part of his world, and – like everything about him – made me feel bigger than my usual self, and more alive. I wanted to climb into his life, to see him in his childhood bedroom as he slept, to be granted visions of his past and future like some kind of Scrooge being educated out of miserliness. Jade, though… That was different. I still flinched from knowing too much about Jade.

When I pitched up at Cromwell Close Mum gave me the usual quick once-over – 'You look well, dear. Gosh, what a lovely bright coat – is that new?' She quizzed me briefly about work and the place I was renting, and then served soup for lunch and fell to talking about Carrie.

'I had a postcard from the Philippines. The Philippines! All this long-haul flying can't be good for her. It wreaks havoc with your body clock, you know. Honestly, you'd think they'd have had a bucketful of it by now, all the jetlag and hanging around at airports, but every other weekend they seem to be off somewhere new.'

After lunch Phil fell asleep in an armchair – he had an enviable knack for napping, and I sometimes wondered if this was one of the secrets of the success of his marriage to Mum. It seemed to be his way of getting through anything he didn't much want to take an active part in. Mum and I decided to leave him alone in the house and went out together.

Mum drove us to Thornley Lakes, a local beauty spot surrounded by woodland. She parked on the muddy lane that led to the woods, and we set off to walk around the calm expanse of water.

'It must be absolute bliss to live there,' Mum said, looking across the lake towards the island in the middle of it, which was covered with a mass of trees and tangled undergrowth. 'I don't suppose there are any predators. No foxes. There's something to be said for keeping yourself to yourself.'

'I guess so.'

Mum always walked very briskly, with her head down; she disapproved of dawdlers of all kinds, along with idlers, people with dirty houses and anyone who tried to beat about the bush. It was a slight effort to keep up with her; I'd got used to walking with Jon, who was neither fast nor slow – or at least, whose pace was a good match for mine.

'So, do you get out much?' she said, and gave me a laser-like sidelong glance, and I knew at once what she was really asking me.

'I try to,' I said. 'I've started seeing someone, and we go out to different places at the weekend.' Even I could hear the apprehension in my voice. Was I really so pathetic as to need my mum's approval for my new relationship? It seemed I was.

'Hm. So... are you going to tell me any more about him?'

'You know him,' I said.

Two ducks chose that moment to start fighting on the lake. It was a surprisingly vicious spat, each one splashing and beating at the other as if nothing mattered more than to get rid of it. It wasn't easy to tell which one was going to be the winner, but after a while one of them suddenly gave up and took off. I waited till the kerfuffle had died down before saying, 'It's Jon Rosewell.'

'Jon Rosewell,' she repeated. We both carried on looking out across the lake, already as calm as if the struggle we'd just witnessed had never happened.

She said, 'How long has this been going on?'

'A couple of months. Since the summer. We bumped into each other in Trafalgar Square and after that... things went from there.'

'Hm,' she said again. Then: 'I suppose you don't need me to point out the potential difficulties.'

'You mean Jade.'

'Jade… and her child. If you really want to make a go of things, it means embracing a certain level of complexity. Especially as nobody likes a step-parent, at least not to start with, maybe not ever. I mean… look at the way you and Carrie are with Phil. You treat him like a kind of boring uncle who happens to share a house with your mother. No, don't bother denying it. Anyway, *is* it serious with Jon? From the way you just announced it, it's as if he's about to suddenly appear from behind a tree and ask for my blessing.'

'Well… we get on really well. He makes me happy. But it's only been a couple of months.'

'That's long enough to know if you like each other, isn't it? In my view people take much too long over these things nowadays. All this going out with each other for years and years and then living together, like your sister. If you can't bear the idea of getting married in the early days, what's the point? It's not as if it's going to get any better when the novelty wears off and you actually know each other.'

'Mum!'

'Oh, Laura, you know me. I speak my mind. Don't pretend to be shocked. I always thought that when you did meet someone, it'd be the real thing. Not like Carrie, with all the endless running about with long-haired layabouts and then ending up with someone who doesn't know why she's glaring at him when he eats with his mouth open. Do you think Jon will want to come back to Kettlebridge? It'd be nice to have you just down the road.'

'Well… he does still own White Cottage. There are tenants in it. But he's got another garden centre in London, and he wants to stay close to Jade and Michelle.'

'Yes, but Michelle's not a little kid any more. One of these days she'll be a teenager and then she'll be leaving home. There may come a time when she doesn't want to see that much of either of her parents.'

'I think you might be getting a bit ahead of yourself, Mum. Michelle's still at primary school. She's got a way to go yet before she's all grown up.'

'Hm. Well, I suppose it might fizzle out by then anyway. But it never hurts to think ahead. So when are you going to introduce us? Formally, I mean? Since obviously we both know each other. How about Christmas?'

'Maybe. I'd have to talk to him. I don't know what his plans are.'

'Complicated, I expect. Jade doesn't strike me as the type to be reliable about custody arrangements. Or generous. Does she know about you yet?'

'I don't think so.'

'Well, when she does, expect a few dates with Jon to get cancelled because he's been called away at the eleventh hour to look after Michelle. But I suppose he isn't a bad catch, if you overlook the difficult first wife.' Mum pursed her lips and glanced over at me. 'Anyway, as a mother, I suppose you have to be grateful if your daughter brings home a man who isn't violent or an addict or something like that. Of course, if Jon doesn't want to come home to meet us… that'll tell you something about where you are.'

Even at the time, her last words sounded like a warning. I thought of them later, when I picked my moment to issue the invitation.

We were having brunch in a café near Richmond Park, where we were hoping to spot some deer. Jon was relaxed, and I knew that what I was about to ask would put him on the defensive. But I still wasn't prepared for the reaction I got.

'So… I told my mother about you.'

Jon added sugar to his coffee and stirred, then folded his arms. 'What did she say?'

'She's suggested you come round at Christmas,' I said. 'Not for dinner or anything, just for tea and a mince pie. Do you think you could bear it? Or we could do it in the New Year if you prefer.'

'Isn't it a little early?'

'What do you mean?'

'Well, you know… things have been going so well. Is it really necessary to drag the rest of the world into it so soon?'

I sat up a little straighter and folded my arms, too.

'It isn't *soon*,' I said. 'It's been nearly six months. And this isn't the rest of the world. It's just Mum. And Phil, but he doesn't really count. I mean, he doesn't say much, and he'll probably fall asleep.'

'What about your sister and her other half?'

'I don't suppose she'll be there. They usually go away at Christmas. Don't worry, I'm not planning to expose you to the whole of my family at once.'

He sighed. Then he reached across the table. 'I'm sorry. I don't mean to be a grouch. It's just… everything's been so perfect.'

I squeezed his hand. 'We can keep it short and sweet. It's not as if I live in her pocket. We don't have that kind of relationship. Look, I get why you wouldn't want me to meet Michelle. But this is different. Mum's not going to have any particular expectations.'

'I find that hard to believe,' he said, and then he paid the bill and we went out and he was chastened and gloomy for the rest of the day, as if I'd just told him off.

In the end, the meeting went off like a dream.

Jon made an effort – not in a creepy way, but he brought Mum flowers and listened attentively to what she had to say and didn't impose himself on the conversation. He even managed to talk to Phil about Phil's twin passions, cacti and financial planning.

It was quite something to see him in that little sitting room in Kettlebridge, with its peach-painted walls hung with pictures of tranquil rural scenery, shelves of knick-knacks, and tasselled lamp-shades. Perched on one of the overstuffed armchairs with a glass of non-alcoholic beer, he looked bigger and more masculine than ever.

Afterwards, when we were on the M40 heading to London with the sunset at our backs, Jon said, 'They weren't at all what I was expecting. I liked them.'

'Why, were you expecting not to like them?'

'Well… I thought it might be harder work than it was. Obviously we were all on best behaviour. I could tell your mum usually likes to speak her mind. I wouldn't like to get on the wrong side of her.'

'She doesn't think much of Stick, as you might have noticed.'

'Well, he *is* called Stick. I don't think being known by a funny nickname by the time you hit adulthood endears you to anybody.'

'True.'

'Anyway, I take my hat off to her. She hasn't had an easy time of it. It's quite something to come through what she's experienced and find a way to be happy afterwards.'

'I suppose it is,' I agreed, and was faintly ashamed of the childish outrage I'd felt as a teenager when it had seemed to me that Mum was replacing Dad with Phil. *Following tragedy with farce*, was how Carrie had put it. She was always willing to be more outspoken than I was.

Jon dropped me back at my little studio flat, but declined to come in. 'We have to say goodbye sometime,' he told me.

And then he sat there in the car just looking at me.

'What is it?' I said. He looked defensive and open at the same time, as if he was building up to saying or doing something that he'd been on the verge of for a long time, something that wouldn't be easy to go back on.

'Oh…'

He inhaled, hesitated. Suddenly I got a sinking feeling that whatever he was about to come out with might not be anything I would want to hear.

But he didn't say it. Instead he shook his head, a gesture on such a small scale that I'd have missed it if I hadn't been watching him closely.

'It was a good day,' he told me.

'Mm. Yes. Could have gone worse.'

He reached forward to give me a quick hug – so quick it was almost as if he was frightened of lingering and wanted to get away as soon as possible.

'Well, we'll speak soon, won't we? Drive safely,' I said, and went to get out of the car.

'I love you,' he said.

The words came out in a kind of rush. He looked startled by them, as if he'd just broken a promise.

'I love you,' he said again, sounding a bit more confident this time.

And I was stunned. It was as if I'd triumphed. As if I'd just been given the biggest and most glorious prize in the world.

'I love you too,' I said.

We embraced again. He said, 'I don't want to lose you. I was miserable before I met you. Now I've forgotten what miserable felt like.'

I couldn't help but be pleased to hear him say that he had been miserable with Jade. I was less threatened by her these days… but still.

'You're not going to lose me,' I told him, and held him tighter. Even though he was so much bigger than I was, it felt like consoling a child.

We kissed, and then we broke off and looked at each other again. He was half smiling and looked much more like his usual self.

'Don't tell me you're still going to refuse to come in,' I said.

He shook his head, more decisively this time. 'You know if I do, I won't leave till morning. And both of us have work tomorrow, and other things to do.'

'Maybe one day we won't have to say goodbye. Maybe one day… we could just go home together.'

His smile didn't falter. If anything, it broadened. 'Maybe one day,' he said.

*

That evening Mum rang up to tell me what she thought of Jon.

'I like him,' she said. 'So does Phil.' Then she said, 'He's obviously very fond of you.'

'I know,' I said.

'I thought I should tell you, by the way, that I mentioned your new romance to your sister. I hope you don't mind.'

'No. No, that's fine. I mean, it's out in the open now, isn't it?'

'Anyway, she says she's pleased for you. The only bugbear is his previous relationship, isn't it? That, and the child who he hasn't let you meet yet.'

'I'm sure we can work it out. Other people seem to,' I said.

'You never want to look to other people for things like this,' Mum said. 'Other people are fine if you're thinking about a new porch or trying to decide what kind of car to buy. But when it comes to affairs of the heart, they're much less likely to tell you if they know they made a bad choice.'

'I'll bear that in mind,' I said, and Mum rang off.

I put the phone back and sat on my bed and looked round at my little flat. The spider plant on the verge of dying that Jon reminded me to water every time he came here. The cream throw that covered the sofa, which was hard and cheap and uncomfortable. A rented sofa. The flower-print duvet Mum had given me for Christmas after I'd asked for dark red – I had imagined that would look seductive, like the bedding in the master bedroom at White Cottage.

My life. Small and temporary and safe. I was almost certain that it was about to change. I was suddenly daunted by the thought of what might lie ahead, but I was thrilled too. I was sure we'd find a way through it. He loved me. He'd said so. And that was all you really needed, wasn't it? Love would be enough.

Looking back, I can see that he'd already missed his chance. That was really the last opportunity to tell me, to set the record straight. Afterwards he was in too deep. We both were. But there's always a point, with any big lie, just before you commit to it, when you can – if you act decisively – escape from it.

Escape comes at a price, though. You have to be willing to leave things behind. You have to be willing to lose.

And he wasn't. He was too proud, and he wanted me too much. He thought he could win. Somehow or other, he had persuaded himself that keeping quiet was the right, the best, the only thing to do. And after that it was too late.

Chapter Eleven

Dani

A shadow fell across the page. Josie was staring down at me, as apprehensive as a lookout who's seen the enemy coming and knows the gang's about to get caught.

'My mum wants to know if she should drop you back home,' she said. 'Or you can change your mind and stay for dinner, but if you do she wants to speak to your aunt first.'

Of course. Of course she would want to speak to Aunt Carrie. Mrs Pye was that kind of mother. The type who doesn't let anything slip through the cracks.

I closed the notebook and let myself stretch. My legs felt weird from having been folded under me for so long. Not pins and needles, but heavy, as if the blood in them had forgotten to keep moving.

'Are you OK?' Josie asked. 'All this time you've barely moved. I thought once or twice you might have fallen asleep. Except every now and then you'd let out an enormous sigh.'

'I'm sorry. I kind of forgot you were there. Anyway, I'm fine.' She looked unconvinced. 'Really, I am. Anyway, cheers for letting me borrow your reading chair. I suppose I'd best head back now. It's later than I thought.'

I put the notebook into my bag. Josie said, 'Are you going to be all right with that?'

'Sure. It's not going to bite, is it?'

Josie pulled a face as if she thought it might. 'So… have you found any clues?'

I shrugged. I wasn't sure if I could bring myself to start explaining about Jade. That woman! Thankfully I'd never had much to do with her. I'd met her a couple of times, most recently at boring Michelle's boring new flat in London. She wasn't exactly friendly. The way she looked – all dark hair and sharp eyes and blood-red lipstick – made me think of a vampire who'd just fed.

What I couldn't be sure of – yet – was exactly what part she'd played in the falling apart of everything before Mum took me off to Cornwall. But she had to have done *something*. Maybe she hadn't actually held Mum's head underwater, but she had some responsibility for the final disaster. I was sure of it.

Josie was still waiting for an answer. I settled for saying, 'My mum really didn't like my dad's first wife. I have to say, I don't much like her either.'

'Oh, second wives never like first wives,' Josie said sagely. 'Probably first wives don't like second wives, either. Like Catherine of Aragon and Anne Boleyn.'

'How do you know they didn't like each other?'

'My mum got me a book about it,' Josie said, then looked nervous, as if I was about to accuse her of being a swot or a weirdo.

'Well, aren't you the conscientious student,' I said. 'Was it interesting?'

'It was, actually,' Josie said, seemingly reassured. 'When Anne Boleyn married Henry VIII, Catherine of Aragon told her ladies-in-waiting not to be too mean about it because one day they'd have reason to be sorry for her. Which turned out to be true.'

A little shiver ran down my spine. 'That's like a curse.'

'Well, she knew what Henry VIII was like, I guess. After all, she had been married to him herself.'

'Yeah, well, Henry VIII had Anne Boleyn's head chopped off, didn't he? And whatever my dad may have done, or not done… he definitely didn't do *that*.'

I zipped up my schoolbag so the notebook was safely out of sight. Josie said, 'Aren't you worried your aunt might find it? I mean, she must have been pretty keen for you not to read it.'

'Yeah, well, probably she knew it would do my head in.' I stood up and shouldered my bag. 'Stop trying to play detectives, Josie. It's not like there's a murder to solve. There isn't even a body.'

Josie's face cleared. 'So there isn't anything… suspicious?'

'No,' I said, more confidently than I felt. 'Not really. I mean, she'd fallen out with my dad. They weren't together. She was thinking about leaving him. That's it, as far as I can tell. As far as I've got.'

Josie stepped forward as if she was thinking about trying to hug me or something. 'Oh, no, I'm sorry, Dani. Your poor dad.'

'Yes, well, that's not a big deal, really, is it? Marriages break up all the time. The big deal is that she's dead.'

Josie flinched. Then there was a knock on the door, and both of us jumped out of our skins.

It was Mrs Pye. She opened the door and peered at us. 'Is everything OK?'

'Yeah,' I told her. 'I'm just going.'

And so I found myself walking along Josie's road in the summer evening sunlight, with my mother's secret life in the bag on my back. I did think about not going back to Aunt Carrie's at all – about just keeping walking or getting my bike and riding off and finding some safe corner far away to finish reading the diary. In the end, though, without really thinking about it, I found myself walking right on up to Aunt Carrie's door as if nothing had changed.

I figured I'd eat my dinner and disappear upstairs and read as much as I could. I'd just have to keep the light off when she came up to go to bed. The last thing I wanted was to be interrupted before I'd finished.

And after I'd finished, I'd know everything there was to know. Surely, at that point, it would become obvious to me what I needed to do.

*

We ate dinner, as usual, on our laps – me on the sofa, Aunt Carrie in her favourite armchair. When the ad break came on she muted the TV and turned towards me – not all the way, but enough to indicate that she wanted to talk.

'So did you go to Josie's house after the park?'

'Yeah, we did.'

'I thought that was what your note said. Your handwriting isn't very clear, you know. You and Josie seem to be quite good friends.'

'Yeah, I guess we are.'

Aunt Carrie hesitated. I could almost hear her weighing up the possibility that I was using Josie as cover for a secret boyfriend, with whom I was most likely going to get into all sorts of trouble that it would take time and money to sort out.

'I don't think I've ever met Josie,' she said. 'Is she in your form photo?'

'Yeah, she is, actually. Do you want me to show you?'

'Yes, just out of interest, why not?'

I put my tray down on the sofa and got the form photo down from its place on the bookcase. I hated that photo. I looked so young and stupid in it, sitting in the front row with my red hair and my pink cheeks, grinning like Orphan Annie after a particularly annoying solo. Josie didn't look great in it either. She was squeezed in towards the end of one of the middle rows, and had her eyes closed and her mouth open as if she was in the middle of a sneeze.

'That's Josie,' I said, pointing her out to Aunt Carrie. 'See?'

Then I put the photo back and picked up my tray, ready to take it out to the kitchen.

Aunt Carrie said, 'I presume it's all right with you if I take an interest in your life occasionally?'

'Well, is it all right with *you*?'

'What's that supposed to mean?'

I knew I should just play nice and not antagonise her. I had the diary upstairs in my room, underneath my mattress; I should be getting back to it, not picking a fight. But Aunt Carrie was such a hypocrite! All these years she'd been carrying on as if she was the sort of person who'd never done anything worse than drop a stitch in the knitting. Whereas actually she'd been quite the rebel when she was younger. And it wasn't even as if she'd been that nice to my mum, most of the time.

Jealous, probably. Because there was Mum, with her smile and her way with words, and her gift for being happy – you could see that in the photo I had upstairs, that she knew how to let herself enjoy the good times when they came along. And then there was Carrie, who had changed from being stroppy into being bitter, but had always been consistent in one thing: being difficult.

'I just mean that you're not that interested, most of the time,' I said. 'You don't even like me. Not really.'

Aunt Carrie said, 'What's brought this on?'

'Nothing. Nothing in particular. But I'm not wrong, am I?'

'I really don't know what I've done to deserve this,' Aunt Carrie said. 'I've always done my best by you. And you haven't always made it easy.'

I knew I should just take the tray out and go upstairs. Instead I found myself saying, 'Did you even like my mum?'

Aunt Carrie's finger was hovering over the sound button on the remote. 'Dani, please. Do we really have to do this right now? It's been a long day, and I'd quite like to just finish watching my programme and relax.'

'Sure. I mean, I guess that answer speaks for itself.'

'She was my sister, Dani. Siblings don't have to like each other. In fact, they very often don't. But I liked her as much as I liked anyone, if that's any good to you.' She hesitated. 'I loved her, of course. But that's something else.'

'So… did you get along? Or did you… you know… squabble and stuff?'

I had her full attention now. She said, 'Why are you asking?'

It was risky… but not *that* risky. She wasn't going to guess that I'd gone up in the loft and found the diary. I still couldn't quite believe it myself.

I put my tray down on the coffee table, but stayed on my feet, looking down at her.

'Josie has a sister,' I said. 'I guess that got me thinking.'

She didn't look entirely reassured. 'Do they get on?'

'Actually, they do. Josie's the oldest. She probably finds her little sister annoying sometimes, but she's too nice to say so.'

'Ah.'

Aunt Carrie looked away from me, at nothing in particular.

'If I'm honest, I wasn't really that close to your mum, not in a day-to-day way,' she said. 'She was younger than you are now when I went off to university, and we didn't confide in each other or anything like that. We had our own lives. Anyway, as you might have noticed, closeness isn't really something I go in for.'

'Then why did you take me in?'

'Someone had to. Your father couldn't cope. From your point of view, I was the best of a bad bunch of options. Now can I watch my programme? Or is there something else you want to know?'

'There is one more thing,' I said. 'While we're on the subject.'

'Oh?'

'What do you think of Jade?'

'Jade? I don't think anything of her, why should I? She's ancient history. Perhaps not as far as your father's concerned, but I haven't seen her for years. Why, has he mentioned her? Have you seen her?'

'No,' I admitted. 'I haven't seen her. It's just… I was just wondering, that's all.'

I stood and picked up my tray. If Aunt Carrie was going to be unforthcoming, what did it matter? Mum had opened her heart ten years ago in Cornwall and written it down. I had more than answers; I had her words, her handwriting – the next best thing to having her come back to life and sit down with me to tell me exactly what had gone on.

As I left the room Aunt Carrie turned the sound on the telly back up and the room was suddenly loud with the sound of soap actors arguing. I left my plate by the sink and went upstairs knowing I was about to do something dangerous. But there was nothing I could do to stop myself and nothing, really, I could do to protect myself, other than leaving my bedroom door ajar so that I could hear Aunt Carrie coming up the stairs, and putting my schoolbag next to it where it would slow her down if she tried to come in.

Chapter Twelve

Laura's Diary

Today is going to be a disappointing day for Dani. She asked last night if we could go back to our special beach, and I promised her we would. But this morning I woke to the gentle sound of steadily falling rain. The sun is up but the light outside is watery and blue, as if the skyline has dissolved and the sea has washed into the clouds. It'll be a day for board games and drawing, and Dani will get bored. She might even start talking about going home.

Home. Where are we going to go? Not White Cottage. And not Cromwell Close, either.

I'll have to get a solicitor. Jon might not let Dani go the way he let Jade have Michelle…

I'll have to tell the solicitor the truth.

But the truth is shameful…

I'll have to let Dani see him. He's her father. But I never want to set eyes on him again in my life.

There were certainly some tensions, even in the early days – and by and by, there were rows, great, furious, unforgiving rows that seemed to blow up out of nowhere. When we argued, I became someone I didn't know – unyielding, uncompromising, never far from hysteria. And he turned into the Jon I'd first met, that New Year's Eve in the master bedroom at White Cottage: cold and scornful and detached.

We only ever rowed about one thing: Jade. The arguments sometimes ended with me crying, at which point Jon would soften and console me, though afterwards he'd be wary for hours or days, as if expecting me to explode into anger again. Other times he walked out, or I did. And then there would be a lull, a grace period of quiet, wary, distant days, during which it was as if we were trying to get to know each other all over again. And then we would make up, and I would be happy again – a powerful kind of happy that seemed to justify the anger and sadness and fear that I'd felt before.

But there was always a snake in the grass in our private paradise, and even though I could sometimes forget about her, I knew full well I'd never be able to get rid of her completely.

Yes, they were divorced, but the connection between them went beyond the vows they'd broken and the contract they'd had dissolved. It was a blood tie. They didn't just have history, they had Michelle. However much he loved me, I couldn't compete with that.

Almost inevitably, I'd thought about the child he and I might have together. I don't know if it's possible to fall in love with a man who has a child already without thinking about that. But I was worried that I would face an uphill battle persuading him that another baby was something he wanted and could risk having; he already thought of himself as having failed as a father because his relationship with Jade had broken down.

Jon's attitude to pregnant women and babies could not have been more different than mine. He could hardly bear to look at them; it was as if they were something from a horror movie that might, at any moment, be transformed into a terrifying threat. I was beginning to find them difficult to look at too, but that was because they filled me with admiration and envy. Fear, too: the fear you feel when you see something you can't quite bring yourself to admit that you want, because then you might also have to admit that you might not be able to have it.

Is love like that for everyone, at the start? Up and down, and fraught with unanswered questions? And for some, does it change eventually into comfort – into being the old couple who go along the street in the sunshine so companionably, so peacefully, that it's impossible to imagine anything could ever come between them apart from death?

And yet it was always too late for us. I wanted so much to believe we had a future. I knew the past was a threat, and I thought I could beat it. But I was in the dark. Maybe that was really what I was fighting. I understood there was something we needed to escape from. In my ignorance, I failed to realise that we would never be able to.

I couldn't bear to think that what I had with Jon was anything like what he might have had with Jade – even though, after a fight, I would always worry that I was reminding him of her in the worst possible way. I hated the idea that they'd had a grand passion that had gone wrong; it needed to have been wrong all the way through, wrong from the start, redeemed only by the fact that it had produced Michelle, who Jon obviously loved and I was trying to.

But as for Michelle… It wasn't easy. I wanted so much for it to work… Too much, maybe. Which was another way of saying that I wanted her to approve of me and tell Jon so. (And maybe even tell Jade, too.) She wasn't the kind of child who is immediately appealing, though. She was the kind of child who – from a teacher's point of view – is no trouble right up until the point where she tells you about something that someone else denies having done, leaving you in a quandary about how to resolve the situation fairly, and wondering who exactly is lying to you.

Physically, she was more like Jade than Jon, but the similarity only went as far as her dark eyes and hair, and perhaps a sulky self-consciousness about her appearance. She wasn't temperamental like Jade, though. She was a watcher and a waiter, and as I was a watcher and a waiter too, our relationship quickly became a wary game of patience in which both of us were wondering whether the other had all the best cards.

Jon drew various lines in the sand around his relationship with his daughter, one of which was a bar on me staying overnight at his flat when Michelle was there. At first, I thought this was fair enough – I understood what a big deal it was for him to let his ex-wife and daughter know I existed, let alone to have me around his place in my pyjamas. But after a year and a half, it began to feel like a block. If I was to be kicked out before bedtime whenever Michelle was there, what hope was there of us ever moving on to what seemed like the natural next stage, and living together?

Was this how Jade wanted it, or did it come from him? When I'd tried to find out, he'd turned cold and defensive. 'If you want more from me than I'm able to give, Laura, maybe this isn't right for you. Maybe you need to find someone who doesn't come with so much baggage.'

This infuriated me all the more because it frightened me – how could he be so quick to suggest that perhaps we should both throw in the towel? That was the last thing I wanted. I wanted to win – to come first – to beat Jade. And it was extraordinary how often he would express concern about our relationship – *maybe this isn't right for you, maybe it's too much to ask, I know it's a lot to take on* – after he'd had contact with Jade.

I might have been in the dark in some ways, but I knew enough to recognise that Jade was a problem. I even challenged him directly about it. I was still operating under girlfriend rules and I believed communication was important. As if you could assume that the other person was also willing to put all their cards on the table, and that it was safe to do so. Wasn't it what you were meant to do, in a relationship – to bring up what was bothering you, as if you were equals? I even tried to choose my moment, the way you're meant to.

We were out for dinner, we'd ordered, and there was nothing to distract him and no easy excuse for him to make for not answering. I said, 'Can I ask you something?'

He was instantly defensive. 'That sounds ominous. What is it?'

'It's just… I was wondering if you ever talked about me with Jade?'

He frowned. 'This isn't about the not-staying-over thing, is it?'

'No, it's not about that. Not really.'

'Not really?'

I knew what that meant: *Are we really going to argue about this again? Please don't. Please let's just enjoy this nice dinner together.* He had a pleading, half-jokingly-hopeful look on his face, like a puppy pleading for a bone. Cute, except I knew it wouldn't stay cute for long if I pressed the point. Then we'd get into shutdown mode: *I'm sorry, Laura, but I have to do what's right for Michelle. And actually, Jade has been very understanding about my relationship with you.*

Understanding? What was there for Jade to understand? I didn't want her to understand *anything* about me. I wanted her to feel as rebuffed and excluded as I did every time Jon said her name.

'Sometimes I feel that you treat me differently after you've been in touch with her,' I told him. 'I wonder if she makes you question your relationship with me in ways that you don't need to.'

Suddenly Jon looked really angry. Angry with me, not her.

'Look, I have to talk to her sometimes,' he said. 'That's just the nature of the beast. It's what happens when you have a child with someone.'

'I understand that, but do you talk to her about me?'

I knew from the way he drew his shoulders together and put his head down that he did.

'Of course I do. I had to tell her you were on the scene, didn't I? And that it was reasonably serious.'

'Reasonably serious? Where does that leave me on a scale of nought to ten? A seven?'

He looked up. 'Laura, don't be like that. I love you. You know that.'

But that time, the magic word didn't work. I didn't feel instantly better, and sure that everything was going to be all right. That was when I knew I needed more from him than love. Perhaps more than he was either willing or able to give.

I wonder now if that was why he proposed soon after. To stop me questioning him. To shut me up. *Look what I'm willing to do for you! I'll even sacrifice my freedom. Now will you believe me?*

The day of the proposal didn't start off particularly well. I was in a bad mood because Michelle was due to visit, and Jon had asked me to stay for dinner, but I understood that after that, he would expect me to leave. As if it would corrupt Michelle's morals to be confronted with the evidence that we shared a bed. Or as if seeing me looking sleepy in the morning would traumatise her any more than the ongoing jangling tension between her divorced parents.

Jade always left us with very precise instructions about what Michelle was to eat, and that annoyed me too. I was pretty sure that back home, Jade was all about the kind of food that was ready to eat after you'd taken off the outer packaging and shoved it in the microwave. I could just imagine her smiling to herself as she emailed over recipes to Jon, having searched at length for something fiddly that she could declare to be Michelle's favourite that week.

And as for Michelle… I had tried, and I kept trying, and that was really the problem: I was pained by my own cringe-inducing insincerity as I tried to bond with her, and she must have been aware of it too. Anyway, she seemed to be immune. I'd taken her out for treats without Jon around – shopping and to the cinema – and that hadn't helped; she couldn't find any clothes she liked, and was bored by the film. Books bored her, too. She was studious, but she wasn't into reading. The thing she liked most of all was playing on the computer, and I was under strict instructions from Jade to ration her screen time.

I was beginning to wonder whether it wasn't the part I was playing in Michelle's life that was the problem – maybe it was just me. We couldn't connect. We were like two elements that stubbornly refuse to react to each other, no matter how much you shake them and heat them up. And I couldn't imagine that it was going to get any better as she got older.

Still… she wasn't due to arrive until the evening, and we had the day up till then to ourselves.

In the morning Jon and I went to the supermarket to buy ingredients from the list Jade had so helpfully emailed over earlier. Once we'd put everything away Jon said, 'Let's go out.'

'Out where?'

He shrugged. 'I don't know. Anywhere. It's a beautiful day. Let's take advantage. Who knows how long the fine weather will last?'

It *was* a beautiful day – crisp and bright and cold, with patches of frost clinging on in the shadows. We went to Hampton Court Palace, which was in walking distance, and after we'd strolled in the grounds we went into the gift shop, where Jon looked comically out of place – a big man in a well-worn hat, standing tall among the themed aprons and crockery and pots of honey. Literally a bull in a china shop.

We drifted round looking at things, or rather, I looked and Jon followed me round, humouring me. I can still picture him now, standing in front of a wooden rack of baubles with his hands behind his back, humming a tune under his breath that was barely recognisable as a Christmas carol. Turning to look at him, taking in this tall red-haired man standing next to me, I felt a sudden, overwhelming burst of love for him.

But I didn't say, 'I wish we could spend all of Christmas together,' which was what I was thinking – Jon was due to pick Michelle up from Jade's place on the afternoon of Christmas Day, which meant I'd have to go back to my own flat that night.

Instead I reached forward and took a Christmas tree decoration off its hook and said, 'This is pretty, isn't it?' It was a bow, made of something rigid and covered with bronze-coloured glitter.

'It is,' he said. 'Why don't we get a couple for the tree?'

We'd put up a tree in his flat – there wasn't really room in mine. It was a real one, a novelty for me because I'd grown up with the same little artificial tree appearing every year. Jon's Christmas tree smelt like a forest, and I loved it.

'They're rather expensive,' I said.

'But they are pretty. As you said. And I guess they'll last.'

I glanced at him. Did he mean what I wanted him to mean – that we might be putting these decorations on our Christmas tree in years to come?

He smiled at me. 'Go on,' he said. 'Get a couple, at least. They won't break the bank.'

In the end I chose four: the bronze bow, a pair of silver bells attached by a slender cord, a golden pear and a pearlised star. The shop attendant wrapped each one in tissue paper, as if it was precious, and I came away feeling as if I had a bagful of treasure.

I had never felt that so clearly before – that solidity. The sense that we could have a future.

Where did it go?

How could we have let it go?

Who knows what will happen to those Christmas decorations now? I don't think I could bear to see them again. Would he feel the same way?

But at Hampton Court on that December day I had no idea that the baubles came with a hidden price tag.

We went from the gift shop to the café, where I ordered hot chocolate and he had coffee. We sat facing each other across a little table in a corner, by a window. The light outside was already beginning to fade.

I said, 'We should head back after this, make sure everything's ready for Michelle.'

And he said, 'I think we should get married.'

It came out in a rush. He kept his eyes fixed on me; he looked like a man who brings a puppy home for Christmas and isn't quite sure whether his gift will bring the happiness he'd hoped for.

I said, 'Did you really just say what I thought you said?'

'I did,' he said. 'I want you to be my wife. I want us to wake up every morning together until we're both old and grey.'

It was an instant high – the kind of joy that makes you feel weightless, just like those dreams where it's suddenly possible to fly. I clasped my hands and leaned forwards and he put his hands round mine and held them.

'That's what I want, too,' I said.

Well, of course I said yes. I didn't have a shadow of doubt. I was dazzled, and I thought he was offering me everything I'd ever wanted. He apologised for not having a ring to offer me, and I said it didn't matter and maybe we should choose them together. And he agreed and then I asked – and I was only partly teasing – if this meant I'd be allowed to stay over with him that night.

He looked momentarily confused, as if I'd reminded him of something he would rather have forgotten. I promptly backtracked.

'Don't worry,' I told him, 'no rush. I know you'll want to tell Michelle in your own time. Probably without me there, I'm guessing? Unless you think it would help. She's bound to have questions.'

I didn't say, *You'll have to tell Jade too*, though of course I was thinking it. She wouldn't be able to dismiss me as inconsequential any more – as a follow-up, someone whose role in Jon's life was only temporary. She'd have to accept me the way I'd had to accept her – as someone of lasting importance, someone who wasn't going anywhere.

'Michelle will probably want to know whether she's going to end up with a little brother or sister,' Jon said. 'Apparently she's been asking Jade about it.'

'Ah. So… how does she feel about that idea? Michelle, I mean.' It seemed to go without saying that Jade would be less than thrilled.

'What does any kid feel about the prospect of having a sibling? I guess she's a bit apprehensive about it. But I'm sure she could be persuaded to see it as a good thing.'

A good thing? Did that mean Jon thought it would be a good thing? I held back from asking outright, but was suddenly hopeful. Hopeful and wary. Sibling relationships were a subject I trod round carefully with Jon; he'd had an older brother who had died in a car crash at twenty. Jon's preferred way of dealing with what had happened seemed to be to talk and think about it as little as possible.

Jon said, 'More to the point, how do you feel about it? Do you think you might want to have children one day?'

I shrugged and nodded. He said, 'That's what I thought. So being a teacher hasn't put you off? You've spent a lot more time with kids than I did before I had Michelle.'

'Well, I'm not planning on having thirty all at the same time. And everyone says it's different when you're a mum.' I drew a deep breath. 'Anyway, I guess I'll be a stepmother before I'm a mum. Hopefully not a wicked one.'

'You could never be wicked,' Jon said. He looked me up and down and smiled as if he had every reason to feel as if the world was at his feet. 'I knew there was something between us the night of the party at White Cottage, when you talked to me in the bedroom. I was scared of it, to be honest.'

'Why were you scared?'

He shrugged. 'I didn't see how it could work. I was still married to Jade then.'

'But not happy.'

'No.'

'How do you think she'll take it?'

He shrugged. 'It would be easier if she was with someone else. Anyway, she'll just have to accept it.'

'Jon… I know you'll need to pick the right time to tell her… but you won't leave it too long, will you? I don't want to have to keep this a secret.'

He looked away from me, down at the table, and his face clouded over. 'That's where we're different,' he said. 'I wish we could.'

And I didn't press him – I didn't ask why. Instead I asked him where he would like to go on honeymoon, and we talked about places we could go and finished our drinks and went outside and kissed under a cold, starry sky. Back at his flat, I put our new Christmas decorations on the tree and stood back to admire them and breathed in the scent of real pine, and I was much too happy to worry about anything.

The following weekend, I found out he'd told Jade.

We were walking by the river – the Thames, the same river that flowed through Kettlebridge, broader and slower as it meandered between the houses of the very rich towards the skyscrapers of Central London. It was the middle of the afternoon, but it seemed like evening; the sun was low but hadn't yet set. We hadn't been talking about getting married or wedding plans, but all of a sudden I found myself saying, 'I spoke to my mum on the phone the other day. It felt very strange not telling her that we're engaged.'

He went quiet for a moment. We carried on walking. Then he said, 'You can tell her whenever you like. Unless you want me to ask for Phil's blessing first. Or hers.'

'But I thought you wanted to wait for a little while… until you'd had a chance to tell Jade.'

'She knows. I told her today, after I took Michelle back.'

'So… what did she say?'

'She said she thought we were a good match.' He paused. 'Then she said she hoped I wouldn't hurt you.'

'*Hurt* me? The only thing that could hurt me – the only thing that can hurt *us* – is her, if she decides to make life difficult for us. I hate that she has that kind of power over us, but she does. Because of Michelle.'

'I know this may sound strange to you, but Jade isn't a monster. She genuinely wants us to be happy.'

'She may have convinced you of that, but she hasn't convinced me. I don't believe for a minute that she wishes us well at all. I think she still has feelings for you.'

'If anyone ever had feelings for anyone else at the end of a relationship, divorce will finish them off. We'd reached the end of the road. We both knew that.'

'Anyway, she's not important enough to fight over.'

'She's not.'

There was silence between us, and suddenly all the other sounds around us were magnified: the crunch of our footsteps, the distant wail of a police siren, the river water rushing to meet the sea.

I said, 'So… does Michelle know?'

'Jade's going to tell her,' Jon said.

I wasn't sure if that was the best way to handle things, but I let it go, and actually, it seemed to work out all right. During the week that followed a card arrived at Jon's flat in the post; it had doves and a diamond ring on the front and said 'Congratulations on your engagement' inside. It was signed by Michelle, in large, careful handwriting.

Jon showed it to me when I went to his place for dinner that Friday, and said, 'It seems peace has broken out.'

'We'd better hurry up and get those rings,' I told him.

And that weekend I stayed over in the flat with Michelle there, and it was fine. Only fractionally awkward – or at least, I felt that *she* found it so. But it wasn't a disaster. It seemed normal, and very faintly embarrassing in the way that family life often is, and I told myself that everything was going to be all right.

Mum was delighted when I told her I was getting married, as I knew she would be.

'Oh! I did wonder… He seemed so very fond of you.' She stood up and we hugged each other, not too tightly; her eyes were shining. 'Well, that is wonderful news.'

Almost as soon as we let go of each other, her thoughts turned to Carrie. 'You will go easy on your sister when you break the news, won't you?'

'Go easy?'

'Well… you know. Don't rub it in. She's older than you, and it won't be easy for her to see you married before her. I know people think things like that don't matter these days, but they do. And things are a bit wobbly with Stick, from what I gather. He has a new job, and he seems to be spending an awful lot of time on road trips with his new boss.'

'Oh.'

'Of course she'll be thrilled for you. I just wanted you to be aware of what's going on with her. If you don't know, it's easy to say the wrong thing, isn't it?'

'I suppose.'

But when I rang Carrie to wish her a happy Christmas and told her Jon and I were engaged she was over the moon.

I guessed Mum must have pre-warned her. I was taken aback: it wasn't like Carrie to be that enthusiastic about anything, and I'd expected her to be much cooler about it. Then she asked if I was going to force her into a disgusting strapless bridesmaid's dress. This was a bit more in line with the kind of reaction I'd expected, but still surprising, since I would have expected her to refuse to wear anything she hadn't chosen herself.

'Wear whatever you like,' I told her. 'Within reason. It's going to be a registry office do, probably quite small. I don't think I'm going to have bridesmaids, but maybe you could be my honorary bridesmaid? Or matron of honour or whatever they call it.'

'What about Michelle?'

'Oh… I don't know. We'll have to see.'

I didn't expect Michelle to want to be my bridesmaid, but I also didn't expect her to say she didn't want to come to the wedding at all. Jon had asked me not to mention it to her directly, and to let him sort it out with Jade. When he finally told me, I was too taken aback and upset to be angry… at first.

'It's Jade,' I said after a while. 'She's got to be the one behind this. She just wants to spoil things for us.'

'I don't think it's like that. Michelle was asked if she wanted to come, and she said she didn't. She has the right to choose.'

'She hasn't chosen. Jade has.'

'We can't *make* her come,' Jon said. 'Don't be too hard on her. It doesn't mean that she doesn't wish us well. It's just that she doesn't feel like being there on the day, that's all.'

'I get that, but… everybody's going to think that she hates me.'

'Well, she doesn't, and what does it matter what everybody else thinks?'

The idea of getting married without Michelle there appalled me. People were bound to want to know why she wasn't coming, and I would have to say that it was because she didn't want to. Jade had found a way of sabotaging the wedding without coming anywhere near it. And neither Jon nor I could do anything to stop her.

Chapter Thirteen

Laura's Diary

When it came to it, Jon deprived me of the chance to have anybody at our wedding – even Mum.

One morning in early February – not quite two months after he'd proposed – he rocked up at my London flat looking pale and pasty and more nervous than any bridegroom with a clear conscience should be. He told me he'd sorted out a special licence – so would I do it? Would I say yes?

One look at him told me that if I didn't agree there and then, the wedding would never happen – that what he was offering was an alternative to a jilting.

I said, 'Yes.' And then: 'When?'

'Now or never,' he said.

He left his car outside my flat, and we took a taxi to the registry office – 'We might want a drink afterwards,' he said. On the way there I told myself we were being romantic. Impulsive. It all went to show that what he really wanted was to be with me – just so long as he could evade the fuss and exposure of a public ceremony.

Anyway, it was Jade's fault, really. If he hadn't been married before – if his first marriage hadn't ended so badly – surely he wouldn't have been quite so phobic about the prospect of walking down the aisle with me.

It didn't occur to me to see his reluctance as a warning rather than as resistance to be overcome. When it came down to it, I wanted to tie the knot at any cost. I saw his ambivalence as my failure, and even though this was a rush and perhaps undignified and I didn't have any control over it, it was a way to win.

In the end, I was married in jeans, a sweatshirt and trainers, and the only pictures of the event were taken on a disposable camera that I picked up at a newsagent's on the way to the pub after we'd said 'I do'.

The whole thing was so downbeat as to be completely surreal. At least it gave us a good wedding story. In the pub afterwards, we agreed that was important. We even practised it on each other. My version tried to be romantic: 'Jon and I eloped! We were planning the usual kind of wedding – a registry office do and fifty people for a reception in a hotel – and then he rocked up one day out of the blue to say he wanted to be married and he couldn't bear to wait any longer.' Jon's account was a bit more to the point: 'Yeah, we tied the knot. We figured the best thing was to just get it over with.'

Looking back, I wonder if that was part of how isolated we became when we were living together as a married couple in his flat. Friends and family were never really part of the mix, were barely even in the background. We weren't the kind of couple that entertains, that hosts dinner parties and attends them in exchange; we didn't go to parties or pubs together – places where we could have shared an audience and practised being our best selves. Both of us had spent too long being lonely to throw ourselves into being sociable together. You can get used to watching the world as an outsider – it feels safer than exposing yourself to it. I'd been like that since childhood, and Jon had turned into a misanthrope when his marriage to Jade broke down if not before, and in that way, neither of us was about to change. Having found each other, neither of us needed to.

We honeymooned in Vienna, where we spent most of our time in our palatial hotel bed, occasionally emerging for *patisserie* and to stroll round grand buildings. By the time we came back I was pregnant – a development confirmed by several tests a few weeks later. I couldn't quite believe it had happened so quickly, so easily.

I was rather smug about it; it didn't occur to me that this might be tempting fate. I felt like I'd caught up – with Jade, with the kind of life I wanted.

But the reality of pregnancy made it hard to stay smug. I was tired in a way I'd never been before. Back at work, I felt sick at morning snack time when the children ate their fruit, and at the same time I kept wanting to eat. As the weather warmed up, my train journey to school – which was longer now I'd moved in with Jon – became increasingly hellish. I began to grumble about how unbearable it was being on my feet all day, and how much I couldn't wait to finish even though I wasn't due to go on maternity leave for months and months to come. I'd always taken pride in my job; now suddenly I seemed to have transformed into someone who wanted nothing more than to stay home.

'Maybe you'll feel differently after you've had the baby,' Jon said.

We both knew that the odds were stacked against me being able to give up work for good. The garden centre business wasn't going brilliantly, and Jon was committed to paying generous child support for Michelle; we were going to need my income. I said he was probably right, but I didn't really believe I'd ever want to go back.

I was still apprehensive about Jade, but I was less vulnerable to being wounded by her than I had been. The first time I saw her after Jon had told her and Michelle about the baby, I half expected her to rock up looking more sultry than ever; it would have been so typical of her – when I was already beginning to put on weight and had lanky hair – to appear as her most glamorous self to drop Michelle off. But she didn't. Instead she turned up looking pale and tired herself, dressed in jeans and an old pale-blue cashmere jumper that had worn patches and bobbles. She still looked better than most people would, though, perhaps unsurprisingly, she didn't look particularly happy.

Michelle went on into the living room and turned on the TV; Jade stayed at the door, as usual, and passed me Michelle's overnight bag and the cool bag with her snacks in it. Jade never tried to come in, and I never invited her.

'Congratulations,' she said, in a not-particularly-congratulatory tone of voice.

'Yes. Thanks.'

She glanced down at my belly, not that there was anything much to see; I was wearing a big, shapeless tunic over leggings.

'I'd appreciate it if you didn't go on about it too much to Michelle. She's fine with it, but it's a bit of an adjustment for her.'

'I wasn't planning to.'

I didn't usually speak to Jade that sharply. She didn't seem to notice. She went on, 'Have you started looking for a bigger place yet? This flat is just about all right for a couple with a kid who stays at weekends. I think you'll find it's a bit of a push to fit in a baby and a load of baby stuff too.'

'We haven't yet. But it's on the cards.'

'Well, I wouldn't leave it too late. If Michelle's going to have a new room to get used to, much better for her to get settled in before the new arrival.' She raised her eyes to my face. 'It's really important for her to know her daddy still wants her, whatever happens. It's not her fault he's decided to have another baby. She still needs exactly the same commitment from him that she had before.'

'He won't let her down,' I said stiffly, though the idea of trying to keep Michelle happy while also looking after a newborn was pretty overwhelming.

I could see what Jade was saying: she wasn't about to let him off the hook. Or me. Well, Michelle had a right to her relationship with her dad, and Jade was entitled to her free Saturday nights. I wondered what she did with them. Went on dates, probably. I couldn't imagine her staying home on the sofa.

Jade tossed her hair. She had freshly manicured nails, painted a glittery dark grey. 'I imagine you'll find it changes a few things. But I want it to change as little as possible for Michelle,' she said. 'Anyway, with any luck it'll put her off getting started too young. Nothing like spending time with a screaming baby to make you grow up careful.'

And with that she turned and went off to her car. I put the snacks from the cool bag in the fridge and joined Michelle in front of the TV, which, according to Jade's strict instructions, I could only let her watch for half an hour.

Later – when Jon got back from whatever crisis it was that he'd had to sort out at the garden centre – he found a moment when Michelle was out of earshot to ask me how things were going.

'Michelle seems fine. We just haven't talked about it,' I said. 'Meanwhile, Jade seems to think that me having a baby will put Michelle off teen pregnancy and will also ruin our romance.'

'Right. That's upbeat,' Jon said.

'Will it?' I asked him.

'Michelle is eleven years old and anyway, she thinks boys are disgusting. I think there's a way to go before I have to start worrying about becoming a grandfather.'

'No, I mean about the romance.'

He pulled me into his arms. 'What do you think?'

'Well, you know what they say. Marry at haste, repent at leisure. Though my mum thinks marrying in haste is the only way to do it, and the alternative is probably not to get married at all.'

'You know, I really don't feel like talking about your mother right now,' he said, and kissed me.

A minute later we were interrupted by Michelle coming into the kitchen to look for something. 'Oh… sorry.'

Jon and I broke off, and Michelle looked at us as if we'd just told a particularly bad and embarrassing joke.

'I just want my fruit,' she said. She rummaged in the fridge and got out the Tupperware box of diced melon and grapes that Jade had prepared for her. Then she found a fork and went off again, head held high, closing the kitchen door carefully behind her.

Jon and I exchanged glances. He said, 'She'll get used to it.'

'Or we'll stop doing it.'

'Us? Never.'

I moved away from him and leaned against the worktop. It was a tiny galley kitchen, with just about room for two; we ate in the open-plan living room. I thought how good it would be to have a kitchen you could eat in, with space for a highchair. And I thought about the kitchen at White Cottage and how perfect it would be if only we could go back there, if only it wasn't for Michelle and Jade.

'Never say never,' I murmured, almost without thinking about it.

'What?'

'Oh, nothing. How's Jade's love life these days?'

He folded his arms. 'We don't really discuss it.'

'Well, you must have some idea. I know you two talk. Look, don't worry, I'm not going to go off on one. I think we're kind of past that.'

He hesitated. 'I think she's given up, to be honest. She wants to set up her own business. A dance school. I think she's going to focus on that.'

'Look, for what it's worth, I actually feel like Jade and I might be at the beginnings of some kind of truce,' I said. 'Or maybe we'll have one once I'm properly in the mum club.'

'Sounds good,' he said. 'It's about time. You know, there's really no reason why the two of you shouldn't get along.'

'Yeah, apart from the obvious,' I said, and went through to the other room, where Michelle was sitting up at the table and eating the snack Jade had provided for her. That was one thing about Jade, she really did love her daughter. It did sometimes cross my mind that she was a little too emphatic about the need for Michelle to keep her weight down, but I'd never got up the nerve to say anything about it to Jon.

A truce. Could we? Would we? I knew it was the only sensible way. The more civilised we could be, the better – for my baby and for hers. And I knew it would please Jon if we tried.

What a fool I was. Jade wasn't civilised, not really – that was what was great about her, and that was what was terrifying about her as well. She must have known perfectly well that she'd messed up her marriage, but that didn't mean that she liked having me around and it certainly didn't mean she was pleased that Jon was having another child.

I thought we were at the beginnings of a truce... but that was just wishful thinking. Really, she was just biding her time.

Chapter Fourteen

Laura's Diary

This morning, when Dani and I made it to the shop at the end of the lane, Mandy was behind the till as usual. She said, 'Someone's been trying to get hold of you.'

I did my best to keep my response casual. After all, she hadn't said 'your husband'. It might not be him. And if it *was* him, was it such a bad thing? Maybe he just wanted to talk to Dani. Maybe I should let him.

'Oh, really?'

'Yes, he sent an email to the lady who owns the cottage, apparently. Saying that he'd tried the landline number and it didn't seem to be working. Do you know if you've got the phone plugged in?'

I carried on packing groceries into my bag – apples, eggs, fish fingers. 'I suppose I'd better check,' I'd said.

'She asked me to let you know, if I saw you. The message was to call him, if you get the chance. It was from a Jon Rosewell.'

Did she know my surname? The woman who owned the cottage would know. She might have mentioned it to Mandy. Would they have gossiped about it? The prospect of a husband on the warpath?

'That rings a bell,' I said. I packed up the groceries and paid, and lead Dani back through the drizzle to the cottage. I put on the ancient TV for Dani and unpacked, and plugged the phone in and looked at it. Then I unplugged it again and sat down at the kitchen table and started writing instead.

*

The beginning of the end was a phone call from Carrie.

She was living in Cromwell Close at the time, supposedly to help look after Phil, who was in the early stages of dementia, but also because she'd been going through a rough patch, as Mum put it; she'd broken up with Stick and lost her job. I had gone back to work and was supply teaching; Jon was trying to keep his business afloat. Usually, we kept in touch through emails or texts: 'You OK?' 'Yes, A-OK here.' We hardly ever chatted. So when the phone rang and it was Carrie at the other end of the line, I knew it was bad news.

She told me Mum had fallen and broken her leg and was in hospital. Then, a few days later, she rang me again, this time to tell me Mum had come down with an infection and wasn't going be discharged after all. And it was Carrie who called to say that Mum was struggling and might not make it through, and I ought to get myself to the hospital as soon as possible. She didn't say *before it's too late*, but I knew that was what she meant.

Mum was in a room by herself by that stage, hooked up to a drip, mostly sleepy but dipping in and out of focus. We were alone. Carrie – who had been a much more regular visitor than I had been – had gone back to Cromwell Close to shower and tidy up, and Phil – whose understanding of the situation seemed to come and go – was at the day centre Carrie had found for him.

The room was bare, overheated and impersonal, apart from the faint smell of the musky perfume Carrie wore. Mum was sleeping. I'd come with flowers and a vase and put them in a corner next to the flowers Carrie must have brought earlier, which were already beginning to wilt. Then I sat down next to Mum and after a few minutes her eyes flickered open. She didn't look at all her usual self; she was thinner, paler, and somehow blurrier, as if she was breaking down.

She said, 'Shouldn't you be with Dani? She'll be missing you.' Her voice was thinner than usual too, but the words were exactly what I would have expected her to say.

'Oh, she's all right, don't you worry about her. She's with her dad. He's probably spoiling her rotten.' It sounded like the way someone might speak about a husband they were separated from.

Mum sighed.

'Your father adored you, you know,' she said.

It was so rare for her or any of us to refer to him that I was almost too shocked to be touched. There was only one reason why she would start saying such things – because she knew she might not get another chance. That meant she knew. She realised she was dying. And this was her trying to tell me something she thought I ought to know, something that no one else would be able to tell me.

She shifted a little on the pillows and paused to rally her strength. She was obviously determined to say her piece; she must have been thinking about this for quite some time. When she spoke her voice was stronger again, more like her old self.

'When you came along, it was hard on Carrie,' she said. 'It always is hard on a little one, when Mum's suddenly wrapped up in a new baby. Your dad picked up the slack. Took Carrie to the park and so on. Then she got quite jealous when he paid attention to you. He had to do it behind her back, as it were. But he was nuts about you. Besotted. It helped that you were a very good baby, of course. Though he'd have been soppy about you anyway. He was like that.' She was looking in the distance, remembering; she was almost smiling. Then she sniffed as if that was quite enough sentiment and it was time for a dose of reality. 'Of course, he wasn't the one changing most of the nappies.'

'Jon wasn't very keen on all that either. He did a few, now and then. But he didn't really think it was his job.'

'Men,' Mum said, and very slightly shook her head. 'Are you thinking of having another one? A baby, I mean, not another man.'

This didn't seem like the time to object to her asking nosy questions.

'Well... we have talked about it. But it's tricky in terms of the finances. We thought it might be best to wait until Dani starts school full-time.'

'Well, you don't want to leave it too long,' Mum said. She was eyeing me slightly suspiciously, as if I might be on the edge of doing something people might disapprove of. 'If you have too big a gap between the first and the second, they might not be so close.'

I cast around for something reassuring to say.

'Well, there's five years between me and Carrie, which isn't that big a gap in the scheme of things, but it's bigger than in lots of families. Anyway, I think that turned out OK.'

Mum's eyebrows went up a fraction.

'You do?'

'Yes. I mean, we've had our ups and downs. But underneath it all, I think we're there for each other.'

But I didn't sound at all convincing. After all, Carrie was the one who had been at Mum's bedside in hospital day in, day out. I was a visitor; she'd somehow become the carer. She was territorial about her role, too: territorial and martyred, as if she was the one who understood our parents' needs and had risen to the challenge of meeting them, while I was too far away and too distracted by work and my husband and small child to be of any use.

'It's good that you feel things have worked out all right,' Mum said.

She didn't sound convinced either. Maybe that was just fatigue; trying to talk was probably wearing her out.

'You're going to need to help each other,' she went on. 'Take care of each other. Somebody's going to have to keep an eye on Phil.'

'Please don't worry about Phil. We'll make sure he's OK.'

'I'm not worried, not really. I know Carrie will see him right. And you too, of course, as far as you're able. I hope you'll come home from time to time. Support her. She shouldn't put her whole life on hold to look after other people. It'll only make her bitter and resentful. And she's still young. Life is for living. While you still can.'

And then her eyes closed and she drifted back off to sleep. Watching her there, dozing in a patch of suddenly strong sunlight, I remembered a conversation I'd had with her years before, back when we'd first moved to Kettlebridge and she'd made me join the amateur dramatic society and I'd been cast in *Macbeth*.

It had been another sunny day; I was sitting at the dining-room table, reading *Macbeth* with the dictionary to one side, and Mum had come in with tea and biscuits. She had been outside weeding, and was in a calmer, more receptive mood than usual, as she often was after she'd been gardening – which was something my dad had loved doing, apparently. Maybe it made her feel close to him again in some way.

She asked me how I was getting on with the play, and I said it was surprisingly scary. 'You think of witches and ghosts as a bit of a joke. But not in this. I guess people still really believed in them then.'

'Some people still do,' Mum said. 'They believe in ghosts, anyway.'

'Do you?'

This wasn't at all the kind of thing we usually talked about. Mum paused to think about it, and that was unusual too: she usually behaved as if she didn't have the time to pause for thought.

'Not really,' she said eventually.

The sun was still streaming into the dining room, and it was warm and bright and there was no reason to be spooked, but I felt the hairs lift on the back of my neck.

'Not really? So… sometimes you do, maybe a little bit?'

'Maybe sometimes feelings linger,' Mum said. 'Intense feelings. Like if a mother is taken from a child before her time, or if her child is taken from her. Sometimes I've been in old houses where things like that have happened, and the place is supposed to be haunted, and there's definitely an atmosphere. But maybe sometimes happy things linger, too. Love. Goodwill. Things like that.'

'So… have you ever felt that?'

Mum shrugged. 'It's hard to pin down that sort of feeling, isn't it? You always wonder whether you just imagined it. But one thing's for sure, death doesn't finish things. It's not neat and tidy like coming to the end of a book. When we go, we don't just vanish off the face of the earth. We leave traces everywhere. Signs, if you like. They're just not easy for the living to make sense of.'

At the time, I thought she was just revealing an eccentric streak that I hadn't known was there. Later, in the hospital, I found it comforting. It was the only time I'd ever had a conversation like that with her, and it seemed like she'd been telling me that I wouldn't lose her, that in one way or another she'd always be around.

But looking back on it now, I think what she said was eerie. Uncanny. It frightens me… to think of what happens at the edge of life and beyond it, and how helpless we all are, in the end.

It means something, to be remembered… depending on *how* you are remembered. You can't control the life you have after life; it's all down to other people. Your fate is totally in their hands.

Can people reach a point where they're ready to let go of life? Was Mum there already when I saw her that day in the hospital, not knowing it was the last time?

I don't know… maybe I'm just tired and being morbid. I haven't slept that well since coming here. But I find myself wondering if I will ever reach that point myself.

It's a terrifying thought… because even when it breaks your heart, life is sweet.

And I have Dani. The way things have turned out, it might not be a huge wrench to let go of the other people in my life, but I can't imagine ever being ready to say goodbye to *her*.

Chapter Fifteen

Dani

I fully intended to finish reading the diary before I went to sleep. But then I only managed a little bit more before Aunt Carrie came up and asked me when I was going to shower. She nearly caught me red-handed; I shoved the diary under my pillow the split second before she came in. She never was any good at knocking and waiting for an answer.

Then, after I'd finished in the bathroom, I lay down on my bed and that was it. I just crashed out – it was like my brain decided to turn itself off and there was nothing I could do about it.

Sleep wasn't much of a break from the day I'd had, though. In my dreams, everything swirled around in a hideous, nightmarish mix. I was reading the diary and then I'd lost it. Dad found it. Aunt Carrie found it. It went up in flames. Gemma and Cherry tossed it into the stream by the bridge, and I watched helplessly as the slow current carried it away to the river and the sea.

And then I was by the sea, on the beach, and she was there. So close. So close. Lying on a picnic rug on her front with a sunhat on, writing, writing. I called to her, but she wouldn't turn to look at me. And the next minute she was gone, and the beach was empty apart from me. But no, it wasn't completely empty, because on the far side of it Dad and Aunt Carrie and Jade were standing in a row, watching me, their faces in shadow so I couldn't see their expressions. Waiting to see what I would do next.

Eventually my alarm rang, and I turned it off and saw that my bedroom was dark, but not really dark. It took me a little while to wake up enough to figure out that Aunt Carrie must have turned out the top light, and I'd slept through to morning.

Then I thought: *I have to go.*

I'd never been anywhere near where she died. I'd barely even been to the seaside. To Dorset, once, for a school trip to look at geological features. I'd always thought it was because Aunt Carrie wasn't the bucket and spade type. Too tidy. Wouldn't have liked the way sand got into everything. I'd never questioned how exactly I knew sand got into everything.

Would I recognise it? Remember it? Would it bring something back?

The notebook was still under my pillow. Still real.

If I hadn't gone swimming in the river when I wasn't supposed to and pretty much forced them into telling me how Mum had died… if I hadn't got friendly with Josie, and if she hadn't helped me up into the attic… if I hadn't clambered across the boards to look in that old trunk under the abandoned wasps' nest…

I might never have found it.

You had to go looking for answers. Otherwise people just gave you what they thought they could afford to give. If you wanted to get at the truth, you had to be ready to take risks for it.

That was when I made my mind up what I was going to do. Once I'd decided I felt very calm. Calm and angry at the same time, like an assassin. I got out of bed and dressed in my school uniform and went downstairs for breakfast as if it was just another normal day.

What was weird was just how normal it was – to sit there eating cornflakes with Aunt Carrie watching the birds in the garden, not talking, not saying anything. It made me realise how 'normal' had really been weird all along. It was enough to make you wonder how many other kids out there were sitting around eating breakfast in houses that seemed normal in every way, but that had the past and its secrets lapping at the doors and windows like the sea that had taken my mother, invisible until someone chose to see it.

I met Josie on the green close to our house. This was a big ask; Josie was always on time for school and the green was a detour that would put her on course for a late mark, especially if she decided to try and talk me out of what I was planning or asked a lot of questions. A late mark would show up on her report eventually and disappoint her parents. But I couldn't help that. Josie had wanted to be my companion in an adventure – and adventure meant risk, and risks sometimes meant consequences. But hopefully, the consequences would be manageable – for her, anyway.

She looked really worried. I shouldn't have been pleased to see that, but I was. It was nice to have someone worried about me for the right reasons – because they actually cared about me, rather than because I reminded them of a whole load of stuff from the past that they couldn't forget and didn't want to talk about.

'Thanks for coming,' I said.

I was sitting on the bench at one corner of the green; she settled down next to me. The grass was all dewy, and she left a trail of footprints behind her. I had too. Evidence, but not the kind that would last. As the sun came up the dew would vanish like steam off a fence. By then I'd be on my way, with any luck, and nobody would be able to stop me. I'd decided not to think about what would happen after: a load of shouting and recriminations, probably. But that was only to be expected.

Josie said, 'What happened? Did you read it all yet?'

'Not all of it. Josie, I'm not going into school today.'

'You're not? Where are you going? Are you running away?'

'No, not really. Running away is when you don't want to face something. I'm looking for something. It's more like… more like an expedition.'

'They'll find out. And then you'll be in trouble. You might even get suspended.'

'So what? Won't kill me to sit around at home for a bit. But Josie, I want you to promise me something.'

She stiffened. Obviously she was afraid that I was going to ask her to lie for me. Maybe she let people push her around a little bit too much, but she was honest. That was a quality I was beginning to appreciate.

'It's OK, you don't have to cover for me. I'm going to cover for myself. But you don't need to tell on me, either, OK? At least not until someone asks. And you don't need to worry about me either. I can look after myself. You know that. But that wasn't what I was going to say. I want you to keep an eye out for Gemma and Cherry, OK? Now here's what you do. You think of something that is ridiculous and stupid about each one of them, and you hold it in your mind. Walk tall – not too tall, just the proper height you are. And you remember how small they are. So small, you wouldn't even notice them if they hadn't been so horrible to you. Don't avoid them, but just keep a weather eye on where they are. If Gemma and Cherry come for you, which they might do, you've got two main choices. Then you've got some other, less good choices, but we'll get into that in a moment. OK?'

'OK,' Josie said doubtfully.

'OK. This is Josie's Law, all right? That's what we're going to call it. Just because you're nice doesn't mean you're weak. If people see that you're nice and make the mistake of thinking that because you're nice you'll let them push you around, they're in for a shock. So shock them. Be nasty right back to them. Words are a weapon and one they're probably too stupid to use. If you can make other people laugh at them, that's the best way of all. All right, so you're little. So what? Be little and vicious. After all, little beats big if little has all the best lines.'

'But if I try to do that… won't it just make it worse?'

'Well, it might do. But I think you'll feel better. Otherwise it's like they're dumping a load of junk on you and you're taking it and saying thank you. Just throw it back at them. I know you've been brought up to be polite and good and tell teacher if something goes wrong. But, you know, you weren't brought up to suffer in silence. All that being good is fine as long as everybody else plays by the same rules, but if they don't – well, your first best line of defence is yourself. I'm not saying that you should go looking for a fight. I'm saying you shouldn't be afraid of a fight if they bring it to you.'

Josie nodded. She still didn't look convinced. She said, 'Why do I feel like I'm never going to see you again?'

'You will,' I said. 'I'm not going that far. Wish me luck.'

'Good luck.'

'Good luck to you, too. Look, you'd better go. I don't think anyone saw us, but if someone did, and you get asked about it, you can say I felt sick and decided to go back to the house.'

'*Do* you feel sick?'

I thought about it. 'Yes,' I said. 'So that part wouldn't be a lie. Now go! If you run, you can still make it before the bell.'

She checked her watch, then looked at me with a kind of fear that I'd never seen on her face before, even when Gemma and Cherry were bearing down on her.

'I don't think you should just go off like this,' she said. 'It isn't safe. I ought to try and stop you.'

'Why should you? I told you I feel sick. I'm just going back to my house. Anyway, I'd like to see you try,' I said.

I got up and walked away, back in the direction of Cromwell Close. At the corner I turned and looked round, just in time to spot Josie running like fury in the direction of school. Then I turned and walked quickly home – quickly, but not as if I was in a panic, more as if I was doing something I was meant to do.

Inside it still looked as ordinary and safe and dull as ever, a place where you wouldn't expect to find any ghosts or skeletons in closets, and where nobody would have any need for hiding places. But there was something stifling about it, and always had been. Something that was very hard to put your finger on. I'd always thought that was in my head – was because of my own bad attitude. But now I realised it was to do with all the things Aunt Carrie didn't want to talk about. Like the circumstances of my mum's death. And the diary hidden in the attic. Not to mention the fact that they hadn't liked each other all that much when Mum was still alive.

In my bedroom, I took off my school uniform and put on clothes I never usually wore: a blue-and-white striped T-shirt Aunt Carrie had got for me in the sale, and a pair of pale blue cotton trousers that she'd bought for herself and had given to me because they were too short for her. (At least she'd known better than to try and fob off anything pink on me.) I checked myself out in the full-length mirror in the hall and saw that from the neck down, I looked pretty much middle-aged. As the starting point of a disguise, it'd do.

I emptied all the books and other school stuff out of my schoolbag and stuffed a hoodie in there, along with a bundled-up waterproof and the cap Aunt Carrie sometimes tried to make me wear on sunny days. Aunt Carrie would have been proud. Except I was bunking off school and taking off without permission, so probably not.

The card for the savings account Aunt Carrie had sorted out for me went into one of the zipped-up pockets inside the bag. At the time, Aunt Carrie had accused me of not appreciating the effort she was making to teach me some financial common sense. Well, I was appreciating it now. I had some cash in a drawer; that went into the other zipped-up pocket.

My old pink piggy-bank looked on blankly from its spot on the windowsill, next to the picture of my mum. All those times I'd dropped in the pennies I'd earned as pocket money for doing chores, from when I was little… And all those times I'd daydreamed about running away. But I'd never thought that I would actually do it. And now I knew what I was going to use my money for.

On impulse, I picked up the picture of my mum and put that in my schoolbag too.

This was as ready as I'd ever be.

It was high time, anyway. It had only taken ten years for me to go back.

It was tempting to just walk out of there. It really was. But in the end, I couldn't do it. Finally, before leaving the house, I left Aunt Carrie a note. I said I'd be in touch and she shouldn't worry about me, but there was something I had to do.

The next half hour or so would be crucial; round here, where people knew me and knew my stupid red curly hair, was where I was most likely to run into trouble. But after that… surely no one would take any notice of me?

Most of the time, people were pretty good at keeping their heads down and minding their own business. I'd seen that at school, when Gemma and Cherry picked on Josie and nobody intervened; I'd seen it my whole life. I just had to hope the same instinct would protect me all the way to my destination, long enough for me to find whatever there was to be found.

I put my helmet on, let myself out of Aunt Carrie's house and cycled out of Kettlebridge as fast as possible on the bike my dad had given me.

If you live in a small town on a river, the only way out is over the bridge. There was no avoiding it, not without going miles out of my way. If someone who knew me spotted me… could they actually stop me? They might try to – they might beep at me, pull over at the side of the road somewhere ahead and expect me to come to a halt. Or at the very least they might have a word with Aunt Carrie.

It was going to be another beautiful summer's day. People in shorts were crossing the bridge on foot, walking their dogs, taking the steps down to the meadows. As I sped past them and over the bridge, I glimpsed the river flowing to either side and underneath me, calm and blue and wide. I never normally thought about it, so maybe it was just because I was leaving, but suddenly it struck me as an idyllic place to spend an hour or two wandering along at the water's edge.

No one tried to stop me. I kept pedalling, along the raised pavement under the old oak trees, round a bend and uphill towards the turning for White Cottage.

White Cottage. Where Mum had met Dad and had fallen for him. Probably a mistake, on paper anyway. And yet... one thing was for sure, she'd fallen for him hard. It had been so strange reading about that, knowing that she had been only a few years older than I was when she had first met him, feeling like I had somehow broken in and was watching them uninvited. Part of me had felt like I shouldn't read on. And yet I had.

If only I could talk to her, just once. If only I could say, *I have never forgotten you, and now I'm doing my best for you the way you did the best you could for me.*

But I had no desire to talk to Dad or hear his side of the story. Every single thing that came out of his mouth from now on, I was going to turn over so I could check both sides of it. Same went for Aunt Carrie, too. And they weren't in control any more. I was.

A mile or so ahead of me was the stretch of river where I'd swum a few weeks before, sending Aunt Carrie into a panic. But I wasn't heading that way today. I turned off the main road onto a smaller road that led through flat fields to another narrow bridge. The chances of being seen here weren't quite zero, but they were much smaller than back in Kettlebridge. It looked like I'd made my getaway.

And it felt good. It felt like I'd broken out of an invisible prison, one I hadn't even realised I'd been in. I'd put them all behind me... Dad, Aunt Carrie, and the other, more shadowy figures that had been a bigger part of Mum's life than mine: Jade, Michelle. Because

I'd been so little when I'd lost her, they'd had me in a kind of trap. I'd been completely dependent on the scraps they'd let me have. And there had been little enough: the framed photo, the occasional stories that I'd clung on to. Like when Dad had told me that they'd called me Danielle because of the story of Daniel and the lion, because Mum thought I looked like a little lion and I roared like one too. Or when Aunt Carrie had said, 'Your mummy will always be your mummy.'

That was something true she'd said, at any rate.

And now I was going to find her. Or at least, I was going to come as close as I possibly could. Soon enough I'd have a long, uninterrupted stretch of reading time, and I'd find out exactly what my mum had been thinking in the last day before her death and what she had been through before she wrote down that last line:

A mother who'd just been hit was the last thing she needed to see.

If I'd had to pay for my ticket at a ticket booth, maybe it would have occurred to someone to wonder why I was travelling such a long way on my own, and whether I ought really to be in school. But as it was, I locked up my bike in the rack outside the station, put my helmet in a left-luggage locker, got my ticket at a machine using my card and passed through the ticket barrier without any problems, and half an hour later I was on the train.

This was the journey I'd made with her by road, ten years before. I couldn't remember anything about it. I wished so much that I could. I'd been in the car with her for hours and hours and hours, and somehow it had left no impression on me at all.

There was so little that came back to me. Was that normal? How much did anybody remember about being four? I'd asked Josie about this, because who else did I have to ask? Josie said she remembered certain toys, the slide at the toddler group she'd gone to, her house, and a thundery night when she'd woken up and come downstairs afraid, and had found her parents side by side on the sofa and they'd let her sit with them till the storm was over. I couldn't remember Mum and Dad together at all, and I couldn't remember the flat in London or the nursery I'd gone to. My memory seemed to start at the beach. And I couldn't really even remember that.

But I remembered the journey back. Sitting in the back seat with Dad driving and Aunt Carrie in front. A long, long drive, and sombre. Dad's car had felt even bigger and darker than usual. Like a hearse, I thought now. As if we'd had her body with us. The diary would have been in a case somewhere, along with clothes and other things from the cottage. Aunt Carrie would have done the packing, most likely. It didn't seem like the kind of thing Dad would have done. And it was probably her who had found the diary. She might not even have told Dad about it. Maybe there was some reason why she would have wanted to keep it to herself.

And then I remembered Aunt Carrie in her kitchen, at the point at which I'd begun to realise that Mum wasn't coming back.

And then starting school – the weird seriousness of it, the little tables and chairs and other children in their uniforms, and the gloomy sense that it was all going to carry on for a very long time.

Then, almost nothing until I'd walked down the road in the sunshine, one foot on the pavement and one in the road, feeling glad to be still alive. The following spring, maybe.

But what about Mum, Dad, the seaside, the sea?

When little kids drew beaches, they had a yellow line for the sand and pretty little blue curves for the waves on the sea. But it wasn't like that. It wasn't like that at all, any more than home was a rectangle with square windows and a triangle roof and flowers outside and Mummy and Daddy as stick-people holding hands. It might be like that for someone like Josie, but it hadn't been like that for me, though I had probably learned to draw it like that, the way everybody else did.

If I were to draw the sea the way I thought of it now, it would be a great scribble of blues and greys and greens that crossed the whole of the paper, with a few tiny black scrawls in the bottom right-hand corner for the pebbles on the beach. And home would be tall and narrow and dark, drawn in black and brown with a sharp, pointy roof, like the kind of tower where a princess might be kept.

I had always known that there were important, mysterious things in the roof. It was where the Christmas tree came down from, and the tinsel. And it was a space where I wasn't supposed to go on my own. But I *had* gone there, and I had stolen something from it – the diary. And I was about to finish reading it.

I didn't open it straight away. I had four hours, longer if there were any delays along the way. The train was fairly quiet – probably because the schools hadn't broken up yet – and the seat next to me was empty. I felt weirdly safe. Not quite at peace, but not that far off it: for now, I'd done as much as I could.

If I'm honest, I didn't want to finish reading the diary. I didn't want to come to the final line, the blank space at the bottom of the last page she'd written on. I'd already lost her once. I was about to lose her again, but this time I'd be conscious of getting closer and closer to the end, of the number of pages and then of lines and then words that were left. And I didn't want to cry on the train. Even though I never normally cried, I thought I might. I could feel the tears building up inside me like an overblown balloon in my chest getting ready to pop. If I lost it suddenly… well, that would blow my cover, wouldn't it? You couldn't travel under the radar if you were howling and sobbing and pounding the back of the chair in front of you with your fists.

The scenery went by: woods and clearings and lonely sheds, horses in fields, grand houses on hills, power lines. Perfect churches. A river with narrowboats moored on its bank. Big birds wheeling against the blue, lightly clouded sky. So much space, and so few people. She'd been grateful of that, in Cornwall. The chance to have nobody around. To think. She'd had me. She hadn't wanted anyone else. All she'd wanted from the rest of the world was for it to leave her alone, at least for a little while.

But it hadn't.

There had been the nosy shopkeeper, looking her up and down as if she wanted to know more, asking questions about what we were doing there.

And Dad had rung her.

I didn't know Dad all that well, but I knew him well enough to know that if he had tried to get hold of her, and failed, he would have made his way down there to find her. I knew that because it was what I was like, and that was why I was sitting there on a train to Cornwall on a Thursday morning when I should have been at school. But instead I was going to read my mum's diary, which had been so well hidden I might never have found it if I hadn't gone looking, and I was going to find out what she'd been thinking in the days before she died. And that seemed like something both my dad and my aunt had wanted to keep from me.

Chapter Sixteen
Laura's Diary

This is the part of the story that I haven't wanted to tell, or even think about. But I'm awake and alone and it's dark outside and gently raining, and the time has come. If I don't write it down now, maybe I never will. I don't kid myself that writing it down will help. It won't change anything. I'll still be here, he'll be there, and he'll still have done what he did. But if I set it down maybe it will begin to seem a little more as if it happened to someone else, and as if it belongs to yesterday rather than today or tomorrow.

At Mum's funeral, Carrie and I sat next to each other and both of us cried – Carrie more than me, which made me feel vaguely ashamed, as if, in the end, she must have been the one who loved Mum best. But I had Dani sitting right next to me and I didn't want to let go in front of her – didn't want to frighten her. The whole thing was already so strange for her, and I didn't feel free to mourn. I was too conscious of needing to keep her calm and still and quiet.

I'd brought Dani's favourite picture books to occupy her, and her magnetic drawing board, and she was managing beautifully but I couldn't be sure how long it would last. My sadness was a heavy, nagging pain that Dani distracted me from, and at the end of the service I was conscious both of the gravity of the moment – the final goodbye – and of relief that Dani had made it through.

We'd agreed that the coffin would lie in a niche at the front of the crematorium chapel during the service and would remain there till everyone had gone. As we were filing out Carrie paused in front of it and I stopped too, and Dani, who was holding my hand, obediently came to a standstill alongside us. Jon held back, waiting for us rather than lining up with us. He'd been like that throughout: sympathetic, supportive, but keeping his distance. Letting us get on with it. As Carrie and I stood together it floated through my mind that he was being *wary*. Scared at the prospect of an outburst of female emotion, perhaps. Or scared of his own feelings; it must all be a reminder of the experience of losing his own parents years before.

Was it normal, in a marriage, to spend quite so much time making little excuses for someone?

Carrie looked as if she was concentrating furiously – as if she was trying to transmit some kind of message. I knew in theory that Mum's body was in that box but I couldn't really believe it – that she could be so close and already be gone. It was as if the funeral was a process of alchemy and she was already turning into something else, and so were we, the people she had loved and left behind.

The coffin flowers were roses, white and pink. Carrie and I had picked them out together – which meant, really, that Carrie had chosen them, and I'd agreed, and then Phil had agreed too. He'd said yes to pretty much everything that had been suggested to him; I couldn't tell whether this showed we'd done a good job of coming up with ideas that he felt were fitting, or if it was because it was too much of an effort for him to disagree, or whether he was as conscious as I was of how keyed-up Carrie was about the whole thing, as if she had something to prove. Maybe he felt it was best to take the path of least resistance.

Eventually Carrie inclined her head in a final gesture of respect and moved on, and Dani and I followed her out, with Jon a step or two behind us.

We emerged into a small, high-walled courtyard with a central water feature, a big bronze cube with a waterfall effect surrounded by a pool. The funeral flowers people had sent were arranged round it – there weren't many, as we'd asked for donations for a wildlife charity instead. It was very quiet, apart from the trickling of the water feature. People were moving around in clusters, looking at the flowers, saying nice things about the service in low voices. Carrie was on her own, standing in front of a spray of rather overpowering lilies that had been sent by a cousin of Phil's, and I took Dani over to her.

Dani was quiet: the sombre atmosphere seemed to have silenced even her. She seemed to be mesmerised by the falling water. Jon was hovering nearby. I turned to him and said, as quietly as I could, 'Could you check in on Phil?'

'Phil?'

Phil was a little way ahead of us, close to the exit, with his cousin – the family resemblance was obvious; she was tall and bony and reserved, just like him. The cousin looked at a loss for words. Phil looked simply lost.

'Please,' I said.

I could see how reluctant Jon was to leave us. He glanced at Carrie as if she was trouble – as if she wasn't to be trusted – then said, 'Sure,' and backed off.

Carrie, who had seemed oblivious to all of us up until that point, turned to me and said, 'Do you think she was a good mother?'

'I'm sorry?'

She looked at me with the slight contempt of someone who is past caring about social niceties and doesn't feel like humouring anyone else's reluctance to speak their mind. 'You heard me.'

'Well, yes, I do. Don't you?'

Carrie turned to study the flowers again. She paused as if weighing up her words, as if she was wondering whether what she was about to say was worth it. Then she turned to me again. 'The problem with you mothers,' she said flatly, 'is that you all worry far too much about what other people are going to think. It's almost as if, deep down, you don't believe you deserve to be mothers at all.' And then she turned and walked off.

Dani tugged my hand and said, 'Can we go home now?'

How I wished I could say yes. But there was still the wake to get through.

'Not just yet,' I told her, and her face puckered up in baffled dismay, which was more or less how I felt, too.

It was pretty obvious from the outset that Dani wasn't going to last long at the wake, which took place at a pub in Kettlebridge that we'd been able to book for the occasion. She was tired, the atmosphere was weird, and she'd had enough of her picture books and magnetic drawing board. I tried signalling to Jon that it would help if he'd take her off my hands for a bit, but he seemed not to clock that we were heading towards potential disaster. Eventually I took her out into the pub garden for a breather only to find Carrie out there, smoking.

Dani said, 'What is Aunt Carrie doing?'

I grimaced at Carrie, who shrugged and said, 'I'm smoking, but it's something you should never, ever do.'

'Then why are you doing it?' Dani demanded to know.

'Because there's often a big, big gap between what people ought to do and what they actually do,' Carrie said, putting out her cigarette. 'Anyway, look, all gone. See you back in there.'

She strode back towards the pub, and Dani watched her go and suddenly, inexplicably burst into tears. Eventually I managed to calm her down and persuaded her to go back inside, but only by promising that I would ask Jon to take her back to Cromwell Close straight away.

I would have expected him to jump at the chance. He was standing by a near-empty plate of sausage rolls, making small talk to my elderly aunt Jemima, my dad's sister, who had travelled from the south coast for the funeral, driven by Kirsty, her fortysomething daughter. Kirsty was picking at what was left of the food with a long-suffering expression and looked as if she'd been ready to leave almost as soon as she'd arrived. Still, I appreciated the effort they'd made to turn up, and Phil's cousin, Mary, too. It wasn't as if we had much of an extended family, and the older generation seemed to set more store by turning up at times like this than my contemporaries did.

When had been the last chance for the wider family to get together? It would have been my wedding to Jon. If we'd invited them. But as it was, it had probably been my grandad's funeral – my grandad on my mum's side, who I remembered only as red-faced and very fat, and living inconveniently in the middle of nowhere with an enormous satellite dish on his roof. And before that, it would have been my dad's funeral, which I hadn't gone to although Carrie had, being five years older and supposedly better able to cope.

Which of them would turn up to *my* funeral?

A morbid thought. But days like this made you think such thoughts – to wonder what people would say about you when your time came. If they would turn up. If they would care. What might they say about me? That I had loved my husband and my daughter and my sister? That I'd loved books and children, which was why I'd gone into teaching, so I could teach children how to read?

That was how it worked, wasn't it? People spoke about the good things; they politely forgot about the bad, or didn't mention it, or didn't know about it to start with. Nobody but Jon would know how threatened I'd felt by Jade, or how hard I'd had to try to build a relationship with Michelle. OK, so we'd had our moments: Michelle had conceded that she liked my Bolognese sauce, and she hadn't objected too much to reading Dani a night-time story once in a while – had even seemed to be quite fond of her. And Michelle was a well-behaved child; she'd never tried to defy me or flown into a tantrum – Dani did a lot more of that. But with Michelle, you always had the sense that she was rolling her eyes the minute your back was turned.

She certainly wouldn't have anything heartfelt to say about me when the time came…

'Sorry to interrupt,' I said to my elderly aunt, then, to Jon, 'Dani needs to go back to the house.'

His face actually fell. And that was really the point at which I recognised that something wasn't right. Something that wasn't to do with me being an insecure second wife, or a stepmother trying to do the right thing but struggling with it, or the mum of a lively four-year-old who sometimes felt overwhelmed by the pressures of work and money worries.

It was just so weird. I'd have expected Jon to be relieved to have the chance to leave, instead of which he seemed to be keen to stay. I couldn't imagine that it was out of affection for my family. He'd got along OK with Mum and Phil, but he'd never really hit it off with Carrie.

He said, 'What, right now?'

'Yeah, I think so. She's really had enough.'

As if to prove the point, Dani kicked me in the shins, rushed over to her dad and wrapped her arms round his legs, weeping copiously.

The polite chitchat going on in various corners of the room dried up. Everyone was staring at us, some of them more openly than others. Aunt Jemima in particular looked horrified. Then she collected herself and said, 'It's very difficult for little ones, this kind of thing, isn't it?'

'OK. I'll take her,' Jon said. He leaned and murmured something in Dani's ear, and she instantly stopped wailing.

'What did you just say to her?' I asked him.

'There's only one word that has that effect on Dani. "Sweets." If only everybody was so simple.' He looked round the room at the remaining mourners. 'Perhaps you could say goodbye for me.'

'Sure.' I passed him the bag of Dani's toys.

'Well, I'll see you a bit later on. I don't suppose we'll be staying long.'

Our car was parked in Cromwell Close; we'd be heading back to London from there. Jon would drive, and Dani would doze in the back, and maybe I'd sleep, too. We would go back to our London lives, and the schools had broken up so I wouldn't be working and I could focus on Dani, and I wouldn't have to worry about Phil or the house because Carrie was here, looking after everything. Time would pass and by and by I would be able to remember Mum differently, not how she was towards the end, not what it might have been like for her knowing that the end was coming, but how she'd been when she was well and strong.

We could just carry on as normal.

There was no reason why we shouldn't… was there?

I looked at Jon – I tried to really look at him, the way you look at someone when you're first falling for them, but don't, so much, when you see them creased-looking and tired every morning, or hungry and grumpy when they come home at night. And he looked back at me, and his expression was almost a blank – as if, whatever he was feeling, he didn't want to let on.

Was it really such a big deal for him to mind our daughter for an hour or so, just while I saw to things at the end of my mother's funeral? It couldn't be just be that. There *had* to be something more.

But then, it would be understandable if he was uncomfortable around funerals, and death – the way some people are around hospitals, a kind of phobia, learned from previous bad experiences. After all, he had lost both his parents when he was still quite young. *And* his brother. Not that I really knew how he felt about all that. He didn't like to talk about it. He was guarded about his feelings, especially if they were painful. Even with me. Even after all this time.

Anyway, there was no call to go hunting for root causes, or trying to analyse him – something he hated. We'd just attended my mum's funeral. He must have been more fond of her than I'd realised. That was reason enough.

'I'll see you back at the house,' he said.

It seemed as if there might be something else he wanted to say, but he gave up on it and gently unpeeled Dani's hand from his leg – she was still clutching him as if her life depended on it – and led her away.

Half an hour later everybody had gone. Aunt Jemima was the last to depart; we saw her out to her daughter's car, helped her into the back, promised to stay in touch and waved them off. Then it was just me and Carrie standing in a near-empty car park with the usual distance between us, and I knew it was the best chance I would get to say something to her.

'Thank you so much for organising it all,' I said. 'I thought it went off really well.'

'Oh. Yeah. Well, it was OK, wasn't it? As these things go.'

'Mum would have been proud,' I said. Carrie grimaced and shrugged slightly and poked at something on the ground with the toe of her shoe. 'The turn-out was pretty good, wasn't it?' I went on. 'I was impressed that Aunt Jemima made it. She must be well on into her seventies.'

'She loves going to funerals, if you ask me,' Carrie said. 'Probably makes her feel alive.'

'Oh, Carrie. Do you have to be so…'

'So what? Honest? I expect we'll be the same at her age. If we make it that far.'

'So *cynical*,' I said.

She stared at me. Her eyes were green and as prettily shaped and unsmiling as a cat's. They were surrounded by dozens of tiny lines and had deep shadows under them. I thought I looked tired all the time and put it down to motherhood, but Carrie looked just as worn down as I did. If not more so. And older. Older by more than the five years between us. She would probably have hated me thinking that. No, she would probably have agreed with me.

She said, 'Why do you always have to be so *nice?*'

'You talk like you see the worst in people, all the time. But I don't think you really mean it.'

'Oh, but I do,' she said. 'Most people are awful. They're selfish and vain and all they think about is themselves and how to get one over everybody else. Except maybe for you. Oh, I know you probably think you're bad in one way or another, but believe me, you couldn't be bad if you tried. Why do you have to be so *good?*'

I thought she might be about to cry, and then I would have been able to hold her and we could have comforted each other and something between us might have been mended, something I'd never quite let myself realise was broken. But instead she turned and went back into the pub, and when I caught up with her she was at the bar and had asked for the final bill, and it was as if the conversation in the car park had never happened.

After we'd paid up we went back out to the car park so Carrie could drive us to Cromwell Close, which was officially now Phil's house but somehow felt as if it was Carrie's too.

'I'll spare you the standard apology,' Carrie said as we set off. 'People always say sorry for the state of their cars, don't they? Either that or they're worried you're going to muck them up. Anyway, neither of us have to worry about *that*.'

'It's not that bad.'

'It's neglected. Usually nobody else sees inside it, so it doesn't matter. That's my excuse. You can blame yours on Dani. Having a kid is a get-out clause for almost anything.'

She pulled out of the car park and onto the road that would take us back to Kettlebridge. I mulled over what she'd just said and tried not to feel hurt by it.

'I don't think Dani's a get-out clause,' I said.

'Yes you do. Why else did you leave it to me to sort out Mum's funeral? Oh, come on, Pinhead.' She hadn't called me that for years. 'I was only joking.'

'You didn't sound as if you were joking,' I said.

'Yeah, well, it's not exactly a light-hearted day, is it? Pardon me if my jokes fall flat. OK, so we've both just lost Mum but you have a family of your own to go back to and I have our ageing stepfather who needs reminding to take his pills and will leave the gas on given half a chance. So I win at misery, OK? You've won at absolutely everything else. But you didn't mean to and you couldn't help it and it's not your fault, so I can't hate you for it and I don't, most of the time. It's *me* who I hate, all right?'

'Well, you shouldn't,' I said.

'Oh, Laura, please just give it a rest, OK? Just carry on thinking the best of everybody. Including your selfish bastard of a husband. If you can keep it up, why not?'

'You shouldn't talk about Jon like that.'

Carrie let out a strained little laugh. 'Loyal to the last,' she said. 'What a good little wife you are.'

And then neither of us said anything more.

As luck would have it, the drive took longer than it should have done. We ended up stuck in one of the traffic jams that the centre of Kettlebridge was notorious for. I imagined Jon getting antsy back in the house, wondering when we were going to show up, wanting to get on our way back to London before the rush hour.

And because we weren't talking, or moving, and because I didn't have Dani with me… I had time to think.

I thought about how Carrie and I didn't confide in each other. We rarely met up, and we hardly ever called each other to chat. We exchanged brief, to-the-point emails and text messages. Mainly, we were polite. Reserved, even. She'd shown more emotion towards me since we'd left our mum's funeral service than in most of the previous years. Not quite love. Love tinged with resentment. But certainly not indifference.

I remembered how she'd always been there, in the background, at all of the key moments when Jon and I had met and it was uncertain whether we'd ever meet again, whether I'd acknowledged her presence or not. Like a shadow.

In the courtyard after the play. The way he'd looked at her. I'd been jealous. Not much, and only for a moment. But still. I'd wanted him to look at *me* like that. And he hadn't, not then. Not till later.

And then, when we'd gone to White Cottage on New Year's Eve…

The way Carrie had folded her arms and leaned against the door jamb and looked down at us. A hard look. Judgemental. Disapproving.

The kind of look I might have expected Jade to give me, if she'd found us there… except Jade wouldn't have stopped in the doorway.

That first Christmas, when I'd mentioned to Jon that Mum had invited us round, he'd said, *Is it really necessary to drag the rest of the world into it so soon?* Then he'd asked if Carrie and Stick were going to be there, and he'd been relieved to hear they wouldn't. *It's just that everything's been so perfect.*

But that was just what men were like, wasn't it? It was normal to want to put off being checked out by someone's family. It made things more serious. More public. It set you on the road to having in-laws, or to being disapproved of. Or possibly both.

In the car on the way home afterwards… what was it he had said? *They weren't at all what I was expecting.*

Even at the time, it had struck me as a slightly odd thing to say. He'd said he hadn't expected to like them. But I'd never criticised them to him. I hadn't said anything negative about them at all, as far as I was aware. Not really. I wasn't the one who was angry with Mum for remarrying, and who had kicked off by rebelling and spent years doing a very bad job of disguising her resentment. That wasn't me: I was the good girl, the one who didn't make waves. Carrie was the one who was down on them. And down on everyone, pretty much, though these days she showed it in a different way.

Except for me.

I'd always known she was fond of me, underneath it all, however moody or distant she was…

But then, when I'd told her I was getting married to Jon, she'd been so weirdly enthusiastic. Joking about how she'd be willing to wear a satin strapless bridesmaid's dress – the very last kind of thing Carrie would ever want to wear – just for me.

Like a martyr.

A martyr who'd been pre-warned and given time to prepare her reaction.

All the years I'd been with Jon, I'd felt – not all of the time, but some of the time – as if I was battling to keep up, or to make up for something. And I'd never really acknowledged it to myself, but at some level I'd believed that I felt that way because I wasn't good enough. As if it would all have been different if I was a different kind of woman; strong-willed and bold and free of self-doubt. Like Jade.

I'd been looking for a reason for something. Something that didn't quite add up. But what if I'd been looking in the wrong place?

It began to rain, and Carrie switched the windscreen wipers on, too fast at first, then, as the rain began to fall more heavily, too slow. One of the blades creaked, and the sound of it seemed to take over and fill the car till the windscreen was so wet and slick that it stopped.

The rain kept falling harder than ever. When we reached Cromwell Close and Carrie switched off the wipers and the engine, the quiet view in front of us, of trees and lawns and the end of the cul-de-sac, was almost instantly blurred as if it was dissolving and vanishing from view.

Which it might as well have been. Or maybe it was me that was vanishing and dissolving. It felt as unreal as falling in love, or saying I do, or gazing at your mother's coffin. As anything that makes you realise you can be living one kind of life one day and a different kind of life, or no life at all, the next.

I could have just walked away. It was still an option, even then. I could have decided that it was nothing and gone back to my husband and child and my home and put the possibilities that were suddenly torturing me out of my mind.

Except how could I have done? When you think you're on the edge of finding out something you didn't know, isn't it natural, inevitable even, that you'll go all the way?

I turned to Carrie. I was determined to speak very calmly, because how did I know what it might be? Also, I didn't want to betray my fear. If I could only be matter-of-fact about this, if I could establish the truth or maybe learn that I was just plain crazy, then I'd be halfway to getting this over with. Whatever *this* was.

'Carrie… the way you spoke about Jon earlier. You know… it was a bit over-the-top.'

She wriggled slightly in her seat, adjusting her position, but she didn't move to get out of the car. That was when I knew for sure that there *was* something, and she was almost ready to let it out.

'Was it? I guess you could say it's been a bad day,' she said.

She sounded resentful. That was par for the course. But more than that… she sounded *hurt*. The way people did when someone set them on edge because once there had been more between them than indifference.

I said, 'Is there something going on between you and Jon? Something I ought to know about?'

There. I'd said it. Just by saying it I'd made it possible. A flirtation. An affair. A crush. It could be that nothing had actually happened. Yes – surely nothing had actually happened. But she was my sister. Whatever it was, even if it had just been the possibility of something, it wasn't nothing.

Carrie's throat made a soft little clicking noise, as if she couldn't quite get it to work.

'You should probably ask Jon about this,' she said.

'Carrie, no. If there is something, you have to tell me now. Don't make me beg you for the truth.'

Carrie hesitated. That was when I realised that she wanted to get it over with too, and had felt that way for a long time, and had wondered if she ever would. And had been afraid of it. Both of telling me and of the prospect of me never finding out.

'There is something, isn't there?' I said, as gently as I could.

And Carrie – my sister, the only person left in my life who had been part of it since I was born – yawned and stretched slightly and said, 'It's really not that bad. It absolutely doesn't have to be that big a deal. I mean, things like this happen in families. Worse things. Really twisted, messed-up things. People get over stuff like this all the time.'

'I can hardly get over it,' I said, 'if you won't tell me what it is. You've come this far. You can't chicken out now.'

'Look, before you get all worked up, it was way before anything ever happened between you and him, OK? Years before.'

'Carrie… what happened?'

She glanced at me. She looked cornered, like a kid in class who's been told on by someone else and isn't ready to own up. She looked guilty. And at the same time I could see the beginnings of the relief I'd witnessed on many of my pupils' faces after they'd been found out for doing something wrong. It was the expression of someone who's been hiding something and no longer has to, and no longer needs to be afraid of the truth coming out, either, since the worst is about to happen and there's no way of avoiding it.

'We had a thing,' she said. 'Years ago, after I'd finished uni. Not when I was working at the garden centre – it was when I'd left that and got the job at the pub. He was still with Jade then, though the marriage was on the rocks and they were fighting all the time. He didn't want her to know, obviously. And I didn't want Stick to know. So we agreed to keep it a secret. You remember that New Year's Eve party you came to with me? We broke up soon after that. We both felt pretty bad about the whole thing, so it seemed like the smart thing to do was just to call it off. But then *you* came along.'

'I didn't *come along*. I met him by chance in London and we fell in love. And he was single. Already divorced from Jade. OK, almost divorced. As good as.'

'Oh, OK. So that's your first reaction, is it? To rub in how much better you are than I am. Fair enough. You win. You're the good sister. I'm the bad one. But we knew that already, right?'

'The point is, he was *free*. Otherwise I never would have got involved with him.'

'If you had known about me and him – if you had known that something had gone on – would it have made a difference?'

I stared at her. 'I don't even want to think about it. It makes me feel sick.'

'That's what I thought,' Carrie said. 'That's what he thought, too. But it wasn't really that big a deal, you know? And there was absolutely no overlap. None at all. There was so far from being any overlap it's pretty much like you went out with a completely different man. Still, I couldn't believe it when he rang me up and told me he'd started seeing you. I mean, what are the chances? I know how you feel, believe me. It's just that I've had longer to get used to the idea.'

I really was feeling sick. Too many funeral sausage rolls and tears. Too little sleep. And this. I couldn't help but begin to try to picture him with her. I knew them both so well. And I could see it. I could see how it would have happened at the time. Two malcontents trying to fend off despair. The disconsolate husband and the bored, lippy barmaid, discovering a mutual spark of attraction and letting it flare up, then allowing it to fade…

If it *had* faded.

But I didn't need to start doubting her… did I?

How could I not, from now on?

It was revolting. Disgusting. They had both been so cowardly. How could they have ganged up on me like this? To put me in this position without letting me know that I was in it?

Carrie said, 'If you had known, would it have made a difference?'

I stared at her. Really and truly, would it have done? His marriage with Jade had seemed like quite enough to contend with. But if I had known that he and Carrie had been lovers once too…

'What do you want me to say? If I tell you it wouldn't have made a difference, that lets you off the hook. But what kind of person would I have to be, to not be bothered about something like that – to just shrug it off like it was perfectly normal? I would have hated it. It's just too… it just feels all wrong. But if I say it would have made a difference… then that means my whole marriage has been a mistake.'

'If you wanted him enough, you would have got over it,' Carrie said.

We stared at each other. Was she right? Maybe she was. After all, she knew me better than anybody. So why did what she had just said feel like an accusation – as if she was telling me that she knew that the man I had fallen in love with would be more important to me than my sister?

'You had no right to keep me in the dark,' I said.

'It's easy for you to take the moral high ground, isn't it? Go on then. Be my guest. I'm sure it's comfortable there.'

'When he told you he was seeing me, what did you say to him?'

'It's so long ago. I can't remember, exactly. I mean, it's not like I've got a transcript.'

'I'm not asking for one. If this is meant to be you coming clean, maybe you could try to be a little less evasive.'

'Look, it wasn't just about you and him. Stick and I were more serious by then, and I knew it would make trouble if he found out I'd kind of cheated on him. Not that it matters now what Stick might have thought, but I cared about it at the time. And Jon was terrified of scaring you off. He really liked you. I mean, he said to me he knew it was something special right from the start, when he bumped into you by London Bridge or whatever. He loves you, Laura. He really does.'

Something about the self-sacrificial way she said this – as if she'd done something noble and honourable in not telling me – made me want to hit her. Or shake her. Anything, to make her shout or cry or scream. To stop her being so supercilious and hardened to it all.

'OK, let's get this straight,' I said. 'You two had an affair, which you decided to keep quiet because he was married and you had a boyfriend. Did you ever tell Stick?'

I could see that she wanted to say it was none of my business but thought better of it. 'No. What would have been the point? In the end, that was nothing to do with why things with Stick didn't work out.'

'What happened, then? I don't think you ever really told me. Did you get bored of him? Or did you go off and have another affair with someone else? One he found out about, this time?'

She recoiled from me. I'd managed to offend her. Good. I'd spent years not judging her, making allowances, cutting her plenty of slack. I wasn't going to do that any more.

'Please don't,' she said. 'Don't be so… so…'

'You don't get to ask me for anything,' I said. 'You slept with my husband.'

'Yeah, before you ever got together with him! It's not exactly a love triangle, is it? I'm like a tiny dot way back in the past, and you two are the perfect duo.'

'But you're my sister, and you always will be. That means that none of it is in the past. Can't you see, because you and Jon had this secret – even though what you had together might not have meant very much and was over years ago – you've both been betraying me all this time?'

'OK, maybe it was the wrong decision not to tell you. It seemed like the best thing at the time, and then it was hard to go back on.

Things moved so fast between the two of you. I didn't expect it to turn out this way, believe me. But, you know… if it hadn't lasted – if you'd dated him for six months and then broken up with him – I could have told you then, I guess. The truth is, Laura, you've been lucky. You have no idea how lucky. You have the prize, don't you? A husband and a child. And I have no one. I'm stuck here, reminding Phil to take his pills.'

'Are you seriously asking me to feel sorry for you? Coming back here was your choice.'

'It was *not* my choice. You think I wanted this life? I was in love with Stick. I wanted to get married to him. That other stuff – you know, the fling – that was just because I was young, and stupid, and he was going off travelling the world without me and I was stuck in Kettlebridge.'

'So why aren't you with Stick now?'

'Because he didn't want me to be the mother of his children,' she said in a small voice. 'I wanted to have a baby, and he didn't want to have one with me. He didn't love me enough, as it turned out. And it didn't take him long to move on. A year after we broke up, he had a baby with someone else.'

'You never told me that.'

'I didn't tell you because I couldn't bear to have you feeling sorry for me. But sometimes I wonder what would have happened if I'd told him about Jon and broken up with him back then. If I hadn't wasted all of that time with Stick, maybe I would have found someone else. Someone who felt differently about me.'

She looked so pitiful, so defeated, that I found I really did feel sorry for her. But I was damned if I was going to show it. Instead I said, 'Does Jade know?'

'Jade? Good God, no. Can you imagine what she would have done? Forget about what she would have done to me, can you imagine what she would have done to him?'

'She'd have killed him. I can't say I would have blamed her. I feel like killing him myself.'

'Don't say that, Laura. He might have done the wrong thing, but he did it for a good reason. He did it because he loved you. And it's not like he's ever been unfaithful. I mean, not to you.'

It was infuriating that she could say that. Maddening. That she knew enough about him to be in a position to say such a thing... that in some ways, she knew more about him than I did.

I said, 'Deep down I bet it was really satisfying knowing you had one over me, wasn't it? That you'd had him first.'

'It wasn't like that.'

'I really, really don't want to know what it was like.'

That was when she began to cry. 'Don't! Don't be like that. Can't you begin to imagine what it's been like for me all these years? He dealt with me like something stuck under his shoe that he needed to wipe off. And then I had to keep on seeing him and dealing with him. Because of you. He treats me with contempt. It could hardly be more obvious that he wishes he'd never had anything to do with me.'

'Are you trying to tell me you thought you were in love with him?'

Carrie sniffed and rubbed her hands across her face. 'He's yours,' she said. 'He's all yours.'

'OK, let's get one thing straight here. You did not give me Jon. He chose me.'

'I *know*,' Carrie shouted.

The urge to calm her down, to console her, was almost impossible to resist. She looked so wretched, sitting there in her black funeral clothes bawling, with her eyeliner smudged and her mascara running and her hair all awry. And she'd got so thin; the T-shirt she was wearing had a scoop neck – cut just a little bit too low – that exposed her sticking-out collarbones. She looked like someone no one loved or looked after. As if she'd given up on herself. I hated to see her like that and at the same time feeling sympathy for her made me furious.

'Everything I ever wanted, you've spoiled,' I said. 'I think you were never going to let the cat out of the bag while Mum was still alive to disapprove of you. Once she'd gone, it didn't take you long to get it off your chest, did it? But you know what? You shouldn't tell lies if you can't stick to them.'

'I didn't lie to you. I just didn't tell you the truth.'

But Jon had lied to me. He'd told me Jade had been unfaithful. He'd never said he had been too. And I had felt sorry for him. And all along, I had thought Jade was the enemy. The one to be jealous of. The threat. And the real enemy had been much closer to home… and wasn't really an enemy at all, was just a woman who knew love was hard to find. My sister.

Sometimes memories play strange tricks on you, like dreams. Something comes to you from long ago that's nothing to do with the present, that seems to be completely disconnected. The heat of summer in the middle of winter. Love when you're lonely. Money when you're broke, and happiness when everything is sad and grey.

That was what happened to me then. A very clear memory, as bright and transient as a bubble. Carrie and me on the carpet of the old house, the house we'd lived in before Dad died, in the time before that happened. An orangey-brown carpet, as carpets were in those days. We were children again, both of us. Me at perhaps five, not all that long after memories begin. Carrie at ten, smooth-faced with a ponytail. My conscientious big sister, playing with me and with the Barbie dolls laid out on the carpet between us.

The dolls' clothes. How I had loved those outfits! They were everything about being grown up, everything that Carrie was five years closer to than I was. In spite of the age gap between us, we had the same favourites: the white flares and pink halter-top and white chunky-heeled boots, and the powder-blue miniskirt suit that looked so good with the best things of all, the blue ankle-strap shoes.

Some of the Barbies were technically Carrie's, though I was allowed to play with them. The outfits were meant to be shared.

But I wanted the very best for my dolls, and we'd squabbled. And there had been some talk of sharing and turns, and then Carrie gave up and just let me have what I wanted.

I'd learned that about Carrie already; if I made a fuss, she usually backed down. And if she didn't, Mum usually told her to. But that little victory hadn't been enough. Later, after we'd tidied up and when no one else was around, I'd retrieved the two best outfits from the box and hidden them in my room. It wasn't enough for me that she'd let me have them that one time. I wanted to keep them somewhere she'd never find them, where they would be only mine. I knew it was a bad thing to do even as I did it – I knew it was wrong – but still, it was darkly satisfying. And I hadn't got into trouble for it. Nobody had ever found out. After Dad had died, when we were packing up to move out of the house – long after I'd forgotten where I'd hidden them, or that I'd ever even taken them – the costumes had come to light. Carrie had said she'd wondered where they had got to, with only the faintest hint of suspicion in her voice.

Perhaps she hadn't really minded that much. Perhaps, after all, she'd been a bit too old for dolls.

But in the end, who was I to hate her?

She was gazing at me. I could see the hope in her face, and I knew she was about to stake her claim – not to Jon, but to me.

'I love you, Laura,' she said.

'I love you too, for what it's worth. I wish I could say I hated you. But I don't. If I'm honest, I understand why you did what you did. Maybe I might even have done something like it myself.'

Her face crumpled up as if she was about to start howling again. She closed her eyes and composed herself, then looked at me and said, 'I'm sorry.'

'Sure you are. But you know who the most important person in all this is? It's not you and it's not me, and it's not Jon and it's not Mum. It's my daughter, and I'm going to get her now and take her home.'

She looked alarmed, as if she'd forgotten that we were about to leave. 'What about Jon? You won't do anything drastic, will you?'

'I'm not going to stick a carving-knife in him, if that's what you mean. I don't think so, anyway. We'll get back to London, and then we'll see. I presume Phil doesn't know about any of this?'

She shook her head.

'OK, so here's what we're going to do. We're going to go back in there and act perfectly normally. Or as normally as possible. I guess there is no normal on the day of a funeral. Especially not a day like today. Jon might smell a rat, and Dani will even if she doesn't realise it, but that's OK. I just don't want Phil being upset. He's been through enough.'

She inclined her head and I felt a faint thrill of power, a sense of finally being in the driving seat, that almost instantly faded away.

'There's just one more thing,' I said.

'What?'

'Promise me you'll never tell Dani, whatever happens. This is one thing she never needs to know.'

'OK,' Carrie said, so quickly it was obvious my request had come as a relief. Which was no surprise, really.

Carrie didn't have all that much contact with Dani, but I knew she was fond of her. She always remembered Dani's birthday and sent her something for Christmas, gifts that were usually either for the wrong age range or slightly missed the spot in some other way, but still, were kindly meant. And if Carrie cared about Dani, it would matter to her what Dani thought of her. And what would anyone think of an aunt who'd had a fling with their dad?

I got out of the car and made my way across the lawn to the house. It had always seemed so normal – an ordinary, quiet, well-maintained suburban house with a neatly kept front lawn, net-curtained, scandal-free. But then, it also looked like exactly the kind of place you might live if it mattered for you to keep up appearances. If you'd decided you could keep going as long as no one else realised that things were not what they seemed or guessed how you might really feel.

Mum had always wanted Carrie and me to be close. To be happy. To protect us.

And now we weren't happy, and we weren't close, and she hadn't protected us from anything.

The front door opened before I reached it. Jon must have been aware of us sitting in the car, talking. He'd been watching and waiting for us to come in. It must have occurred to him to wonder what we had been talking about. Or had he just assumed Carrie would never break her silence, especially not today?

He looked a little worried. But not nearly worried enough.

He'd taken off his jacket and tie and undone the top button of his white shirt. Seeing him there, his familiar body in the unfamiliar funeral clothes, was like an insult. It took a conscious effort not to remind myself what that body had done to my sister, all those years before. What she had wanted him to do to her. And what he had wanted, too.

He said, 'Is everything OK?'

'As OK as it's going to be,' I said, and brushed past him without a kiss or a smile, or without even meeting his eyes.

They'd put the TV on for Dani, who was sitting on the carpet watching cartoons. Phil was in the armchair, sound asleep. He was waxy pale and barely appeared even to be breathing. But then, why shouldn't he look like death? He'd just lost the last person he would ever really love. Maybe that should have been a lesson to me, a way of putting things into perspective. A reason to forgive. But I didn't have that in me, not then. I still don't know if I have it in me now.

I wanted to scoop Dani up, hold her close, lose myself in the comfort of loving someone who had never done anything to hurt me. But that would have to wait. First, we had to get out of there.

'Dani, love, it's time for us to head off. You should go to the bathroom before we leave,' I said, and turned the TV off. Normally she would have protested, but she didn't. Perhaps she knew I meant it. She got to her feet and went obediently off to the downstairs cloakroom.

'We don't have to rush off,' Jon said. 'You can take your time. As much as you need.'

'I thought you were keen to get away before the rush hour. Anyway, it's been a long day for Dani, and you've got work tomorrow. We should make a move.'

Carrie had gone through to the kitchen. I could hear her moving around, tidying up. Trying to stay out of the way. If there was going to be a scene, she wouldn't want to be part of it.

'Laura,' Jon said, 'are you sure you're OK?'

'I'm fine,' I said in a tone of voice that challenged him to contradict me. 'Just tired.' That much at least was true. 'I'll get Dani's stuff together.'

'I can do that.'

'You'll miss something, and then Carrie'll have to post it and it'll just be a nuisance.'

'Trust me,' Jon said firmly. 'You look like you need to sit down.'

And I did. My legs suddenly felt unsteady under me, and I sank into the nearest armchair.

Jon said, 'If you want you can check up on me before we go. How hard can it be? Round here, kiddy stuff sticks out like a sore thumb.'

He knelt on the carpet to scoop up the toys I'd packed for Dani and put them into the bag we used to cart her stuff around. I didn't want to think about it, but I couldn't help it – the picture just presented itself: me packing Dani's bits and pieces for a visit, the way Jade must have got Michelle's stuff ready so many times, weekend after weekend. And then handing her over to him.

How could I possibly carry on loving a man who'd turned out to be such a liar?

And yet... what would life be like if I didn't?

'Her cup's probably in the kitchen,' I said.

'Yeah. Sure.'

He went off to fetch it. I wondered whether Carrie would take the opportunity to try to tell him what had just happened, or whether she'd keep her head down and leave it to me to do it. Probably the latter. She'd probably be too scared of him to broach it. He wasn't going to be pleased with her when he found out. He'd want to blame somebody, and he didn't have a great track record when it came to finding fault with himself. Problems were usually somebody else's fault. The economy, the internet, the stupid government, other drivers, other people. The weather. The whole world and the various ways it kept tangling with him and putting obstacles in his path, slowing him down, making him poorer, less healthy and more stressed, and forcing him to stumble.

I couldn't face talking to him. Not yet. Anyway, he'd probably figure it out soon enough.

Dani had gone into the kitchen too. I could just about make out what she was saying, something about there not being any soap in the cloakroom. She sounded self-important, as if she was enjoying making the point about how good she was at washing her hands. Anyway, there was no need for me to move to help her; she already had Jon and Carrie at her beck and call.

I reached for the magazine on top of the coffee table and began to leaf through it. Dani was chattering away to her father now, like a nervous guest at a dinner party. 'Look, Daddy, the handwash bottle doesn't work. The pump is stuck. It's not very well made, is it, Daddy? Maybe Aunt Carrie has another one. She should take this one back to the shop. Daddy, can you fix it?'

Can you fix it? He would surely want to. The question was, could I bear to let him?

'Daddy? Daddy, will you help me with my shoes? I want you to help me.'

Then the low rumble of Jon's voice: 'I thought you could do the buckles, Dani. After all, you're a big girl now, aren't you?'

'I am big,' Dani said. 'But I'm not *that* big. Not all the time.'

He'd been a good dad to her. He loved her. He wouldn't want to let her go.

He'd told me once that he regretted letting Jade have primary custody of Michelle, that he should have pushed for more. What if he decided to fight me for Dani?

And Dani would hate it if we broke up. We were her world. There was nothing relative about parents, not for a little kid. No point of comparison. Your mother wasn't just a mother: she was *the* mother. The only one who mattered. And the same for your father.

And your sister, if you had one. Or maybe you didn't. You might not have a mother or a father either. But you'd have someone. And that someone, at least to start with, would be all you had.

I turned the pages of the magazine. It was a travel supplement from the Sunday paper; I imagined Carrie leafing through it, fantasising about getting away. She didn't travel much these days; she'd told me she didn't want to go away on her own, and anyway, she didn't want to leave Mum alone to cope with Phil. That had struck me as an excuse. Somewhere along the line, she'd lost her nerve.

What had happened was so tawdry. So humiliating. Like something out of a soap opera. I had done nothing wrong, and yet I was ashamed.

The magazine on my lap was open at a picture of a seaside village. The sky was warm and blue; the sea was a deep shade of turquoise, calm and almost still, washing up on a sandy beach in a sheltered bay. The surrounding hills were the kind of green that you only see somewhere with plenty of rain. They were topped by patches of yellow gorse and sturdy white houses.

Cornwall. I'd never been. It was somewhere you heard people talk about; I'd always had it in mind as somewhere we might go to one day.

Jon put his head round the door. 'We're ready if you are,' he said. I put the magazine aside and got up and went into the kitchen to say goodbye to Carrie.

Somehow, we got through it. It was all so ordinary, really, as long as you carried on going through the motions, just as you might have done at the end of a normal visit. I didn't embrace Carrie, but I did manage to speak to her, and to ask her to say goodbye to Phil, who was still asleep.

Carrie made no attempt to hug Dani or Jon, but then, she wasn't really a huggy person at the best of times. She did come into the corridor to see us off; she held out her hand to us and waved, a stiff little gesture that kept us at arm's length. I was trying to avoid meeting her eyes but glimpsed her expression. She looked shattered. She looked as if she couldn't have felt any worse.

And then we were in the car. Jon's car, a huge thing that I was terrified of driving – I'd nearly scratched it once or twice and he had not been impressed. But what right had he ever had to get annoyed with me about anything, given what he'd been hiding from me right from the start?

'We didn't have to rush off quite so soon,' he said. 'You could have had more time.'

'It's been a long day. I don't know about you, but I'm ready to go home.'

He shot me a quick sideways look; I could almost hear him wondering if Carrie had said anything. 'Is everything OK?'

'Under the circumstances, yes.' My voice sounded shrill. Like a nagging wife. An unreasonable wife, who might make a big deal of a long-ago fling her husband had tried to spare her feelings about. So what if it was with her sister? After all, it was before they'd even started seeing each other.

'I suppose things are as all right as they've ever been,' I added.

Jon shot me another quick look and then set off without saying anything else. He'd probably concluded that I couldn't possibly know, because I wouldn't have been able to keep it to myself for a minute if I had. After all, nagging wives weren't known for their restraint.

Well. Jon wasn't the only person in our relationship who was capable of having a secret. It was just that, until then, it never would have occurred to me to keep something from him.

Chapter Seventeen

Dani

Until then, it never would have occurred to me to keep something from him.

I read those words and looked up from the page and saw the sea.

It took me a while to move. I couldn't bring myself to close the diary and put it away in my bag; couldn't do anything other than sit and stare at the view sliding past the train window.

We were passing through holiday country, along the coast, far south and west of Kettlebridge. I saw an estuary crowded with bobbing boats and fancy homes with balconies and bay windows and sunrooms. There were clusters of white cottages in distant green valleys and buildings nearer the shore painted in bright colours that had faded and peeled in the salty air. And then the train whisked us past gardens with palm trees and pampas grass – plants I associated with hot countries overseas – and across a bridge over a broad stretch of greenish water, more the colour of the sea than of river water, into Cornwall.

That was when I began to feel properly distant from home, not quite as if I'd escaped, but certainly as if I'd left and wouldn't be going back – or wouldn't be the same when I did.

I realised that I'd felt trapped without really being aware of it, or recognising that it might be possible to live a life where you didn't feel that way. It was a taste of freedom, and it seemed so natural – as if being free was something I'd had but had lost and had then forgotten about. Maybe it was how I'd felt in the front seat of the

car with Mum driving us down the motorway to get here, coming
away with her for an unexpected holiday that seemed a bit like the
kind of thing you weren't usually allowed to do.

We travelled inland, away from the sea, past great curves of
the river and huge, rolling hillsides dotted with sheep, and onto
a remote valley covered in a forest of fir trees. The light seemed
different here, as if the sun was travelling through a different part
of the sky, or maybe it was just that there was more of it, more of
everything that wasn't people or buildings or roads. She must have
noticed that too, as she got closer to the end of the journey. *Our*
journey, except she hadn't made it back.

It was no wonder, really, that she had wanted to get away from
other people. Everyone except me.

But Dad had been on his way to her or maybe had even been
with her when she died.

I could ask them about that. Aunt Carrie, and Dad. There would
be a version of events. It would come from Dad, most likely, and
then Aunt Carrie would most likely corroborate it. Funny how
often they'd acted in cahoots, those two, even though they made
out that they didn't much like each other.

The question was: would I ever be able to trust either of them
again?

Which was pretty much what *she*'d been thinking in the days
before she died.

And now I was nearly there, closer than ever to the truth of it
and to the place where it had happened, and I was afraid because it
was such a huge and terrible thing – the drowning, the death, and
all the secrecy and guilt that had prompted her to come here in the
first place, and that had grown up all around the memory of her in
the years since. But I had to keep going, too, because I had yearned
for her for so long – my mum, with her smile and her brown eyes
and her hand in mine, and her love for me that had been so very
real that I could still feel it.

I had forgotten so much else. I had forgotten almost everything. And maybe in some ways it was easier to forget, and dangerous to remember.

What might I have seen and heard, at the cottage and on the beach? Had he come for her – for both of us? What had I been a witness to – and would going back to the cottage and the beach bring it back? Was it possible to recover memories you had buried, or once they had gone, were they gone for good?

It would have been a comfort to think there was nothing to lose by carrying on, but I didn't believe that. There was a huge amount to lose. I'd already found out that Dad and Aunt Carrie had been cowards and that they'd lied. What if there was worse to come?

Sitting by the window on the train, hurtling towards the scene of Mum's death, I hated the pair of them. All those years I had thought Dad was distant and Aunt Carrie was gloomy because we had lost Mum. Now I knew there was a cloud of guilt over both of them. But what if they had even more reason to feel guilty than Mum had been able to tell me?

I wasn't even sure what I was accusing them of, really. Murder? Conspiring to kill her? She had drowned. But when she went under, where had he been? Where had I been? And what had he told Aunt Carrie afterwards?

It all seemed so far-fetched, to be sitting there imagining that my dad could even begin to be capable of doing something so terrible as letting my mum die. Unthinkable. Anyway, why would he have done it? To keep me? In which case, why had he shown so little interest in me since… as if even coming near me hurt him?

It was crazy to even think about it. But I did.

He was someone I didn't know, who had done something Mum hadn't known about till years after. Maybe all grown-ups were like that – shadowy collections of little things you were familiar with and bigger things that were hidden from you.

But Mum hadn't been like that.

Mum had loved him, she had loved Aunt Carrie and she had loved me. When she ran away from everything else, she'd taken me with her. It was me and her against the world. It was still me and her against the world; it was just that we weren't together any more.

The least I owed her was to find out as much as I could about what had happened to her.

And soon I would. I was getting closer to the blank pages at the back. Mum was about to run out of time.

My heart was pounding. It felt as if the train might be about to come off the rails, as if everything was about to whirl out of control.

I looked down at the diary, at her handwriting which had become familiar now, and wasn't so hard to read. Familiar and strange at the same time. I don't know why, but it seemed as if this was my last chance to read what she'd written to the end. As if I was running out of time too.

Chapter Eighteen
Laura's Diary

It has not been a good morning. OK, so it could have been worse. Nothing catastrophic has happened. But still…

Maybe it's because I haven't slept. I still feel antsy. Or maybe it's because we're at the halfway mark now, and in a few days' time I'll have to hand back the keys and pack up and drive back to London and face the music. Which means Jon, really. And I'm not ready to face him yet. I don't know whether I'll ever really be able to forgive him. Or her.

And yet part of me feels I should be able to forgive both of them. For Dani's sake. If it wasn't for her, I'd be off. I'd never go back. Or at least, it would be much easier to leave.

To top everything off, Dani's bored and it's still raining.

We went down to the corner shop, for something to do as much as because we needed anything. Dani talked me into buying her one of those overpriced magazines with plastic toys stuck on the front. As I paid for it, I tried and failed to remember the name of the woman behind the till, and attempted some small talk anyway: 'Miserable weather, isn't it?'

'It'll pass,' she said. 'Anyway, it lays the dust.'

Lays the dust. Perhaps that was all this was, the whole trip. All that dust from the past, now washed away. The chance for a clean start. Or a clean break. One of the two. Or both.

Mandy. That was what she was called: Mandy. So there – I could still function, could get by in the world, do all the small, necessary things that are part of everyday life. Names. Shopping. Greetings. That was a measure of how much of a shock it had been – that I'd come to doubt myself to that extent. In a sudden rush of confidence, I decided to keep talking.

'We went to a beautiful beach the other day, and Dani's desperate to go back. We're just waiting for the right weather,' I told Mandy. 'St Angel's Cove. She loved it. It was really quiet, considering the time of year. Bit tricky to find, though. We took a couple of wrong turnings.'

'Anywhere that's easy to get to is always going to be crowded,' Mandy said.

'I don't suppose you know why it's called that, do you? It's a lovely name.'

'I don't know, I'm afraid. But I can tell you there's a song about it. "St Angel's Air." It's about meeting a lady in a veil on the beach and falling in love with her. Then the singer has a big surprise, because the mysterious lady in the veil turns out to be his wife.'

'Oh dear. I guess the wife probably isn't very pleased with him.'

'The song just ends there. Guess the moral is it's easy to fall in love with anyone as long as they keep a veil on.'

Was that how everybody felt, if they stayed married long enough? As if they'd stared in the face of reality and learned to live with it?

I was suddenly conscious of my bare hands: I'd left off my rings that day. I hadn't let myself think about it too much; I just hadn't put them on, as a kind of experiment. It didn't really feel all that different. I'd almost forgotten I wasn't wearing them. I was only noticing their absence because I was aware of Mandy noticing it too.

'Well, anyway, it's a beautiful beach,' I said. 'I've never actually been to Cornwall before. This is my first time. Hers, too.'

I gestured towards Dani, who was standing by the magazine rack and eyeing up the magazines she'd reluctantly rejected in favour of the one I'd just paid for. If we loitered here too long, she'd want another one. It was probably time to go. And yet… It was a while since I'd made conversation with another adult. I was reluctant to break off so soon.

'What made you come here?' Mandy asked.

'Oh… it was just a last-minute thing. I looked on the internet, and there'd been a cancellation and the cottage was free, so I snapped it up.'

'You were lucky,' Mandy observed.

'Yeah.' I glanced over towards the windows; the rain was still trickling down them. 'And we've been lucky with the weather, mainly. So far.'

'I think it's meant to brighten up later.'

'Really? Oh well, if it does, we'll probably go and try to find St Angel's Cove again.'

'Yes, well, drive carefully, won't you? There's some nasty hairpin bends on those roads, if you're not used to them.'

'I'll take it slowly. Anyway, you'll know where to send the search party if we don't reappear.'

Dani interrupted us with a plaintive request for another magazine. She knew she wasn't likely to succeed, though, and she didn't kick off when I said no. Instead she came over to the till and started eyeing up the sweets.

'She's a dear little thing, isn't she?' Mandy said, as if Dani wasn't right there and more than capable of understanding her. 'I'm guessing her daddy has red hair.'

Was it an intrusive thing to say? But that was what happened when you started talking to people; they took it as a cue to try and find out more about you, and you couldn't really blame them. Anyway, she was right.

'He does,' I agreed.

Dani picked up a packet of sweets and waved it at me. 'Mum? Maybe a little treat, if I'm very good?'

'OK,' I said. Jon was always buying her sweets; usually I tried to resist, but just this once wouldn't hurt, would it?

I paid for the sweets and Mandy said, 'Hope the sun comes out for you. Enjoy the beach if you get there.' And then I put Dani's hood up and ushered her out and got the umbrella up, and we made our way back to the cottage.

It was only once we got there that I realised I'd missed a call. Not on the cottage landline, which I'd left unplugged, but on my mobile – for some reason it had gone through to voicemail. Reception was spotty round here; maybe you couldn't get a signal from inside the shop.

It was Carrie. She'd rung twice, actually. First time she hadn't left a message, second time she'd steeled herself to say something.

'Hi, Laura. Look, I know you're going to be angry with me, and I don't blame you. But Jon drove up to see me and I told him where you were. I really felt I couldn't refuse. He's been tearing his hair out. I'm just leaving this to warn you, because you might hear from him.'

Typical. Absolutely typical. I should have known.

I'd asked her to do one thing. Just one. To keep quiet.

All those years when she couldn't bring herself to open her mouth. Yet the minute I'm the one who asks her to keep something to herself, and Jon's the one trying to get her to talk… she cracks.

But maybe I had known, deep down, that sooner or later he would ask her where we were, and she would tell him.

Maybe I wanted to rub it in, to make it plain to her that Dani and I were the ones he really cared about. Maybe I shouldn't have run away the way I did, taking Dani with me… Leaving the two of them to figure out why.

The truth is I wanted them both to suffer, the way they've made me suffer. It may not be reasonable. It's not kind. But that's how I feel.

And yet I can't help but feel sympathy for her, in spite of myself. The way she's lived her life over the last few years, she's punished herself already.

Jon, though… Jon is a different matter.

The instinct is there all right: the urge to make him pay. I'm just not sure it's a good one.

Maybe we shouldn't have come. But after what happened just before I left – once the initial shock had passed and the truth had begun to sink in – it seemed like the only option. To run away… if only for a little while.

I told Mandy that I came here because I found the place on the internet, which is true. It's where people find all kinds of things, isn't it? Answers and temptations, long-lost lovers, old friends. I found a cottage by the seaside that just happened to be free for a week in August. But I didn't tell Mandy what prompted me to sit down and search for it. There's a *deus ex machina* in this story, something that forced me into action I might not otherwise have taken. Or rather, someone. Jade.

The evening after we got back after Mum's funeral was filled with the usual domestic things: making dinner, clearing up, getting Dani in the bath, putting her to bed. After that I came downstairs to find Jon yawning. He said, 'I think I might turn in. I've got to be at the garden centre early tomorrow. If we have another couple of good Saturdays, it'll really help. Problem is, it's almost too hot to go to bed.'

'I think I'll sleep on the sofa tonight.'

'Really? Why?'

'I want to be on my own.'

He stood up. 'Laura… are you sure you're all right?'

'No. I'm not all right, actually. But I don't think there's anything much you can do about it.'

He hesitated, moved forwards as if to attempt to give me a hug, then thought better of it. 'Jade's bringing Michelle round tomorrow. You won't forget, will you?'

I had completely forgotten. 'No, of course I won't.'

'Look… I should be the one to go on the sofa.'

'No, it's OK. I have a feeling I'm not going to sleep much anyway.'

And I didn't; it took me forever to drop off, and then I was woken up by Dani's face peering down at me. She looked as if she wasn't quite sure whether this was a joke. 'Mummy! What are you doing down here?'

I sat up and did my best to compose myself. Bluffing is essential when you have a kid. I could bluff well enough to fool Dani, surely.

'That is a very good question. Silly old me. I was up late watching TV, and I just fell asleep.'

'Then why have you got a pillow and a sheet?'

'Well, I decided to get really comfy before I started watching my programme.'

'Was it a scary programme?'

What had I watched? I couldn't even remember. 'Not particularly, no. Why?'

'Because you were shouting, just now. Like you were having a bad dream, the way I do after I see something a bit scary.'

'What was I shouting?'

'It sounded like, "Get off! Get off!"'

'Oh. I don't remember any dream.'

'You're forgetting a lot of things,' Dani observed.

I got up and fixed her breakfast, and by and by Jon came down. He was never at his best in the mornings; it was the time when he was least likely to want to talk. He looked very tired. Usually I would have been sympathetic, but I just wanted him gone.

He made what was an effort, though, for him. He always made his own coffee in the morning – I never got it quite the way he liked it – and after he'd plunged the cafétière he turned to me and said, 'You OK?'

I shrugged. 'Same as yesterday. Not really.'

'Have you got anything planned today?'

'Not really. The park, maybe, before it gets too hot. If it's going to be another stinker we'll want to be home in the cool from lunchtime.'

'If you need anything – if you want to talk or something like that – you call me, OK? I can come back. And if you want some time to yourself over the weekend… just tell me. You could go to a film or something, go shopping, whatever. I can babysit.'

'It's not babysitting. It's taking care of your daughter. Both your daughters, since Michelle's going to be here too. It's harder work than you might think.'

'I know it's hard. And it's not an easy time.' He gazed at me with that expression I'd come to know so well: watchful and wary. Now that I knew a little bit more about what might be going on behind it, I saw it as calculating. 'Have I done something to annoy you?'

'You haven't annoyed me. No.'

'Because I know things have been tough for you lately, but you're being cold with me and I'm not sure what I've done to deserve it.'

Dani, who was sitting at the kitchen table drawing, suddenly piped up: 'You annoy Mummy when you don't put your stuff in the right bin, Daddy.'

'All right, all right,' Jon said. 'It's get-at-Daddy time, I see.' He drained the last of his coffee. 'I'm going to have to go,' he said. 'I hope you have a good day. Or least a peaceful one.'

He came over and kissed me rather self-consciously on the cheek. He didn't embrace me – he had obviously picked up on the vibes that a hug wouldn't be welcome – but he patted me on the shoulder. I'm sure he was trying to be comforting, but it didn't feel it. It just felt like a touch I didn't want.

'I'll see you later,' he said.

The answer that presented itself to me was, 'Don't count on it,' though up until then I hadn't consciously thought about running away.

On his way out he stooped to look at the picture Dani was drawing – it was her in a swimming pool, a happy stick figure in a square of blue – and praised her, and she beamed at him with that special, uncritical adoration that young children have for their parents, and older children never do.

She was so very far from being disillusioned with him. How would she be able to understand it if I took her away from him? How would she ever forgive me?

'Call if you need me,' he said as he was leaving, and again I didn't answer.

It was a relief to have him gone. Although not that much of a relief, because I carried right on having the discussion with myself that I hadn't had with him. What should I do? What did I want? What was best for Dani? What was the right thing to do? And so on and so forth, as I sorted out the laundry and mopped the kitchen floor and cleaned the oven for good measure.

Dani and I were just about to set off for the park when my phone went off. It was Jon.

'Laura?'

At least he cared. He cared enough to take time out of a busy day at a busy time and check up on me.

'Look, I'm sorry to bother you like this, but I thought I'd better give you advance warning. Jade wants to come round.'

'Jade?'

'Yeah, she wants to pick up something Michelle left here last weekend. A swimming costume. Do you have it? I mean, do you think you'll be able to find it?'

It was briefly tempting not to be helpful. But I did know what he was talking about; Michelle had left a plain black swimming costume on the drier the weekend before, and I'd left it on her bed for her.

'Yeah, I know where it is. But what's the urgency? Michelle's going to be here tomorrow. Can't it wait till then?'

'She's going to someone's pool party this evening, and that's the only costume she feels comfortable in, apparently. I mean, you know what she's like – she's not exactly confident. Jade said to tell you she's setting off now, so she'll probably be with you in half an hour or so, if the traffic's good. Is that all right?'

'I'm just about to go out to the park with Dani. You can tell Jade to call me on my mobile if we're not back when she gets here. See you later.'

And with that I finished the call. Dani said, 'Who were you talking to, Mummy? It sounded like it was someone you don't like very much.'

'Actually, it was Daddy,' I told her, and steered her out of the house.

In the end we were back home well before Jade showed up.

She looked bad-tempered and resentful, but that was how she usually was when I saw her and there was nothing else to indicate that she'd just been stuck in traffic for the best part of an hour. She was wearing a close-fitting T-shirt and tiny shorts and was toned and tanned; she had hardly any make-up on but still glowed with good health, and her dark hair was as glossy and bouncy as if she'd come straight from a salon. However bad-tempered she was, she was hot, there was no doubt about it; sexy hot, not the sweaty kind. I felt a pinprick of jealousy prompted by nothing more personal than seeing a woman who, like me, was a mother – who had a teenage daughter, for heaven's sake – and yet who wasn't mumsy at all, who was still confident in her own attractiveness and had every reason to be.

'I think this is what Michelle wants,' I said, and handed over the carrier bag I'd left by the front door with the swimming costume in it.

Jade peered inside as if she half expected me to trick her by putting in something that was completely irrelevant. 'Thanks. This is a big deal for her, you know? It's so difficult at that age. Before you're really sure of yourself.'

I thought things would probably be a lot easier for Michelle if she didn't have a mother who looked like Jade. But I decided not to say so.

'Are you OK?' Jade went on, looking me up and down. I couldn't imagine that she was impressed by what she saw.

'Oh, you know. As well as can be expected.'

'Well, at least it's over, right? The funeral bit of it, anyway. Believe me, I know how hard it is. It's like having a wedding to organise when the person you love is dead. And then it's all so formulaic. All those people saying, "I'm so sorry for your loss." When my mother died, I felt like saying to them, "What do you know about my loss?" Actually, I felt like punching them on the nose.'

'I think that might have been what I said to you.'

'Oh, everyone did. But seriously… are you sure you're OK? You don't look so good.'

I didn't have the energy to take offence. 'Bit hot. We just got back from the park.'

'Tell me about it. I could hardly sleep last night. Tossing and turning all the time. Would you mind giving me a glass of water? I'm so dehydrated. I like sunshine as much as anyone. When it's at the beach. But this, in London… It's too much.'

I hesitated. She never normally came in. And then I stepped back and said, 'OK.'

Once she was inside and settled at the kitchen table, Jade asked for ice and a flannel too, and wrapped the ice in the flannel and pressed it against her cleavage. Dani came in and looked at her askance and then turned to me as if to say, *What is* she *doing here?* Her reaction was such an honest version of what I was feeling that I had to suppress the urge to laugh.

'Mummy, isn't it our lunchtime?' she said.

'It will be in a minute, sweetie.' I drew the line at inviting Jade to stay for lunch.

'I hope it's a short minute. I'm very, very hungry,' Dani said warningly.

'Hi, Dani,' Jade said pleasantly. 'Don't worry, I'm not staying.'

Dani didn't look convinced. She gave Jade a baleful glare and withdrew to the living room to carry on playing.

'She's a cute little thing,' Jade said.

'Well, she wasn't especially just then. The heat doesn't suit her.'

'She's tired, I expect. And, you know, picking up on stuff, the way kids do even if they don't really understand. Maybe you should get away. Take her down to the coast for a few days. Or go north, where it's cooler. Anywhere's better than London in a heatwave.'

'Yeah, well, we can't really get away. Jon's got a lot on at the moment.'

Jade rolled her eyes. 'I would have thought, after all these years, he'd be able to step back once in a while. To have somebody deputise.'

'It's high season. This is when they make their money.'

'Sure. Well, I guess it's none of my business. But you're a teacher, right? You've got the whole summer off. You and Dani could go somewhere, couldn't you? Even if Jon can't get away.'

I shrugged. Normally I might have said, *It wouldn't feel right to go away without him*. Now I wasn't so sure.

'You should think about it,' Jade said. 'Why should you stick around here, in the heat? Maybe you could go with a friend or something. Or your sister. You have a sister, don't you?'

'I have a sister. I'm not going to go on holiday with her.'

I hadn't mean to sound aggressive, but I did. Jade frowned. 'What, did you fall out or something?'

'You could put it like that,' I said. And then – because it was hot, because I wanted to shock her, because who else would care? – 'I found out about something she did.'

Jade's perfectly groomed eyebrows went up. 'Something she did? What, has she got some ex-boyfriend's body in the freezer? Don't look at me like that. It's a joke, OK?'

She put the flannel with the ice cubes in it down on the table and raised her hands in a gesture that could have been either mocking or a sign of surrender. Her nails were, as ever, manicured and gleaming, painted a deep, shiny red.

'Go on, then. What did she do that's so very terrible you won't go away with her?'

'She slept with Jon.'

Jade's mouth dropped open. Then it curved in a slight but unmissable smile.

She was shocked... but she was amused, too. And that could only mean she hadn't understood.

I'd seen that expression plenty of times before, on the faces of kids at school when someone did something that broke the rules and was about to get in trouble for it. If someone transgresses, one of the natural reactions, along with disbelief, is to laugh – as long as you think it doesn't affect you.

'The dirty dog,' she said. 'He had an affair with your sister? That's quite the betrayal. Not an easy one to forgive and forget.'

The ice I'd given her was already melting; a small, glistening patch of water was already spreading from the flannel, darkening the wooden surface of the table.

'It was before I got together with him,' I said. 'At the time, the only person he was betraying was you.'

Her reaction was as instantaneous as a cat pouncing or a hawk descending on a mouse, talons extended. She stood up, reached across the table and slapped me across the face.

The sound of it was so loud my first thought was that Dani would come running in and I'd have to find a way to explain. But the only person staring at me was Jade, who'd straightened up now and was looking down at me with the closest thing I'd ever seen to pure murderous hate.

'You're a liar,' she said.

'You were seeing other people, weren't you? What makes you think he wouldn't do the same? There's no motive like revenge.'

For a moment I thought she was going to slap me again. 'We might have had our problems, but Jon's a good man,' she said, and I was taken aback by the slight tremor in her voice – as if she was upset as well as angry, as if she needed to think of him that way, as a virtuous victim of her own bad behaviour. As if it distressed her to hear him accused by someone else.

'You might not want to hear it, but that doesn't mean it's not the truth. Why would Carrie lie?'

'You tell me. Because she's desperate and jealous and a loser and a fantasist. Because she's gone nuts. Maybe she even believes it. How should I know? She's your sister. Your problem.' She pointed at me. 'You have to sort this out, Laura. I don't want Michelle coming round here, being stuck in a poisonous atmosphere, wondering what on earth's going on. I get that you're grieving, and it's a difficult time. But you need to talk to Jon. Clear the air. And maybe you should believe in your husband a little bit more. Sure he has his faults. He's selfish and obsessed with his business and I don't think he's ever enjoyed a party in his life. But he's not a cheater.'

With that she stooped to pick up her handbag and the carrier bag with Michelle's swimming costume in it. Then she walked out, slamming the door behind her.

I picked up the flannel she'd left on the table, wrapped it into a ball and squeezed it. The ice cracked between my fingers; water dripped onto the table. I pressed the flannel to my stinging cheek to cool it and thought how easy it would be to get so angry that you could do someone real harm – not just a slap, but the kind of harm that draws blood or breaks bones.

In a minute Dani would remember that she was supposed to be hungry and come in asking where her lunch was. She needed everything to be as normal as possible, the same as usual in spite of the heat; she needed to be able to carry on believing that what adults did made sense. I hoped she wouldn't notice the mark on my face, that it would have faded enough by then to be inconspicuous. A mother who'd just been hit was the last thing she needed to see.

Chapter Nineteen
Dani

The trees thinned out and there were more fields and then the train began to slow down. We were approaching Bodmin. There were little planters with flowers at intervals along the platform; it was shaded with trees and it was quiet. There was one man waiting there, holding a bike, wearing a hat and a paint-stained shirt. He got on with his bike at a carriage further along the train and I got off and slammed the door shut behind me.

It would have been nice to have been met there – to have someone come along to pick me up and take me on the next leg of my journey – but who would I have wanted to meet? Nobody. Nobody who was still alive, anyway.

My legs felt a little weak, but they would have to do. I made my way out of the station to the taxi rank.

Nothing.

There was a sign with a number you could call for a cab; I rang it and someone said it would most likely be a half-hour wait.

It had just gone three; normally I would have been looking at the classroom clock and counting the minutes till home time. There was nowhere to sit, so I squatted down with my back against the wall and settled in to wait.

My phone rang before the taxi came. Predictably, it was Aunt Carrie. I didn't answer. She rang again. Then she sent me a message:

Just tell me where you are and that you're safe.

I tapped out a message, hesitated, then pressed send.

Don't pretend you care.

I knew I was being childish. Vindictive, even. But she'd kept Mum in the dark for so long. Me, too. Why shouldn't I keep her in the dark now?

There was a pause. It was warmer here than back in Kettlebridge; I was beginning to wish I'd worn shorts instead of the blue trousers. I drank a bit more of the fizzy drink I'd bought on the train. Not the kind of thing Aunt Carrie approved of. Well, Aunt Carrie could go stuff herself.

Another message:

When are you coming home?

I pictured her pacing round the house, torn between anger and the usual guilt. Wanting me back so she could shout at me, most likely. Well, she deserved to pace. She deserved to worry. Why should I put her out of her misery?

Then I was holding the phone and my finger was moving across the screen and I couldn't stop myself and didn't want to.

When were you going to tell me about Mum's diary?

I pressed send.

There was really no reason for me to be afraid of her. There was much more reason for her to be afraid of *me*.

I watched a dandelion seed floating on the air, circling in the eddying breeze and drifting down towards the ground. And then I waited and waited, but there was no answer.

Maybe she was making her way up into the loft so she could check for sure that I'd taken it. Maybe she'd fallen through the plaster and broken her neck. Who cared?

But it bothered me as time went by, and another train pulled in and moved on, and I still didn't hear from her.

I was retracing Mum's steps in more ways than one. I'd been dead set on getting away, but I didn't really have much of a plan for what I was going to do when I got there. I knew I wanted to find the shop and the cottage and the beach… but that was about it.

Finally my taxi driver appeared. I got to my feet and he pulled up at the empty taxi rank and wound down his window.

'Going to Port Mallion?'

He made it sound like the most normal, ordinary destination in the world, like he was just about to drop me off at a shopping precinct or a leisure centre. A place that was tame and safe, not somewhere darkened by bad luck and bad faith and maybe even deliberate malice.

Maybe even murder.

But I didn't really think that, did I? Her death wasn't anybody's fault. It was an accident. A tragic accident. Wasn't it?

And Dad had tried to save her, and he had failed. Or so he had told me. But what the diary had told me was that he wasn't to be trusted.

I climbed into the back seat of the taxi and the driver accelerated away. I sat holding onto my bag as tightly as I could, because everything I had to remember Mum by was in there.

I'd never got a taxi before, certainly not on my own, not with anybody as far as I could remember. The driver didn't seem at all curious about me, which was just as well because my small talk wasn't great at the best of times. He had the radio on, so it wasn't like there was an awkward silence. I tuned out the music and tried to figure out what I was going to say to the people I would meet when I got there.

Ten years ago, there was a woman staying at a cottage up the road who drowned. She had a little girl with her, a little girl with red hair.

Or would it be better to come straight out with it: *My mum was staying around here ten years ago just before she drowned at St Angel's Cove. I'm trying to find people who might remember her…*

But as we headed out of town I stopped worrying.

At first the Cornish landscape reminded me of home – the softness of it, the low, flattish fields you find in a river valley. But then the road ahead began to rise and was enclosed by hedges and trees to either side, so that we were travelling through a green tunnel which occasionally opened up to offer a glimpse of rolling hills and distance, turning blue at the horizon. Next we emerged into a different kind of countryside, higher and harder and more exposed. There were fewer trees lining the road, and they had been bent out of shape by the wind. And finally we rounded a bend and the sea came into view on our right beyond the curve of the hill.

It was an intensely deep-blue mass reaching to the horizon, in contrast to the paler blue overhead. The sky was hazy and floaty and dreamy – the sea looked like something only a fool would try to cross. It wasn't at all a cosy little blue holiday sea that you might paddle in. It looked formidable and indomitable. Well, it was the Atlantic, wasn't it? My geography was hit and miss, but I was pretty sure of that.

The scale of it made me feel weirdly calm. Next to *that*, the power of it and what it had done, what was there to be afraid of? I was more sure than ever that I was heading in exactly the right direction.

I asked the taxi driver to drop me off as close as possible to the sea. I thought I might as well take a look at it up close. Besides, I wanted to walk round a bit and get my bearings before actually attempting to talk to anyone.

The lanes that led down to the harbour were narrow and busy with holidaymakers strolling along, on their way to get ice creams and postcards and take in the views and whatever else people did on holiday. In the end, I got the taxi driver to pull over, and paid out a chunk of my savings to cover the fare. And then the taxi went and I was on my own.

I made my way down to the harbour. It was small, with a few brightly painted rowing boats lined up on the jetty next to stacks of plastic crates and mesh-covered boxes that looked as if they were designed for catching things, or keeping them – lobsters maybe, or something else that lived in the water. The tide was out, exposing mud flats striped with long cracks that reached almost as far as the breakwater across the mouth of the bay. From here, the sea looked almost tame – a calm pool of shallow turquoise water on this side of the breakwater, a glimpse of deeper blue beyond it.

The air was like nothing I'd ever breathed before, light and clean and salty, reviving in the same way that sunshine in January is reviving. It didn't seem menacing at all; it seemed idyllic. It didn't seem like a place that could kill you, somewhere you might visit and not return from.

My phone rang.

It was Dad.

Part of me really, really wanted to ignore him. But another part of me had been waiting for this ever since I'd cycled out of Kettlebridge, and that was the part that won.

I answered the call. He said, 'Dani. Where are you?'

'I'm looking at Port Mallion harbour. It's very pretty. Did you ever get to see it?'

He exhaled. It was hard to tell if he was relieved or angry. Or both. 'What are you planning to do next?'

'Oh… I thought I'd take the place in. The sights. The sounds. Soak up the atmosphere, you know?' I paused. 'Then I thought I might see if there's anyone around who I can talk to. You know. Someone local, who was living here ten years ago. Someone who would remember.'

'Don't do that,' Dad said.

'Why not? I'm here. I might as well.'

'You don't want to go talking to strangers in a strange place. Look, why don't you walk along the beach? Get an ice cream, eat some fish and chips or something. Have you got money?'

'Yeah, I've got cash.'

'Be careful, all right? Keep yourself to yourself. People can be dangerous, OK?'

'I know,' I said, but he carried on as if he hadn't heard me.

'You end up going off into somebody else's house, you never know what could happen. So don't. I'm going to come and get you. Depending on the traffic, I should be with you early evening. I'll take you out for dinner somewhere, and we'll talk. I know you read the diary, Dani. I know what's in it, and I know you have questions. Whatever you think of me right now, I am the best person to answer them.'

'Yeah, well, I'm not sure I feel like listening to you right now. I mean, I guess it's nice of you to drive all this way to come and get me. I guess it shows you care. Or maybe it just shows you feel bad. And maybe you *should* feel bad. I mean... Aunt Carrie. It's kind of hard to get the thought of you two out of my mind, you know? It's disturbing. Anyway, at least now I know why Mum came here. It was about as far away as she could get from the pair of you without actually leaving the country.'

'Oh come on, Dani. Really? You really think we deserve to be punished like this? For what? For something that happened before you were born, before I was seeing your mother? What kind of judge and jury are you? It is ancient history, Dani. It has nothing to do with anything. And it's no reason to do what you're doing now.'

Suddenly I felt very tired. 'You should have told her,' I said.

'Maybe, but I can't do anything about that now. And if you stop to think about it, Dani, I think you'll understand why we didn't say anything to you.'

My tiredness was rapidly mutating into being on the verge of tears. 'Yeah, because you were embarrassed and ashamed. So many times I've seen that look on your face. I thought it was because of me. I thought there was something wrong with me. Whereas all along, it was because of *you*.'

'Oh, Dani… I have never, ever been anything but proud of you.'

'Well, I can't say the same for you,' I said.

I ended the call and set my phone to silent and put it back in my pocket. Then I stood and stared at the harbour for a while, at the breakwater and the boats moored by the jetty that were aground on the mud flats for now but would be lifted off them by the incoming tide. I listened to the sound of seagulls and it struck me as harsh and sad. I thought about Dad getting ready for the long drive here – getting in his car and setting off – and I felt bad but not bad enough to call him back.

When I'd been staring at the sea for long enough to be sure that I wasn't about to burst into tears, I turned and started making my way up the steep narrow road that led away from the harbour and into the heart of the village.

I didn't feel at all brave. I felt crazy, like someone in a gale looking down from a cliff or a tall building; like a person at the edge of everything.

The shop at the end of the lane was still there, and it still sold sunhats.

There was a whole rack of them: straw ones, plastic visors, caps that said things like 'Captain' or 'Captain's Mate' and little cloth hats for kids, like the one Mum had got for me. I stood there for a while just looking at them. I probably looked at them for longer than she had; she'd had me to distract her.

It was quiet in the shop and if the girl behind the till had been paying attention my behaviour would probably have struck her as pretty weird, but she was busy playing something on her phone and didn't look up. People go on about phones like they're the world's evil, but sometimes they save the day. I was left in peace to look around at the displays of snorkels and flippers and beach toys and swimming costumes and children's magazines and imagine myself here with Mum, ten years before.

I didn't remember the place at all, not even vaguely. There was nothing particularly special about it. Still, I liked standing there. Because she'd written about it in her diary, it felt like I knew it. It even felt as if I had some kind of stake in it. Like it belonged to me, just because it had been part of her story and was now part of mine.

Before I left, I went up to the girl and asked her if she knew Mandy, who'd run the store ten years ago. She looked blank. No, the store wasn't owned by anybody of that name any more. No, she didn't know where Mandy might be.

Then I asked her where Curlew Cottage was, and she stopped looking quite so blank and started looking vaguely suspicious. 'Why do you want to know?'

'My mum brought me here for a holiday when I was little. We stayed there. I just wanted to see what it looks like.'

'Why don't you ask your mum?'

'Because she's dead. So are you going to tell me or not?'

We stared at each other. The girl didn't look embarrassed or unnerved. Perhaps she was used to intense strangers. Perhaps this kind of thing happened a lot if you worked in a shop that a lot of tourists passed through.

'If you come out of here and walk up the lane you'll see it,' she said. 'Just keep going, it's near the end. There's a family staying there at the moment. I wouldn't hang round there for too long, they'll think you're up to no good.'

I thanked her and turned to go. She said, 'How did your mum die?'

'She drowned. It was just along the coast from here. The cottage was where she'd been staying before it happened,' I said and walked away quickly, without looking back.

*

The cottage was the first thing that really me feel I'd been there before. It was something about the size and shape of the windows; it was like coming across a clip from a TV programme I'd watched as a little kid and knowing I'd already seen it.

Mum had described the place as if it was a refuge, miles away from anywhere. It wasn't quite as remote as I'd expected, but still, it was a good walk uphill from the shop. It was just as well the girl had mentioned it was towards the end of the lane, as otherwise I'd have assumed I'd gone wrong.

But there it was, just as it had been ten years ago: Curlew Cottage, set back from the lane and surrounded by slightly overgrown hedges, with a picture of a fat little bird with a long beak on its nameplate.

No wonder Mum had reported that I'd slept well there; even at fourteen, the walk up the hill was enough to leave me out of breath. I was surprised I hadn't whinged more, to be honest. It might not have been the first choice of place to take a four-year-old. But then, she'd booked it on the off-chance. She'd thought herself lucky to find something. She *had* been lucky, finding somewhere in peak season at short notice. It was just that not very long after, her luck had run out.

I'd half expected the cottage to be spooky. Grey and ominous, overgrown with briars. And it wasn't. It was charming. How could it not be? A little white-painted cottage under a blue seaside sky? It was a place where other people had been perfectly happy. People who had normal, lucky lives, where the worst thing that happened on holiday was hitting a bit of traffic on the way home or forgetting to pack the suncream for the beach one day and having to go back for it.

There was a family staying in the cottage, just as the girl in the shop had said. Their car was parked on the gravelled area in front of the house, and a couple of the windows were open. I could even see one of them: a boy a bit younger than me, sitting on a bench next to the pub-style table on the lawn at the side of the cottage.

He was wearing one of those short-sleeved wetsuit-type tops that parents at the splash park in Kettlebridge put their kids in when they're worried about sunburn and skin cancer, and he was sorting through something – football stickers, maybe. A girl about my age, dressed in a frilly-sleeved T-shirt and shorts, came out of the house carrying a cake on a plate and said something to him. Something rude, judging by his reaction. She sat down opposite him and pulled a face at him and then their mum came out, carrying a tray of tea, and she was all smiles.

It was then that I knew I wasn't going to try to speak to them. How could I? How could I darken their day by reminding them that people could die here, people not so very different from themselves? Instead I withdrew slightly to the side of the hedge, so I'd be harder to spot if they happened to look round, and I spied on them.

The mum was pretty and blonde and fit and toned. She reminded me a bit of Josie's mum, though she had longer hair, the kind that lots of girls have but not many women. Her kids looked more athletic than Josie and her sister, though, and maybe a bit more competitive. I was glad to see there was a little bit of friction even in Paradise. The girl seemed to be at odds with her brother, and he looked as if it baffled him when people, especially his sister, got annoyed with him – as if it was hard to understand why everyone couldn't just adore him the way his mother did.

The dad came out with a bottle of beer. He was wearing a patterned, short-sleeved shirt and shorts, probably louder clothes than he'd have worn at home. Fun clothes. He was a fairly successful businessman type, likeable, easy-going up to a point that was probably hardly ever reached. Pleased with his lot, and why not? Money, health, love: if life was a lottery, it looked as if these people had won it.

Most likely *he* hadn't slept with his wife's sister before getting married.

Watching that other family, I could almost find it in myself to feel sorry for Dad. Poor old Dad. He'd only gone and fallen for the wrong woman. In the wrong way. *Twice*. You couldn't afford to make that kind of mistake if you wanted a picture-perfect life. You couldn't afford to make any mistakes at all.

I'd never seen Dad relax. He was wary and guarded and you always had the feeling that he was thinking more than he was saying, more than he'd tell you. And probably he was.

Another word for him came to me as I stood there watching somebody else's dad lean back and swig his beer and soak up the sunshine, then break off to quiz his children in that way some dads have, as if it's essential to keep them primed for success.

Dad was *haunted*.

Maybe we all were. Maybe being haunted wasn't about an apparition in a white sheet at the end of the bed. Maybe it was about memory, and fear and guilt. Maybe you could be haunted by someone who hadn't been scary at all in life: someone who'd been warm, who had smiled at you and held your hand. Someone you'd loved. And who had loved you back.

Where had all that gone? How could it just disappear?

A wave of sadness crashed over me. The other family looked so safe. So untouchable. I hated them a little bit, but only because I longed to be like them. I wanted to be like that. And I never would be. I was the person on the outside, the watcher, the one who lived in the aftermath of a disaster that nobody wanted to talk about.

All of a sudden, as if she'd sensed me watching her, the girl turned and looked straight at me.

I bolted. There was no way I was going to present myself or go into explanations. First off, they'd be freaked out, and then, if they believed me, they'd feel sorry for me, and then they'd start asking questions about who I was with – they looked just the sort for that. The kind of people who liked to do things officially. Josie's mum had felt sorry for me but that was OK because I'd stuck up for Josie and Josie looked up to me. But a family like that, faced with a runaway? Let's just say I didn't want to give them any more reasons to feel great about themselves.

I didn't stop till I reached the end of the lane. Then I fished out the card the taxi driver had given me earlier and rang up to get a ride to St Angel's Cove.

The woman at the other end of the line told me that there was nothing available for at least the next two hours. And no, there wasn't a bus service or anything like that.

Then she said, 'If you don't mind walking, you could always try the coastal path. Probably take you about forty-five minutes? Lovely views.'

I thanked her, said goodbye and checked the map on my phone.

A dotted line marked out the path along the cliff-tops. Mum had managed to get lost when she drove me there, but if I just followed the edge of the sea it wouldn't really be possible to go wrong.

I'm definitely not a long-distance kind of person. Cross-country was my idea of hell; slow and tiring and boring. Sprinting was all right, or cycling, anything where you could go fast. Or tennis, where you could whack the ball but didn't have to be in a team with a captain and a load of other irritating people yelling at you about what to do.

Swimming wasn't really my thing either – unless it was to cool off. I could get by, but nobody would have put me in a gala. As for hiking... forget about it. Walking for pleasure was for old people and people who had too much time in their hands. I did it because I had to, to get from A to B, and as soon as Dad had given me my bike I'd used that instead.

But if you had to walk somewhere, well... that cliff path to St Angel's Cove wasn't a bad place to start.

For a start, you had to watch your step. It was up and down all the way, and sometimes there were little holes in the path, or near it, that had probably been made by animals. I had the land to my right and the sea on my left. The cliff-edge wasn't very far away, and the sea was a long way down. It wasn't quite as dramatic as walking on a high wire, but still, I had to concentrate.

After a while, I sank into a kind of trance. I wasn't thinking about anything apart from the next step and what I was seeing and hearing and feeling; the sun on my skin, the soft sound of my footsteps and breathing and the waves, the green grass and blue sky and deeper blue of the sea.

It had clouded over a little, enough to give a bit of respite from the heat although the sun kept coming out again. Once or twice I stopped and sat down to take in the view and drink a little more of what was left of my fizzy drink. Each time it was harder to get up again. But that was fine; that meant a little less energy for thinking about everything and trying to work out what I ought to be thinking about it.

Every now and then I'd pass somebody; a family with kids and a dog, or young people in vests and shorts, or an oldish couple with bandannas tied round their necks and athletic-looking walking sticks, thin metal poles with a spike at the end. They said hello to me, and I said hello to them and walked on. I guess it looked as if what I was doing was wholesome: why should they have been concerned?

Finally, when it had begun to seem as if I would never get there and the whole of the rest of my life would be spent trudging along the cliff path, I rounded a bend and there it was. St Angel's Cove.

There was a well-worn sign announcing it, a sign with two warnings underneath:

DANGER – CLIFF EROSION.
STAY WELL BACK FROM THE CLIFF EDGE
AND BEWARE OF FALLING ROCKS.
DANGER – STRONG CURRENTS.
THERE IS NO LIFEGUARD AT THIS BEACH.
NOT SAFE FOR SWIMMERS.

Underneath the warnings was another sign:

Please take your litter home with you.
Please don't let your dog foul this beach.

I guess if you survived the rocks and the water, the least you could do was to tidy up after yourself.

Had the warning sign been there before Mum had drowned? Perhaps they'd added it after.

What if she had *wanted* to die? This was something I'd never let myself think before. It didn't sound like something she was contemplating in the diary – but what if the urge had suddenly overtaken her? Was it possible for something like that to happen? Could her frame of mind have changed so dramatically between putting the last full stop at the end of the last sentence and arriving at the beach that day? And if so, why?

She wouldn't have abandoned me. Or would she? If she had suddenly somehow been overwhelmed by despair, and had given into a violent impulse, something she would never have done if she'd been in her right mind? Had kept on swimming, until it was too late to go back...

It felt like a betrayal of Mum to even consider it.

I came to the path that spiralled down to the beach. Here and there it had flights of steps or stopping places, but most of it was rough earth, baked hard by the sun. I began to make my way down.

Who would choose to drown, anyway? To force themselves through the moment of awful panic when what flowed into your lungs was water and not air, and there was no stopping it? To choke and sink and know your life was ending? It would hurt. It wouldn't hurt like a bullet or a knife or like burning or falling, but it would be agony all the same. I couldn't believe she would have done that to herself... not Mum, who had laughed and held my hand and looked back over her shoulder at my dad and his camera as if to say,

Remember this. Who'd had so much of her life left to live. Who'd had *me*… so who cared if Dad and Carrie had let her down? There was no need to let them destroy her. She should have defied the lot of them: taken me and told Dad and Aunt Carrie to get lost. Especially Dad. And she should have hired the meanest divorce lawyer she could find and taken White Cottage off him as well.

Surely that's what she would have done, if she'd lived? Maybe not the mean divorce lawyer part. Still… why not? What was the thing Aunt Carrie sometimes said? *Don't get mad, get even.*

What if it hadn't been like that at all?

Dad was a strong swimmer. I knew that, just as I knew he'd won races and played rugby when he was younger. But Mum might not have been.

What if they had swum together… and he'd left her out there, knowing she wouldn't be able to make it back?

But that was a terrible thing to think. Maybe he had told me the truth – that he had tried to save her and had been too late.

I made it to the bottom of the path and stopped to look out across the beach and take it in.

It was beautiful all right. It was the perfect cove, with a curve of soft, smooth, creamy sand enclosed by rough grey cliffs. Even if it didn't already mean so much – even if it wasn't at the heart of the mystery that I still didn't quite know how to solve – it would have made a big impression on me.

It seemed like a secret place; you could imagine smugglers here, or anyone who wanted to escape unseen. The sea was an impossibly deep blue, fading to turquoise closer to the shore and then breaking into silvery white foam where it met the sand. It was gorgeous, and it was easy to see why Mum had brought me here. It would have been like something from a dream… if only I could have had it to myself. But a few other people had discovered it too.

There was a family on the far side – Mum, Dad, two smallish kids and a sandcastle. A younger version of the family that I'd seen back at Curlew Cottage. Always there were families, wherever you went, squabbling or being happy but being together. You couldn't get away from them.

In the middle of the beach there were two girls in bikinis; one of them was posing while the other one took a picture. It made me think of Gemma and Cherry, posting pictures all the time as if they might cease to exist if they didn't. Which wouldn't have been a bad thing, in my opinion. I hoped that back in Kettlebridge, Josie would remember my advice and stand up to them as much as she needed to.

I found a spot where I could look out to sea without either the bikini girls or the family group getting in my line of sight and settled down on the sand to watch the waves rolling and breaking. Such small, harmless-looking waves. I could see why Mum might have been tempted to swim. The idea of a dip would have appealed to me too, if not for the sign by the cliff path, and if what had happened to her hadn't been like an invisible hand holding me back.

A dead hand.

I drew up my knees and folded my arms on them and rested my head on my arms. Then I closed my eyes and listened to the sound of the waves breaking and sucking at the sand as they moved back. It was the softest sound I could ever have imagined, and yet it was the strongest and the steadiest. It just kept going, like an unstoppable heart. I supposed it would be like that forever, quieter sometimes and louder at other times, right up until the end of the world.

There was so much I hadn't known. And there was so much I had forgotten, so I knew no more about it than a stranger would even though I had been there at the time.

All the way, I had been expecting St Angel's Cove to be terrifying. For it to be a dark, haunted place, or to seem like that even if the sun was shining. I'd expected my reaction to it to be a more intense version of what I sometimes felt at Aunt Carrie's house: that there was an oppressive force circling all around us, something that you couldn't see but that filled you with instinctive fear, taking the light out of the air and making it hard to breathe.

But it wasn't like that at all.

It was bright and the sand was soft and the waves were the most soothing thing I'd ever heard, and it felt just as safe as if someone had been right there looking out for me.

I shifted so that I was lying curled on my side, with my bag under my head as a pillow. I closed my eyes and breathed deep. And then I let myself go back.

They weren't memories so much as moments – split seconds cut off from the time before and after them. They could have been dreams. I remembered how I had felt, but what I could see was hazy and imprecise. I couldn't be sure what order they came in, or where I had been.

In the first moment I was on my dad's shoulders, and he was walking, and I was very high up, as if on an elephant. There was sand underfoot and clear air and a kind of emptiness around us. I wasn't happy, exactly. I felt like he was paying me my dues. Like he owed it to me. Like when you ask for something and an adult gives you something else to shut you up, and you're won over for the time being, but you're still not really satisfied.

The next moment was a shock.

I was wet. Wet through, right to my underclothes. Small and wet and cold and shivering. And I was alone. Nobody was touching me or keeping me warm. Nobody was telling me what to do. And nobody could hear me, either. There was sand under my feet and the ground was all that was holding me up, and the sky reached all the way down to where I was standing, and the only thing wrapped round me was air.

And that was all.

That was all there was.

My heart was pounding. I kept on breathing, felt the warmth of the sun on my skin, reminded myself I was here and now and safe and those moments were long ago… if they were even true, or anything more than strange little tricks of the mind.

I tried so hard. I came all this way. And I still don't know what happened.

Then it was as if I was listening to an echo, or the kind of words you sometimes hear when you're on the edge of drifting off: *You know there's nothing to be afraid of, though. Don't you?*

Chapter Twenty

Right there on the beach I did something really stupid. Stupid and dangerous. I fell asleep. Deeply asleep, into the kind of sleep where you don't dream and you're not conscious of anything.

I didn't stir until I realised that someone had hold of my shoulder and was shaking me and I heard Dad's voice saying: 'Wake up! Dani, come on, it's time to wake up!'

And then I came to and saw his anxious face and took in the sand and the waves and heat and remembered where I was. And in spite of everything I was glad to see him.

Perhaps that was really why I'd run away, when it came down to it. Because I had wanted to find out whether he would bother to come and get me. And how I would feel when he did.

It took a little while for the shock to wear off. Once I was sitting up and had pulled myself together the first thing I said was, 'Have you got anything to eat?'

'No, I haven't. Sorry,' he said.

He was fiddling with his phone, sending a message. To Aunt Carrie, probably. *Found her, safe and sound.* I supposed she'd be relieved. Or maybe not. Maybe she would have quite liked never to have to deal with me again. In which case the feeling was definitely mutual.

Dad put his phone away. 'I'm parked up at the top of the cliffs. I'll take you somewhere to eat. Are you done with Port Mallion? Because I could do without going back, if it's all the same to you.'

'I think so,' I said, yawning and stretching. 'Have you just been there?'

'Yeah. Carrie told me the diary you found mentions the cottage, and I thought you might have gone there. I asked if they'd seen you and one of the kids said a girl with red hair had been lurking round there about tea-time. They were pretty concerned, actually. The guy was all for coming and helping me look. Made me take his number and promise to call him if he could do anything and to let him know when I'd found you.'

'Well then, you'd better put him out of his misery.'

'All in good time.' He looked me up and down. 'What are you wearing? Is that your idea of a disguise?'

I patted the pale blue fabric of my trousers. 'It was enough to get me out of Kettlebridge.' Then I pulled a strand of my hair. 'I thought this might get me spotted, but I had my bike helmet on.'

'Yeah, Carrie said you'd taken your bike.'

'I left it at the station. Locked up in one of the racks. And the helmet's in a left-luggage locker.' For some reason it seemed important to assure him that I had been careful.

He let out a sigh. 'I guess you know she's been worried sick.'

'Well then, she doesn't need to worry any more, does she?'

'She's not going to stop worrying just because I've found you.' He shaded his eyes and looked out to sea. 'Why'd you fall asleep? It was a pretty silly thing to do. You could have been robbed. And you could have had a nasty shock when the tide comes in.'

'Someone would have woken me up.' The bikini girls had gone, but the family were still there.

'I would have thought you'd have learned by now not to rely on other people to keep you from getting into trouble.'

'You know what? I can't quite believe that after everything that's happened, you're giving me a lecture about falling asleep on a beach.'

'You can't use other people's mistakes as an excuse for your own stupidity. Or you can, but it won't help you much when things go wrong. So, what do you think?'

'Think of what?'

'This place. The cottage. The beach.'

'I don't feel what I thought I would. I don't know what to feel. You?'

He shrugged. 'Like I said, I'd rather not have had to come back.'

'Dad… how did it actually happen?'

He kept his eyes on the skyline. 'Freak current. She wasn't actually in that deep, but it carried her out.'

I said, 'Where was I?'

'You? You were on the beach.'

'Did I see it? I mean, did I see her being swept away, and you going in to get her? Because I don't remember it. I don't even remember the beach, not really.' But as I said this it seemed to me that I *did*, that it was coming back – the dark cliffs looming behind me, and something terrible in front of me. Something I couldn't see. 'It's like my memory starts with the drive back from here, and Aunt Carrie being in the passenger seat and being in Aunt Carrie's kitchen. But before that, there's hardly anything. I remember going on your shoulders and I think that might have been on a beach, but I can't be sure. And then I remember being really wet through, but with all my clothes on, and crying and it seems like there was nobody there. But I don't know when that was.'

He was looking at me oddly. Almost as if he was scared. 'They say that memory tries to protect you. You were very small, Dani. Don't torment yourself trying to remember. It's for the best if you don't.'

'If I can't remember, then you have to tell me. I know you probably don't want to talk about it, but you're only person who can.'

'It's just… I don't know where to start.'

'Believe me, I don't want to hear about all the stuff with Aunt Carrie. Start when you got here. How did Mum react when you showed up? Going by what she said in the diary, it's hard to predict.'

Dad hesitated. Was he trying to think of a way of describing it that would spare my feelings, or getting his story straight? Or both? And if you had to stop and think to put your facts in order… did that mean that you were lying? Or just that it was hard to tell the truth?

'She wasn't best pleased when I arrived, to start with,' he said. 'But then she kind of warmed up. She always found it hard to stay angry. And she could see you were pleased. So then she said we might as well all go down to the beach together. It was a lovely day.' He turned to look at me again. 'It was a freak accident, Dani, that's what you have to remember. It was really unlucky, the equivalent of being struck by lightning. There's never a good time for something like that to happen. It shouldn't have happened, but it did. And at the point when it happened – just before that – the three of us had been together and she was happy because *you* were happy, Dani. You mattered more to her than anyone else in the world. More even than me.'

My nose had started running and I had to blink back tears. Stupid tears! What good would crying do? Everybody knew it did no good at all.

'I wish you could have saved her,' I said. 'I know you tried. I just wish you could have managed it. I wish we'd never found this beach. I wish it had carried on raining that day and we'd stayed home. I wish we'd never come here, that we'd gone somewhere else where there wasn't any sea. Or that Aunt Carrie had just kept her mouth shut. If Mum had never found out about all that, she'd probably still be alive. And what did it matter, anyway? Some stupid fling, ages and ages ago. Nothing like as important as Mum carrying on being alive.'

'Believe me,' Dad said, 'you're not saying anything about it that I haven't thought already. It was stupid and it was unlucky and it was tragic, and it never should have happened. And if things had turned out just slightly differently, it wouldn't have done. But we are where we are, Dani. We can't go back and we can't change it.'

'I know that,' I shouted. 'You don't have to tell me. It's so obvious.'

And then I started really crying, louder than I ever had before, louder than I would have thought was possible. I was crying too hard to be aware of anything or anybody else. Then I realised Dad was awkwardly shifting a little closer to me and putting his arm across my shoulders, very tentatively, as if he half expected me to lash out if he tried to touch me or at the very least to shrug him off. I was conscious, too, of the family of four a little way across the beach, looking in our direction and wondering whether to intervene.

Finally I wiped my face with my hands and got a tissue out of my bag and blew my nose. Aunt Carrie had always been big on me carrying a packet of tissues. For once, I was actually grateful to her.

I got to my feet and glared at the other family, who politely looked away, and said to Dad, 'I'm ready to go now.' Then I set off across the sand at such a pace that he had to hurry to catch up with me.

It wasn't until we'd made our way back up the cliff steps and were in the car that he said what he must have been waiting to say all along.

'Can I see the diary?'

Now it was my turn to hesitate. 'You said Aunt Carrie had mentioned it. Have you ever even seen it before?'

He shook his head. 'After what happened, Carrie came up by train to help me with everything. She packed up all your stuff. Then I had to go back again later to sort out getting rid of your mum's car. Anyway, she was the one who found your mum's diary. But she never told me about it.'

I didn't want to hand it over. I really didn't. But I couldn't bring myself to say no. Instead I leaned down and unzipped my bag and took it out and handed it over to him.

His hands were trembling. Trembling badly, like an old person's, like someone who needed looking after. He looked at the cover, at the doodle of the dancing couple. Then he glanced at the first page and the last, just as I had done, and closed it.

'Thank you,' he said. 'Is it OK with you if I take care of it from now on?'

I stared at him. 'You can't do that. It's mine.'

'I'm afraid it isn't,' he said, so gently that I knew he meant it and there was no way I could talk him out of it. I had a brief, wild impulse to snatch it right out of his hands – but how could I beat him? He was bigger and stronger and more sure of himself. And he was still my dad.

'Carrie should never have had it,' he went on. 'She should have given it to me. You should never have had it either. Carrie stole it from me and then you stole it from Carrie, and I understand why you did and I'm not angry with you about it, but now I need you to let me keep it.'

'It's not my fault Aunt Carrie didn't give it to you,' I said.

'I know,' he said, and reached behind him to put the diary on the back seat.

I felt dreadful. As if I'd betrayed Mum – and as if I'd lost some big game that I hadn't even been aware I was playing. I was suddenly sure that he hadn't told me the whole story about what had happened that day. In which case… how could he be trusted with the only piece of evidence that was left?

He said I'd stolen it. I hadn't. I'd found it. But maybe I would get the chance to steal it back. Maybe there was something in there that I'd missed, some other crucial clue…

'You'd better take care of it,' I said. 'You can't just leave it on the back seat. What if someone stole the car? It'd be lost forever.'

He said, 'Don't worry, when we get to where we're going I'll make sure it isn't left behind.' Then he started the car.

I meant to remind him that I needed to get something to eat, but then I must have closed my eyes and drifted off again, because next thing I knew we were on the motorway and the light was beginning to fade.

We stopped soon after that and got a twin-bedded room at a cheap hotel just off a main road somewhere. I was glad to see he took the diary and put it in the safe in the wardrobe. Then we went out for burgers. I ate fast and so did he, and neither of us spoke.

*

Back in our room I watched TV for a bit before falling asleep without brushing my teeth, still wearing the same T-shirt I'd been in all day. He was sitting up in bed, reading the diary, backlit by the reddish light of the bedside lamp. He was still reading when I next woke up – it must have been hours later, in the middle of the night. He told me to go back to sleep. When I next woke up it was light outside and neither he nor the diary were anywhere to be seen.

Chapter Twenty-One

I didn't seriously think that Dad had walked out on me and disappeared. Well, only for a minute. The first thing I did was look for the diary, but there was no sign of it. The safe was locked – in a way that was a good sign, since presumably it meant he was coming back – and I tried several combinations, but none of them worked. Then I gave up and went off to the dodgy en suite and used the shower, which didn't drain properly. For a first ever stay in a hotel this was no great shakes.

The shower made me feel better, but not much. I didn't feel at all like the me who had gone up in the loft and found the diary and read it and decided to run away. I was more like some wobbly-lipped little kid who starts crying in the cornflake aisle in the supermarket because her mum has started chatting to someone round the corner, just out of sight.

Pathetic. Lost. Waiting for Dad to come back and tell me what to do next. But what other option was there?

I put on yesterday's clothes and sat on my bed and played on my phone, and about five minutes later he came in, carrying something in a paper serviette that he put down on the plywood desk by the door. He looked pretty rough, like someone who'd had a big night out and was facing up to the consequences with a hangover.

'I brought you a croissant,' he said. He didn't sit down. 'Help yourself to a hot drink if you want one,' he added, and gestured towards the kettle on the desk, which had a little dish of sachets of tea and coffee and mini-cartons of long-life milk next to it.

'Can't I go and have breakfast downstairs? Isn't there other stuff?'

'We should get moving. It's gone nine. You had a long sleep.'

'Well, duh. I'm a teenager. Sleeping's my speciality. Given half a chance.'

'You should eat something,' he said. 'I have to make a phone call. I'll be back in a minute.'

And with that he went out again, and I obediently got up and went over to the desk to eat my croissant.

It was an effort to finish it. It didn't taste of anything much, and I was beginning to feel really nervous – too nervous to be hungry.

I wouldn't have expected Dad to come over all loving and apologetic and keen to make it up to me. But I also wouldn't have expected him to be quite as preoccupied and distant as this.

When he came back in he said, 'OK, time to go.'

'What's the rush? I don't suppose Aunt Carrie's that keen to have me back.'

'Do you really want to hang out here?'

I looked round our hotel room. It was nothing special. There were probably hotels like this in every town and city in the country. So why was I suddenly reluctant to leave?

'Guess not,' I said, and we went out and down the stairs to reception and checked out, and headed out into the car park.

It was going to be another sunny day, though it hadn't got hot yet. Back in Port Mallion, the family at Curlew Cottage would probably be having a nice, leisurely breakfast at the table in the garden, talking about their plans for the day. They might not even mention the red-haired girl they'd seen the day before – the runaway whose dad had come looking for her.

I said, 'Did you ring the other dad?'

'Which other dad?'

'The one at the cottage. The one who wanted you to let him know that you'd found me and everything was all right.'

'Oh, him. Yeah, I told him. Not that it was any of his business.'

'It was nice of him to be worried.'

'He was just doing the kind of thing that people do so they can think of themselves as nice. There's a difference.'

He unlocked the car. I hung back. All of a sudden I didn't feel much like getting in.

He said, 'Dani, come on. We have somewhere to be.'

I had a sudden, wild impulse to run away. Not that I would get very far. Hadn't I just tried that? And I'd lasted barely a day.

He opened the car door for me, held it open wide. 'Let's get this show on the road.'

I gave up and got in and he slammed the door and got in the driver's side. My heart was racing. As he turned the key in the ignition I said, 'Are you OK? You seem kind of weird.'

He pulled out of the parking space. 'I'm fine. A bit tired, but I've had some sleep and plenty of coffee.'

'When I woke up in the middle of the night you were still reading the diary.'

He let out a sigh. 'Yeah. That was...' He paused, apparently at a loss for words. 'It's quite something to think that she was capable of doing that.'

'What do you mean, *capable*? Of course she was capable. She could write, couldn't she? And she had a mind of her own.'

He turned onto the main road. 'There's no "of course" about any of those things.'

'I don't get it. What do you mean? Surely you don't think she should have just put up with whatever you lot had got up to and not told her about? She was never going to do that. I never got the chance to know her, but I know enough to be sure of that. And you should be, too. And if you've forgotten who it was you were married to, then the diary should have reminded you. She wasn't a doormat like Aunt Carrie who'd go along with whatever you wanted her to do. She was brave, and she was going to face up to things and do what she thought was best for *me*. Which is something you don't seem to have thought about very much at all.'

'I'm here, aren't I? And I haven't forgotten her, believe me.'

'Then why are you talking about her in this weird way? It's like you're talking about a totally different person. And why you do normally never talk about her at all?'

He didn't answer. He just carried on driving. I was angry with him for being so untouchable, for being able to keep going, watching the road and checking his mirror and indicating and finding our way. I would rather he'd have swung the wheel and yelled at me and skidded and nearly crashed the car.

Then I remembered to feel bad for him. He'd had a chance to rescue her from the sea – though realistically, it might not have been much of a chance – and he'd failed. It was so obvious; he felt guilty because he hadn't managed to save her. He was ashamed.

'I'm sorry,' I said. It felt strange apologising to him, but suddenly I really *was* sorry. 'You shouldn't blame yourself. Like you said, it was a freak accident. I'm sure you did everything you could.'

But then he said, 'Who are you to tell me what to feel? You don't know what happened. You don't remember.'

'Of course I don't. I was only four. That's why it matters what you tell me about it.'

'Yeah, well, maybe there are some things it isn't possible to explain. Maybe some things you have to see for yourself.'

'Yeah, but you can't do that if it happened ten years ago, can you?'

'Always with the ready answer,' Dad said. 'Did it ever occur to you that there are some things people don't tell you because they know you're not ready for them?'

'Yeah, I'd love to think that's the reason you didn't tell me you had a fling with Aunt Carrie before you settled down with Mum. It was just to protect me, right?'

'Watch your step, Dani.'

'Oh, OK, we're back to that, are we? The absent-dad-does-discipline thing. So when are we getting back to Kettlebridge? Because I can't wait for you to dump me back at Aunt Carrie's after all of this.'

'We aren't going back to Kettlebridge. Not yet.'

'Right. OK. Then where are we going?'

'You want to know more about what happened to your mother, right? That's what all this is about. Well, I'm going to take you to a place where you can find out.'

'What do you mean?'

'It won't be long now. We're nearly there.' He gave me a quick sidelong glance, then went back to watching the road ahead. 'Just sit tight and I'll tell you more about it when we get there. I'm sorry it's come to this, Dani. I really am. But I think when you know, you'll see why I couldn't have told you earlier.'

'Just tell me what it is, Dad. You can't make me wait like that. It's cruel. And anyway, you already told me what happened to her. Unless you were lying. What exactly are we talking about here?'

But he just shook his head.

'I could never bear to tell you,' he said, and he sounded tired and terribly sad. 'You've waited this long – it won't hurt to wait a little longer. Like I said, some things you have to see for yourself.'

And after that I didn't ask him any more questions. I was too scared. Scared of the answers. Scared of him not answering.

Mum had written in the diary that she didn't know whether she could trust him any more. Did *I* trust him? How could I? I was glad that he'd come all this way to pick me up. But I was beginning to feel as if he'd caught me rather than rescued me.

Still… at the same time, I didn't seriously believe that he meant me any harm. And so I carried on sitting there next to him in the car, because what else could I do?

Chapter Twenty-Two

Laura

I hear them talking about me. The fat little blonde who does the night shift – I know that isn't nice but I'm past caring if it's wrong to call someone fat, and anyway, it's not as if she's ever going to find out. And isn't it OK to think mean things about your jailer? Though she isn't the one who's keeping me here. Anyway, when the changeover happens and the brunette comes in, they always have a bit of a chat. I think they're friends. Or what passes for friends in this place.

Did I have friends, in the old place, the place where I was before? It seems to me that I didn't. Not really. I kept myself to myself. Out of choice? Self-protection? No choice about it now, anyway… I have such trouble remembering and when you can't remember, nothing in the world makes sense.

Everything is strange here, almost all the time. Including myself. Even day and night don't always make sense. They come and go, and I lose track. But I love the light from the window that glows on a patch of the wall. I could watch it for hours. Light! Air! These things are so precious that only a fool would take them for granted.

I can see, I can breathe. When they come at me with the spoon I can eat. But there's no flavour. Just texture. And sometimes it revolts me and I spit it out – *No no no no* – but the words don't come and then they look so disappointed, and fed up, like a cross between angry mothers with a naughty child and people who are having a really bad day at work. And that annoys me even more because I hate the way they talk about me then: *Better give up on that. That's it, she'll do. It's obviously going to be one of those days.*

They don't talk *to* me. They talk *about* me, as if they don't think I understand. And when I try to tell them I can hear them, they react as if I'm mad, and then I get angry and in here, getting angry never does any good.

In the other place, when I got angry, I had so much power. More power than I ever realised! I had so many words – I was like an assassin, a girl who could go out and change everything, and the words were my weapon of choice. And I could use the words for so many different things. I could shout and scream. I could reproach. I could persuade. And I could see what my words did to people.

I used to have such lovely clothes. There was a dress, a brown dress. I wore it to walk under a row of blossom trees. The spring before I died. But I don't like to think about that. It makes me shake and then they come and it's the crisis thing like in a hospital drama except I'm the body they're doing things to and then everything goes black. And it stays black for a long time and when it's black you really don't know where you are.

How many times can one person die and be reborn?

I died once. As good as. I saw myself on the bed, hooked up to all the wires. I was quite calm about it. Fatalistic. It was so obvious it was nearly all over and there was nothing I could do about it. I was fading, I was floating. But then I remembered…

I remembered why I had to stay.

But I don't want to think about that either. Not now. No, I have to stay calm. I have to stay calm and look at the light and only think of the happy things. Because there were happy things. So happy. So many I couldn't have counted them and didn't notice them. Or didn't notice them enough.

I was so lucky! But I still am. We all are: just to be here, with the air and the light. Me, the blonde and the brunette. Everybody. There is so much dark. And who knows what happens when you really give yourself up to it, when you go in so deep there's no coming back? Nobody in this place, that's for sure.

I'm scared of the dark. Of course I am. Who wouldn't be? It is unbearable to think of it. Anyway, how can I go when there is something here that I still have to do?

Back to the cherry trees.

He took a photo. I saw the picture later and I was surprised by myself, by how happy I looked. Like someone who it would be easy to love.

Him. The red-headed man. Husband. Bluebeard, with the wives. He's my jailer.

Back then, in the other place, we were lovers and all of that. A different world. I was beautiful then. Beautiful to him. I do not think I am beautiful now. But I am here. I am alive and that is enough.

And I am waiting… waiting… but I do not know what for. If only I could remember… if I could taste my food… if I could get up off my bed without the blonde or the brunette helping me… if I could dress myself. If I could walk on my own. If I could get up and walk right out of here.

If I could only speak.

Chapter Twenty-Three

Dani

After half an hour or so – though it felt like forever – we turned onto a side road and pulled up in a car park in front of an ordinary-looking brick-built building, perhaps thirty or forty years old.

It was the nowhere kind of place you would normally go past without really noticing and that nobody would ever queue up to get into. But it didn't look dangerous. It didn't look like somewhere to go for a good time either, but given the events of the last twenty-four hours, that's the last thing I would have expected.

It was coming up for ten in the morning. This time the day before I'd been on my way to catch the train and head west towards the coast. And now I was here, a long way from the beach. And a long way from home, too. A kind of no man's land. We'd learned about that a couple of years ago, when we did World War One: the space between the trenches where each side was dug in.

Perhaps, in a way, it was where I'd been all these years. Though if there had been a battle going on, it was a pretty uneven one. Mum hadn't exactly been in a position to lay claim to me.

Dad unbuckled his seatbelt and I did the same.

I said, 'What is this place? Is it a prison?'

'I guess it is, in a way,' he said.

'Dad… why are we here? Are we here to see someone?'

He sighed. 'There's something you don't know about your mother, Dani. Something you never could have found out from that diary.'

'Well… what is it? Did she do something bad to someone? Did someone hurt her?'

'No, nothing like that.' He sighed again. 'Dani, the thing I never told you about your mother is that she's still alive.'

I caught my breath. Everything seemed to be rushing towards me. There was a ringing in my head. Then it stopped.

I was still exactly where I'd been just a moment before. Sitting in the passenger seat of my dad's car with him next to me, outside an unfamiliar building that was tucked away out of sight. The sun was still shining. Nothing had changed.

But at the same time it was as if the world had turned itself round, as if we were in a kaleidoscope and the pieces were still settling, but I couldn't make out the new pattern just yet.

'I was always afraid that you might go looking for her one day,' Dad went on. 'I just didn't think it would happen quite so soon.'

I said, 'Why didn't you tell me?'

'You might not want to believe this, Dani, but we did it for the best. She survived, but she's not who she was. Her body's still alive but part of her died that day at the beach. The part of her that made her who she was. She can't talk. Can't feed herself. Can't do anything without help. It's not much of a life. She would have hated knowing that this was how she was going to end up. She doesn't know who I am, Dani. I've gone there once a month for the last ten years and she's never so much as said my name.'

'But she drowned. You both told me she drowned.'

'She did. But she came out of the water alive. Just. Then she had a kind of massive stroke afterwards. It's something that can happen to survivors of drowning. She has brain damage and neurological damage – that's damage to the way her nerves work. I've seen a scan of what's going on in her head and there are big patches where there's nothing there – nothing – when it should all be lit up. But it's just dead tissue. Pitch black. The light's gone out and it's never coming back. That's what it's like when you see her. She'll never recover, Dani. She's been like that for years, and she'll be like that till she dies for the second time.'

No man's land. That was where we were – that was what the building in front of us was. It wasn't me who'd been stuck in no man's land: it was Mum. Lost somewhere between the sea that had nearly taken her life and the life we'd lived.

I said, 'Is that place a hospital?'

'Kind of. But it's for people who are never going to get better. It's a nursing home. They take good care of her, Dani, I promise you that.'

'Maybe it'll be different when she sees me. When she realises who I am.'

'She won't. Don't put that burden on yourself, of hoping for a miracle. Miracles don't happen. Not on this Earth. Look, she sleeps most of the time, and she's doped up to the eyeballs to stop her from having fits. She doesn't respond to much, and when she does respond it's not always the kind of reaction you might hope for. She can be quite aggressive, sometimes – she can try to lash out. But most of the time, she just seems completely oblivious.'

'What does she do all day, then? Apart from sleep?'

He shrugged. 'She just lies there. Or sits there. Every now and then she reacts to things. Makes noises. She responds to some kinds of stimulus, like people talking to her or the TV being on, but only from time to time. They think that she doesn't really know where she is. She's only processing information at the most basic level, and even that isn't consistent. Sometimes she'll sit and look at a patch of light on the wall as if it's the most interesting thing in the world. Other times she doesn't seem to care if it's light or dark.'

'You're talking like you think she'd be better off dead.'

'I'm just saying this so that if you do decide you want to see her, you're not shocked.'

'Obviously I'm going to see her. Why wouldn't I?'

'I'm not going to force you, Dani. I brought you here. But it has to be your choice. I just want you to know that your aunt and I chose to protect you for a reason.'

'You weren't protecting me. You were protecting yourselves. You lied to everyone. My teachers at school. People in Kettlebridge. Everyone. Or did they know, and it was just me you decided to keep in the dark?'

'We didn't lie. Not that much. You'd be surprised by how little we had to lie. Dani, let me tell you something about people. They don't ask a whole lot of questions. They talk about the things that everybody else is talking about and they leave everything else well enough alone. Especially difficult things. Things like death. They don't know what to say. Someone tells them something's happened and they say they're sorry and probably they feel sorry too, but they're at a loss for words and they're actually a little bit grateful if you just change the subject. Either that or they'll cross the road to avoid you because they can't cope with another awkward conversation. After a time things just get accepted. They are as they are.'

'Yeah, well, even if the people you knew in London didn't care, I can't believe that people in Kettlebridge would have been like that. I mean, they knew her. She'd gone to school there.'

'There are people who remember her. But they tend not to persist when you make it obvious you don't want them to. They usually leave me alone. And I think Carrie's learned to avoid cosy chats.'

'I suppose she's had to. I guess this was your idea, was it? Not telling anybody. Keeping quiet about where Mum was and what state she was in. And Aunt Carrie went along with it.'

He didn't answer. I said, 'What about Phil? The stepdad? What did you tell him?'

'He was pretty confused by then,' Dad said. 'He wouldn't have made much sense of anything we told him. Betty's death had knocked the stuffing out of him, and he'd gone into a bit of a decline. Betty was your grandmother – your mum's mum. And

Carrie's mum too, obviously. Carrie had already started looking for nursing homes for him. He didn't last much longer.'

'Oh, well, that was convenient, wasn't it? You know what you did was wrong, don't you? You must know. You lied, and you took advantage of people to do it. You took advantage of them being too tactful and kind to ask many questions – or being like Phil and not knowing what was going on. And you took advantage of me, being too young. All because you wanted her tucked away out of sight. Because you were ashamed of her, I suppose. Because it was easier just to pretend she doesn't exist. But whatever she's like, however she behaves, she's still my mum.'

'It's easy to judge, isn't it?' Dad said. 'You might feel differently once you've seen her. Dani, she hasn't been able to be a mother to you. The person who's done that is Carrie.'

'Carrie! She is *not* my mother. Even she has never said that. Does she ever bother coming to visit? Or did she decide it was more convenient just to go along with the story you two had come up with?'

'She doesn't come. She finds it too upsetting. It's not because she doesn't love your mother. It's because she did.'

'She always carried on like such a martyr. Mum deserved better. From everybody. Didn't anybody even ask about the funeral? Didn't they send flowers?'

'I can't remember about flowers, Dani. All I can really remember is seeing her after it had happened. After we'd really lost her. And crying.'

'You cried?'

'Of course I cried. We were in shock. Carrie led people to understand that it had all been dealt with very privately. Close family only. Which was her and me.'

'Dealt with?'

'That's what all this is about, isn't it? Dealing with a body. Dead or alive. I think there were a couple of donations, if that makes you feel any better.'

'Donations? To what?'

'The lifeboats. Royal National Lifeboat Institution. They're volunteers. Every year, they save people who are drowning.'

'Oh. Well, that's touching, I suppose. That it meant something to people. Something more than nothing, anyway.'

'There's no point being angry,' he said. 'I promise you. Being angry will eat you up. Look, Dani, let me tell you something about small towns. People think they're hotbeds of gossip and everybody knows everybody else's business. They're not. You want all that, you live in a village. But everyone in a small town wants his bit of privacy. And the only way you can have that is if everybody gives it to everybody else. It's "do as you would be done by". If you don't stick your nose into other people's lives, maybe they won't stick their nose into yours. And most people are just trying to get by. They don't go looking for things they don't know are there. Anyway, the truth of it is that the thing your mother left behind – the most important thing, the mark she made on the world – that was *you*. Dani, to all intents and purposes, your mother really did die on that beach. She never made it back.'

'I can see that's what you want to believe,' I said. 'Maybe it's easier for you that way. But that doesn't make it true. Because she did come back, Dad. She's been here all this time. And you hid her from me.'

'What could we have said? You were four years old. What were we meant to tell you? Neither of us ever actually sat you down and lied to you, you know. Carrie said you asked her about it. Not directly, but in your own way. You said, "She's gone, isn't she? She's not coming back." And she said yes. Was that such a terrible thing to do?'

'It's no different to a lie.'

'Look, have you ever wanted for anything? Food? Clothes? A roof over your head? Somewhere warm to sleep at night?'

'Well, no, but…'

'Then I don't think we did so badly by you. Did we?'

'That is not the point and you know it. You could have tried to explain what actually happened instead of just locking it away and making it impossible to talk about.'

He couldn't meet my eyes. That's how ashamed he was. He was trying to bluster his way out of it, to justify himself for his own benefit as well as mine. But he couldn't. He desperately wanted me to tell him that it was OK, that I understood and it wouldn't really have made that much difference anyway. And I couldn't do that. I wanted an apology and he wanted forgiveness, and neither of us could begin to offer the other what was wanted.

'We should go in and see her,' I said. 'Does she know I'm coming?'

At that he looked up. His expression was very cold and cut off. I thought of the panic he must have gone through on the beach, trying to get the water out of her lungs, giving her mouth-to-mouth, calling for help. Alone with the dead or dying wife who had been about to leave him and the small child she'd been determined to keep.

No, I didn't feel any pity for him. I wanted to kill him for having failed.

'Dani, she has no idea you're coming,' he said. 'That's what you don't understand. She doesn't understand anything.'

He got out of the car and I tried to follow him, but it was like one of those nightmares where the waters rise and you're rooted to the spot. My legs had turned to jelly.

And then I thought of the one thing of Mum's that I still had in my bag, the picture of her in the brown dress holding my hand and smiling, and that was what made it possible to move towards her.

Chapter Twenty-Four

Laura

I pity him from the depths of my heart. But I can't console him.

He can walk and talk and do all of those things. But he can't forgive himself. And I can't help him to. I can see how broken he is. He can barely bring himself to look at me and I know it's because of how ashamed he feels, and how much he blames himself.

What a pair. What a pair of fools. There was always something that came between us. In the other place we never could be honest with each other. And now I'm here... well.

He is my husband still, I think, as far as I know. I don't think of myself as a wife. That sounds like a dressing-up costume I used to play in, back in that other life. A wife belongs to someone, lives with someone, and I don't really live with anyone. This is alone, in here. Alone with what's left in the inside of my head, which is a kind of ruin. There are bits that are broken and have crumbled, and other parts are still standing. But only just. A few arches. A pile of stones. All overgrown.

Somewhere there is sand and the sea. I was there, in a cottage by the sea, at night. While the child slept and it was dark all around. I wasn't afraid of the darkness then. Or not so much. I didn't really know what it was like. I'd never sunk into it, never let it into me. Never been taken over and blotted out by it. I didn't know what it could do.

And I was writing, writing. So many words. I set them down with a pen on lined paper and they flowed and it was so easy, the words and the movement of my hand, the curves and lines and dots on the page. The tiny waves of words and the spaces between them.

The space between is where I am now, I think.

Years ago, when I was a kid in the other place, I had a book about a girl who went through a mirror into a different world. It was all different and weird on the other side and yet it was the same. Because perhaps none of it ever made any sense.

This morning, in the bathroom, I caught sight of my reflection. A shock. Then the name of that book came back to me. *Alice Through the Looking-Glass*. I don't think that's what's happened to me. No one can really pass through a mirror – you'd get cut to pieces. But still, it was very weird to see myself. I almost didn't know who I was.

I looked so tired. Tired and pale and worn out. I looked ill, to be honest. The lighting wasn't the most flattering, but still. Surely I hadn't always been like that? In the other place, hadn't I leaned forward to put on lipstick, adjust my hair? But now I have the face of someone who no one looks at. Or not for long, anyway. Not the way you look at someone because you want to.

The people who are with me start saying things about hurrying up so they can finish helping me and take me down for breakfast, and then I'm back in my chair in my room and I'm not hungry any more. I'm in front of the TV, which I don't mind too much even though it doesn't make a lot of sense because I can just tune out whatever it is they're saying and laughing about and watch the shapes moving across the screen.

It tires me out, though. I can't watch it for too long. And then I come to and the light has changed and something else is happening, and I have no idea what I've missed.

Yesterday a new person came and tried to get me to look at squares with letters on them. I couldn't look. My eyes wouldn't do it. They wouldn't go the way I wanted to. I understood exactly what she was trying to do. She was looking at me as if she knew I could hear her, and she talked to me the same way. *If you can look at these, Laura, you'll be able to talk to us. You'll be able to tell us what you want.* But I couldn't do it and I cried out in frustration and then she stopped. She looked so disappointed. Like a teacher with a naughty child. *Never mind. We'll try again.*

If only I could have done it. Imagine how freaked-out they would have been! It would have been like a ghost sending a message through a Ouija board. *Hello, yes, I heard you the first time. It's awfully boring in here. I think I'm ready to leave now, if it's all the same to you.* And then I could have wheeled myself right out of there while they were still all pinned to their seats in shock. The doors would have flown open as if by magic and I'd have been gone – out into the air and freedom and life, to do whatever it is that I still have to do.

This morning the blonde and the brunette were talking about me again.

'I don't know why the speech and language therapist still bothers,' the blonde said. 'It's obvious there's no one there.'

'I guess she still thinks there could be some kind of breakthrough,' the brunette said.

'Oh, come on,' the blonde said. 'After all this time?'

So that was her: the one who grumbles. The bad one, who finds fault and says it won't work out, and there's no point even trying. And then the brunette was the optimist, the one who doesn't quite give up hope. I'd known other people like that, once. But which had I been like, the blonde or the brunette? The sweet one, or the one who says how bad things are? Just another of the things I couldn't remember.

'Yes, but the brain is still a bit of a mystery, isn't it?' the brunette said. 'Nobody really knows that much about it. I guess they're just waiting for something to connect.'

'Yeah, well, you can have all the technology in the world, but you won't get a connection if there's nothing to connect *to*,' the blonde pointed out.

'You know they tried getting her to look at letters on a screen. They thought maybe it didn't work because the computer couldn't register her pupils. Too dilated, apparently, because of all the meds. That's why they thought the old-fashioned way might work better.'

'Oh come on. How long have they been asking her to look one way for yes and the other for no? And then she gets distressed. Well, she does, doesn't she? That's what you told me. It's not so bad for me on the night shift, but you ought to watch yourself,' the blonde said. 'She's strong, and I wouldn't put it past her to suddenly lash out when we're least expecting it. Every once in a while, she looks at me and it gives me the shivers. I think she's angry. I would be too, if I'd spent years of my life in here.'

'Well, I guess she wasn't always that way. Her husband's always ever so gentle and patient with her. Still comes to visit her, like clockwork once a week,' the brunette said.

'Yeah, and I still visit my Aunt Nancy at Christmas,' the blonde replied. 'I should think he comes out a sense of duty and that's all.'

'Poor man.'

'I know. Everybody says he's lovely. A true gentleman. I'm surprised he hasn't married again. Surely he deserves a bit of happiness.'

'He must really have loved her,' the brunette said wistfully. Then: 'We should cut her hair soon. It's getting long.'

'She has lovely hair, doesn't she? She must have been pretty, back in the day,' the blonde said.

I shouted out, *I can hear you! How dare you talk about me like that!* but all that came out was a groan, not even loud enough for them to notice.

The brunette said goodbye and I heard the blonde's footsteps in the corridor and then there was nothing.

Peace. Except I didn't feel blissful. I felt like knocking everything down and screaming. How could they?

She must have been pretty, back in the day. Nothing to connect to. Every once in a while, she looks at me and it gives me the shivers.

And then it came back to me.

Carrie. My sister. Always so angry. The dark eyeliner. The bad attitude. But that was just a shell. I knew it was, because of the way she held me after our dad died. I knew how sad she was. She smelt of sadness. A smell like damp tears mixed with fear.

How could she have lied to me?

But I knew. I knew why. She knew I was in love. She wanted me to have that – to have what she hadn't found. Love. She didn't want to spoil it. She didn't want to risk it. She didn't want to risk losing me, either. To have me not see her in the same way.

She kept me in the dark. She must have thought it was for the best. And so did he.

Him. The red-haired man. Big, broad-shouldered, moody. Alone in the bedroom at the party that his wife walked out of. A woman I was scared of. Dark shiny hair, dark eyes, and that edge of menace. *Don't mess with me and mine or you'll be sorry*. Had she said it out loud or had it just been in the way she looked? Handing over her daughter for the weekend. Hating me. As if hating me was in her blood, like a blood feud.

Wife. I had been a wife, once. Was I still?

There was something so defeated about him. And then: sparks. Magic. His touch, making me beautiful, turning me into someone else.

And then her.

Our baby.

I hadn't forgotten. I could never forget. No one could forget what that was like. To hold her in my arms, so small and so perfect and smelling of milk. Her tiny face. Fingers. Toes. The eyes with their delicate fringe of lashes, opening cloudy blue.

The red hair. Only a trace at first. A fine down on the almost hairless scalp. Then curls. And her energy! Into everything, crawling, walking. No stopping her. Always wanting to swing higher, to stay longer, or to go faster. She amazed me. Sometimes I really could have believed she'd been dropped in my life by a stork; she was so different, so much herself. A miracle. A small, busy miracle with a mind of her own.

My little lion. Dani.

Him with his camera on a sunny day in London. The seductiveness of that conversation. Walking by the river, not knowing where it would lead us. Not wanting to say goodbye. And then fate intervened in the shape of a bag thief, and we ended up in each other's arms.

He had come to the cottage by the sea. Tracked us down to where we were. Carrie had told him. I ought to have known she would. Maybe she thought it would help. Probably she hoped to play a part in fixing us up. Maybe that was it, all along; she wanted to think we were *her* doing, that she'd made it possible for us to get together in the first place and then, when history caught up with us, had been the one to make it possible for us to reunite.

He'd knocked on the door.

I had known exactly who it was and what he would want, and I had let him in.

I remember all of that now: it comes back to me quite clearly, as clear as day. But what happened after?

It's still sunny outside, and I can see a square of light on the wall by my bed. I know I've noticed it before and have sat here and studied it and been amazed by it. It's so bright and glowing it looks as if the wall is melting, as if it might be possible to walk through.

Then – as if somebody's pressed a switch – I'm somewhere else. Somewhere as terrifying and familiar as a nightmare.

Darkness. Up above somewhere there's light. Light that can't reach me. I'm sinking and falling, and I know I'm lost. I know with absolute certainty – with the kind of pure clarity that it is usually impossible to have – that I am going to die. And the strangest thing about this is that I am glad at the same time. Euphoric. I am drowning and at the same time I know I have escaped my worst fears.

She is going to live. I am not. That is the deal I have made. It was the only deal I could have made. Because how could I have lived without her?

How could I have carried on living otherwise, if he'd chosen to save me instead of her?

You never know, with a man. Whether they'll do what you say. You try to tell them. So often they don't listen. You never know if they'll listen when it matters. Or what's really in their hearts. Which way they'll jump when the tide comes in. Who they'll abandon, and when they'll stay.

Chapter Twenty-Five

Dani

The nursing home was nothing like what I would have imagined.

The first thing that surprised me was the security. Dad had to sign us in at reception, and then we were allowed in through a set of double doors, like an airlock on a spaceship on TV. Or security in a prison. Instantly I felt shut in. On the other side of the doors it was weirdly stuffy, as if the air was barely moving. Like a classroom on a particularly dull day, except with no prospect of the bell ringing to let everyone out.

My school had security too – special barriers across the side entrances that went down after we were all supposed to be inside to register, so you couldn't sidle in late but had to come through a series of doors at the front. But those barriers were more to keep intruders out than to keep us in, and school didn't feel anything like as cut off from the outside world as this.

At the end of the day at school, everyone went home. But this was a place where people were expected to stay until they died. I could see, in a way, why Dad found it hard to come here, and why Aunt Carrie had given up completely. Already part of me hated it, and just wanted to get out.

We were shown into a small side room. If it was a waiting room it obviously wasn't used very much. There were no magazines, no toys or books for visiting children – none of the things you might see in even the most rundown, unloved doctors' surgery, or at the dentist's. It was bare. Weirdly, deliberately bare, as if everything had been cleared away from it so that nothing could be ruined or destroyed.

Maybe they just didn't have the money for magazines and so on.

Or maybe there just weren't that many visitors. Because why would there be? If people were here for any length of time, anyone who cared enough to visit would be likely to come less and less often, for ever shorter lengths of time. You'd find excuses. You might even believe them. But the truth was, the place felt hopeless – in a contained, medical, caring kind of way. And who wants to keep coming face to face with a hopeless case? Nobody. We all want to think we can make a difference, after all. Otherwise what's the point in being alive at all?

But Dad had kept on coming. He could have given up, but he hadn't. I had to at least give him that.

At any rate, I was no worse off than I had been. I had believed she was dead. Now I knew she wasn't. Yes, Dad had said that she might as well be, but still… if that was really how he felt, why did he still visit her? He couldn't have given up on her. Not really. Not as completely as he'd made out.

Who was being kept safe, here, and who was a threat to who?

After all, Dad had said Mum could be quite aggressive and unpredictable. I began to feel afraid. And at the same time I knew this was wrong. Very wrong. I was about to see my mum for the first time in ten years. I had found her. I should have been elated. So why did I feel as if I was about to meet someone terrifying? It felt as if I was about to see a murderer in prison, not someone who'd drowned and been damaged and survived.

Dad couldn't keep still. He obviously hated the place even more than I already did. He sat down for a bit, looked around, jiggled his foot, got up and paced around. He looked nervous and bored and miserable. About as miserable as it's possible to be without being in actual physical pain.

It felt like a long wait but it wasn't really, of course – it was nothing compared to how long I'd already waited. A nurse in pastel green overalls came in and said, 'Sorry for the delay. We have to be very careful about access, because some of our clients are a flight risk.'

Clients? Flight risk? Did she mean that some of the people they kept in there would run away given half a chance? And what was it about this place that meant it needed its own special language?

'I'll take you up now,' she went on, and smiled at Dad and I saw that she remembered him from when he'd been before. She had long brown hair tied back in a ponytail, and her ears were pierced but she didn't have any earrings in. Was that a precaution? Might someone have tried to yank them out? Or maybe she had just forgotten.

Dad grimaced back at her. I had never seen him so uncomfortable. Then the nurse smiled at me too. A sympathetic, encouraging smile. The way you might look at someone who's in trouble through no fault of her own.

I said, 'We didn't bring anything. We should have got some flowers or something.'

Dad exhaled sharply. 'It would have just been a waste of time and money. This isn't like visiting someone in hospital, Dani. I keep trying to tell you.'

'All the same, it doesn't seem right to turn up empty-handed,' I said.

We went out with the nurse and along the corridor and up a flight of stairs, and through another set of double doors. Dad said to her, 'How has she been?'

'Stable,' the nurse said. I guessed that was another code word. Code for 'the same'.

We stopped at the door at the end of the corridor. I said to Dad, 'Do I look OK?'

He glanced at me, but not for long enough. Too preoccupied to be irritated. He said, 'Sure you do. But Dani… she's not going to care. She's not even going to notice. She's not going to throw her arms around you and say, *Haven't you grown?* She can't talk and she can't move, not like that. And she won't know you're there.'

'I get that. You told me. I know she's out of it,' I said.

The nurse glanced at Dad, then at me. I wondered what she was thinking: *Why is this man bringing his kid into this situation?* maybe or, *Why didn't he bring her before?* She didn't look obviously disapproving, though. Or curious. She looked like a less depressed version of Aunt Carrie – like someone who might have kids back home and who would be strict with them, but not too strict.

'You look fine,' she told me. She glanced at Dad again. 'You ready?'

'Why not,' Dad said.

His voice didn't sound like his. It was flat and strange, as if he didn't want to give anything away.

The nurse knocked at the door. There was no response, of course. I wondered why she bothered. But maybe it was part of the rules of the place, like talking about clients and flight risks and being stable. She pushed the door open wide and we went in.

Mum was sitting in a chair by the bed, staring into space.

I felt the shock of it all through my body. It was like when someone turned the sound system up loud at the school disco and you could feel the floor shake and the vibrations travelling up through the soles of your feet through your bones and spine through to the top of your head. I had thought about her so often, dreamed about her, tried to remember her and imagine her: the smiling woman with brown hair and eyes, the one who had held my hand in the photo that lived on my bedroom windowsill. And there she was – the same woman. But older. Paler. And blank, as if somebody had sucked all the life out of her and locked her away.

Dad said, 'Hi, Laura.' He obviously didn't expect her to react, and she didn't.

The nurse said, 'I'll bring you another chair.'

'Sure. Thanks,' Dad said.

'She's had her breakfast and her meds and she's been toileted this morning, so you should be fine. Any concerns, just press the buzzer.' The nurse gestured to the alarm button set in a panel of different high-tech-looking controls at the head of the hospital bed. 'I'm going to leave the door slightly open. As you know, it's our standard policy for visits on this ward.'

'Fine,' Dad said, as if this was all perfectly normal, and she went out.

But he still didn't really seem to be at ease. He didn't go over to Mum and try to kiss her on the cheek. He didn't go anywhere near her. She might as well have been in there for something contagious. Instead he moved the chair that was against the wall so it was closer to Mum and said, 'Take a seat, Dani,' and I sat down.

I'd got it wrong; she wasn't staring into space. She was definitely looking at something – just not at me, or Dad. She was gazing at the wall opposite her, at the patch of square light that fell there, the shape of the window by her bed.

Dad said, 'Dani's here to see you, Laura. She's fourteen. She went all the way to Cornwall to find you.'

Mum began to move her head from side to side. I thought maybe she was nodding, or trying to communicate something. Then I realised she was still staring at the square of light on the wall. It was as if she was trying to move the light rather than talk to us – or make it look as if it was moving, anyway. Maybe she was just trying to blot us out. To focus on something else.

'Say something, if you want,' Dad said. 'You have to try and think that it doesn't matter if she doesn't respond.'

'I don't know what to say.'

He looked at me with his eyebrows raised. Not unsympathetic. But too *I told you so* for comfort. *You came all this way and now you have no words?* Well. Maybe he had a point. It was pathetic, to have come so far and to have so little to give…

But I had absolutely no idea where to start.

Here was my mother who I had thought was dead and who had turned out to be alive but who didn't know I was there. Was there a magical formula, an abracadabra or open sesame that would make it possible for us to connect? Or was this it: the two of us in a room with the door slightly open and a buzzer only one of us could press for help, with her looking at the light on the wall and me looking at her?

And my father looking on. Her husband. You thought of marriage as rows and boredom – or at least that was the impression I had of it, based mainly on the soaps Aunt Carrie liked to watch. Or if you were a bit more romantically inclined, it was posing for the wedding photo and then turning into the kind of sweet old couple that walks down the street together in the afternoon. But not this.

The nurse came in with a chair for Dad. She said, 'Can I get either of you anything? Tea? Coffee? A glass of water?'

'No, thanks,' Dad said.

The nurse put the chair next to mine, and Dad sat down. We were all facing each other now, sitting at the three points of a perfect triangle, but Mum was still looking at the wall. She let out a low groan. It sounded almost exploratory, as if she was surprised to find she was capable of making sound at all.

'She does vocalise from time to time,' the nurse said to me. 'We're not sure if she's aware of the sounds she makes, but we think maybe it gives her some kind of sensory feedback in her throat and palate.'

Vocalise. I said, 'What if that's her trying to talk?'

'She's not trying to talk,' Dad said gruffly. 'She's just making noises to pass the time.'

'Well, that's talking, isn't it? How often do you say something because you actually need to? How often does anyone?'

'Dani,' Dad said, 'there has never been any evidence of intent to communicate. She is less able to tell us what she wants than a newborn baby. At least a baby can cry when it wants something. She doesn't even know when to cry.'

'It's difficult to keep going when there isn't any response, or when the response isn't what you expect,' the nurse said. 'But that doesn't mean there's no point in trying. Just call me if you need anything.'

She went back out, and the three of us were alone again in the weird semi-silence. It was quiet, but not peaceful: it sounded muffled, as if there were things going on close by that you couldn't quite make out – monitors beeping, and staff pacing and saying soothing words and dispensing pills, and patients struggling to reach for things and knocking them down, or not managing to reach them at all.

'So how do you normally play this?' I said to Dad. 'Do you tell her stuff? If people are in a coma, aren't you meant to play them their favourite music and things like that? Or get some celebrity they fancy to come and say hello?'

'She isn't in a coma, and she isn't going to wake up. The only thing that might happen to her is that she might get worse. That would mean she would stop being able to do some of the things she can do now, like swallowing.'

'Well, how are they going to feed her if she can't swallow?'

Mum's head sagged. She started to make a different sound, a long, low hum, as if she had a tune in mind but was limited to two or three notes. Her right hand, which had been resting on the arm of the chair, turned palm upwards and flexed.

'You can feed people with a tube through the nose if you need to. It's amazing what you can do to keep people alive,' Dad said. 'Anyway, we'll worry about that when we need to.'

I stared at him. It seemed to me that he was avoiding my eyes just as much as she was, though for different reasons. I said, 'Do you wish she really had died on the beach? Was that why you lied to me, because you were telling me what you wanted to have happened?'

Mum went quiet. Dad said, 'Dani, you have no right to talk to me like that. How can you even say such a thing?'

'Seems to me someone has to start saying the unsayable round here. After all, it's not much of a life for her, is it? Stuck in here.

Even her own sister can't bring herself to visit. And you obviously hate coming. And you thought the state she was in was so awful that I'd be better off thinking she was dead than seeing her. Like she'd turned into a monster.'

'I never thought that.'

'Well, she's not a monster, is she? She's still a person.'

'Is she?' Dad said. 'If she can't speak? If she can't remember anything? If she has no idea who she is, and where she is or why?'

There was something pleading about the way he said this, as if I might be able to tell him something he'd lost sight of. As if I might be able to comfort him.

I said, 'I'm not here to reassure you. Not after you kept me out of it all these years. I'm not going to waste my words on you.'

His face puckered up as if I'd just stabbed him in the heart. Good. Serve him right. I was starting to feel really angry, the way I'd felt when I'd seen Josie's frightened face and confronted Cherry and Gemma by the stream. But more powerful than that, with a kind of dam-breaking energy that wasn't really under my control.

I turned back to Mum. 'Look, they all think you can't hear or understand what I'm saying. And maybe they're right. But since I'm here, and since there's nothing to lose, we might as well carry on like you do know what I'm saying, OK?'

Nothing. Her hand was still open, palm upwards. She was staring at the light again. Perhaps there was a very faint hint of a frown on her face. Or perhaps she was just squinting.

'I'm Dani. Your daughter. Fourteen years old.' Might as well start with the basics. 'Anyway, that doesn't really matter. I'm sure Dad forgets how old I am half the time. Though he did remember my birthday. I thought he'd forgotten, but he hadn't. He got me a bike and I rode it to the river and swam, and Aunt Carrie gave me what for and that's how I found out you'd drowned. I live with Aunt Carrie, did you know that? Dad drops by every now and then. He's like the opposite of a helicopter parent – you know they're the ones who hover over you all the time? He's more like one of those medivac helicopters. Most of the time he's somewhere else, and he only shows up if it's a matter of life and death. Like now. Because that's what this is, isn't it?'

No response. I ploughed on. 'I found the beach, you know. I walked there, all the way from the cottage. And it was beautiful. I could see why you took me there. A really special place. But I don't remember it. I have no memory of what happened. I guess I wiped it. You and me both, right? Well, there is just one thing I remember. Two things. Going on Dad's shoulders, and me standing there crying, wet through and feeling like I was completely alone. But I don't know for sure if that was on the beach. It might even be a memory from a dream. Or a memory I've made up. I bet you'd know, though.'

Her mouth opened and some drool ran down the side of it. I looked away; I was shocked, and a little bit revolted, and I really didn't want to be. Dad got up and grabbed a tissue from the box on the cabinet by her bed and wiped her face. Then he sat down with the tissue balled in his hand ready to do it again if he needed to.

'She does that, sometimes,' he said. 'It's fine. No big deal.'

I hesitated. Just as suddenly as it had flared up, my anger was beginning to die away, along with the will to keep on talking. I glanced at Dad and even though I'd hurt him, and it was obvious the pain I'd caused him hadn't faded away, he looked more pitying than wounded.

'Keep going,' he said.

I turned back to her. I said, 'I'm not doing all that well without you, to be honest. I'm not like a credit to you or anything. My teachers don't like me much and Aunt Carrie puts up with me because she has to. And Dad doesn't know what to say to me any more than he knows what to say to you. But, you know, I made a friend, kind of. She's this skinny kid at school called Josie Pye. Two other girls were bullying her and I kind of had a go at them. I don't mean to make out like I'm noble or anything. I just hated to see it. They were enjoying it so much. That's the worst thing about bullies. They love what they do.'

Mum settled back in her chair and let out a small, contented sigh. I thought for a wild moment she was maybe agreeing with me. Then her eyes closed.

'She's going off to sleep,' I said to Dad.

'It's OK. She does that sometimes. She just kind of dozes off.'

'OK. Well, guess I might as well carry on anyway.'

I turned back to Mum. It seemed like the visit was about to run out on us both. The big chance I'd come so far for, slipping away like sand through a timer. Like a woman underwater with her lungs filling up with fluid. Or like a patient on a hospital bed with the circuits in her brain being blotted out, going out like the lights in a city at war.

'I read your diary,' I said. 'Aunt Carrie had it hidden in the loft at Cromwell Close, in a trunk under an old wasps' nest under the eaves. Josie helped me get up there and then I had to climb across all the beams to get it. I know about the stupid fling Dad had with Aunt Carrie, and that they didn't tell you. I know Jade didn't believe you and hit you when you told her. But there's something you might not know. Since what happened to you on the beach, Dad's never loved anybody else.'

'Dani,' Dad said. 'There really is no way she can hear you.'

And it was true. Mum was soundly, peacefully asleep. Oblivious.

'There was something else in the trunk, too,' I said to her. 'A paper bag with some Christmas decorations in it. Really fancy ones. Old-fashioned. I don't know if they were anything to do with you, or if they were just left there from some other time.'

She didn't respond. Dad looked sadder than ever, so sad that it was as if he'd frozen and would be like that for ever. Then he pulled himself together and said, 'Those were ours. Laura chose them. I asked Carrie if she'd like them, that first Christmas after what happened on the beach. I didn't realise she was just going to hide them away somewhere. I guess, I don't know…' He swallowed. 'I guess it was too much of a reminder for her too.' His face crumpled and I thought for an awful moment that he might be about to cry, but then he shook his head and composed himself and stood up. 'We should go. I ought to get you home.' He started to move towards the buzzer by the bed.

'No! No. I'm not ready to go back. Not yet. Let me try one more thing.'

I reached for my backpack, rummaged in it, took out the photo of Mum holding my hand underneath the cherry trees. I pressed it into her hand and folded her fingers round it.

At first she didn't grasp it. Dad said, 'You shouldn't do that, Dani. That's not a good idea.' Then her hold tightened very slightly, and that gave me the courage to go on.

'That's you and me, near where we lived in London,' I told her. 'Ten years ago, before the accident. I don't remember it. Maybe you do. We were happy then, I think. Maybe we didn't realise it. You know I dream about you? Sometimes I'm trying to find you. Sometimes I do, and we sit there and talk and we're together. But I always have to wake up.'

'We really should go,' Dad said, but he still didn't press the buzzer.

And then I said the thing people always say when they want to put things right, or remind someone why they're there, or stake a claim to someone. It's not abracadabra, it's the opposite. It's what you say when you know it could be your last chance. When it's time to say goodbye.

'I love you, Mum. I love you.'

She clenched the frame tightly and her eyes shot open and met mine.

There. It was there. Just for a moment, I saw it. Her. Peering back at me, seeing me just the way I was seeing her.

And then there was chaos.

She hurled the picture across the floor and let out a long, guttural howl. Her body splayed out and extended so that her back was braced against the chair and she began to pound her head against the headrest. Her arms reached out and her hands lashed out as if she was hitting someone, or would if she could.

I was rooted to the spot. I couldn't believe what I'd conjured up. Dad grabbed hold of me roughly and dragged me back into a corner as the nurse charged in. I tried to wrestle him off and screamed, 'Let go of me!' But he wouldn't.

'It's not your fault, Dani,' he kept saying. 'Please believe me, it's not your fault.'

And then I stopped struggling and began to cry and he held me and I let him.

The nurse came over and said, 'I'm so sorry, I think it might be better if you left,' and Dad's grip loosened and I realised there was another nurse in the room too, and that Mum was still bellowing and moving in her chair as if she was in a rage with absolutely everything and would have attacked all of us and trashed the place, if only she could have done.

'OK, Dani?' Dad said. 'Are you ready to go?'

'OK. I'm ready.'

I let him take me out. It wasn't until much later, when we were about an hour along the road back to Kettlebridge, that I realised I'd left the picture of me and Mum on the floor of her room.

Chapter Twenty-Six

Laura

The light was still there but closer to the door than the window, and I was in bed and couldn't move. Something taped to my finger. A monitor beeping. Not good. No, definitely not good.

And then something extraordinary happened.

That smell. Sweetish, like fruit. Like fruit sweets, or apricot yoghurt. A bubblegum smell.

But I hadn't smelt anything for so long. I didn't know how long. So long ago I had forgotten what it was like, hadn't really been aware that my sense of smell had vanished. And here it was back again. And here was the smell, like something from another life, or at least from the other place.

It smelt like me when I was young. Like the deodorant I'd worn. But why?

Other smells, too. An apologetic sort of smell. Anxious man. Slightly musky.

Him.

Had he been here or was this something else? A mixing of the other place and here? Like time dissolving, so that scent and maybe other things could seep through?

Pine disinfectant. Well, that could be here. I'd used something like it, once. But not so much.

The brunette nurse came in to check the monitors.

'Well, that doesn't look too bad. Bed rest for you,' she said. 'Doctor will be round later.'

A gentle voice. Not expecting me to reply. Yes, this is the kind one, the one I like. But why do I need to rest?

She went out again and then I saw the picture someone had left on the cabinet in the corner.

A woman with brown hair, smiling, laughing, holding the hand of a sweet little girl.

Me. It was me.

My daughter.

Dani.

Dani, who smelt like bubblegum and apricots.

I love you, Mum.

Here.

And then I remembered. I had everything, all of it right there at my fingertips, and I knew all of it at once. What had happened and why he had stayed away. And I knew he hadn't told her.

I knew it was him before I opened the door of the cottage.

He looked very tired. He looked dreadful. And something happened to my heart. Pity. A little extra twist of the knife. Still love, maybe.

'I'm sorry. I had to see you,' he said. 'I couldn't bear waiting, not knowing where you were or how you are, or what you were thinking. I missed you. Both of you.'

'I've been doing a lot of thinking,' I said. 'We need to talk. But we can't do that here.'

'Laura… Do you think you can forgive me?'

'There's a difference between forgiving you and carrying on as we were,' I said.

And then Dani shouted, 'Daddy! Daddy!' and rushed up to him.

She pretty much hurled herself at him. He didn't have much option but to catch her and hold her. And I stepped back and said, 'OK, come in.'

*

I made him coffee. My heart was pounding. Had it been a mistake to let him in? He looked so desperate. But how could I have turned him away?

He was still wearing his wedding ring, and I couldn't help but be conscious that I wasn't wearing mine. I knew he'd noticed, but he didn't comment on it. He sat at the table with Dani and she showed him her drawings, expecting him to admire them. He seemed distracted. She pouted. Then inspiration struck. Something that was bound to impress him.

'Will you come to the sea with us, Daddy? To our secret beach? We found a new one, a special place to go.'

I said, 'Oh I don't know, Dani. I'm not sure it would be such a good idea.'

'Oh please, Mummy? Please?'

'Daddy isn't staying long. He has the business to get back to.'

'Ohhhhh…'

They both looked at me beseechingly at exactly the same time. And what of it? We were still a family, after all. Whatever happened to me and him. What harm could one walk by the beach do? It might be the last time we walked as a family, together.

Or it might not be the last. But anyway, it would be easier than talking.

'OK,' I said. 'But Daddy will have to go back to London after that.'

'But that's too quick!' Dani protested. She never did know how to quit when she was ahead. 'It's not fair.'

'It's as fair as it's going to get,' I said.

OK, so it was a long drive. But he could find a hotel, couldn't he? What business was it of mine where he slept? I got up and set about gathering together the things I would need to take to the beach.

*

He drove. Already I'd got out of the habit of being driven. The luxury of being a passenger. I have to admit, I liked it. Not quite enough to feel comfortable, or safe, or to relent and tell him he could stay. But it was a change, anyway.

Would this be the last time? It might be. I wondered when I would find the courage to make it clear to him what I'd decided. That it was over. That we could be cordial and civilised and work things out and do everything we could to make it easy for Dani, but we couldn't be man and wife any more. I knew he would know why; I knew he would understand. The lie had been too big. It wasn't even about what he had done. It was about him not telling me, year in, year out, until Carrie broke it to me. All that time, both of them had both known something they had chosen to keep from me. Carrie had kept her distance. But Jon had never really been as close to me as I had allowed myself to believe.

He parked on the cliff-top and turned to me and said, 'Thank you for this. It means a lot. It's good of you, better than I deserve.' And I realised he already knew what I was going to tell him.

We made our way down to the beach. Another beautiful day. There was no one else there – too early. High tide. An idyll. Man, woman, child. It could have been paradise.

Dani asked to go on his shoulders and he obliged even though she was getting a bit too big, then set her down after a few paces. She scampered ahead and we walked along together behind her. He seemed calmer, maybe because of the contact with Dani. Or maybe he was already becoming resigned.

But then he said, 'I just can't believe this is it. I can't believe I've lost you. Can you tell me honestly that you don't love me any more? Because I think you do.'

'You didn't make me happy,' I said. 'I don't trust you any more.'

'I'll make it up to you.'

'Jon… it's too late.'

'It's never too late. I don't believe it. I just don't believe this is it. Not for you and me. It can't be. If I had told you… if I had told you back then, when we first met… do you think you would have given me a chance?'

'I don't know. How can I possibly know? We can't live on might-have-beens.'

He screwed up his face as if he was about to say something that was difficult to admit. 'You can live on next to nothing, believe me. As long as you don't know what you're missing. I did, for all those years before I met you.'

He reached out to take my hand. I shook him off and hurried along the beach to catch up with Dani, leaving him behind.

Little Dani with her red curls and yellow sunhat, the only one who really mattered. Blissfully oblivious to what was about to happen. The thought of it hurt me as it would no doubt one day hurt her. Was I a monster, to take her from her dad over a few qualms?

But it wouldn't be like that. It didn't have to be like that. He'd see her often. I'd make sure of it. She'd spend plenty of time with us both. She'd know it was nothing to do with her, that it was just us.

She wouldn't need to know about the business with Carrie. We hardly saw Carrie anyway. It wouldn't make much difference if we saw her even less.

And if she could see Jon… it would be different, wouldn't it? It wouldn't be anything like my childhood, like losing my dad.

Dani wasn't even that close to the shoreline. And then the wave came in and knocked her off her feet and curled over her and pulled her back into the sea, as quickly and easily as a cat's paw pouncing on its catch.

I was in almost before I knew it. There she was, an arm, a trace of red hair. If I could see her then why couldn't I get to her? Now, right now, before it was too late. Before the sea took her further and further away, and there would be no chance.

But I couldn't reach her. The water was carrying me further and further away, washing salt into my eyes and nose, putting a distance I couldn't cross between me and her.

And then I saw him, plunging into the water towards me. Always a strong swimmer. I screamed as loud as I could: 'Dani! Get Dani! Just leave me! If you don't save her I'll never forgive you!'

I saw him hear me. He hesitated a split second before changing course, and then I couldn't see him any more and I couldn't see her either.

There was just sea, and the line of the land and I couldn't begin to reach it, couldn't get any closer. My lungs began to burn. Another wave swept over me and I went down, and I saw the light above me and everything was burning, everything was hurting, and I thought how strange it was that drowning should feel so much like burning and that I should hold my breath and then I couldn't keep myself from gulping for air, but instead of breathing I was choking and all the darkness and the salt and the burning rushed in and blotted me out.

...And then I came back. But not as myself.

At first I didn't understand what I was seeing. I was overhead and looking down, and nothing made sense. It could have been a dream.

I recognised the woman on the bed, though I couldn't have said where from. She seemed unreal, like someone you know who comes to you in a dream. Her face was ghostly pale and her hair fanned out across the pillow like a dark halo. She looked as if she hadn't moved for hours, or maybe days.

There were tubes coming out of her, and she was hooked up to various beeping monitors. Still alive, then, presumably. But apart from the machines keeping an eye on her, and me floating overhead, she was all alone.

Shouldn't someone be there with her – someone who cared, who was willing to keep watch, who wouldn't let her slip away from the world unattended?

But there was only me, and I was as light as something lifted on the air, and I had no idea how long I was going to be able to stay.

I was adrift but not quite gone, hanging by a thread. It would have been so easy to let go, to fade into the haze and the brightness that was waiting at the edges of the room. Like smoke drawn upwards into sunshine, or a shell washed away by the sea…

It had been such a beautiful morning. You couldn't take that for granted, not in Cornwall. The weather could change so quickly. You had to make the most of it. He'd come such a long way, and Dani had been so happy to see him, so keen to show him our special beach. How could I have sent him away?

It's never too late. I don't believe it. I just don't believe this is it. Not for you and me. It can't be. If I had told you… if I had told you back then, when we first met… do you think you would have given me a chance?

The diary. Everything I'd written about what had happened and why I had left. Who would find it? Would anyone?

The woman on the bed was moving, thrashing around, her limbs shaking as if she was having a seizure.

The memory of the beach vanished, and the world exploded into noise. Alarms, people hurrying, voices. The room was full of panic and doctors. And just like that I was plunged back into myself, my life, and I was fighting for it.

For Dani.

It was too soon. I couldn't leave her. She was so little.

She wouldn't remember.

I had to protect her. She needed to understand that none of this was her fault.

And most of all, she had to know that it wasn't his fault either.

*

I waited. I waited so long…

I never quite gave up hope.

And then she came back. My daughter. Dani. The feel of that little hand in mine. Bigger now. Almost adult. Her touch. Closing my fingers around our picture.

So big. And so fearless! The way she talked. To her father. To me. Taking no prisoners. That girl!

Suddenly my heart is huge with love and pride.

She doesn't need me any more. Not really. A girl like that. A girl who is brave and who looks for the truth and doesn't give up. A girl with a heart. A girl who knows not to believe everything everyone tells her. Who has learned to question and look for her own evidence and find her own way.

A girl with a mind and a voice of her own.

I love you, Mum.

As the square of light by the door begins to darken, I have one question left, but it's more of a hope. Does she know that I love her too?

Chapter Twenty-Seven

Dani

The road home took us past Stonehenge. I'd never seen it before. It seemed weird that you could just drive right past it, like it was a service station or a holiday camp or any other kind of landmark.

The traffic crawled, so I had plenty of time to look at it.

Tall stones, in a circle, on a hillside. I'd read somewhere that nobody quite knew how the long-ago people who'd put it there had managed it, or what exactly it was for. I decided not to ask Dad if he knew anything about it. As usual, he didn't seem to be in a talking mood.

One thing was for sure, the stones had been put there to be seen. Seen and found and remembered.

Eventually we got past the gridlock and Kettlebridge started turning up on the road signs. I said, 'Are you taking me back to Aunt Carrie's?'

'Come to White Cottage if you want. Your choice.'

'Nah. All my stuff's in Cromwell Close.' The thought of shutting myself away in my bedroom was suddenly powerfully appealing. Not to mention sleeping in my own bed. 'It's home, I suppose.'

'I'm glad to hear you say that. You should think of it that way. You've lived there most of your life.'

I decided not to tell him I'd only said that to make him feel better. What was the point of getting his back up? Especially now, after my attempt at running away had ended in such disaster. He'd been right all along, and I was an idiot. It would have been much better if I'd left well enough alone… never gone up in the loft and found the diary, never run away. I should never have intervened to help Josie, either. I should have kept myself to myself.

But how could I not have helped her? And having done that, how could I not have done everything that had followed?

I said, 'Do I have to go back to school on Monday?'

'Well. You probably ought to.'

'My education comes first, right? Better just carry on as normal. Much the best thing.'

He didn't answer. The road kept rushing past, the flat green countryside, the cars. All those people going about their business, so very far from the sea.

Then he said, 'Tell people what happened if you want. If that will help. If that's what you need to do.'

'What, because at this point you're past caring what they think of you?'

He sighed. 'Pretty much.'

'I don't know whether I will say anything,' I said. 'What's the point? Nobody really cares, anyway. It doesn't matter to them if she'd dead or alive. They didn't love her the way we did.'

He didn't reply. After a while he made an odd snuffling sound and took one hand off the steering wheel to wipe his cheek, and I realised there were tears running down his face.

I didn't know what to do; I thought it might embarrass him if I said anything. I should have felt sorry for him, but I was too desolate for that. I felt like I didn't have any heart left to give. So I kept quiet, and he carried on driving, and neither of us said anything more.

When we got back to Cromwell Close Aunt Carrie came to the door straight away to let us in and we stood there awkwardly in the hall, not embracing.

'You made it, then,' Aunt Carrie said.

'Yeah. We saw her,' Dad said.

'How was she?'

Dad shrugged. 'Much the same.'

'Well, now you know,' Aunt Carrie said to me. 'I hope you can understand why we kept it from you.'

I could tell that part of her wanted to say sorry, but she couldn't bring herself to any more than he could. She didn't want to admit to me – or to herself – that what they had done might have been wrong. And part of me wanted to forgive her, to hold her, to reassure her that I was OK and it was a tragic situation and I could see that they'd done what they thought was the best thing at the time. But another part of me didn't want to give either of them anything at all.

'I'm kind of tired,' I said. 'I don't really feel like talking about it. Is it OK if I go to my room?'

Dad and Aunt Carrie exchanged glances. 'Sure,' Dad said, and I went off up the stairs.

Everything was exactly as I'd left it, as if nothing had happened – except that the picture of me and Mum was missing. But otherwise, it was spookily the same.

It was actually cosier than I remembered. More homely, after the starkness of Mum's room.

I messaged Josie to let her know I was back and then turned off my phone. Last thing I needed was her – or anybody else from school – trying to find out exactly where I'd been and what I'd done.

Time to escape the best way I knew how. I turned on my laptop and sank into a game of Sims. Where I could control everything, even the ghosts… I set about remodelling my favourite family's house and making them as rich and happy as possible. Somebody had to have a happy ending.

I wanted to weep for Mum, but I couldn't. I was too burnt-out to do anything other than lose myself in the details of the game. It was as if I'd climbed a mountain to find myself on a plain with miles and miles still to go, and all the people around me were making it pretty obvious that they wished I'd stayed right back where I'd started.

After a while Aunt Carrie called me down for lunch. It was one of those excruciating meals you can only have with your close family – the absolute opposite of the kind of family meal you see on happy adverts on the TV where everybody tucks in and chats and smiles as if it's the best feast they ever had in their lives. Aunt Carrie had made some kind of salad and pizza (slightly burnt). Dad looked as if he didn't want to eat it any more than I did, but didn't know what else to do with himself. It seemed that all of us were still trapped, in our different ways, just as we had been ever since the accident on the beach. All that had changed was that I understood why. Knowing the truth, as it turned out, was not at all the same thing as being free.

After we'd finished I said goodbye to Dad and went back up to my room, and that evening Aunt Carrie and I shared another awkward meal together, though at least this time we had the TV on to distract us.

She didn't attempt to say anything to me until after we'd finished, when she was washing up and I was drying. Then all she said was, 'I suppose I'd better take you to the station tomorrow, so you can collect your bike and ride it home. If it's still there.'

'Oh. Yeah. Sure. I mean, I guess I could get the bus if it's too much hassle.'

'It's fine, Dani. It's really not a problem.'

Her voice was sharp, as if she was offended by the suggestion that she would object to going out of her way to help me get my bike back. But her nose had turned pink and her eyes were wet, as if she was about to burst into tears.

What right did she have to cry? Or to speak to me sharply, come to that?

She said, 'Is this what it's going to be like from now on?'

'Like what?'

'You giving me the silent treatment. Resenting me. Blaming me. As if it was all my fault.'

'I don't think it was all your fault, as it happens. If it makes you feel any better, right now I'm actually more angry with Dad than with you.'

I hung the tea-towel up in the usual place and turned to go. Then I felt Aunt Carrie's hand on my shoulder, yanking me round.

'I'm talking to you. You can't just walk away like that,' she said.

She was that close to losing the plot – she had the face that teachers have just before they blow up completely, when being upset suddenly gives way to rage. It's scary to see an adult like that. Adults aren't meant to explode, they're meant to be in control. But some little demon in me wouldn't let me stop needling her.

'Don't tell me what to do,' I said. 'You're not my mum and I'm glad that you're not. You're a coward and a liar and Dad's just as pathetic as you are. I hate you both for what you've done. You deserve each other. You're well suited, actually. I don't know, maybe the two of you have been at it all along.'

Her arm moved and I flinched as if she'd slapped me. But she'd just hit herself, whacking her hand against her thigh as if to show me how much force she had, and how much of an effort it was to restrain it.

'You stupid child. You don't know what you're saying. He loved her. He still loves her. He has never got over her. Is it so hard for you to have a tiny bit of sympathy for him?'

'Harder for me than for you,' I said. 'I don't feel sorry for him. I feel sorry for her. I don't know, maybe I'd feel differently if he'd made a bit more effort all these years. But let's face it, he's not exactly been around much, has he? You couldn't say he's done his best to make it up to me.'

'Can you not see how guilty he feels? He feels so guilty sometimes it makes it hard for him to look at you.'

'Yeah, well, maybe sometimes guilty people should feel guilty.'

She folded her arms and stared at me. She looked less angry now, but colder. I stood as tall as I could and stared back at her.

'You shouldn't talk about your dad like that.'

'Yeah? Well, I happen to disagree. I think after what's gone on round here, I've got the right to talk about him however I like. The two of you can't exactly start claiming the right to respect now.'

'Not respect,' she said, 'not for me, anyway. But you do owe him something.'

'You mean because he gives you money to pay for my food and stuff? Yeah, well, I guess that's better than absolutely nothing. I know he isn't exactly rolling in it these days. He had to sell the other garden centre, didn't he? The one in London that he'd just set up when he got together with Mum. I suppose it's not surprising it went belly-up. It must be hard to focus on running a business when you've got a bad conscience. Probably quite a distraction from doing all the things you know you ought to be doing. Like taking care of your family.'

'He does take care of you, Dani.'

'Barely.'

'He saved you, Dani. He saved your life. Is that enough for you?'

'What do you mean? He didn't save me. He tried to save Mum. But he was too late.'

'Dani, that's not how it happened.'

'But… that's what Dad told me.'

'Well, he didn't tell you everything. If he had, you would feel differently about it.'

I couldn't speak. All I could do was stare at her. She was just a few inches away from me and the kitchen floor was under my feet. But everything was simultaneously unsteady, as if I was underwater and powerless against the current, deafened by the water and unable to scream.

'It was that day at the beach,' she went on. 'You got caught by a wave. You were so little, and you couldn't swim. It knocked you off

your feet and dragged you out to sea. Your mum waded in to get
you and a freak current caught her and carried her out. He couldn't
save you both. She screamed at him to get you, and he did. But by
the time he went in for her it was too late.'

I stepped back. My hands had formed fists as if I was about to
defend myself. I said, 'So it's *my* fault.'

'Of course it wasn't your fault. You were four years old. But he
did rescue you. I thought you should know that before you decided
to give up on him completely.'

'I never gave up on him,' I said.

And just like that, the fight went out of me.

I was still angry – not just with Aunt Carrie, with everything. But
at the same time I could picture it almost as if I was there watching:
the child swept out to sea and the woman following, and the man
on the beach being faced with a choice. An impossible choice.

And then the man had come out of the sea with the child in his
arms and the woman had been left behind in the water, gone for
too long, disappearing from view.

I could see how fast it had happened. He'd had no chance to think
and reflect and weigh up the options. He'd had to decide in next to no
time, and then act. How long had it all taken? A matter of minutes.

But he hadn't decided on his own. Mum had screamed at him
to save me, and he had done it.

When I'd been alone on the beach, wet and cold, watching
something that I didn't understand – that was when it had happened,
then. That was when we had lost her. And had got her back again,
though not the same as when she had gone.

'He's thought about it a lot, you know, over the years,' Aunt
Carrie said. 'In time, he decided there was no way he could have
saved you both. And if he hadn't gone in and got you the way he
did, he might have lost both of you. But you know what he's like.
He makes his mind up fast – for good or ill – and then sticks to it.
And pays the price for it. You're like that, too, I think.'

'Do you think… if it hadn't happened… that they would have got back together?'

She shrugged. 'Who can say? I don't think anybody else can understand the inside of someone else's marriage. But he thinks not. He said Laura only agreed to the walk to humour him, so you could all spend some time together before he left again. He said she was pretty quick to get him out of the cottage, and it was made clear that he wouldn't be welcome back. But I think they would have tried to do the right thing by you. He *has* tried to do the right thing by you… and maybe he hasn't succeeded. I can understand why you're angry with him. But I don't think he deserves your hate. We made mistakes. People do. Whatever age they are.' She hesitated. 'I'd like to think I don't deserve your hate either,' she said.

I could tell she wanted to sound strong, but the wobble in her voice gave her away. I said, 'Is that your way of saying sorry?'

'Is that what you need me to say?'

Suddenly I felt very tired. 'I keep feeling like you want me to forgive you and tell you it's all right. But it's not my job to make you feel better. You're meant to be the one who looks after me. We can have a truce if you like. I'll let you off the hook if you leave me alone. And now I really don't want to talk about it any more.'

I turned away from her and went upstairs. I thought that maybe I heard her crying before I closed my bedroom door. And I did hesitate before shutting it… but not for long. I was too numb to find it in myself to do anything that wasn't already a habit. And so I sat down in front of the computer and put my headphones in and went back to my game.

For a little while, I was almost able to forget about the bad things that had happened just because I'd once walked down a beach at the wrong time and the wrong distance from the waves.

*

That night Aunt Carrie didn't so much as knock on my door to remind me how late it was getting. Eventually I realised she must have gone to bed already. It was weird to think that only the night before last I'd stayed up late in secret, reading Mum's diary. Now I'd lost the diary, but it seemed as if I could stay up as late as I liked and not bother pretending to be asleep. Even if everything around me looked the same, this really wasn't the same life that I'd been leading before I ran away to Cornwall.

When I finally turned in, I slept for what felt a long time and deeply. My dreams were a mix of things that almost – but not quite – woke me. I dreamed about being underwater, the weight of it and how the pressure grew as I drifted further down, with no hope of ever making it back to the light. I dreamed about running home as the sky pressed low overhead, ready to fall and crush me. And I dreamed about being surrounded by people who couldn't hear me and opening my mouth to scream at them only to find that I couldn't make a sound.

Then all of that cleared, as if I'd just woken up.

I was in the car, with Mum driving, and there was music playing on the radio, not too loud, a tune that I recognised but couldn't put a name to. We were on a winding country road leading between green hills and fields – the kind of road that criss-crosses Oxfordshire, like the one that heads east from Kettlebridge past White Cottage and Rosewell's Garden Centre, on to the village where I broke my promise to Aunt Carrie that I wouldn't swim in the river and beyond.

I said, 'What are you doing? You can't drive.'

'No, and I can't talk either. Or at least, that's what everybody seems to think.'

Her voice! She sounded just exactly the way I would have imagined. Soft and light and warm and very slightly hesitant, as if she didn't really expect anyone to be that interested in what she had to say. She was wearing the brown dress she'd had on in the photo that I'd lost, but she didn't look quite so young any more – she had a few white hairs and a few lines around her eyes.

'You're older,' I said.

'Comes to us all. If we're lucky,' she said, and took a sudden right turn.

We were instantly in Cornwall, driving along the narrow lane that I had trudged up to find the cottage. She slowed down as we went past the gate so that I could see: the family I'd watched there were all sitting at the picnic table in the garden and they smiled and waved at us as we went past.

'We had a pretty good time, you and I,' Mum said. 'Didn't we? I'm sorry I had to leave so early, though. It was very hard on you. Hard on me, too, come to that.'

'Well, you know, I guess I got by.'

She flashed me a quick sidelong smile. 'Oh, I think you did a lot better than that.'

Then we were driving down towards the harbour, and she pulled up in the empty car park that looked onto the bay. The water was blue and calm, just as it had been when I saw it, and the tide was in. There was no one else around, nothing to see apart from the water and the sky and a little rowing boat with a white sail, which was moored to the jetty.

We got out of the car, climbed up onto the jetty and walked towards the boat. I could feel the sun and the breeze on my skin and hear the gentle rush of the waves, and I could still make out the tune that had been playing in the car, even though the car was now nowhere to be seen.

I said, 'I've never been in a boat. I might get sick. And I don't know how to row. Or sail.'

'You learn these things when you need to,' she said. 'Anyway, you're not coming, not yet.'

She climbed into the boat and put her hands on the oars. She wasn't wearing the brown dress any more, but was dressed instead in the T-shirt and jogging bottoms she'd had on at the nursing home.

I said, 'You can't go off somewhere without me. Not again.'

'It's not forever. You'll manage. You're my daughter, remember? You can cope with anything. I need you to help me cast off.'

I looked down at the rope tying the boat to the jetty. It was wrapped around a wooden post and tied up with an impossibly complicated knot.

'I'm never going to be able to undo that,' I protested.

'Just try,' she said, and I bent over the knot and began to work at it.

To my astonishment, as soon as I'd made a start, the whole thing seemed to slither along and undo itself. I looked up at her with the rope in my hands; she was shielding her eyes from the sun. The tune I'd heard in the car was still playing. Some old folk tune. A sea shanty, perhaps.

'What now?' I said.

She pulled a face as if to say, *Come on, you know*, and I threw the rope down into the bottom of the boat, where it landed in a perfect coil. She was already moving away, rowing as if she'd done it a million times before, and the sail was filling out with the breeze. She paused to wave at me and blow me a kiss, and then set off again.

I watched her row right through the walls of the sea defence and out onto the open water. The sail got smaller and smaller and more distant and eventually merged into the haze and brightness of the horizon, and I realised the tune I'd been listening to had stopped and I couldn't even remember any more what it had been.

I was woken by Aunt Carrie, who was sitting on my bed. Her face was covered in tears and even as I struggled upright, before I could make out any of what she was trying to say, I knew what she was going to tell me.

'She's dead. She died in her sleep. They found her this morning. I'm so sorry, Dani. You finally met her and now she's gone.'

Chapter Twenty-Eight

Dani

In the end, we brought Mum back to Kettlebridge and Dad scattered her ashes at the Wildcroft Hills.

It was a beautiful day, just on the edge of autumn; the colours of the leaves were just beginning to change, and a few had already fallen. We stopped at a bench near a flat, carved block of stone that told you all the landmarks to look out for on the horizon and how far away they were, like a map. We didn't bother with the map, though. We just looked out at the view spread out like a gift at our feet.

There was a cluster of houses, an old church spire, and stretches of water, but mainly there was the land, green and quiet and peaceful as it must have been for centuries. There was nothing here but a sense of time and space, and of things quietly growing. It was like being on another planet – one far, far away from the everyday world of news and routines and timetables and traffic.

Dad said, 'There's an old legend about this place, you know. There's supposed to be a bird trapped here by the hill, and if you could find it and free it, there would be eternal spring. There's meant to be a hoard of treasure, too, with another bird guarding it.'

'There certainly are a lot of birds,' I said. There was birdsong coming from the wooded crest of the hill behind us; the wood was fenced off, perhaps because it was supposed to be unsafe, or maybe to protect the wildlife.

Dad went off with the urn that had Mum's ashes in it, and I stayed sitting on the bench and thought about the service in the crematorium near the nursing home.

There had just been three of us there: me, Dad, and Aunt Carrie – one more person than in the story Dad and Aunt Carrie had agreed to pass off as true, when they had told everybody she was dead before her time had come. It didn't seem like many mourners. It seemed as if she should have had more.

Dad hadn't wanted to say anything, but Aunt Carrie had thought we should have some readings. She'd picked out a poem for herself, something about lapping water and finding peace on an island, and she'd talked me into reading some Shakespeare.

'Fear no more the heat o' the sun,
Nor the furious winter's rages…'

The lines she'd chosen didn't exactly make sense, not in the normal way, but then the words were hundreds of years old and I could see that they were beautiful, even if they weren't easy to understand. And it wasn't as if I was in school, where people were likely to laugh at you if anything that sounded strange or not quite right came out of your mouth.

Just before the end of the reading I'd had to pause because of the loudness of the land gulls squawking and circling overhead, as if they had chosen just that moment to pay their tribute.

'Ghost unlaid forbear thee!
Nothing ill come near thee!
Quiet consummation have;
And renownèd be thy grave!'

It was eerie, that sound of gulls crying. Wordless and haunting. But it was comforting too, because it didn't feel as if it was only us who were grieving, or who had come to mark her passing.

Aunt Carrie hadn't wanted to join us to scatter her ashes. We'd agreed that I would come this far, and then Dad would go off and finish it on his own. As I sat there on the bench and waited for him those final words from the reading came back to me, but this time no gulls cried. They were rare here, this far from the sea. There was just the rushing sound of the wind in the long grass to remind me of water, and the distant blue of the river and the lake.

After a while he came back and we went down to the car park together and he drove me to White Cottage. We didn't say anything on the way, but for once it seemed all right to sit together in silence.

When we got to the house he muttered something about how he'd be back in a minute and left me in the kitchen to make coffee – he didn't have any tea in the house, unlike Aunt Carrie who treated the stuff as if it were the elixir of life, or as close to it as it was possible to find. I made the coffee and wiped a few surfaces and did a bit of desultory washing-up, then pulled myself together and went out through the sitting room and up the narrow stairs to find him.

Strange to think that when Mum had first seen this house, it had been packed with people. It was silent now. I couldn't hear anything apart from the creak of the stairs underneath my feet; I could easily have been the only living thing in the place.

When I came to the landing, I saw that the door to Dad's bedroom was slightly ajar.

'Dad? Are you OK?'

No answer.

I went closer. Knocked gently, once, twice. Still no answer. I pushed the door open wide.

He was kneeling in the middle of the floor with a cardboard box to one side and a photo album open in front of him. There were five photos on the spread he was looking at – five photos and a gap where one was missing. The photos were carefully arranged and stuck in place under transparent plastic and were all of me as a child, or Mum, or both of us.

He looked up and said, 'I'm sorry, I was going to bring it all down. But then I got distracted.'

I knelt down on the floor next to him and studied the pictures. There was me in a pair of yellow dungarees, holding a rapidly melting ice cream; me with Mum on the swings somewhere; me and Mum at a table in a pizza place, her looking determined to have a good time, me obviously ready to leave. In that picture she was wearing the familiar brown dress from the photo that had lived on my bedroom windowsill, the one of her holding my hand underneath the cherry trees. The picture I'd taken all the way to Cornwall only to lose it in Mum's room on the way back.

Then, at the bottom of the right-hand page, was the conspicuous empty space.

Was that where my picture had come from? Dad had asked if the staff at the nursing home had found it, but it had gone missing and had never come to light.

He said, 'That was such a beautiful spring day. We took you out for lunch. You played up a bit, as I remember.'

'Yeah, looks like it.'

'She did all this. I took the pictures, she put the photos into albums. I don't think anybody bothers to do that these days. And I haven't picked up my camera for years.' He gestured towards the box next to him. 'It's all in there. All the old photos and stuff. After what happened, I packed up our old flat and moved back to White Cottage. Jade thought I might as well. I had to flog off the garden centre I had in London anyway, it was about to go bust. And Michelle had a boyfriend by then, and more of a life of her own, and she wasn't so keen on staying overnight at my place any more. She didn't need me, really. Or not as much. I mean, I still saw her, obviously. But I don't suppose I was a lot of use to her. Or to you either, come to that. Anyway, that was the one box I couldn't bring myself to open. It's been sitting in the bottom of a cupboard for years.'

I pointed to the album in front of him and said, 'Can I have a look?'

He pushed it over to me. 'Sure.'

I turned back to the beginning. There I was again, dressed in a round pumpkin costume that matched the colour of my hair.

'There seems to be a lot of me in it.'

'Well, of course.'

'I made your coffee. It'll be going cold.'

'Sorry. I sort of lost track. I'll bring it up.'

He got up and went downstairs. Next to the door there was a bright patch of sunlight, a square of yellow that faded almost as soon as I'd noticed it. It was a changeable day. Then I heard a snatch of music somewhere; Dad humming, maybe? But it wasn't like him to hum. Maybe I had imagined it.

I bent over the album again.

There I was on a little red bike with stabilisers, pedalling furiously, with Mum standing by and applauding. I remembered that bike! Though I hadn't thought about it for years. As I turned the pages, I was struck by how happy Mum looked in every picture. Me, too, mostly. But her especially, as if she'd had a gift for it.

The photos looked like long ago, like history. And this day would be history one day too. It made me sad to think of that, as if she was at one end of a tunnel and I was at the other, and the tunnel was getting longer and longer and she was getting further and further away.

Dad came back with his coffee. He sat on the edge of the bed to drink it and watched me turning the pages.

'Have it, if you like,' he said when I'd finished. 'Have all of it. There are some prints in packets in there, too. The ones that didn't make it into the albums. I'll put the box in the boot and we can take it over to Carrie's when I drop you back.'

'Are you sure?'

'I'm sure. You should have it. She would have wanted you to have it. You can look through it all at your leisure. Show the albums to Carrie, if you like. Or keep them to yourself. I just... I can't do any more today.'

'That's OK,' I said. 'I'll take care of them.'

I closed the album and put it back in the box. It was about half full. There would be plenty to look at. More than I had ever imagined would come my way.

Dad put his coffee cup down on the bedside table and said, 'There's something else I thought you might like to have, too.'

He got up and I stood too, and he took a folded-over envelope out of his pocket and passed it to me.

'They're her rings,' he said.

I peered inside and glimpsed the dull shine of gold and the glint of a diamond, then closed the envelope again and put it in my own pocket. I'd never really thought about it before, but he was still wearing his wedding ring. He always did.

'I promise I'll take good care of them,' I told him.

'I know you will,' he said. 'I'll take the box down for you.'

I nearly told him I could manage, but I could see that he wanted to carry it for me. He picked it up and we stood facing each other.

'Thank you,' I said.

'You're welcome,' he told me. He looked both hopeful and crushed – as if he wanted more than anything to make it up to me and knew he never could.

'Aunt Carrie told me you rescued me from the sea, that day in Cornwall,' I said. 'She said Mum shouted at you to save me and not her.'

He was shocked – properly shocked, as if I'd just let something slip that shouldn't have happened. 'There wasn't any need for her to go telling you that.'

'Don't be angry with her. I'm glad she told me.'

He looked me straight in the eyes. I saw how much regret he lived with, and how resigned he was to it – how he had come to accept it, as if it was a punishment he just had to take, whether it was fair or not.

'I got her out as fast as I could. But it was too late. I failed.'

I reached out and rested my hand gently on his arm, which was folded round the box. The gesture felt odd: we never usually touched or embraced each other. But I had to do something, and it was as far as I could go.

I said, 'You shouldn't be so hard on yourself.'

He managed a faint smile. 'Maybe we could have a pact. I won't blame myself if you promise me you won't blame yourself either.'

I could see that he was just trying to get me off the hook, and wasn't about to let himself off so easily. But I smiled back and said, 'OK, it's a deal.' And then I withdrew my hand and helpfully collected his coffee cup, and we went down the stairs together.

When we got back to Cromwell Close Dad carried the box into the house for me. Aunt Carrie came rushing into the hall as if we might have been a couple of intruders hell-bent on robbing her and stood looking at us with a mixture of fear and suspicion.

She said, 'What's that?'

'Old photos of Laura,' Dad said. 'I thought Dani should have them. Dani, where do you want them?'

'You could put them on the dining-room table,' I said.

Aunt Carrie pulled a face, as if I'd suggested something unhygienic, but didn't say anything. She followed us into the dining room and stood to one side as Dad deposited the box on the table and turned to me to say goodbye.

He said, 'I'll see you lunchtime on Sunday, then. Do you want picking up?'

'No, no worries. I'll cycle over.'

'You can help me do some sorting out in the garden if you like.'

I knew this would be infinitely preferable to him than sitting round making conversation, or, even worse, revisiting things that were painful to talk about.

'OK.'

He glanced over at Aunt Carrie as if he'd only just remembered she was there. 'Well, I guess I'd better be getting out of your hair.'

'I'll see you out,' I said.

Outside in the hallway we gave each other a quick farewell hug. He wasn't really a hugger. Neither was I, come to that. But there had been a time when I would have just kept my distance and he would have let me, and I didn't want to be like that any more. I had to be capable of saying goodbye to my dad without being standoffish and sulky, without it being awkward. Maybe what it needed was for me to accept him and me for what we were – not estranged, and not broken, but just a father and daughter who had learned to cut each other some slack.

He got into the car and I waved him off, and it didn't feel too bad. It felt like we might be able to fall into some kind of rhythm of coming and going that wouldn't be a reminder of how much both of us had lost.

I went back into the dining room and saw that Aunt Carrie had taken the album that was on top – the most recent one, the one I'd just been looking at – out of the box. It was open on the dining-room table, and she was leafing through it.

And she was crying. She was crying the way she had the morning she told me Mum had died, as hopelessly and quietly as Josie that day by the bridge, the way someone cries when they don't expect any comfort from anybody.

Suddenly it was like I'd turned into somebody else or discovered someone else who had been living inside me all this time. I went over to her and put my arms around her and held her tight, and my own tears ran down my face and soaked into her dark hair.

A Letter from Ali

Thank you for choosing to read *My Mother's Choice*. If you would like to keep up to date with all my latest releases, just sign up at the following link. Your email address will never be shared and you can unsubscribe at any time.

www.bookouture.com/ali-mercer

In the late 70s, when I was about four years old, I was knocked off my feet by a wave on a beach in North Cornwall. My dad, who was a strong, confident swimmer, went into the sea to fish me out. A couple of years later he and my mum separated and then got divorced, and I grew up with him living abroad. When I asked him about the incident years later he brushed it off as no big deal. 'You were just rolling round in a couple of inches of water,' he told me.

I think he was being self-deprecating – he didn't want what he'd done to be seen as heroic, or as anything out of the ordinary. But it is what it is: he rescued me from the sea, and I know this only because it's what I was told afterwards.

What I remember is the miserable shock of being cold and wet through. I also remember my family donating various items of clothing so I could have something dry to wear on the way back to my grandparents' bungalow – this was tricky, because everyone else was so much bigger than I was, and I ended up with a crazy hotchpotch outfit and no pants. And the other thing I remember is going on my dad's shoulders on the long walk home. That seemed like a special treat; I was probably a bit big for it at the time.

I have no recollection of being in the water, only of being safe afterwards. My brush with the sea turned out all right – became one of those anecdotes that form the fabric of family life, a close shave, an escapade, a 'do you remember when?' But what if it hadn't? If every life is a series of lucky escapes, what happens if your luck runs out when you need it most? What if that happens, not to you, but to someone you love?

Three years ago, when I was deep into an early draft of a novel about a fractured family, I read Richard Beard's powerful memoir *The Day That Went Missing*. It's an exploration of the loss of his brother, who drowned during a childhood holiday in Cornwall. This was never spoken about in the family afterwards, and the memoir is an account of trying to piece together exactly what happened, like a detective, and to make sense of the aftermath.

I had just written a scene in which a young woman nearly drowns when I went along to Mostly Books, one of the two bookshops in my hometown of Abingdon, to hear Richard talk about his memoir. The bookshop was packed and the atmosphere was extraordinarily intimate and intense. There was grief in the air, but there was a kind of collective energy, too – a compulsion to listen and to share. I've tried to capture some of the feeling in that room in the book you've just read: the weight of sadness, and the driving force of the urge to remember and reclaim something that has been lost.

The near-drowning scene I had written before that evening in the bookshop didn't make it into the story I was working on at the time, which eventually turned into my most recent novel, *His Secret Family*. But it turned out to be a kernel, and *My Mother's Choice* grew out of it.

The sea can be lethal, but it is magical too. Both Dani and Laura in *My Mother's Choice* run away to the sea, something we surely all daydream about doing from time to time. My dad actually did it, as a teenage stowaway on a ferry to France. He was always at home by water. At his funeral in 2018 one of the readings was John

Masefield's poem 'Sea Fever', and when I stood to read the end of T S Eliot's 'Little Gidding' – which is full of references to the sea – the sound of gulls squawking overhead, above the chapel, was so loud I could barely make myself heard. It seemed like a kind of tribute, as if they were claiming him as one of theirs. It was eerie. But also, being reminded of what he had loved was comforting.

My Mother's Choice is a novel about missing someone you can't see, about memory and forgetting and trying to recover what you can't remember, and about how love persists between people who can't meet. One of the ways love persists is through words, whatever technology you're using – whether it's Zoom or the phone or email or pen and paper. But words are not the only way, and sometimes the words you need are impossible to find.

As readers of my previous novels will know, difficulty with communication is a subject close to my heart. My son, who is thirteen now, is autistic, and was diagnosed at the age of four. These days, he expresses himself freely and loves to tell jokes – he has a vast repertoire, learned from his prized collection of joke books – but language didn't come easily to him. That has made me acutely aware of how difficult it can be to put what you think and feel into words, and how hard it can be to know what is going on in other people's heads. Because what if they can't tell you, or even show you? What if you can't make assumptions about what someone understands on the basis of what they are able to say?

Appearances can be deceptive, but if you can't go by appearances, then what have you got? You're left with uncertainty, doubt and guesswork. And maybe hope and faith, if you're lucky.

I'm writing this at a strange and sad time; the daily death toll from coronavirus keeps climbing, and we are in the midst of a calamity with no idea of when or how it will end. In the windows of many homes – my own included – there are rainbow pictures, bright little tokens of the possibility of a better tomorrow. Somewhere in that future, you are reading this. I hope it is safer than today. I wonder how it will be different to the days before the pandemic, when we had so many freedoms we saw as normal – to travel, and gather, and visit each other's houses, and hug each other if we wanted to.

I hope *My Mother's Choice* has been an escape, and has moved you and taken you out of yourself. If you enjoyed it, I would be very grateful if you could write a review. I'd love to know how you felt about the characters and the choices they make. Also, it's really helpful for other readers when they're looking for something new.

Do get in touch – I'm often on Twitter and Instagram and you can also contact me through my Facebook author page. I love hearing from my readers.

All good wishes to you and yours,
Ali Mercer

 AliMercerwriter

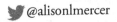 @alisonlmercer

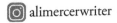 alimercerwriter

alimercerwriter.com

Acknowledgements

While I was writing this book something pretty wild happened to me: my previous novel, *His Secret Family*, became a bestseller. I'd be lying if I said I'd never dreamed of such a thing happening, but there's a big difference between daydreaming and thinking that your dream might actually come true. I owe a huge, heartfelt thank you to everyone who made that possible.

Thank you to all my readers and everyone who has supported my books: all the book bloggers and reviewers and members of book groups – whether you meet in person or talk on Facebook, Instagram or Twitter, or get together in a mixture of different ways, both online and off-screen. Your appetite for stories is an inspiration. And your recommendations are powerful!

Thank you to the starry team at my brilliant publisher, Bookouture. Thanks to Cara Chimirri, my editor, and to Kathryn Taussig who got me on board, and to Noelle Holten and Kim Nash, Bookouture's tireless publicity managers. Thanks to Jon Appleton. And thank you to all the Bookouture authors for your cheerleading and encouragement. We rock!

Thank you to Judith Murdoch, my agent, and Rebecca Winfield, who looks after my foreign rights.

Shout out to North Cornwall Book Festival (the novelist Patrick Gale is its artistic director): the book lover's perfect getaway.

Towards the end of working on *My Mother's Choice*, I took the plunge and became a full-time writer (gulp). Thank you to my former colleagues for your support of my other career, and for all the kitchen chats down the years.

Thanks to my friends and family. Thank you to Neel Mukherjee, who has provided so much encouragement along the way, and to Luli and Nanu Segal and Helen Rumbelow. Thank you to David Mercer. Thanks to my mum, to whom *His Secret Family* was dedicated. And thanks to Gary, Katie, Sam, Emma and Laurence. Mr P, Izzy, Tom: it's a privilege to share lockdown with you.

And finally, thanks to my dad for fishing me out of the sea when I was a kid. If you hadn't, I guess this book might never have been written.

CPSIA information can be obtained
at www.ICGtesting.com
Printed in the USA
LVHW031605241022
731423LV00003B/284